SECRETS OF THE WYRDE WOODS
FORGOTTEN ROAD

By Nisse Visser

Secrets of the Wyrde Woods Book One
FORGOTTEN ROAD
Amsterdam/Houvin-Houvigneul/Brighton
ISBN/EAN 9789082323818
Netherlands NUR Code 334

A C.B.S. Green Man Publication
Cider Brandy Scribblers
Burnham-on-Sea, Somerset, England

Ingram Spark Edition first published in print in the UK 2015 as:
Secrets of the Wyrde Woods Book One FORGOTTEN ROAD
ISBN: 9789082323818

First published digitally on Amazon Kindle in 2015 as:
Secrets of the Wyrde Woods Book One FORGOTTEN ROAD
ISBN: 9789082322965

Cover art by Corin Spinks (Corinography) featuring Anna Orgers with a Fairbow Vertex bow and Melissa Spinks. Illustration by Kayleih Kempers.

Instructions for use: Start at the beginning and read all the words one after the other until you come to the very end and then stop. WARNING: Reading can cause serious damage to ignorance

For Thallie
(you're not forgotten)

Pledge: 50% of the royalties received for The Wyrde Woods: FORGOTTEN ROAD have been pledged to the Abington Ferret Refuge in Northhamptonshire.

CONTENTS

For Anna & Rozemarijn

For there is no friend like a sister
In calm or stormy weather;
To cheer one on the tedious way,
To fetch one if one goes astray,
To lift one if one totters down,
To strengthen whilst one stands.

(from *The Goblin Market*, by Christina Rossetti)

For Jack, Gerrit, Richard & Marcel

There was once a road through the woods.
It is underneath the coppice and heath
and the thin anemones.
Where the ring-dove broods,
and the badgers roll at ease,
there was once a road through the woods.

Yet, if you enter the woods of a summer evening late,
when the night-air cools on the trout-ringed pools,
where the otter whistles his mate,
you will hear the beat of a horse's feet,
and the swish of a skirt in the dew,
steadily cantering through the misty solitudes,
as though they perfectly knew
the old lost road through the woods ...

(from *The Way Through the Woods* by Rudyard Kipling)

Prologues

27 May 1940
Maskall Farm
Wolfden, Sussex

Dear Mum,

I hope you are well. ~~I miss you so much I can't sleep at night.~~ I am well. Sometimes ~~I feel very lonely~~ I miss you a little. ~~I don't like being an evacuee very much.~~

Gran and Gramps are nice like you said they would be. ~~They are funny. I mean in a nice way.~~

~~I miss London so much it hurts~~ The countryside is very different from London.

~~School is utter rubbish~~ I try to do my best at school. ~~It isn't always easy. I haven't got any friends.~~ It's in Wolfden. ~~There is a horrible teacher and the other chavvies call me dwarf.~~

Gran said you attended the same school. ~~It's the only thing I like about it. I sometimes wonder if I sit behind your old desk.~~ That's nice, isn't it?

Please write back soon. All my love to Dad. ~~I miss him a lot too.~~

Your loving daughter,
Maisy Robbins

29 May 1940
Maskall Farm
Wolfden, Sussex

Dear Dad,

I hope you're keeping well. I wish you were here sometimes so we could go on an adventure. Do you remember them? I remember all of them. Which is your favourite? Do please write to tell me Dad? Your letters don't need to be long or anything. It's just that I think I will hear your voice when I read them the first time and that would be cracking. Have you found work yet?

You wouldn't believe the nickeys at school sometimes, the local chavvies are very slow but most of the chavvies are evacuees like me. But they are from WEST LONDON!!! Would you believe it? You wouldn't like them at all, I am sure. ~~They don't like me very much either.~~

The farm is cracking and all. I like the animals a lot. There are a lot of stables and workshops and sheds and lofts, some of them look like they haven't been visited in years. I already have three secret lofts. We should play hide and seek when you come to visit me and we can start a secret club in one of my secret lofts .

Pass my love to Mum. I miss both of you a lot.

Love, Your Maise

1. Maisy

It could not have been the light. The four children were huddled around a single book in the corner of the classroom, right next to a tall latticed window which let in plenty of daylight. The act of reading was a big problem though. Maisy decided that she simply had to do something about it before she suffered from spontaneous combustion. Relieved that she had come to a decision she jumped up from her seat.

She approached the teacher cautiously. Maisy had got along with most of her teachers at her old school in London – they had lived in the same community on the Isle of Dogs and knew Maisy well enough to handle her abundant enthusiasm for life. So far, Sister Mary – who taught in Maisy's new school in the Sussex countryside – had not shown the same measure of empathy.

A few chavvies chuckled softly as Maisy passed and she threw them a quick glare. She was far shorter than an eleven-year-old was expected to be. The vast majority of her new classmates continued to turn their ceaseless fascination with this fact into mockery.

Maisy's exceptional lack of height was emphasized by the height and bulk of Sister Mary, who towered over all the other teachers at school. Maisy had dubbed her 'The Abbess' though she had not found anyone in class to share that with yet.

The nun had caught Maisy's movements out of the corner of her eye and slowly turned to face the girl; astonishment written all over her face.

Maisy took a deep breath and put on her best smile. "Ma'am, I don't meant to *chaunt* but either these chavvies are *glocky* or else I am real *jemmy*, innit?"

Maisy pointed at the corner of the classroom. The three boys pretended to continue struggling with the day's reading assignment but their full focus was on Maisy's encounter with Sister Mary. They all looked puzzled. There was not a single person in the classroom who had understood what Maisy had just said, though Maisy was blissfully unaware of this. She looked up at the teacher and continued her best smile. It was part genuine, Maisy really hoped the problem could be solved.

"Pardon me?" Sister Mary asked, her eyes bulging. "You are deviating from your set task, Miss Robbins."

"The reading," Maisy nodded. "That's what I'd like to talk about, Ma'am."

"Deviation leads to the Devil," Sister Mary spoke sternly.

Maisy nodded again. Sister Mary said those words an awful lot. They did not make sense to Maisy. Sure, she deviated from the other chavvies in the class, but they deviated from her too. There was no way to do things right in this scenario and Maisy thought it was rather silly. She half suspected that Sister Mary considered Maisy's height an offensive deviation too. Whenever she directed speech at Maisy she spoke loud and slowly using only simple words as if Maisy's brain had been slow in growing too.

The girl suddenly felt foolish standing there smiling away and she brushed her long dark hair with a hand to conceal a facial transition to the sort of serious expression Maisy had seen actress Margaret Lockwood use in *The Lady Vanishes* at the pictures.

"You will speak when you wish to communicate, not nod or shake your head," Sister Mary said.

"Yes, Ma'am."

"You will address me as Sister Mary," the nun spoke sternly and drew herself to her full height. An imposing sight reinforced by her considerable physique.

"Yes, Sister Mary," Maisy nodded. "As I said this lot are real *nickeys*. I don't mean to *beef*, do I? But it'd be dead clever of you to shift me to a faster group, innit? My old teachers in London all did, didn't they?"

"*Nickeys*?"

Maisy nodded. "Proper halfwits, Ma'am."

Sister Mary's jaw dropped and Maisy tried not to flinch; it was not a pretty sight. Instead she tried smiling again.

"To my desk, Miss Robbins."

Maisy nodded her agreement and followed the nun to the desk, pleased that the teacher was going to look into the problem.

"Your hands on my desk top please, Miss Robbins," the nun picked up a thin bamboo cane from her desk.

"Oi! What's that for?" Maisy exclaimed in surprise.

"Since your parents forgot to teach you manners, Miss Robbins." Sister Mary intoned loud enough for the whole class to hear. "I shall be forced to do so."

Maisy folded her hands behind her bottom. "I didn't hold no candle to no Devil did I? All I did was ask…"

"I will have NO talk of the Devil! WICKED CHILD!"

"The dwarf is *afeared*," a boy sniggered. Some in the class dared a short laugh at that.

Maisy ground her teeth, the voice belonged to one of the three *nickeys* in her reading group; a large bulking bully with narrow eyes and a mean streak which was on a par with the most vicious chavvies back on the Isle of Dogs.

"You don't understand…" Maisy stalled. It was just a saying. Sister Mary referred to the Devil all the time but Maisy figured it would not be a good idea to bring that inconsistency to attention now.

"SILENCE!" Sister Mary was seething. "Hands on my desk."

Determined to show she was not scared Maisy laid her hands on the desktop. She braced herself. Sister Mary aimed at Maisy's knuckles and brought the bamboo down half-a-dozen times and the pain was bad. Maisy kept her jaws locked, determined not to cry out.

"You may remove your hands now," Sister Mary said with satisfaction in her voice.

Maisy forced her hands to her sides, though she really wanted to rub her stinging knuckles. She stared at Sister Mary dully; not comprehending the cause of this unexpected punishment at all.

"I will not tolerate little uncouth brutes in my classroom, do you understand, Miss Robbins?"

Maisy nodded, fighting back a tear. The 'little' stung. She really did not need constant reminders.

"You have been assigned to a study group according to my assessment of your intelligence, Miss Robbins," Sister Mary spoke self-importantly. "You will stay there until I deem otherwise. Now get back to your desk."

Maisy walked back to her desk with her head held high. One or two pupils grimaced in sympathy as she passed but many more smirked nastily and the rest ignored her.

Maisy held herself together – ignoring the sneers of the *nickeys* – but desperately wished she could get herself *boated* back to London.

§ § § § § §

Back on the Isle of the Dogs, in London's East End, Maisy used to fly home after school in heady exhilaration. Now she shuffled despondently as she followed the road out of the Sussex village of Wolfden; wondering what had gone wrong in class. She knew she was known as a bit of a mouth but Maisy had made a genuine attempt to avoid using the words which had sent the Abbess off the handle on previous occasions.

Maisy had also figured it would be reasonable to ask about something that would improve her schoolwork. By which Maisy understood motivation; her old teachers had known how to motivate her, and a motivated Maisy was a force to be reckoned with. Her English teacher had allowed her to write scenes of film scripts instead of creative essays. She had nearly finished her first complete motion picture script, fuelled by that encouragement alone. She had been hesitant to ask Sister Mary for feedback and now knew for sure she had better not.

Maisy suddenly stopped, closed her eyes and tapped her heels together three times.

There's no place like home,
there's no place like home,
there's no place like home.

Though her ears told her of the absence of London's busy street noises she still opened her eyes hopefully only to see the Sussex countryside. The tall hedges and glimpses of fields and edges of woodland all seemed mightily indifferent to Maisy's plight. London was not like that, London always seemed to manage to reflect Maisy's own mood somehow.

She snorted and walked on. *So much for the pictures. Thanks for nothing, Dorothy.*

There was a pub at the end of the road, one of those old fairy tale ones, with dark beams criss-crossed across loam walls and a sagging tile roof which gave it a desolate appearance. The long north-south road which bypassed it meant there was usually farm traffic there, long waggons parked in a row alongside the road with patient draught horses being watered outside whilst the carters had a quick pint. Now and then there would be a lorry or a car too. Maisy's grandfather, Fred Maskall, was waiting for her outside the pub; seated on the driving box of a large farm waggon, holding the reins of three draught horses harnessed in single file.

Despite her mood Maisy granted the horses an appreciative glance. They reminded her of home. The sound of hoofs on the cobblestone streets on the Isle of Dogs had always drawn her out to watch the drays loaded with large barrels of beer from Whitbread's Brewery. Mum always encouraged Maisy to follow them with bucket and a shovel so she could collect the droppings which Mum used as fertilizer for her tiny allotment out back. Maisy had loved the Whitbread horses; their enormous hooves and great height were imposing. The well-groomed animals had coloured ribbons knotted into their plaited manes and big leather halters around their neck with ornamental emblems which shone like gold on a sunny day. Her grandfather's horses were fine animals too although they wore no ribbons in their manes and the halters were practical working farm halters; no fancy brewery stuff here. London seemed worlds away.

"How do, Maisy?" Fred Maskall greeted his granddaughter jovially.

"Fine, thank you, Gramps," Maisy said dutifully and clambered onto the driving box to sit next to him, throwing her school satchel and gasmask container onto the empty cargo bed behind them. "You?"

"Scratching along," Gramps answered as he always did. It was one of those odd local sayings which had caused Maisy to be in a perpetual state of bafflement when she first arrived in the Sussex Weald a few weeks ago. The rural natives used very strange words which varied from district to district; village to village even, or so she had been told. She was getting used to it though, somehow many of the words made sense even if she did not know them. Others resembled words she knew. The Sussex *chavee* was a chavvy – that was one she liked. Better than the 'child' used by teachers at the school. That was fine for the toddlers, not for clever eleven-year-olds.

Gramps was in his late fifties; tall and strong. He had a kind face with mischievous eyes and his chin and cheeks were usually covered in grey stubble. His hair was cropped short under the cap he wore. He was dressed in his usual old fashioned tunic which Maisy had seen other farmers wear as well. He flicked the reins and the waggon grumbled and creaked into movement as the horses responded to his instructions.

"How was school today?" He asked it casually but Maisy sensed he was keen. She had already figured out that her grandfather was a bright one, a proper *jemmy*. She had tried to hide her unhappiness at the farm from both Gramps and Gran because they were doing their best to be nice but she suspected they knew anyway.

"I got into trouble," Maisy mumbled.

"What did you get in *moil* for?"

"All I did was point out my reading group were dead slow," Maisy conveyed outrage in her voice. "I finished both reading pages a dozen times, Gramps. And they were still on the first bleeding page, weren't they?"

"So you told your teacher you're a quick reader?"

"Yes," Maisy nodded. "I thought she'd put me in a faster group or something."

"More of a challenge for you?" Gramps asked. "*Mayhap,* it was the way you told her?"

"Could be," Maisy admitted. "The Abbess can't mouth a word of proper English I reckon. Speaks like a Toff, innit?"

Fred Maskall looked away biting his lip.

"*Mayhap* that is a problem," he said at last. "So she's an Abbess?"

"Well no, but I call her that because she's humongous; the size of an abbey."

"Do you think it's a good thing to poke fun at a person's size?" Gramps looked at her with raised eyebrows.

"Yes! No! I don't usually, Gramps," Maisy gestured wildly. "But she keeps on calling me 'little' and she always lets the boys call me 'dwarf' and pretends she doesn't hear them, innit?"

"Tis unaccountable," Gramps nodded his understanding. "Do you reckon you'll be able to learn her how to speak proper *Sheere-Folk* English? Like you yourself speak, Maisy?"

Maisy shook her head with conviction. "It's teach, Gramps; I teach, you learn, innit? Nah, she won't let me teach her, she reckons I'm *downy* and *gammy*, doesn't she?"

"Tis 'learn' in Sussex," Gramps said stubbornly. "I recollect from my schooldays that some things were middling unfair."

"Blooming unfair and all!" Maisy confirmed wholeheartedly.

They passed another waggon heading north and Gramps exchanged a greeting with the carter. There were woodlands to either side of the road here. The woods on their right were lighter and interspersed with small irregular fields or dirt roads leading to small farmsteads. The woods on their left, the Wyrde Woods, were dark and forbidding; unbroken by roads or gaps.

Gramps turned his attention back to Maisy. "*Howsumdever*, there was little to be done about it. All you could do was put up with it and try to stay out of *moil*."

"Did you get into trouble, Gramps?" Maisy demanded to know.

Her grandfather sighed deeply. "That is a *gurt* big state secret, lass. *Bettermost* we don't talk about it. Your *gammer* will skin me alive if I tell you, so she will."

Maisy laughed. Gran probably would too.

"I said 'try' to stay out of *moil*," Gramps shrugged. "If I were you, I'd accept that communication is hampered – lost in translation as it were."

Maisy nodded reluctantly, "That does seem better, dunnit?"

"When you're done reading; daydream," Gramps suggested. "Think of other stories."

Maisy wrinkled her nose though the task was not hard. A chavvy on the Isle of Dogs did not have much in the way of toys; street games and make-believe were the order of the day. That and visits to the pictures provided plenty of storylines but Maisy sensed an opportunity.

"But I'd have to read those stories first, innit?" She said with a sly grin.

"Stories aplenty. Have you seen my bookshelves?"

"Yes," Maisy nodded eagerly. "But Gran said not to touch them."

"My Betty is a dear," Gramps nodded. "She *kens* those books are middling important to me."

"I could read one at a time, innit?" Maisy suggested hopefully. "I'd be dead careful and all."

"*Geemeny*," Gramps smiled. "That might well work, I'll have a word with your *gammer*."

Maisy smiled; life had just got a bit more bearable. Gramps had more books than anybody she knew, maybe as many as a hundred even.

The horses turned right without any encouragement, they knew the way home and pulled the waggon onto the narrow dirt road that was framed by two copses of ash before these were replaced by the wheat fields which fronted Maskall Farm.

§ § § § § § §

Maisy had hidden herself on top of the haystack, burrowing in deep so that only her face was showing. She had felt a morose mood brewing like a summer storm and needed to be on her own so as not to expose her grandparents to it.

The haystack was in a corner of the central farmyard that was surrounded by the farmhouse, the barn and various stables and sheds. There was a ten foot gap between two of the lower stables through which the haystack could be reached and Maisy had positioned herself so she could overlook the farmyard.

She needed time to think, time to make sense of it all. Though she had been here for a few weeks already she was still overwhelmed by the sense of space. It was not as if she knew nothing except the narrow cobbled streets on the Isle of Dogs; she got around and knew the great muddy expanse of the Thames by the wharves and for all its abject poverty there were ample parks in the East End. Even the damp airey her parents lived in, accessible only by a narrow set of steps leading down from the street level, was adjacent to a big park. There was a proper playground there, with swings and slides and a roundabout which would spin at breakneck speed if there were enough chavvies around to propel it. There were loads of grassy areas as well for picnics and games. However, all the wider expanses of space had been securely framed by buildings at one point or another. Here in the Sussex Weald there were no such frames; the countryside rolled on and on like a multi-hued green ocean. It had made Maisy dizzy at first, now it just added to her general sense of misery.

"Maisy?" Gramps called from the farmhouse door.

The hay rustled as Maisy dug herself in deeper. If only Gramps and Gran were not so nice. They had been kind and patient ever since she had been exiled from London. Their warmth made it difficult to wallow in proper misery which Maisy considered justified because it was all so blooming unfair. It was all the bloody Nazis' fault, them and their bleeding bombers. London had been abuzz with the need to evacuate the chavvies and although Maisy had fought the possibility tooth and nail Mum's concerns had prevailed in the end.

"Maisy!" Gran's voice this time.

Maisy shut her eyes. When the train had chugged out of Victoria Station she had been determined to hate Sussex in general and Maskall Farm in particular. Mum had been on the verge of enthusiasm; trying to instil into Maisy the cheer of her own childhood memories of growing up on her parents' farm. There had been a longing in Mum's voice which had unsettled Maisy because it reminded her that German bombs were not the sole threat to the little family trying to make ends meet in the dank underground airey they called home.

"Where can that lass be?" Gran's voice suddenly sounded close.

"I don't *ken*," Gramps grumbled. They had wandered into the farmyard and ended up by the haystack and Maisy held her breath for fear of stirring the hay.

"She *baint* happy here, Fred," Gran said softly and Maisy felt a stab of guilt.

"She just needs some more time, Betty," Gramps tried to sound cheerful.

"That's what you said *somewhen-the-other-day*, Fred, and afore that too," Gran pointed out gently.

"I was so looking forwards to having her stay here," Gramps suddenly sounded forlorn and Maisy pulled a face. "Reckoned we'd hear *chavee's* laughter on the farm again, *surelye*."

"Aye, I recollect you saying so," Gran answered.

"Liz should *naun* have gone to *Lunnon*."

"You gave your blessing, Mus Maskall. We both did."

"Twere what Liz wanted," Gramps answered. "Full of young hopes and dreams they were. There *baint* much left of them and I don't reckon Liz is very content there *naun* more."

Maisy's eyes grew large. She had not realized that her grandparents were aware of the difficulties at home.

"Well," Gran said. "What's done is done, *surelye*."

"You're right once again, my nightingale," Gramps' usual cheer sounded in his voice again. "Tis unaccountable how often you are right, my love. I'll *gwoan* check the barn."

"I'll have a gander by the paddock, she's drawn by those ponies often enough."

Maisy waited till their footsteps died away and then allowed herself a small audible sob.

§ § § § § § §

School was not much better the next day. The local village and farm kids seemed to exist in a universe of their own; talking at length in their broad Sussex drawl about topics which Maisy either did not understand at all or found dull to the extreme. She had hoped that the influx of evacuees from London would yield some kindred souls but they were all from west London; in many ways further away from the Isle of Dogs than some of the exotic worlds Maisy had seen in the pictures. Most knew each other for they had attended the same schools and they took their cue from the teachers who accompanied them. These regarded Maisy warily; as if she was a captive animal likely to revert to unpredictable rabid aggression. Some teachers, like Sister Mary, were downright hostile and the London pupils regarded this as an encouragement to shun Maisy.

Reading was the usual hell, now made worse by the foul looks the three boys gave her.

"You said we are *chuckle-headed,*" the big bulking bully called Bill growled at her.

"Chuck-what?" Maisy shook her head in confusion.

"*Nickeys,*" one of his mates hissed. "You called us *nickeys.*"

"Oh!" Maisy said brightly. "But that wasn't meant as an insult."

"*Naun?*" Bill sounded surprised.

"Course not," Maisy expounded happily. "It's only an insult if it aint true, innit? It's right nasty to call a regular person a *glock*, he'd be a right *nickey* if he weren't insulted by that, dontcha think? But to call someone who is *glocky* a halfwit is just stating a fact, innit? Not meant as an blooming insult at all, more a recognition of their special *glocky* status."

She smiled brightly at Bill as he looked bewildered by her train of thought. It occurred to Maisy that figuring out what she had just said might take him as long as it took him to finish a reading assignment and she decided to help him somewhat by adding: "A *glock* is someone simple in the head, innit?"

"Miss Robbins?"

Maisy rolled her eyes, despite her great size the Abbess possessed the ability to sneak around the classroom in total silence until she spoke and by the sound of it she was standing right behind Maisy.

"Yes Ma...Sister Mary," Maisy answered dutifully. She looked around.

Just about all the pupils had focused on Sister Mary and Maisy now; anticipating the renewal of their conflict with gleeful grins. One girl surprised her by flashing Maisy an encouraging smile. The girl's seat was at the back of the class and usually she kept to herself as if she were blissfully unaware of the *nickeys* and *glocks* around her. Maisy returned the smile hesitantly. Despite her aloofness the girl seemed kind and Maisy thought she was pretty enough to feature in the pictures; proper tall with a cascade of deep red hair.

"What did you just say?" The nun's voice rumbled like an ominous storm cloud.

Maisy turned her attention back to the Abbess and thought fast. She had no idea how much the Abbess had overheard so it was not wise to deviate from her words. She decided that honesty was the best course of action.

"I were telling Bill here that it's okay to be a halfwit, innit?"

Some of the local kids dared a grin. The red-headed girl smiled.

"Reading is not the time to chatter like a little monkey," Sister Mary said reprovingly. "Although it is very kind of you, Miss Robbins, to share your first-hand experience of being halfwitted."

The class laughed dutifully and Sister Mary shot Maisy a triumphant look. Maisy just lowered her head, relieved that the teacher considered her remark sufficient punishment for the time being. The bamboo cane was far more painful.

The boys, however, were not finished with her yet. Bill's two mates and some others followed her out of Wolfden to the pub at the crossroads; name-calling all the way. Mostly 'dwarf' and 'gnome' for creative originality was obviously not their strong point.

Maisy ignored them, the London gangs were far worse and she had stood some of those off. It was just a matter of showing them who was boss and she reckoned an opportunity would soon arise, especially if they continued to follow her further and further away out of the village.

None-the-less, she was despondent as she trudged southwards along the broad dirt road which led to Maskall Farm. She missed her own London gang; the group of kids from her street who would congregate to play in the parks or roam about the wharves.

A curious sight greeted her when she got to the farm. Gramps was up on a ladder by her bedroom window, fidgeting with some sort of contraption which he had installed.

"Gramps?" Maisy asked curiously as she reached the ladder.

"How do, Maisy?" Gramps looked down and smiled.

"Scratching along," she used the response which he always gave, she was not quite sure what it meant but it seemed to illustrate her new countryside existence perfectly.

Her grandfather laughed and climbed down the ladder. He stood next to her, looking up with a proud look on his face. Maisy could not make out what he was looking at. A wood bracket had been attached to the wall by her bedroom window and something boxy hung from it but she could only see the dark underside.

"Watcha built, Gramps?"

"You said you had trouble sleeping at night," Gramps answered. "*All-along-of* the lack of proper noise and light."

"Yes! The street is always busy," Maisy said as she nodded. "You hear people's feet real well in the airey, cause their feet are at our head height, innit? And buses drive by and there is light and rumbling and shaking. Oh! There is a pub by the park entrance and you hear people come out singing and all!"

"And that helped you sleep?" Gramps looked incredulous. "'Tis unaccountable."

Maisy shrugged, it was hard to explain how the utter darkness at Maskall Farm pressed on her at night. There was no lack of noise on a farm but they were all made by animals and it had taken her some time to learn to become familiar with them. They had sounded monstrous during the first sleepless nights.

"Well, this might help," Gramps beamed and worked a rope that hung down from the contraption above and slowly lowered the rectangular shape to the ground.

Maisy's mouth dropped open when she saw what it was. Gramps had built a wood replica of a double-decker bus. It had small glass windows and was painted bright red and he had used labels from tins to create advertisements on the sides.

"Roof opens like a lid," Gramps explained and demonstrated by swinging it open. "There is space for a candle, see? It works like a lantern. I blocked the windows facing outwards because of the blackout."

He turned to her and smiled, pride evident on his face. "I reckon we can light it at night and you'll have yourself a proper lit-up *Lunnon* bus outside the window to help you sleep."

Maisy was speechless and felt her eyes water.

"Well?" Gramps looked at her expectantly. "What do you think of it?"

Maisy bit on her lip and wiped an eye. Then she turned and ran away as fast as she could.

§ § § § § § §

Gramps joined Maisy when she had finished crying, huddled up against one of the barn walls with a tearstained face.

Without saying a word he lowered himself and sat next to Maisy. He handed Maisy a clean handkerchief and the girl accepted it gratefully and began to clear the mess on her face.

"I am sorry," Maisy said in a small voice. "Shoulda said thank you, innit? It's a real cracker, really, it is."

"*Baint* easy, is it?" Gramps asked.

Maisy shook her head.

"Is it Betty and myself?

"No, no, you're both cracking, innit?" Maisy shook her head. "I just miss London."

"I can imagine."

"Have you ever been there, Gramps?"

"Just the once lass, to visit your mum and you after you were born, we both went."

"Did you like it?" Maisy asked eagerly.

Gramps stared in the distance mulling over his answer.

"I felt middling lost, adrift in a strange world I could *naun* understand and utterly helpless. *Naun*, lass, I didn't like *Lunnon*, truth be told."

Maisy nodded. Although it was beyond her comprehension that London held no appeal for Gramps she understood the rest of his feelings all too well. She reckoned it also meant that Gramps understood what it was like for Maisy. *Adrift in a strange world.*

"I didn't mean to be ungrateful, did I?" Maisy said softly.

"You're a good lass, Maisy," Gramps smiled.

"Really?" Maisy was puzzled. She had never reflected on her behaviour much in London but since coming here she had felt like a bull in a china shop more often than not; mouthing off and forever launching herself into trouble.

"Aye, *naun* doubt about it," Gramps said firmly.

Maisy sighed and shifted so that she leaned against him. He folded a big strong arm around her and she felt comforted. They sat there for a while, overlooking the green fields which swept down at a shallow angle before rising more sharply to meet the edge of the woods. The fields were dotted with sheep grazing contentedly, pausing only to add to the chorus of bleating which broke out every now and then.

"It aint half bad here, really," Maisy said dreamily. "Right pretty, innit?"

"*Zackly*," Gramps nodded. "The Wyrde Woods are middling fair. *Bettermost* with good company though. Have you tried to make friends at school?"

Maisy snorted.

"I'll take that as a '*naun*'," Gramps sighed.

"The London kids are snobs, innit?" Maisy protested. "They look down on the likes of me. Proper West End Toffs. And the local chavvies look at me like I escaped from London Zoo."

"Hmm," Gramps responded. "*Mayhap* those are first impressions? I remember in *Lunnon*, all of them *Sheere-folk* seemed the same to my eyes at first. Then I got to know some of the carters, *scorsed* horse talk with them and they took me to their pub for a pint."

"No carters at school," Maisy declared. "Just a bunch of *nickeys* and *glocks*."

"There are always exceptions," Fred Maskall shook his head. "It's a matter of having a closer look, I reckon. Have a gander at the quiet ones, you *baint* the only one that doesn't fit in, *surelye*."

Maisy nodded but she was unconvinced.

"Meanwhile," Gramps continued. "I could use your help, lass, so I could."

"Really? With what?"

"It's top secret," Gramps warned.

Maisy cheered up, she liked top secrets. "I aint a *blabber* and I don't *chaunt*, do I?"

Gramps caught her gist and nodded. "I have these…little friends, *somewhen* folk bring me more. One came in *disyer* morning. Lamentably mistreated though, and *afeared* of menfolk by the looks of it. Perhaps she'll respond different to a woman's touch?"

Maisy beamed. 'Little friends' sounded intriguing. "I can try!"

"Let's *gwoan* see her then."

Maisy was up in an instant and held out her hand to offer Gramps some support as he scrambled to his feet. He smiled his thanks and then took her to the mysterious long shed which she had seen tucked away behind the barn. She had noticed it before but the single door had been doubly padlocked and there had been so many stables, sheds, workshops and other outbuildings to explore that she had not paid it much attention yet.

Gramps unlocked the padlocks and opened the door. "Welcome to my secret kingdom, Maisy."

Maisy grinned broadly, she liked secret kingdoms too, and then stepped inside full of anticipation.

§ § § § § § §

"Catcha later, Gramps," Maisy jumped off the waggon at the timbered pub.

"I won't be here to pick you up after school, *naun* today." Fred Maskall answered.

"That's alright," Maisy said while she retrieved her satchel and gasmask, much more careful than usual. "I'll walk again. I know the way to the farm."

"Maisy?"

She looked at him questioningly.

"Do you recollect what we talked about? Trying to make some friends?"

Maisy frowned. "I got Valkerie now, innit?"

"Aye," Gramps laughed. "That you do and Valkerie sure took a liking to you. Just try to get to know some of the *chavees* as well."

"I'll try," Maisy said dubiously.

"Good lass," Gramps smiled. "Now, be *gwoan*, off to school. Try to avoid *moil* if you can."

Maisy nodded with a bright smile, but when she turned to walk towards Wolfden the smile faded fast as she considered the prospect of another day lost at a school full of halfwits.

2. Joy

The girl was tall for her eleven years. She walked barefoot and was dressed in a simple white dress which reached down to cover her knees. She had a dishevelled mane of red hair that reached halfway down her back. Her mum combed and brushed it endlessly but it never stayed proper very long as individual hairs frizzled out one by one until her hair seemed to reach out each and every way.

"Witch! *DRAGGLE-TAIL* WITCH!!"

The girl's cheeks coloured slightly and she bit her lip as she resisted the temptation to increase her pace.

"Your mum is a witch Joy Whitfield! *Chance-born* like yourself!"

Joy clenched her teeth. The village lads were unusually hostile today. A group of them – a core of some half-dozen with occasional followers – had long made it a sport to walk behind her, taunting her as she left the village of Wolfden at the end of each school day. Her strategy had always been to ignore them, departing the village with as much dignity as she could muster.

She sensed the clod of earth which flew through the air and ducked just in time. It flew past her head but the next one hit her back. Joy was closing in on the Raven's Roost and she knew that once she had passed the morose looking pub she would be safe. She would cross the North Woods Lane into the area of the Wyrde Woods known as Shims Copses and none of the village kids would dare to follow her there; they were all afraid of that part of the Wyrde Woods.

Another clod of earth flew past her but then the bombardment ceased. Joy turned to see if the boys had lost interest, they usually drifted off somewhere between the last farm cottage which marked the village boundary and the Raven's Roost.

The boys had not drifted off though, they had spotted new game in the form of a girl who was walking up the road behind them. Joy stopped, unsure what to do. She recognized the girl, she was one of the evacuees – *Sheere-folk* from abroad - who had arrived a few weeks ago. Joy had paid them little attention because she kept to herself at school. No one liked witches much. She had taken a bit more note of this particular new girl because she was quite short. When she had first walked into the classroom Joy had figured she was one of the younger *chavees* who had got lost. A closer look though had revealed the girl was about her own age despite her lack of height. She had long black hair and dark intelligent eyes. She had not seemed very happy in class – and got into trouble with the teachers a lot – but Joy had not minded that a great deal. To her mind being content and attending school were opposites at any rate.

"Look, it's that dwarf," one of the lads shouted.

The short *Sheere-girl* looked up and grinned cheerfully. "Look, here are the village idiots, innit?".

Joy smiled at the fearless answer. The boys took offence though and straightened their backs and broadened their shoulders. The *Sheere-girl* did not appear to be in the least bit intimidated and walked resolutely forwards – possibly unaware that the village idiots were intent on giving her a sound beating. Maybe they did things differently in whatever *Sheere* she was from. The lads were as confused about this as Joy was; put off by the *Sheere-girl's* total lack of concern. They hesitated.

It was time to even the odds.

Joy rushed forwards and started screeching like a *scritch* owl. "EEEEEEEEEEEEECCCCCHHHHH!"

The boys spun around, alarm on their faces. Joy stopped, dropped into a crouch, looked around the half circle and then hissed at them. At least half of them looked extremely uncomfortable and shifted about edgily. She had already noted that it was mostly the younger ones in the group today, the older more audacious ones were absent and she might be able to scare this lot off.

Aware that she was taking a risk Joy closed her eyes, stretched out her arms in front of her – forming claws with her hands – and started mumbling incoherent nonsense. She resisted a great big smile when she heard the first boys back off and then run away; followed by more shuffling of feet and murmurs of 'witch'.

"Cor, you didn't half scare them didya?" The *Sheere-girl's* voice was close now and full of admiration.

Joy opened her eyes. She could see the lads scampering back to the village, it was just her and the *Sheere-girl* left.

"Tis in their own mind," Joy answered. "They call me witch, *mayhap* they believe it."

"I'm Maisy," the girl offered her hand and Joy looked at the outstretched hand with some surprise. Had she not just dropped a hint as to her reputation?

"Joy," she answered and decided to shake Maisy's hand.

"Why did those boys call you a witch? They were horrid, innit?" Maisy asked.

Joy smiled hesitantly. Maisy was straightforward, most locals preferred to take some time getting to the point they were making. *Scorsing* pleasantries along the roadside could take a good half hour in the autumn and winter when the main work on the land was done. Joy did not mind though, it gave her a chance to tell Maisy that Joy was not considered very likable in Wolfden and Maisy could then go on her way.

Before I start to like her.

"My mum aint married, I'm *chance-born*," Joy shrugged.

"A bastard?"

"Aye, that's what *Sheere-folk* call it," Joy felt tense for a moment but was relieved the truth was out.

"Fiddle-dee-dee," Maisy laughed. "You're not alone, I'd say half of London is *chance-born*, innit. I'll take you there one day when we're done smashing up the Nazis."

Joy smiled, Maisy moved fast, already planning a trip to *Lunnon*. Joy had never even been to Brighton; and Stancaster just the once. The nearby markettown of Odesby formed her most regular impression of life outside of the Wyrde Woods. They started walking again.

"You're from *Lunnon* are you?" Joy asked.

To her surprise Maisy launched into a song.

Maybe it's because I'm a Londoner, that I love London so.
Maybe it's because I'm a Londoner that I think of her wherever I go.
I get a funny feelin' inside of me just walkin' up and down.
Maybe it's because I'm a Londoner that I love London Town.

"Proud of *Lunnon*?" Joy smiled in confusion. Generally to call someone a *Lunnoner* was derogatory; it had never occurred to her that somebody might actually be proud of the place.

"Greatest city in the world, innit?" Maisy confirmed happily.

"Full of *Sheere-folk* and a middling stride from Sussex," Joy pulled a face. "You might *naun* want to sing that song too often down here, *surelye*."

"Bollocks," Maisy decreed. "We're all English, there's a war on dontcha know?"

"War?" Joy frowned and then realized what Maisy meant. "Oh, *all-along-of* the fighting in France and such? France be a middling stride from Sussex too."

Maisy looked at her in amazement.

"Where have you been this last year Joy?"

"*Dereaways* in the Wyrde Woods," Joy stopped and pointed straight ahead of her.

They had come to the crossroads with the North Woods Lane. In the old days it used to be a crossways – the Raven's Carfax it had been called then. The North Woods Lane ran north to the village of Mordrove and south to the village of Nickleby and the old road had intersected it on an east-west axis. Only the west road that led to Wolfden was used these days, all that was left of the east road at the crossroads was a narrow footpath leading into Shims Copses. It was on Joy's route to the Owlery; the cottage where she lived with her mum on the other side of Shims Copses.

Joy stopped where the signposts used to be, indicating the directions of Wolfden, Mordrove and Nickleby. They had been removed recently because of the war.

"I *gwoan* straight here," Joy told Maisy.

"Well that's a blooming shame, my granddad's farm is there," Maisy pointed south and frowned.

At that moment her gasmask box started making thumping noises. Joy looked at it with surprise.

"Why dontcha come for a visit?" Maisy suggested, ignoring the racket in the box. "Come have a cuppa?"

"Your box," Joy pointed. "It's making noises."

"That'll be Valkerie," Maisy nodded. "She does that."

"Your gasmask has a name?" Joy was puzzled.

Maisy laughed long and loud.

"No, I left it at home innit?" She said when she was done laughing. "Lots of stuff you can carry in the boxes, like a sarnie for lunch. Or…"

She fidgeted with the lid of the box and started opening it. Before the lid had even opened a quarter of the way a sleek white ferret wormed its way out and ran up Maisy's arm.

Maisy cradled it and the ferret rested on its back and let Maisy tickle its tummy. Joy smiled.

"Hullo Valkerie, didya have a nice day at school? Rubbish weren't it?"

Valkerie did not pay Maisy any attention, she had spotted Joy and was stretching her neck this way and that as if to see Joy from different perspectives with her little red eyes. Joy smiled and reached out her hand.

"Better not, Joy," Maisy warned. "She'll nip you for sure."

Joy withdrew her hand. It seemed incongruous for the little furry creature looked friendly enough but Joy knew to heed an animal's human companion when they gave such warnings.

"Called her Fluffy at first," Maisy said cheerfully, then turned her face to the ferret. "Didn't I you little rogue?"

The Ferret-Formerly-Called-Fluffy looked back at Maisy then twisted her lithe body in an instant and clambered up before curling herself around Maisy's neck, half concealed under the girl's dark hair.

"Together, we're salt and pepper," Maisy grinned. "Renamed her Valkerie cause she was a bit like them vampires in the pictures. Dead set on biting anything in her reach. Weren'tcha, little bugger?"

"Bad imprint?" Joy asked Maisy who looked surprised and then nodded.

"Yeah, you know about that?" Maisy asked.

Joy nodded.

"Anyhow, come visit? We're mates now, innit?" Maisy repeated her invitation. "Mates drop by."

Joy had never had a friend apart from Thallie and wondered if there had been some sort of friend-making ritual in her interaction with Maisy which she had missed. Best to assume Maisy knew about these things. She studied the girl who looked at her brightly with a cheeky grin.

A house meant other people; adults who were like as not to disapprove if Maisy casually inserted the likes of Joy into their household. She felt a stab of bitterness. Most of the folk in Wolfden would have seen Joy's mum Sarah in their very own homes. If someone in their house was sick or wounded Sarah would be asked to come since Wolfden had no doctor and the nearby town of Odesby was a fair stride away. As far as Joy was concerned Mum should just let them suffer their ills and pains. It was their just reward, for surely it was impossible that the adults in the village had never witnessed the daily verbal abuse Joy was subjected to. Mum always shrugged when Joy complained about it and said it had always been so and Joy should rise above it.

However, Maisy had mentioned a farm and many of those who lived beyond the village boundaries still followed the Old Ways to one degree or another. Sarah Whitfield was respected at some of those farms. Joy was also greatly curious as to what it was like having a friend and she also thought she perceived a very subtle pleading in Maisy's eyes. The *Lunnon* girl seemed confident enough but Joy reckoned she might be lonely. Her short size made her odd and odd was something the village *chavees* found hard to cope with on a good day. Mum would not mind, she would assume her daughter was wandering about the Wyrde Woods again. There was no set time to be home at the Owlery as long as chores got done.

"I'll *gwoan* with you," Joy decided and Maisy looked delighted.

The girls started walking southwards along the North Woods Lane, Valkerie content to ride on Maisy's shoulders.

"The Nazis are the greatest evil bastards ever," Maisy declared, not quite done with the war yet. "Chased me outta London didn't they? That's why I am here, to stay with Gramps and Gran, me mum reckoned it's safer here."

"Ah," Joy said. This did not seem so bad, so far Joy was rather pleased that Maisy had been chased out of *Lunnon*.

Maisy burst into another song.

Hitler has only got one ball,
Göring has two but very small,
Himmler has something sim'lar,
But poor old Goebbels has no balls at all.

Joy burst into laughter.

"You must've heard the song before, the whole of London is singing it these days," Maisy said.

"*Naun*, never," Joy shook her head.

She knew the country was at war, fighting the Nazis on the continent but that was about all. So far the war had had little impact on the folk living in the Wyrde Woods apart from the first evacuees and the rationing. Joy and Mum produced most of their own food at the Owlery anyhow and soon harvesting truffles in the woods would mean some under the counter trade in Odesby.

"I know lots of war songs," Maisy chattered happily. "Me dad taught me, he fought in the Great War, some place called Wipers in Flanders."

Oh, oh, oh, it's a lovely war,
Who wouldn't be a soldier, eh?
Oh, it's a shame to take the pay;
As soon as reveille is gone,
We feel just as heavy as lead,
But we never get up till the sergeant
Brings us breakfast up to bed.

Joy giggled again. Maisy was full of balderdash.

"I'll teach you if you like," Maisy suggested.

Joy nodded happily; she could sing some of them next time the vicar came to talk to her mum about attending church services. Vicar Framsfield always said he liked music.

"What can you teach me?" Maisy asked.

Joy pointed at the trees to their left without hesitation. "The Wyrde Woods," she said. "I'll learn you about the Wyrde Woods."

Maisy looked dubious. "Woods, filled with trees and most of it's bleeding green," she shrugged. "Gramps also wants to teach me about them woods."

Joy stopped and Maisy followed suit. Joy captured Maisy's eyes with her own bright green ones. Valkerie stuck her head out of Maisy's hair to sniff at the reason they had stopped.

"There is a lot more to it, Maisy," Joy smiled. "There are whole *wurrelds* in there."

"You've got a deal then," Maisy nodded after a moment's thought. "I'll teach you my dad's songs, you show me those worlds of yours."

Both girls looked pleased as they continued on their way and before long Joy could sing soldiers' marching songs and the two sounded like two drunk sailors on shore leave, albeit with higher voices and more interruptions for rounds of giggles.

§ § § § § § §

Maisy led Joy up a dirt road to their right and soon the trees began to clear before being replaced altogether by the fields and orchards which surrounded a small thatched farmhouse and various outbuildings.

Dogs began to bark in one of the sheds and a tall man emerged from it. He wore a wool smock that fell down to his knees and had wide sleeves. He was not wearing a cap and his short grey hair was uncombed, there was grey stubble on his cheeks and chin. Two lurchers slipped past his legs and ran forwards to greet Maisy, wagging their tails.

"There's a secret in the sheds," Maisy whispered conspiratorially as she petted the lurchers. "Tell you later. Hullo Hugin! Hullo Munin!"

As the man came closer Joy noted that his smock was green. Generally she saw the blue ones which shepherds wore or the black ones favoured by carters and ploughmen. The embroidery across the chest that always depicted aspects of the trade of the owner showed only a pattern of acorns and oak leaves. Joy liked it and realized she had seen it before. This was Mus Maskall whom she had seen wandering around in the Wyrde Woods every now and then. On those occasions they had stopped to *scorse* pleasantries and her impression had been that he liked to play a jolly bumbler but that his eyes were alert and watchful, betraying a keen intelligence. His wife Betty was one of Mum's friends and sometimes called at the Owlery.

"Why, it's Goody Whitfield's lass," Mus Maskall said and smiled at Joy. "You are welcome here, Joy Whitfield."

"*Bethanks,*" Joy smiled back gratefully. The formal welcome was important and he had shown no hesitation giving it. This was not so bad after all. "How do, Mus Maskall?"

"Scratching along," Mus Maskall nodded. "How was your day at school Maisy?"

"Smashing!" Maisy beamed.

"Well that's middling good," Mus Maskall said, looking genuinely pleased.

Suddenly he frowned and Joy followed his gaze to Valkerie whose white head slowly emerged from the dark curtain of Maisy's hair. The ferret sniffed at Mus Maskall curiously.

"Oh blooming heck," Maisy pulled a face. "I plain forgot."

"There I was thinking I had Valkerie safe and sound in the long shed," Mus Maskall frowned. He scratched his head and looked puzzled. "A shed that's locked with the *bettermost* padlocks on sale in Odesby."

"I...," Maisy turned red.

"I reckon Valkerie must have *loped* out of the shed," Joy said quickly. "Tis a good thing Maisy found her scurrying *atween* here and North Woods Lane then, aint it Mus Maskall?"

"A middling fine find," Mus Maskall winked at Joy. "*Bethanks* Maisy, tis a wide *wurreld* out there for a little ferret."

"I am not in trouble?" Maisy asked suspiciously.

"*Naun*," Mus Maskall said. "*Howsumdever*, a Top Secret *baint* a secret for too long if you take careless risks, *surelye*?"

Maisy looked down and nodded.

"And...," Mus Maskall continued, "...the next time you pick one of my locks..."

He lapsed into a meaningful silence and Maisy looked up at him and pouted.

"Good, I am glad that's clear," Mus Maskall said. "Now, Joy, can you keep a secret better than my own flesh and blood?"

Joy nodded.

"Let's take Valkerie to her home, then see if my Betty'll treat us to a cup of tea."

Maisy's grandfather led the girls behind the barn which had a long shed built along its entire length. He tutted as he unlocked the padlocks and opened the door. Joy followed Mus Maskall and Maisy in. There was a musky smell in the shed though Joy was surprised it was not far stronger when she beheld cage after cage filled with ferrets. Each cage was as big as a small stable stall and held about a dozen ferrets; some curled in a heap and fast asleep, others wild at play. The latter ceased their activities to come to the edges and throw curious looks at the small procession. Maisy greeted those by name, Joy had no idea how she could keep all of them apart. Mus Maskall opened one of the cages.

"This lot I call the Hooligan Horde," he said as the occupants of the cage stirred into curious activity. Maisy peeled Valkerie off her neck and the ferret jumped into the cage to be greeted by her fellows.

"*Bettermost naun* tell anyone about *disyer* shed Joy," Mus Maskall said, looking at Joy.

Joy shook her head. Mum had dropped the occasional hint as to Mus Maskall's activities in the Wyrde Woods and the ferrets seemed to confirm that. She would not tell a soul.

"I won't Mus Maskall."

"Good lass, come, let's *gwoan* say hello to Maisy's *gammer*."

The girls followed the farmer outside. Joy and Maisy exchanged a glance and a grin as he locked the door and then followed him to the house.

Betty Maskall was pottering around in the kitchen which was dominated by a big table in the middle of the large room. She was broad though Joy suspected that was mostly muscle as the wives pitched in with the hardiest work on the smaller farms. Joy sometimes visited the Hornsby farm on the other side of the woods. The family had half-a-dozen children and everything she saw indicated a tight-knit family operating the small farm as a team. She suspected the Maskalls were like that too.

Goody Maskall wore a green dress which contrasted nicely with the silver grey strands of her long hair.

"By *Geemeny*!" Betty exclaimed. "Sarah's lass! You're welcome here Joy of the Owlery."

"*Bethanks*, Goody Maskall," Joy smiled brightly.

"Owlery?" Maisy asked.

"It's the name of the cottage where Joy lives with her mum," Mus Maskall explained.

"Right, in the Wyrde Woods," Maisy said.

Mus Maskall sat down behind the table and Joy and Maisy followed suit.

"Oi! The Daily Express!" Maisy spotted a folded newspaper on the table.

"It's a few days old," Mus Maskall said.

"Anything important in it, Gramps?" Maisy asked.

"Aye," Mus Maskall nodded. "Good news. The *Lunnon* Minister said wheat prices are to rise to sixty shillings a quarter, up by more than ten. Livestock *gwoan* fetch more too."

Maisy shrugged but Joy nodded. That was good news for the farmers in the Edgelands of the Wyrde Woods, especially the small ones struggling to get by.

"There's plenty of news on Dunkirk too," Goody Maskall added, "You'll be wanting a gander at it, Maisy."

"Dunkirk!" Maisy brightened and promptly acquisitioned the paper.

"Dunkirk?" Joy asked curiously.

Goody Maskall provided everybody with a steaming mug of tea and set a large pitcher of fresh creamy milk and a small bowl of sugar on the table before sitting down herself.

"You've *naun* heard about Dunkirk?" Mus Maskall asked Joy.

Joy shook her head.

"Tired, dirty, hungry they came back – unbeatable!" Maisy read out loud.

"They got the *sodgers* out of France, *e'enamost* all of them, twere a middling miracle," Goody Maskall said. "Easy with that sugar Maisy, tis all we have for *disyer* week."

"Blooming heck!" Maisy exclaimed, pouring most of the sugar in her teaspoon back into the sugar bowl. "I thought Tommy Atkins were all done for. Listen to this: An army that has been shelled and bombed from three sides, and had to stagger backwards into the sea to survive. An army that has been betrayed, but never defeated or dispirited!"

"Does that mean the war is over now?" Joy asked. It made sense to her, if the British army had withdrawn from France then all this silly war business could stop.

"*Naun* lass," Mus Maskall shook his head gravely. "Them Nazis will *naun* settle for less than our surrender. Tis a good thing Winnie is in *Lunnon*. He was educated in Sussex, did you know? In Hove-on-Sea. He aint bad for a *Sheere-man*. *Some-one-time* that does happen."

"Ships of all sorts…local skippers who know the Channel better than the land. Without fear they went into the blast and hell…an inferno of bombs and shells!" Maisy vividly relived the evacuation.

"But…" Joy frowned. "If our *sodgers* are gone from France what can the Germans do?"

"Oh, they'll invade," Maisy said. "The Huns will try to cross the Channel and we'll have to smash 'em into tiny bits, innit?"

"Invade England?!" Joy asked with disbelief in her voice.

"Aye," Mus Maskall nodded. "Invade England. They'll be sending those parachutists of theirs over our sky like they did in Holland and Belgium. Landing their *sodgers* on our Sussex beaches, more like than not."

"A grin on their oily, bearded faces. They were exhausted. They had not slept or eaten for days," Maisy continued reading. "Many tramped off in their stockinged feet. Others were in their shirt sleeves. Many had torn uniforms, and their tin hats blasted open like a metal cabbage!"

"Well, I'll *naun* be having them German *sodgers* in the Wyrde Woods," Joy said with fierce determination.

"Don't you be thinking you can take on Jerry *sodgers*, Joy," Goody Maskall said. "Tis bad enough *disyer* old man be applying for the LDV."

"LDV?" Joy asked.

"Local Defence Volunteers," Maisy said. "Like a home army, Granddad is going to be a proper soldier. Stop Hitler from coming further inland, aintcha Gramps?"

"Have you ever heard such *oakum*, Joy?" Goody Maskall shook her head. "Fred doesn't even *ken* Hitler, how would he recognize that *scrowse* madman *atween* all of them other Jerry *sodgers*?"

"Winnie gave a speech today, in the House of Commons in *Lunnon*," Fred said to Joy. "Why don't you stay for tea and we can listen to the radio after. I'll take you home in the waggon afterwards."

Joy nodded happily, her mum was unlikely to be worried and listening to a wireless would be a rare treat.

Both Maskalls left on various errands in and around the farm and Maisy continued to study the paper. Joy joined her.

"Look!" Maisy pointed at a cartoon picture of a German bomber strafing a pram and a teddy bear. "Machine-gunning helpless women and children."

"Where?" Joy asked as she studied an illustration of an immaculately groomed cocker spaniel called Flush the Plus Dog. She felt sorry for Flush, the dog did not look very happy being all pretty.

"*Amjins*, in France," Maisy said with expert authority.

There was also a picture of a boy and girl which caught Joy's eye. Their clothes were dirty and they were being scolded by an aproned woman with folded arms, presumably their mother. The woman stood in front of a washing board but her hair was styled in perfect waves. When Mum asked Joy to do the laundry the steam from the copper or tubs would cause her hair to hang down bedraggled and wet. The woman must have some sort of secret, Joy concluded.

Maisy turned the page.

"Ha!" She declared triumphantly. "This chap, Brig-Gen. Deedes says he likes East End people the best!"

"Brig-Gen?"

"Brigadier General, dead important," Maisy assumed a look of dead importance. "Says here Deedes lives in Bethnal Green, near Vicky Park. I used to play there, Joy! Me dad took me there sometimes on Sundays, didn't he? Deedes says he likes us better than West Enders."

Joy smiled although she had no idea why Maisy considered this to be important. Joy's eyes wandered over the pages as Maisy continued to read bits and pieces, especially if they concerned London. The paper revealed a wondrous world of which Joy knew little. Chappie Dog Food, Vita-Wheat Crisp-Bread, Black Cat Medium Cigarettes, Barratt Shoes, Willerby Suits, Pelletink Pens, Rowntree's Cocoa, Harlene Cremex Shampoo, Mick McQuaid Tobacco, Mentholum Balm, Bile Beans, Zambuk Skin Remedy, Brooklax Chocolate Laxative and Robbialac Paints. Joy had never heard most of the names before and the Whitfields got by at the Owlery without any of them, even though the ads seemed to suggest life was incomplete without them. Maisy probably knew them all, being used to the complexity of life in a city.

"The way those Huns machine-gunned women and children made us mad!" Maisy read. "For an attack on Britain Hitler would probably pour bombs on us from the air, drop paratroops and attempt an invasion by sea. Oh look! There's something on French women joining the French airforce as auxiliary pilots!"

"Women who fly aeroplanes?" Joy asked in surprise.

Maisy looked indignant. "Us women can do anything we want, innit! Me dad took me to Croydon Airport when I was six to watch Amy Johnson take off in her Percival Gull."

"She flew a gull?" Joy was bewildered.

"It's an aeroplane, she flew it to Cape Town and back! She was the first aviatrix to fly to Australia. 11,000 miles in a Gypsy Moth, innit?"

"Gypsy-Moth being another aeroplane?" Joy guessed, then added dreamily: "I'd like to fly."

"You and me both," Maisy confirmed happily.

§ § § § § § §

Maisy took Joy to her room and went to the window first to show Joy the London double decker which served as her night light. Joy was impressed, especially after she found out Mus Maskall had made it for Maisy because she had trouble sleeping.

"'Tis *bettermost*," Joy said. Mus Maskall seemed a good man.

"Innit just?" Maisy sat down on her bed, retrieved a battered suitcase from underneath it and turned it over on the bed; causing all manner of things to cascade out.

"Look, I've got a proper Hubley Cap Pistol! It's American and all."

Joy smiled. She had never been in another girl's room before but the storybooks at school always depicted them as filled with dolls, little play stoves and the like. Maisy was clearly not like the girls from the books, Joy decided as she scanned the items on the bed; marbles, a spinning top, various stubs of coloured paper, cigarette cards, a yoyo, aviation magazines and comics. Apart from the magazines Joy had seen several books in the room and she was glad that Maisy seemed to like reading.

"Mum and Dad had a proper row about that," Maisy admired the toy gun. "It was dead expensive, but he won big at the races, the only time ever, and he used it all to buy Mum and me an expensive present each. She were well cross, but I was really pleased. Used up all the caps in half-an-hour."

"This is pretty," Joy picked up the only soft object amongst Maisy's scatter. It was a folded yellow handkerchief, quite large.

"Oh yeah, Sue gave that to me," Maisy nodded.

"Who is Sue?"

"She were my best mate in London," Maisy answered. "Always thinking of games to play, she likes the pictures, just like I do. You know what the pictures are, right?"

"I've heard of them," Joy nodded. "Moving images, right?"

"Never seen one?"

Joy shrugged.

"I would go all the time. Just a penny for the cheap seats, innit? Then, after, we'd play the picture. Sometimes Sue would drape herself in a red curtain and wear old red shoes and stand on the steps and sing like Judy Garland. Or we'd go to the Island Gardens, there's a round iron lift there that takes you down into the tunnel under the river. The tiles were always wet in the tunnel and we'd play that it would crack and let the Thames flow in and we would scream real loud, cause there's an echo there, and then run real fast. Real Hitchcock moments but we never drowned!"

Joy smiled as Maisy sped on to describe various adventures in her old haunts in *Lunnon*. Most of what Joy knew about *Lunnon* was from books and the exasperated headshaking that always accompanied any mention of *Lunnon* in the Weald.

"There is something of everything and everything of something in *Lunnon*," folk would say.

Listening to Maisy it sounded like the capital city could be a fun place to live. Maisy got round to explaining that she had worn the yellow handkerchief around her neck when she played someone called US Cavalry *Leftenant* Blanchard when they had played *Stagecoach* for months on end. Sue and Maisy had even acquired an old squeaking wheelbarrow and painted it red and black so it could serve as a stagecoach. It could easily seat four or five 'chavvies' - Maisy's word for *chavees*. Invariably some would fall off as the wheelbarrow was raced around but that just added to the play. Those who fell were pounced upon by the Apaches who subdued them with horrible tortures; tickling in particular.

Joy was listening to Maisy spellbound as the *Lunnon* girl painted a picture of adventures in *Lunnon* when Goody Maskall rang the large bell next to the front door to let everbody know that tea was ready.

§ § § § § § §

After tea Mus Maskall announced that he had a chore in one of the sheds.

"I'll come too," Maisy jumped up and winked at Joy.

"After you've helped wash up lass," Goody Maskall said as she started clearing the table.

Maisy pouted.

"I'll help you Goody Maskall," Joy offered. "Then Maisy can help her *gaffer*."

Maisy gave Joy a grateful smile and followed Mus Maskall out of the door before Goody Maskall could respond. Joy helped

Maisy's grandmother clear the table and then joined her by the sink. There was a single tap with running water and Goody Maskall added hot water from a kettle which stood on the great coal-fired oven. They had one at the Owlery too and there was a similar one at Hornsby Farm. It could be used to cook on and bake in and kept the kitchen warm.

"It's middling kind of you to have me over," Joy said shyly as she dried the first plate Betty had washed in the old cracked sink.

"*Oakum*," Goody Maskall said. "I've been a guest in your home more than once Joy, you're welcome here as I said. Your mum, Mus Maskall and myself have been friends for a long time."

She looked sideways at Joy.

"Is something bothering you lass? You're *timmersome* all of a *suddent*."

Joy nodded.

"I don't think Maisy understands what it's like in Wolfden," she confessed. "I like her a *gurt* deal Goody Maskall, *howsumdever*, if she is seen with me…"

"Oak's Acorn, child!" Goody Maskall emptied her hands, wiped them dry on her apron and turned to Joy, laying her hands on the girl's shoulders. "You need *naun* be worried *all-along-of* that, sweetie."

"I am worried though," Joy persisted.

"Listen lass," Goody Maskall's eyes conveyed concern and sincerity. "It's Maisy's choice to invite you over. She's a clever lass if somewhat rash, if she likes you tis *naun* important what the village *chavees* think of you. Let them *bellick* all they want. Maisy has been lamentably unhappy at school; *disyer* day, tis the first time she's come home smiling. I reckon that is *all-along-of* yourself Joy and I can tell my Fred reckons the same. You can bide here anytime you like. Do you understand?"

"I think so," Joy nodded.

"Good," Betty Maskall turned back to the dishes. "That's the third time I welcome you in my house lass, don't ask again, it would bring ill luck and I might change my mind."

Joy grinned.

"I won't," she promised.

§ § § § § § §

The BBC radio presenter gave his listeners more details about Operation Dynamo, including descriptions of the hellish conditions at Dunkirk. Then he mentioned Prime Minister Churchill's speech. Winnie had been defiant to say the least, it was clear that there was not a single hair on his balding head that was considering surrender to Germany, he intended Britain to fight on just as he had promised in the speech he had given in May. Only this time he indicated that this fight might well take place on English soil.

The wireless presenter read out a part of the speech:

We shall go on to the end. We shall fight in France, we shall fight on the seas and oceans, we shall fight with growing confidence and growing strength in the air, we shall defend our island, whatever the cost may be. We shall fight on the beaches, we shall fight on the landing grounds, we shall fight in the fields and in the streets, we shall fight in the hills; we shall never surrender.

§ § § § § § §

"He forgot to say the woods," Joy murmured.

"*Quiddy?*" Goody Maskall asked.

"He said fields and hills and the like," Maisy said. "He oughta have added the woods, innit?"

"Aye," Mus Maskall agreed. "If needs be, we'll fight them Jerries in the woods. I just hope it'll *naun* come to that."

Joy nodded and said: "We shall fight in the hills; we shall fight in the Wyrde Woods."

"And NEVER surrender!" Maisy added cheerfully. "Bleeding marvellous innit?"

3. The Owlery

Fred Maskall stopped when he and Maisy reached the Raven's Carfax. He was wearing a long leather trenchcoat and carrying two stout linen satchels. The lurchers Hugin and Munin circled Maisy and her grandfather expectantly, eager to go in any direction Gramps chose. To Maisy's left the familiar Roreford Road stretched out to Wolfden. She looked at it with distaste. Gramps indicated the path to their right.

"Shims Copses," he looked at her. "The fastest way into the Wyrde Woods. Used to be a road *datyer* way, the Wolfden Road."

"The Wolfden Road leading to Wolfden," Maisy remarked. "Is there a Roreford for the Roreford Road?"

"Clever lass," Gramps beamed and ruffled her hair. Normally Maisy made her distaste for this gesture known with the speed of lightning. She was not a cute pet just because her much yearned for growth spurt was taking its bloody time. Once, one of Dad's mates had persisted till he yelped and withdrew his hand; looking in astonishment at the indentations left by Maisy's teeth. Dad had just about died laughing and called her his fierce warrior. It was alright when Gramps ruffled her hair though, it was even nice. She knew he took her serious so she did not bite him.

"Twere some time ago that folk lived in Roreford," Gramps said. "'Tis *naun* but ruins now, a whole ruined village."

Maisy was intrigued. She quickly worked out a plot in which she uncovered an obscure reference in one of Gramps' books which would lead her to the discovery of a cache of hidden gold and silver coins somewhere in this ruined village. Valkerie would have a role to play of course, vampirical ferrets might well have the ability to sniff out precious metals. Joy would be in it too.

Gramps led the way onto the narrow path which led eastwards into the woods. It did not seem to be used much as small branches and twigs frequently barred easy passage as if trying to ward off unwanted visitors. The path widened some after a hundred yards and the trees changed into ones which seemed to slither out of beds of decomposing leaves and then subdivide into a multitude of tentacles which snaked upwards. The bird chatter which they had heard walking along the edge of the woods had ceased abruptly. The only audible birds cawed and croaked as their black shadows flitted to and fro in the oppressive menace which blanketed the woods.

"Some folk are *afeared* here," Gramps remarked. "It *baint* a shame to take the longer way around into the Wyrde Woods, if you prefer."

"Blimey, no!" Maisy shook her head. "It's cracking, it really is. Good scenery for the rescue scene."

"Rescue scene?"

"Me and Joy come to rescue you, innit," Maisy nodded. "After you've been tied to a tree by German parachutists. We'll need loads of mist though, several mist machines."

"Tied to a tree?" Gramps chuckled. "Machines to make mist?"

"Well, yeah, that's what they'll do to the LDV, innit? Tie 'em to trees."

"*Howsumdever*, we also get rescued by our granddaughters. It's a good arrangement, *surelye*."

Maisy laughed. "We won't let a Jerry hurt you, Gramps. I'll take his bollocks off with a blunt axe and he'll be dead sorry he tried to invade England, innit?"

Gramps raised an eyebrow. "You'll do what?"

"Cut his…"

"Never mind, never mind," Gramps shook his head. "You're a bloodthirsty little savage, has anyone ever told you that before?"

"A few times," Maisy confirmed with a pleased grin.

The path narrowed again and they had to walk single file as the path took sharp left and right turns.

"I thought it was 'copse', Gramps, for a bit of forest, innit? But you keep on saying Shims Copses, dontcha?"

"*All-along-of* there being more than one copse. A whole string of them we have, from the twin hills by Nickleby all the way around to Mordrove."

Maisy nodded, that made sense then.

"Why are people scared? It's just a wood innit?" Maisy asked, though part of that was bluster. She would not want to walk here all by herself after sunset.

"They believe Shims Copses to be haunted."

"By ghosts?" Maisy's eyes grew wide.

"Aye, *shim* is our word for a ghost. *Shims* and other critters of the woods," Gramps said lightly.

Maisy looked around appreciatively, she regretted not trying to sneak Valkerie along. A vampire ferret would feel right at home here, but there was no way she would be able to conceal Valkerie from Gramps for long. Besides, she had no idea where they were going. All she knew was that it was Saturday morning and that her grandfather had shook her awake before dawn to ask her if she fancied going on a jaunt in the Wyrde Woods with him.

Maisy had been instantly awake. It was impossible to stay here long and not hear mention of the Wyrde Woods. Sometimes it was used as the name for the whole area, but Maisy had come to understand that Wolfden and the long line of farms between Mordrove and Nickleby were also called The Edgelands and that the Wyrde Woods proper were on the other side of the forest they called Shims Copses.

It all depended on the intonation, she had concluded. When folk meant the wider area there was nothing remarkable in their voice but when they referred to the Wyrde Woods proper there was always a short pause and then either a tone of reverence or one of disdain. There must be something special about these woods then. There was for Maisy at any rate, because she knew Joy lived somewhere in the Wyrde Woods. Her mate would be right surprised if she was collecting berries – or whatever she did in the woods – and saw Maisy strolling by for a picnic lunch.

Maisy had deduced the picnic from two satchels Gramps carried. They looked well laden and were often sniffed at by Hugin and Munin as they ambled to and fro. Maisy's belly grumbled appreciatively, breakfast had been a hurried and minimal affair.

The path suddenly straightened out. Some twenty yards ahead it was flanked by two low crumbling stone walls which rose to meet the porches of a gateway. Half an actual gate still hung listlessly from rusted hinges; it was made of wrought iron and sported numerous fleur-de-lis decorations. The latter had once been painted in bright colours but the colours had faded, even though their paleness still formed a contrast with the dark serpentine patterns of the rest of the gate.

"Well that used to be dead fancy, innit?" Maisy marvelled. "What is it, Gramps?"

"A boundary," he answered. "Shims Copses this way, the Wyrde Woods on the other. It marks the edge of the land owned by the Malheur *fambly*, they live in the big castle at the end of *disyer* road."

"There's a big castle?" Maisy asked happily.

"Aye, moat, towers and all," Gramps nodded.

They passed the gate and Maisy's eyes had to readjust for the shadows of the dense sinous trees in Shims Copses were replaced by more open mixed woodlands and Gramps and Maisy were suddenly bathed in bright sunlight.

The path too changed, it broadened into a dirt road with grassy verges which ran on for a considerable distance before taking a gentle turn far ahead.

"The Wolfden Road?" Maisy guessed.

"Folk call it the Forgotten Road nowadays."

"The Forgotten Road," Maisy liked it. "A secret road!"

§ § § § § § §

"Trees are a bit dull, innit?" Maisy declared, waving at the surrounding forest. "Just stand there frozen like bleeding palace guards."

They had been walking on the Forgotten Road for some time and Maisy had concluded that these woods were just woods. She had never been in a woods before and did admire the sheer profusion of trees but after a while it became a little boring, or so she thought.

"Standing around is all they do?" Gramps smiled.

"All day long and then some," Maisy nodded.

"Follow me," Gramps led Maisy off the path and onto a large bed of moss surrounded by ash trees. He dropped to the ground and rolled onto his back. Maisy laughed. She dropped to the ground too and settled on her back.

"Now what?" She asked.

"Look up," Gramps lifted his face to the sky and Maisy did likewise.

The sky was unbroken by clouds and the intricate lacing of branch, twig and leaf formed an irregular contrast of shadows against a clear blue backdrop. Maisy then heard the soft whisper made by the rustle of leaves as the twigs swayed in a barely perceptible breeze. To her astonishment Maisy noted that the thicker supporting branches swayed lightly too. That led her eye to the boughs, and then even to the trunks. These moved more slowly as the trunks approached their roots but moved none-the-less. Each part of the tree gently bending this way and that in a slow graceful dance. All semblance of solidity seemed to be gone for every tree within her sight was now swaying to a slow beat she could not hear and only the blue sky was constant.

"Blimey!" Maisy jumped up. "It's like they're gonna fall down right on top of us, innit?"

Gramps rose slower. "Aye, but they will *naun* do so. Well, lively enough for you?"

Maisy nodded. "Are there more dancing trees in the Wyrde Woods?"

Her grandfather smiled. "All trees dance, folk just never take the time to see 'em proper, *surelye*."

"They aint patient like me," Maisy grinned and Gramps chuckled.

"*Somewhen* it be useful to be quick about things," he admitted.

"Sure it is," Maisy nodded happily. "Is Roreford at the end of this road?"

"Aye."

"Then I'll find the treasure first, cause I'm quick, innit?"

Gramps raised an eyebrow. "Treasure?"

Maisy just grinned and then started sprinting down the road.

"Last one in Roreford is…!" She turned to shout back at him but to her surprise her grandfather was right behind her. He was not running particularly fast but took long consistent strides, the satchels swaying to and fro from his shoulder. Hugin and Munin ran to either side of him.

Maisy nearly stumbled but caught her footing and then redoubled her effort as Gramps threatened to overtake her. She groaned inwardly when she saw a sharp bend up ahead, he had the inside of the bend and drew level with her. Right in front of them the road seemed to disappear in a large smudge of dark brown mud which spilled over the sides of the road and was interspersed with the sun's reflection on water.

"MUDBERG! DEAD AHEAD!" Maisy screamed though she did not slow down; if he slowed down first she would have won the race.

"JUST A BIT OF *STODGE*! FULL STEAM AHEAD!" Gramps hollered back and plunged straight into the mess; splashing into puddles and kicking up droplets of mud.

Maisy had no choice but to follow and her lighter step allowed her to gain distance in the mucky obstruction. She laughed happily as her footfalls sent explosions of water and mud spraying every which way.

When they cleared the muddy obstacle at last Gramps careered onto the soft grass of the verge.

"Gramps?" Maisy turned and ran back to him.

He heaved himself up on an elbow, gasping for breath.

"No…more…running." He grinned foolishly. "You…win."

Maisy raised her arms in the air and cheered. She liked winning.

§ § § § § § §

Joy leaned against the sturdy trunk of an oak, feeling the bark scratch the back of her head as she closed her eyes and lifted her face to the warm caress of the sun. She was nervous. Joy knew that Mus Maskall was bringing Maisy to the Owlery as a surprise for the *Lunnon* girl this morning. Mum had told her at breakfast. She was looking forwards to the visit but also dreaded it a bit and was unused to experiencing this particular anxiety.

"Something to explore," she told Thallie, who was perched six feet up the tree.

"Kleak-kleak," Thallie agreed.

The Owlery received a fair number of visitors. No one had ever visited specifically to call on Joy though. Sometimes one or two of the Hornsby children would accompany their fathers Jeremy and Jasper when they came calling on Mum, and those visits were memorable, they had been fun but that was somehow different. Joy was aware that her life was divergent from that of most *chavees* in the Edgelands but that was mostly a matter of social outlook because Sarah openly adhered to the Old Ways. Other than that Joy knew that the townies from Odesby – who generally considered themselves clever – regarded the Edgelanders to be just as backwards as the woodfolk.

Joy was much impressed by Maisy's *Lunnon* stories. She had always been curious about the wider world and sometimes hiked all the way to Odesby to read about it in the town's small library. Until now the books had satisfied her curiousity but Maisy had spurred a new interest in the foreign world beyond the boundaries of Sussex. Secretly Joy already longed for the day that Maisy would show her around in this *Lunnon* of hers. She had been slightly envious of the admiration in Maisy's voice when the *Lunnon* girl had spoken of her friend Sue who could apparently organize an adventure at the drop of a hat. As a result Joy now had a strong desire to show Maisy that the Wyrde Woods were a splendid place for adventures too. She did not feel that she was anywhere near as good in telling stories as Maisy was but if Joy could just show Maisy then she could share just as well.

Joy just hoped her new friend would not turn her nose up at the Owlery. She had always thought of the Owlery as a warm home but this was the first time she had tried to view it from an outsider's eye and that had revealed a life of such simplicity that someone savvy to the busy streets of *Lunnon* might consider it outlandish.

Before long she could hear the approach of Maisy's chatter and Mus Maskall's occasional interjections. Joy stood up, brushed imaginary dirt from her dress and walked to the edge of the path. She was wearing a leather shoulder patch fastened with straps and Thallie glided through the air to settle on Joy's shoulder.

§ § § § § § §

Gramps had led them off the Forgotten Road to follow a path which wound northwards. Maisy noted that the woodlands around them changed, dominated now by a variety of 'needle trees' as she opted to call them as well as the occasional open stretch of meadow, brightly coloured by a profusion of wild flowers. The path rose deceptively, it did not seem steep but Maisy felt all sorts of muscles in her legs protest the prolonged climb.

"So where are we going to, Gramps?" Maisy asked.

"To the Owlery," Gramps answered.

"That's where Joy lives!" Maisy was delighted.

Her grandfather nodded and then pointed straight ahead of them. Maisy followed his gesture and saw a girl in a white dress standing by the side of the path up ahead. There was something pale on her shoulder, momentarily giving Maisy the impression that Joy had grown another head. Maisy waved excitedly and Joy raised a hand in greeting.

As they came closer Maisy gasped.

"Gramps! She's got an owl!" Maisy tugged Fred Maskall's sleeve.

"*Baint* called the Owlery for *naun* reason," Gramps smiled. "This one is a *scritch* owl. *Sheere-folk* call it a barn owl."

Maisy had never seen a real owl before and she was so taken by the sight of it that she almost forgot to say hullo to Joy. The owl scrutinized Maisy without a discernible expression on its white heart-shaped face. Maisy tried to count the colours which blended into its plumage; on first sight it seemed sand-coloured but seeing it up close she realised there were numerous hues and patterns that made up the whole.

"This is Thallie," Joy said proudly.

"Hullo Thallie," Maisy kept a respectful distance.

"Kleak-kleak," Thallie said, then spread her wings and lifted off into the sky most gracefully.

"Cracking!" Maisy said.

Joy smiled happily. "Come, the Owlery is *anigh*, *naun* more than five minutes away."

§ § § § § § §

Maisy loved the Owlery from the moment she set eyes on the little white-washed thatched cottage in the middle of the woods. The path they had followed joined a dirt road which ran past a low stone wall behind which a single row of trees grew from an expanse of grass fronting the cottage. They walked through the front gate but instead of heading for the front door Joy led them around the cottage and Maisy held her breath when she saw the riot of colours in a well-filled flower garden. Behind the flower beds was a small courtyard; shaped by the end of the house and a series of outbuildings it was framed by doors and windows on three sides. Deeper into the garden was a fenced-off vegetable patch and an orchard where a few thethered goats nibbled at the grass.

"It's beautiful, innit?" Maisy said appreciatively.

Joy, who had been looking edgy, broke into a broad smile.

"Why, *bethanks* for your kind words," A woman's voice sounded. The owner of the voice rose from the greenery in the vegetable garden where she had been weeding. She had dark red hair like Joy and a shrewd face wrinkled with laugh-lines. She seemed to be in her mid-forties, older than Maisy's own mum.

"How do, Sarah," Gramps greeted her fondly.

"Middling, Fred," the woman answered. "How do, you old *scaddle*?"

"Scratching along and a proud grandfather," he answered.

The woman directed her gaze at Maisy who suddenly felt shy; those emerald eyes seemed to pierce right into her soul.

"I'm Sarah Whitfield, Joy's mum," the woman said. "And you'll be Maisy, *naun* doubt?"

Maisy nodded and piped: "Pleased to meet you, Missus Whitfield."

Missus Whitfield wiped her hands on her apron and shook her head as she looked from Gramps to Maisy and back.

"Well, look at the state of you both, tis unaccountable," she said. "I hope you don't expect to be invited into Grace's sty, that porker has more class than the both of you put together, *surelye*."

Both Maisy and Gramps looked down and took note of grass and moss stains as well as considerable amounts of dried mud.

"We've been walking in the Wyrde Woods, innit?" Maisy said, then added proudly: "My first time."

"I see," Missus Whitfield looked at Maisy thoughtfully. "I hope your *gaffer* taught you some woodlore on your way to the Owlery, *naun* just his *oakum* tom-foolery."

"Tom-foolery? Me? Never!" Gramps protested.

"I learned," Maisy rubbed her forehead as she sometimes did when she was thinking. "I learned that trees dance."

"You mean to say that you saw a dancing tree?" Joy smiled.

Maisy realised how odd it suddenly sounded, but Joy and Gramps were curiously strange of their own accord, they would not laugh at her, she was sure. "Sure, a whole bunch of them, innit? Like Ginger Rogers and Fred Astaire in the pictures."

Missus Whitfield gave Gramps an approving smile and Maisy was delighted to receive a proud look from her grandfather.

"You're welcome here at the Owlery, Maisy of *Lunnon*," Missus Whitfield told Maisy. Then she turned to Joy. "Would you mind fixing a cup of tea for our visitors?"

Joy nodded, took hold of Maisy's hand and pulled her towards the open door.

"Shoes off," Gramps called after Maisy.

"Shoes off, roger!" Maisy dropped on the step in front of the door and pulled at one shoe while Joy pulled at the other. Joy herself was not wearing any shoes as usual. When that was done Maisy followed Joy into the Owlery.

§ § § § § § §

Joy busied herself in the kitchen. It was large and contained a big woodstove and cracked sink, as well as an old table with a variety of rickety chairs. There were also shelves all around, each of them stocked with labelled jars and tins. Numerous bundles of dried herbs were suspended from hooks and there was a pleasant fresh crisp fragrance in the air.

Maisy tried to read the labels on the jars while Joy poured the tea and then helped Joy to carry the steaming mugs into the living room. Mum and Mus Maskall were seated on an old sagging couch in front of the fire, talking about a Pig Club arrangement which would see some of Maskall Farm's porkers lodged at the Owlery. Hugin and Mugin had settled closer to the fire and seemed fast asleep. From the corner of her eye Joy watched Maisy look around with wide eyes at the room which was filled with tattered looking furniture and open boxes high up on the walls, all of them inhabited by owls of all shapes and sizes.

"Thank you, dear. I'm to attend Jenny Hornsby today, at their farm." Mum told Joy.

Joy nodded. Goody Hornsby had scalded herself badly when the copper in which she had been boiling a wash had tipped a few weeks ago. Mum had been called in to treat her and had gone back regularly to replace the soothing poultices which she had applied to Goody Hornsby's leg.

"I will *gwoan* with Sarah," Mus Maskall smiled. "See if Jeremy and Jasper Hornsby need a helping hand feeding that wild tribe of *chavees* of theirs."

He patted his long leather coat and Joy smiled. The Hornsby larder would be well filled, she suspected.

"Please say hullo to Leon and the rest," Joy said, referring to the Hornsby children. Leon was the eldest and the leader of the lot. He had been to the Owlery a few times and Joy had relished in his good humour and bright laughter, though she had been shy in his presence.

"What about us?" Maisy asked.

"Well, we don't know if we will be back today or tomorrow," Mus Maskall answered. "So it's up to you. Joy has promised to bring you back to Maskall Farm if you want to return today. You can also wait here till the morrow. Your *gammer* packed some of your things, just in case."

Mus Maskall passed one of his satchels to Maisy who looked delighted.

"I'll stay here, innit?" Maisy said quickly, then looked at Joy's mum. "If I may, Missus Whitfield?"

Joy was pleased that Maisy seemed eager to stay.

"You're more than welcome," Mum smiled. "Joy has spoken much of you."

Joy and Maisy exchanged a brief glance filled with gleeful anticipation.

Mum's smile was replaced by a short stern look at Joy. "I'm trusting the both of you."

Joy nodded.

"Good," Mum nodded back. "You'll need to mind the animals, don't roam too far into the woods."

"A gift from Betty," Mus Maskall handed the other satchel to Mum who opened it to take out a large cured ham.

"*Bethanks,*" Mum smiled. "Maskall hams are the bettermost hams in the Wyrde Woods."

§ § § § § § §

Maisy looked around the living room. They had just fed a bewildering amount of chickens, geese, rabbits, mice, goats and a large pig called Grace. Maisy stoked the fire while Joy was busily distributing dead mice to some of the owls in their boxes in the living room. When she had first seen the living room Maisy's impression had been that there had been uncountable owls but now she realised there were only six permanent residents. Joy said that Thallie had her own box upstairs.

The furniture scattered around the living room showed rips and scratches.

"Owl play," Joy commented.

One of the walls running along the length of the cottage sported two small windows and the front door, though Joy had said nobody ever used that. Visitors went around the back of the house to the small courtyard by the kitchen door. The far outer wall had no windows. The short inner wall was composed of the enormous hearth and the passage to the kitchen. The other long wall puzzled Maisy, there was an alcove of sorts, partitioned off by thick curtains which were now draped to either side to reveal a large bed.

Maisy called up a mind's eye view of the Owlery. The main building was definitely rectangular.

"I'm missing part of your house," she remarked to Joy.

"Where'd you lose it?" Joy grinned.

Maisy pointed at the far corner of the room. "Shouldn't there be something on that side of the alcove? Like a proper corner?"

Joy gave Maisy a thoughtful look.

"You're right," she said at last.

Joy walked to the far corner and lifted up a threadbare wall-hanging to reveal a small door.

Maisy clapped her hands gleefully. "A secret passage! Can we go in?"

"Mum would feed me to Grace if I took you in," Joy said.

"I like Grace," Maisy said. The large sow had uttered a range of satisfied grunts when Maisy had scratched her head and the pig had wagged her curly little tail. Maisy did not need more encouragement than that to fall in love with an animal. She had also befriended a comical looking goat called Nancy on account of the animal nibbling at the hem of her dress.

"Don't tell Mum, but I call Grace 'Bacon'," Joy grinned and walked to a set of drawers.

Maisy laughed. "That's cruel!"

"Grace doesn't mind," Joy assured her. She opened a drawer and took out a long key.

Maisy's eyes widened. "I thought you said…"

"Do you always do what you're told?" Joy said with a mischievous sparkle in her eyes.

"I'd rather be dead, innit?" Maisy grinned. She walked towards the door as Joy slid the key into the keyhole. There was a loud click and Joy opened the door. The two girls stepped into a cubicle in which shelves reached to the very ceiling. They were overflowing with books and scrolls of paper, except the top two shelves which contained more jars with dried herbs or liquids in them. There was a trapdoor in the floor.

"That leads to the cellar," Joy pointed at the trapdoor. "Naught but food storage down there. Those..." Joy pointed at the highly placed jars, "...are the more powerful herbs and potions Mum uses to heal folks, and the books are full of secrets."

"About treasures?" Maisy asked eagerly.

"Treasures of sorts," Joy answered vaguely. "Do you want to see my room?"

She led Maisy to the small hall between the living room and the kitchen, there was a steep half-ladder which led up to the loft. The loft ran along the entire length of the house though a division was created by the broad chimney stack right in the middle of it. The narrow openings on either side of the chimney were partitioned off by blankets and Joy's space was behind the blankets, in the part of the loft over the living room below. The dual-pitched roof and the blankets made Maisy think of a tent. There was a window in the gable and a large low bed stood below the window, surrounded by some chests and a low set of shelves. The shelves held a few books, feathers and rocks. There was an owl box in the corner by the chimney.

Joy looked at Maisy shyly. "It *baint* much..."

"It's wonderful!" Maisy was delighted.

"You have far grander rooms in *Lunnon, surelye*," Joy offered.

"Some people do, innit? Mum, Dad and I live in a cellar, just the one room and we all share it."

"Really?"

"Yes. There's five families that live in our house, each family has one room. Maskall Farm is the first time I've had a room of me own."

"I thought *Lunnon* was middling grand," Joy shook her head.

"Streets are paved with gold and it rains diamonds," Maisy nodded. "But not where we live, in the East End. It's..." Maisy searched for the right word: "Squalid. Still home, but proper squalid, innit?"

"So this *baint* bad?" Joy looked around her own room as if it were the first time she saw it. "You don't mind sleeping here tonight?"

"This is perfect," Maisy grinned and Joy smiled happily.

§ § § § § § §

"You're awfully silent," Joy told Maisy teasingly.

Maisy grumbled. Joy had awoken her before dawn and dragged her off into the dark's chill, all the while promising that Maisy would not regret walking the woods in darkness. Thallie sailed overhead, her pale shape gradually losing contrast as the eastern sky began to change its hues.

"It isn't much further," Joy encouraged her when the track they followed began to get steeper and steeper.

"What isn't much further?"

Joy twirled in circles around Maisy, her eyes bright. "Adventure!"

"Oh?" Maisy rubbed the sleep out of her eyes. She could hear the distant rush of a river. "What kind of adventure?"

"The *bettermost* adventure there is," Joy promised.

"It better be."

It was.

There seemed to be a gate of sorts up ahead, two long jagged shadows rearing high above the route of their path. When they got closer Maisy could see they were two pinnacles of rock.

Joy grabbed Maisy's shoulder to slow her down. "We *gwoan* to be real careful now, Maisy."

"Why?"

"*All-along-of* us being at the very end of a cliff," Joy grinned.

"Cliff?"

It was at that moment that the sun rose over the Wyrde Woods and Maisy gasped.

The cliff they were on jutted outwards over the woods some hundred feet below. It had a twin on the other side of a gorge. The gorge was all darkness still, enclosed as it was by high cliff walls on both sides. The river that spilled out of the gorge rushed into the forest and past a clearing on its right bank which contained irregular grey shapes huddled around a small square tower. Further on the river seemed to suddenly disappear from sight amidst the trees, though Maisy could catch occasional glimpses of it as it meandered through a great expanse of woods towards distant patches of lighter green. To the east the woods climbed a series of low ridges and to the south they enveloped and then spread beyond three high hills. To the west the green canopies seemed to flood towards the very distant church spire of Wolfden. To the north they could just make out the spire of Mordrove's church and a long flat-topped hill behind that.

"You're welcome in the Wyrde Woods, Maisy of *Lunnon*," Joy beamed.

"Cor blimey…" Maisy shook her head as she watched the morning's sunshine dance over the treetops. She pointed at the roofless church, "Is that Roreford?"

"Aye, that's Roreford, and the Farisee Bridge over the Rore River. The Forgotten Road crosses that bridge and then leads to Malheur Hall and the Carfax Alus on the other side of the Wyrde Woods. You can just see the Blood Stone on Gallows Hill too, and the Giant's Grove, of course."

"Giants? The castle! Gallows Hill?"

Joy nodded. "The Giants are really tall trees. Gallows Hill is a bad place, it's where they used to execute people. Yonder, beyond the bridge, is where the Falls are. You can hear them from here. There's a lake by it called Fey's Pool. *Bettermost* for swimming. And you see that there?"

Joy pointed southwest and Maisy saw that the canopy dipped and rose along an irregular line. Maisy nodded.

"That's Willikin's Drove, it's a gorge of sorts, *naun* as *gurt* as Hood's Gorge though, which is where we are now."

Maisy shook her head again. The Wyrde Woods seemed huge, there was so much to explore that she did not even know where to begin.

"We can play here?" Maisy asked.

"I do all the time," Joy smiled.

"Cracking, I want to see the ruins."

Joy shrugged. "The animals need feeding."

"Of course," Maisy recalled Missus Whitfield's instruction not to wander too far off. "Another time?"

"Another time," Joy agreed wholeheartedly and Maisy felt wonderfully happy. If only the chavvies from the Isle of Dogs could see this! Maisy surveyed the Wyrde Woods again and decided with a grin that she would just have to see all of it.

4. Cynthia Chesterton

Cynthia Chesterton was ushered into an elegant reception room by one of the maids while her luggage was carried deeper into Malheur Hall by other servants. She noted with approval that the furnishings of the room spoke of a refined cultured taste that avoided the ostentatious display of luxurious wealth so often favoured by new money. The Malheurs were an ancient family and so far Cynthia had been impressed by their ancestral home. Malheur Hall was a brick Tudor palatial county residence which had clearly been built for grandeur and comfort rather than defensive purposes, though it incorporated the hallmarks of a castle such as defensive towers and an imposing gatehouse at the end of the permanent bridge which crossed the broad moat.

Cynthia peeled off her white gloves and walked slowly to one of the tall windows which offered a spectacular view of the well-maintained castle grounds. She was not interested in the ornamented lawns though, her gaze was drawn by the far wilder nature which formed a continuous green expanse beyond the castle grounds. A frown appeared on her forehead, one that acquaintances would have recognized as a signal that her sharp mind was at work. It was that mind, or so Oswald had claimed, which was her most attractive feature though he had been most eloquent in singing praises of her refined face and classical beauty as well.

Poor Oswald, misunderstood and now reviled. Cynthia had known that their affair would not be lasting; Oswald used his charm and attraction as a tool to further his political ambitions and she had never been under the illusion that there had been true emotional attachment on his behalf. None-the-less, she had felt flattered for it meant recognition as one of his young female protegés whose opinions carried weight in the organization, one of the rare institutions in Britain that she knew of where a lady was appreciated for merit rather than looks or inheritance. It was this recognition of her talents more than the actual politics which inspired her devotion and loyalty to the party and in this she was not alone. With many of the men now interned or under house arrest it was the dedication and capacities of the young women which kept Oswald's dream of a better Britain alive.

She heard the door opening and turned around to see Sir Mortimer Malheur walk into the room. She had met him very briefly on a few party occasions in London but even then she had been struck by his suave manners and handsome features. Cynthia supposed him to be in his late thirties and upon seeing him again decided he might well be a rather pleasant perk of her current assignment.

Sir Mortimer seemed to return her appreciation as he took her in.

"Miss Chesterton, how delightful to see you," he said. "I trust you had a good journey?"

"Sir Mortimer," she purred. "I cannot thank you enough for hosting me."

"You know my politics Miss Chesterton, the war is an unfortunate inconvenience, but I will do what I can to support Oswald."

As long as it is not too public, Cynthia thought somewhat sourly. A great many influential supporters had withdrawn into anonimity and that in turn had affected the dwindling public support for the party.

"I would have stayed at a hotel in Odesby, Sir Mortimer, but one simply cannot move into the south coast counties these days without an official permit."

"As my guest you shall not owe anybody an explanation Miss Chesterton, you are welcome to stay here as long as you need to," Sir Mortimer smiled. "I sincerely hope your work will allow you occasional moments for socialisation. I look forward to making your further acquaintance, it is always pleasant to have civil company. I trust you will join us for dinner tonight?"

Cynthia gave him a genuine smile, there was potential promise in his words which she looked forward to exploring as long as it did not distract her from her mission.

"I am grateful for your gracious invitation Sir Mortimer and humbly accept," she said and then turned businesslike again. "Have you been informed as to the risks, Sir Mortimer?"

"Yes indeed. I am prepared to take them." There was no sign of doubt in his voice and Cynthia rewarded him with another smile. She turned back to the window.

"Those are the Wyrde Woods?" She asked.

"Those are the Wyrde Woods indeed Miss Chesterton," Sir Mortimer answered. "*My* Wyrde Woods. Lord of the Wyrde Woods is an ancestral title. It may not be recognized elsewhere but carries a modest degree of weight in our corner of Sussex. I do hope the Wyrde Woods contain what you seek."

"Oh, but they do Sir Mortimer," Cynthia answered. "The *Stellvertreter des Führers* has assured me so in person."

5. Sister Mary's Bloomers

The Wolfden School stood on the foundations of an old medieval inn – some of its outer walls still dated from that time. The inn's former importance dictated its position in the village; facing a triangular clearing at the heart of Wolfden which was called Stone Square, for it was centred by a ten foot tall rectangular standing stone called Cross Stone; crosses embellished with vines and roses chiselled into all of its four faces.

Three roads led away from Stone Square; one leading westwards as opposed to the other two points – the lower road leading east towards the Raven's Roost and North Woods Lane and the upper road heading north-east towards the hamlet of Mordrove. The school was on the south axis of the triangle. On the eastern face of Stone Square was a small church; St Lewinna's Church. It was said that this was the first Church ever built in the Wyrde Woods and the Saint herself had preached there. The roughly hewn sand stone walls of the church had lost all its ochre pallor and faded into a pale grey.

A grandiose building on the northern perpendicular looked out of place; two storeys high with a tall roof it towered over Stone Square. Two half columns rose alongside tall chestnut doors which was reached by nine stone steps. In times past it had been the Deighley Bank, founded by an illicit son of a 17th century Malheur Lord. In its heyday – which lasted several centuries – there had not been a single farm or home in the Edgelands which was not in debt to the bank. These days faded letters on a wood panel above the door read: *Wolfden Town Hall*.

The villagers had taken to jokingly calling Stone Square 'the schoolyard'. The initial trickle of evacuee children had swelled to four score and more were due to arrive. There was not a home to be found without a few forlorn London children either having the time of their life or being poignantly miserable. The two class-roomed village school had been overwhelmed; there had been three teachers and forty pupils before the sudden expansion. Many of the groups from London had been accompanied by teachers from a variety of London schools and this went some way to solving the sudden acute shortage of staff. As for space, the Wolfden Village Hall and St Lewinna's Church had been given over to the school. The Mayor had set up office in the Raven's Roost where the Home Guard had their Headquarters as well and the Vicar retained ownership of the church on Sundays. There was still a shortage of staff and space though and most of the pupils spent several hours a day lounging about Stone Square waiting till it was their turn for tuition.

The old inn which had preceded the schoolhouse had been accompanied by a coach house and a long row of stone stables which lined the square courtyard behind the main building. The stable doors had long been bricked in, the reddish bricks forming an odd contrast to the grey-ochre sand stone walls. The entry was on the other – outer – side now for the stables had been converted to a pensioner's row of tiny cottages half a century ago by Oscar Malheur. Sir Oscar had been a notorious madman but a generous philanthropist. He had broken the power of the Deighley Bank and gifted its Wolfden dependency to the village parliament as well as founding the pensioner's row and an orphanage in Mordrove.

The row of cottages, commonly known as Grumpy Row, faced a disused meadow and now housed the additional teachers who had accompanied their pupils when these had been evacuated from the capital. Maisy was in the meadow, sitting in the grass. It would be another hour till her next class and she preferred not to linger about in Stone Square like the others, especially because Joy was absent from school this day.

"Tis the Harvest Club," said Katie Rye, a slender nine-year-old renown for shyness. The timid lass was generally left to her own devices because she simply never talked to anyone which many – including the teaching staff – found disconcerting. It had not bothered Maisy in the slightest; she could talk for six and happily jabbered away at Katie who had seemed to appreciate the attention for she shadowed Maisy like a puppy whenever she could.

Katie's response to Maisy's renewed lamentations regarding Joy's absence were the first words Maisy had ever heard her say.

"Say what?" Maisy inquired incredulously.

Katie blushed at her transgression, then shrugged. "The *chavees* that live on farms stay away when there is work to be done at home. They're called the Harvest Club."

"Just stay away from school?" Maisy's eyes grew wide. "And this is allowed?"

Katie nodded. "Joy will be out in the Wyrde Woods today, harvesting."

"I live on a farm!" Maisy declared happily. She would negotiate an increased position of usefulness at the Maskall Farm with her grandparents and then take Harvest Club days off school when the prospect of listening to teachers talk and talk to fill the day was just too much to bear. Which was most of the time so this Harvest Club business could work out real well, she figured.

Something caught her eyes and demanded full and immediate attention.

One of the tiny cottages on Grumpy Row had a washing line in front of it with bedclothes swaying lightly in the breeze. One of the items looked odd though. Maisy jumped up and wandered over, Katie followed curiously.

"Cor blimey," Maisy's eyes shone brightly. "That aint a pillow case, it's a pair of bloomers innit? They're bleeding huge!"

She marvelled at the gigantic drawers, they must have belonged to Sister Mary, she was about the right size for these. Maisy looked at the cottages and spotted the narrow chimney stacks which protruded high over the shallow sloped roof. The bloomers would make a fine flag on those she decided; there was even a ladder propped up against the roof edge of the corner-most cottage.

Maisy felt in her pockets till she found some string, then unfastened the wood pegs and took the bloomers off the line. Katie tugged at her sleeve and Maisy turned to see an alarmed expression on Katie's face.

"It'll be fun," Maisy promised reassuringly and pointed at the roof.

Katie shook her head nervously.

"I can do it *on the fly*," Maisy made calculations whilst looking at the chimney stacks. She vaguely understood Katie's anxiety but was driven by an imperative need to hoist the colours. Maisy fetched the ladder and placed it against the roof edge of the centre cottage.

Katie tugged Maisy's shirtsleeve again, a pleading look on her face.

"It'll be fine Katie," Maisy gave her a warm smile, "Why don't you go back to the field, stay down low, be my look-out, innit?"

Maisy scrambled up the ladder like a proper *flue faker* and crept over the ledge after which she made her way over the roof tiles on all fours, keeping her head low. She figured that the chimney stacks would half conceal her when she had to rise to tie the bloomers to them. If she was lightning fast she would not be seen at all. Instead, the children inside the classrooms would be treated to the sight of Sister Mary's bloomers waving proudly from the cottage roofs. It would brighten up a dull day for everybody, Maisy reckoned, all but Sister Mary who never ever smiled anyway. Maisy bared her teeth; nobody called her 'little' again and again. It was totally unnecessary and Sister Mary's continual reminders smarted Maisy.

"MAISY!" Katie suddenly called out from her vantage point in the meadow behind Grumpy Row. Maisy turned to give a bright wave to poor little Katie but then her eyes grew wide. Bill Hare had just lumbered around the corner of Grumpy Row followed by a few of his cronies. Maisy froze but the bully had already seen her. He looked puzzled for a moment but when his brain had made sense of the unexpected sight of Maisy on the roof he brightened and gave a nasty grin.

Speaking a few low words to his compatriots he directed them towards the ladder.

"Don't you dare," Maisy hissed loudly.

Bill Hare just looked back at her with a triumphant smile. His mates were now out of Maisy's sight but she knew exactly where they were when she saw the ladder move just a little bit and then swing out of sight.

"OI! RAT ARSES!" Maisy rose to her feet and shook her fist. "PUT THAT BACK YOU ROTTEN FISH FACES!"

There was laughter as the boys ran back to Bill Hare and huddled around him, directing vicious grins at Maisy.

"YOU! Girl!" A man's voice sounded unexpectedly. Maisy turned. The mathematics teacher, a frightful dullard from London, was striding across the courtyard towards the cottages, peering at the roof through his glasses. The windows of the two classrooms filled with inquisitive faces as pupils realised something was happening outside.

Maisy ducked, even though she already knew it was in vain. Resignedly she rose again.

"Yes you! Stand still girl."

Caught red-handed.

"Damn and blast," Maisy wrinkled her nose.

"What are you doing up there girl?" The mathematics teacher came to a halt and shook his head in disapproval. "Get down at once."

Bill Hare's crew guffawed loudly behind her but Maisy ignored them. She had spotted Katie disappearing into the tall grass so she knew her friend would be alright and the boys were no longer the immediate threat. That was now formed by other teachers emerging from the backdoor of the school to join the mathematics teacher.

"Maisy Robbins!" Sister Mary was amongst them and Maisy thought she detected a satisfied look of vindication on her face.

"In for a penny, in for a pound," Maisy grumbled to herself and then raised her right arm.

"I SURRENDER!" She hollered loudly and began to wave her improvised white flag over her head.

Sister Mary came to a standstill and her face first turned white with anger and then red with embarrassment when she recognised them.

"I SURRENDER! FLAG OF TRUCE!" Maisy bellowed and continued to wave Sister Mary's bloomers over her head. The children behind the classroom windows whooped audibly and children on Stone Square came streaming around the corners of the school building to see what all the noise was about. They too started cheering.

Maisy was having the time of her life now and performed a dramatic curtsy towards the courtyard which she then followed with a deep bow – all the while waving those sizeable bloomers over her head.

She started prancing along the roof. "Raise the anchor! Hoist the mainsail!"

The courtyard was filling up now as the children in the classrooms took advantage of the general mayhem and spilled out of the building to join the others in the courtyard.

"Hi-ho me Hearties!" Maisy waved at the newcomers in the manner she reckoned Errol Flynn would have done.

She had to shout loud now for the teachers were fuming; either bellowing at Maisy who blithely ignored them or else hollering instructions at the horde of yahooing pupils who thought the whole scene to be splendid entertainment. It had dawned on Maisy that she had worked herself into a whole world of trouble which was only getting worse as she prolonged the act but she was driven by a stubbornness to see it through. Fuelled by all the frustration of being plucked out of the East End and deposited in a place which seemed as alien to her as the faraway planets she had seen in sci-fi pictures. Besides, the chavvies were all cheering her on and that appreciation lifted Maisy to new heights.

The mathematics teacher had found a ladder and placed it on the roof's edge. He crept up the ladder ever so slowly, his hands shaking as he peered over the roof.

"BOARDERS! ALL HANDS ON DECK!" Maisy shouted defiantly as he and another teacher negotiated their way up on the roof and started taking tentative steps towards Maisy. The girl started to back up, obstinately waving her flag and enjoying the cheers until she had reached the far edge of Grumpy Row. She glanced down; she might have dared a jump but the ground below was overgrown with vicious looking stinging nettles which seemed to be reaching for her, eager to get her in their grasp. Instead she waited until the livid teachers were but a few feet away from her and only then did she stop waving Sister Mary's bloomers in the air.

The teachers on the roof stared at her furiously but their stock of teacher-to-pupil communication lacked the appropriate words for piratical mutiny.

Maisy smiled as innocently as she could and held out Sister Mary's bloomers as a peace offering.

"Parlay?" She suggested.

§ § § § § § §

The stinging nettles might have been a better option, Maisy decided as she continued to rub her painful bottom on the way out of Wolfden. The mathematics teacher and Sister Mary had arranged instant public punishment in the courtyard. The lack of a fair trial meant that her bum was still smarting; the teachers had not been gentle to say the least and Maisy had needed to grit her teeth so she would not cry out. The pain of shame might have been worse – in that sullen circle of now silent pupils – but Maisy had just kept on replaying the scenes of her epic performance in her head and had managed to grin through most of the spanking. She had thrown occasional murderous looks at Bill Hare and his mates though. They had arranged front row seats to enjoy Maisy's punishment.

At least the punishment was over with, Maisy figured as she left the village. She would think of a way to get even with the bullies yet. First she wanted to savour the reward; she had been suspended from school for a whole week. Now she would be free to head out into the Wyrde Woods and see what all this harvesting business Joy was occupied with was all about. Maisy grinned happily.

Her grin faded as she saw a familiar figure approach from the Raven's Roost. It was Gramps in his Home Guard uniform; Maisy had not thought him to be so near the village. She had counted on being the first to present an explanation of the day's events back at Maskall Farm but she could tell by the look on Fred Maskall's face that he had already heard about it.

6. The Maskall Touch

Betty joined Fred by the fence of a small paddock behind the farm. Maisy was riding a chestnut pony bareback around the paddock. The girl had a look of concentrated determination on her face that was mirrored by the pony, a bad-spirited New Forest.

"Aint Maisy supposed to be mucking out the sheep stalls?" Betty asked Fred.

"Aye, that she is," he answered, keeping his eyes on his granddaughter.

"Aint that the old Hare pony?" Betty frowned as she looked at the animal.

"Aye, that it is," Fred nodded.

He had bought the New Forest from Silas Hare on the spur of the moment a few months before. Silas had been leading it into Wolfen to bring to the butcher's, claiming it was messed in the head and out of control. Fred had taken pity, the poor animal looked mistreated, its coat dull and scratched bare in places and Silas had been willing to part with it for a bargain price. They had sealed the deal with a pint at the Raven's Roost as was tradition.

Neither man had enjoyed it as much as one ought to appreciate a fine ale in the timbered and smoky interior of their regular, they did not have a great liking for each other. Tradition was tradition though and they were both NCOs in the Wolfden LDV. Unity in the Wolfden community was frail as it was, without some of the most influential members of the main two factions discarding all civility by failing to honour a deal.

Unfortunately, Fred had been unable to make much progress with the animal; it had a vicious temperament and he had reluctantly concluded that the butcher's might be the best option. In the past, Maskall Farm had seen many such outcasts. Fred's father and older brother Wilfred had been able to strike up a friendship with most, after many patient hours. The few they had not been able to reach had always been granted a graceful retirement in Moody Meadow, at the top rear corner of the Maskall Farm lands. Fred had always continued that tradition. He used to tell folk his 'viabilities' added to the happy spirit of Maskall Farm. The war had put an end to all that though. There was a mandatory livestock limitation and frequent visits by a War-Ag inspector who, Fred had grudgingly admitted, knew what he was on about.

Fred simply could not afford to keep stock which did not add to the meagre war income. They had ample food, the land was good and produced an abundance of natural wealth: Apples, pears, cherries, a wide range of berries, hazelnuts, honey from the bee hives and Betty worked wonders in her vegetable patch. The woods provided as well. Actual cash, however, was very tight and there were bills to pay.

None-the-less, Fred kept on finding reasons to postpone the pony's last trudging journey to Wolfden. The beast had repayed him with angry glares and spitting fury. Its temper was parralled by its countenance, the elegance of its breed distorted by unaligned features which suggested an unwholesome nature.

"You let our grandchild in a paddock with an animal that bites and kicks anyone who comes near to it?" Betty raised an eyebrow.

Fred marvelled at Maisy as the pony made sharp turns at the corners of the paddock. She had learned to read the pony already and adapted her position and movements to his without effort. The beast looked chagrined but obeyed her directions without hesitation. Maisy's face was pure sunshine, she was fully concentrated but also in the thrall of sublime joy. She was the spitting image of her mother and in her radiant beauty at that moment he could see the youthful countenance of his Betty when he had fallen head over heel for his faithful life companion all those many years ago. There was not a *Pook* in the Wyrde Woods guileful enough to entice Fred to let his grandchild into a paddock with a ruined animal.

"*Baint* my doing," Fred shrugged. "The lass is headstrong, she takes after you, I reckon."

"She rides well," Betty watched Maisy and the pony thunder around a corner of the paddock. "Did she ride in *Lunnon*?"

"*Lunnon*?" Fred raised an eyebrow. "*Naun*, as far as I recollect the lass has never sat on a pony or horse *afore* this day."

Betty laughed. "Then, by the looks of it, she has the Maskall Touch."

"Aye," Fred nodded. There was pride in his voice. "That she has. Your Pilbeame looks but some of my Maskall traits, *surelye*."

"Tis unaccountable for a man your age to be flattering me, Mus Maskall," Betty tutted.

Fred grinned.

"Gramps! Gran!" Maisy urged the pony towards the fence and brought it to a stop. She jumped off and walked forward to stroke the pony's straw coloured mane. The pony turned its ugly head and nuzzled Maisy's face.

"You've finished mucking out them sheep stalls?" Fred tried to sound stern.

"In a minute," Maisy said. "Promise. Cross me heart and hope to die. Did you see me ride?"

"Aye, that we did," Fred nodded, impressed by the pony's demeanor towards Maisy. "Tis unaccountable, *surelye.*"

Maisy looked at Fred with eager eyes. "There's fire in him, innit?"

"Aye," Fred nodded. "That there is."

"Can I call him Spark?" Maisy looked at the pony with pure adoration in her eyes.

Fred sighed but inwardly he smiled. The War-Ag inspector might accept the pony as a recreational addition to Maskall Farm. "I suppose it's *bettermost* that you do. Now, about that muck…"

Maisy grinned, looked downcast and elated, nodded and shook her head all at the same time.

Her grandparents smiled.

7. Little Savages

"I like what you did Maisy," Joy grinned when Maisy told her of her adventure with Sister Mary's bloomers. "*Howsumdever*, I'm surprised Mus Maskall didn't thrash you to the *Sheeres* and back. *Ken* he that you're in the Wyrde Woods today?"

Maisy, Joy and Bacon were making their way eastwards towards the extensive oak woodlands which covered most of the north-eastern corner of the Wyrde Woods. Thallie was shadowing them and now and then Joy caught a glimpse of the owl's pale form gliding soundlessly on a parallel course. She adjusted the shoulder strap of the linen bag she carried and swung a small empty basket in her hand.

"He knows," Maisy waved her hands to indicate the whole universe and then some. "It's Thursday innit?"

"Meaning?" Joy looked confused.

"Bloomer Day was on Monday," Maisy explained. "There was some muck-raking Gramps wanted done, weren't there?"

Joy laughed. "Deep in muck were you?"

"Bleeding hell, Joy," Maisy pouted. "I was covered in pig, sheep and chicken shit, innit? I didn't even know there could be so much of it."

"*Naun* ferret poo?"

"Off-limits till the mucking were done," Maisy looked miserable for a second but then brightened up. "But instead of five days at school this week, I only had the one, then two days of bloody muck but I got Spark now and I'm free as a bird."

"That you are," Joy agreed with a smile. Maisy had told her all about the New Forest pony in jubilant detail.

"Free as a...," Maisy scanned the sky for an inspirational bird and then jumped to a whole new subject. "Maybe the Huns will come today."

"From the sky?" Joy looked up as well. There was some scattered cloud cover but little sign of much else.

"It were blooming horrible, innit?" Maisy orated. "Those poor Hollanders and Belgians never knew what hit them when the Jerries came."

They passed through Roreford's ruins. A maze of ivy covered walls standing guard around a small ruined church to one side and a smaller jumble of roofless buildings by the river. Maisy sounded awestruck comments and then they crossed the old stone Farisee Bridge, where the Forgotten Road led further eastwards towards the north-eastern end of the Wyrde Woods around Malheur Hall.

Maisy found a new subject. "You oughta bring Bacon to London when you visit after the war. We don't see a lot people walking pigs, you'd be a spectacle in Vicky Park wouldn't you?"

"Only if you come along," Joy retorted. "With a gasmask container full of ferrets. We don't see a lot of that in the Weald. Tis an unaccountable fashion in *Lunnon*?"

"How did you know?" Maisy's hand flew to her gasmask container.

"Maisy, don't tell me you brought Valkerie," Joy laughed.

Maisy grinned sheepishly.

"*All-along-of* your promise to Mus Maskall that you wouldn't pick his locks again," Joy said more seriously.

"I didn't did I?" Maisy protested and rapped her fingers on her gasmask container which promptly thumped back a few times.

"You didn't bring Valkerie?" Joy smirked at the gasmask container. "Which one did you bring then? Is it one of the Hooligan Horde?"

"I said nothing of the sort did I? I meant to say I didn't pick any locks. Granddad forgot to lock the shed door this morning."

"*Mayhap*, Master Dobbs."

"Dunno no Master Dobbs, do I?" Maisy grinned happily. "But Valkerie said she fancied a walk, so she did."

"Just keep her out of Thallie's sight," Joy frowned.

"They won't be best of mates," Maisy pouted, then brightened. "Not like us."

"*Naun* like us," Joy confirmed with a smile.

They came to a crossing.

"There's a stone circle *datyer* way," Joy pointed left at the northbound path, and then indicated the dirt road which headed south. "The Guardians this way and Tuckersham Church anigh. We still *gwoan* straight here along the Forgotten Road."

"They used parachutists didn't they?" Maisy found a previous train of thought. "The skies of Holland and Belgium were filled with the parachutists. I'll need to see that stone circle. Jumping outta planes and then sailing to the ground, innit? Armed to the bloody teeth. What are the Guardians?"

Joy smiled. She was getting better at following Maisy in conversation; quicker to make the jump with Maisy to some previous or new topic. The topic of the war was never ending and Maisy had happily taken on the role of expert.

"I'll take you to see the Shy Maidens one day, that's the name of the stone circle. The Guardians are three rows of standing stones."

"Some of 'em were dressed up. Not the standing stones. The Jerry soldiers innit? Like Dutch or Belgian soldiers; nurses, tram conductors, monks and nuns even!"

"Nuns?" Joy was incredulous.

"Nuns," Maisy confirmed. "Came floating down from heaven in their habits, innit? Nobody suspected a thing."

"*Naun* suspicion?" Joy found this hard to believe. "Nuns with parachutes jumping from aeroplanes and *naun* found it outlandish?"

"God works in mysterious ways, innit? Anyway, it was all over the papers." Maisy clarified and Joy chose to accept this since she could not tie head or tail to church stories; there might well be parachutists in that book of theirs. Perhaps Angels were heavenly paratroopers.

She led them onto a narrow footpath to their right. The undergrowth was dense here, part of the young oak copses which encircled the large expanse of older oak woodlands which dominated this corner of the Wyrde Woods. The girls and pig walked single file and on occasion the girls had to bend low to avoid overhanging branches.

"This is one of them deer trails innit?" Maisy guessed. "Gramps uses these too. You don't want to be seen, do you?"

"*Bettermost* if we're *naun* seen," Joy agreed. "Old Lady Malheur she doesn't mind, but her son is back now and him would just as lief build a *gurt* big fence around the Wyrde Woods to keep the likes of us out."

"Are the truffles his?" Maisy asked.

"In a manner of speaking..."

Maisy laughed; this truffle business was more interesting than she had expected. "So what are these truffles we're looking for?"

"Summer truffles. Size of small apples, but all brown and black like a turd," Joy explained. "Oh, and covered in warts so they are."

Maisy pulled a face, "They taste good?"

"A little like nuts, but we're *naun* supposed to taste them. They're fancy folk food, rich people pay well for their truffles."

"Good," Maisy said happily and looked around her. "So what does a truffle tree look like?"

Joy laughed. The undergrowth had thinned and they came to a clearing. Joy put down her basket and got a metal muzzle out of the linen bag. Bacon stood still and was patient as Joy used the leather straps of the muzzle to secure it to the pig's head.

"*Otherwhile* Bacon will eat the truffles," Joy explained to Maisy who was watching in astonishment. "She is a fancy pig, likes fancy folk food. Truffles grow in the ground like taters."

Joy gave Bacon a gentle nudge and the pig made for the nearest patch of earth in front of a gnarled oak. The animal poked her nose into the earth and began to root around until she grunted happily and Joy walked over to retrieve a truffle. She held it out to Maisy.

"No thanks. It does look like a turd, dunnit?"

Joy carefully put the truffle in her basket and continued to follow the irregular circuitous route Bacon was taking along the oaks which edged the clearing. Now and then Bacon would stop and grunt or snort and Joy would add another truffle to the growing collection in the basket. Joy was pleased with their seeming abundance in this area this year; she could almost see the broad smile that would brighten Mum's face if she could hand over a full basket at the end of the day.

"Anyhow," Maisy said. "Them Hollanders and Belgians got a big surprise, innit? Those fake nuns took out machine-guns after they landed and started shooting at everything that moved. **RATTATTATATAT! RATTATTATATAT!**"

The birdsong in the trees ceased abruptly at the loud intrusion of Maisy's machine-gun fire and Bacon stopped rooting the ground to give Maisy a curious look. Maisy's gasmask container sounded a concerned knock or two and Joy laughed.

"Aint no laughing matter," Maisy shook her head. "Bloody hell Joy, they shot women and chavvies; old grannies who could barely walk and they bayonetted babies right in their prams."

"Parachutists have bayonets?" Joy asked curiously.

"Course they do, I told you, they're blooming armed to the teeth. They had grenades too and whenever people had a litter of puppies or kittens they tossed a grenade to blow them up!"

"Puppies?" Joy asked incredulously.

"And kittens. They're right bastards, I keep telling you, don't I?" Maisy was in full swing now. "Nazi Nastiness knows no bounds, that's why we have to fight them when they come here, don't we? We will never surrender!"

Bacon grunted a few times and stomped the ground.

"We're done here," Joy picked up her basket and linen bag and followed Bacon for the pig had decided to start heading for the next clearing already. "If them Jerry *sodgers* come to the Wyrde Woods we'll fight them."

"Oh but they will," Maisy promised. "To get them truffles. That bastard Hitler loves English truffles. He likes them for breakfast and tea."

"He can pick his own German truffles," Joy said. "We can make spears and stick any truffle thieves in the bum."

"Up their bum till the tip sticks outta their throat," Maisy said bloodthirstily. "We can make bows and bleeding arrows as well! So we can shoot any nuns walking about in the woods. Maybe Sister Mary is a German spy and we'll shoot her too."

"We could," Joy said carefully. "*Bettermost* not shoot the vicar though, *all-along-of* him walking in the woods sometimes."

"Humbug, I know the difference between a vicar and a nun, don't I?"

"This one has boobs," Joy pointed out. "He's a *gurt* big fat man with boobs."

"Oh!" Maisy looked downfallen for a second. "In that case we'd better be careful with Jerry parachutists who look like fat nuns then."

"Aye, that would be *bettermost*," Joy agreed. They came to a second clearing where Bacon immediately proceeded to start rooting in the ground.

"Skinny nuns now, we'll slit their throats straight away, no questions asked," Maisy decreed. "Fat ones; we'll jump from a tree and knock them to the ground and ask them to talk to see if they have a Jerry accent or talk proper."

Joy burst out laughing at the thought of the startled vicar unexpectedly pushed onto the ground whilst Maisy jumped up and down on him demanding that he bid them a good afternoon in flawless English. She bent down to retrieve another truffle.

"We'll have to practise loads with bows and arrows," Maisy decided. "Become Amazons."

"Amazons?" Joy liked the sound of the word.

"Women warriors, from way back," Maisy nodded. "They lived without men didn't they? Fought their own battles with proper armour and weapons and all."

"But," Joy frowned. "Without menfolk…"

"Oh, they captured good-looking prisoners to make babies with. But they were the boss." Maisy said earnestly.

Joy collected another truffle at Bacon's signal. "Good, we will be Amazons then. Beware Jerry *sodgers*, fat nuns and vicars."

"And captured prisoners!" Maisy added gleefully.

"Oink!" Bacon's head shot up and she trotted away out of the clearing and down a path with sudden determination.

"Bacon! Come back here you middling *scaddle*!" Joy grabbed her things and ran after the pig.

"Runaway pig! Runaway pig!" Maisy shouted and followed as fast as she could; carefully holding her gasmask container in both hands so poor Valkerie would not bounce around too much.

"SCCCCREEEEEEEEEEEEEEEE!" Thallie's interest had been aroused by the chase and she flew over Maisy towards Joy.

By the time Maisy got to the next clearing Joy was standing at the edge of a huge mud pool, hands on her sides and shaking her head. Thallie was perched on Joy's shoulder and seemed to be dozing as if she had not just participated in the pig chase. Bacon was in the middle of the mud pool; squirming on her back and grunting with pleasure as she sank deeper into the goo.

Joy had already deposited her bag and basket by the side of the path and carefully started moving forwards into the mud pool, calling Bacon's name.

"Eeech!" Thallie protested as her perch started moving and the owl shifted to increase her grasp on the leather shoulder patch.

The pig ignored Joy's approach and continued to happily roll about in the mud. Maisy sat down and put her gasmask container next to the base of a broad beech tree. She shouted encouragement: "Go for it Joy!"

"You could lend a middling hand," Joy grumbled.

"Can't swim, can I?" Maisy answered.

Joy was taking her steps very slow now; the mud swirled around her feet and became ankle-deep when she reached Bacon. The girl reached out for the pig which squealed a protest, turned and made a break for freedom. Thallie screeched annoyance and fluttered upwards. Joy threw herself forwards to wrap her arms around Bacon. The pig's skin was wet and slippery and she squirmed itself out of Joy's grasp leaving the girl to slubber face down into the mud Bacon had just evacuated.

Maisy's laughter rang out loud and clear as Joy scrambled to her feet, her entire front – from head to toe - covered in clinging mud.

"Damn pig!" Joy shouted and made a dash for Bacon but slipped again, this time falling into the goo sideways.

Joy got up slowly, dripping mud, not sure if she wanted to laugh or cry. She turned to face Bacon in order to give the pig a piece of her mind when she heard splashes behind her.

"WHEEEEEEEEEEEEEEEEEE!!!" Maisy shrieked and took a less than graceful dive into the mud. She landed on her belly with a splash and splattered both Joy and Bacon with mud spray.

Joy laughed. "Maisy!"

"What?" Maisy got to her feet.

"You forgot your face," Joy said gleefully and produced a handful of mud which she smeared across Maisy's face.

"You blooming louse!" Maisy bent down to scoop up two handfuls of mud and Joy ran to the edge of the mud pool as quick as she could. She dashed down a path and was half hit by one of Maisy's handfuls of mud which sailed through the air.

"Gotcha!" Maisy hollered and Joy squealed and ran faster. Maisy was surprisingly fast though and came pounding down the path behind Joy. Maisy caught up with Joy just as the path intersected the Forgotten Road and tackled Joy so the two tumbled onto the dirt road; rolling around and around as Maisy tried to reach Joy's face with the remnants of her last handful of mud, both of them laughing. When they came to a halt – the dry dust of the Forgotten Road now clinging to the sheets of wet mud which covered them – they rolled on their backs and panted like pups after chasing a rabbit.

"Ahum," a man's voice startled them out of their happy reverie and they rolled around to see who was behind them.

§ § § § § § §

At first Joy saw only hooves and horse legs. She got up on her hands and knees as she looked up. Two horses towered above her, they were magnificent beasts and eyed the girls curiously. Joy and Maisy rose to their feet and now came eye to eye with the man and the woman who were riding the horses. The man, dark-haired and dignified, looked every inch the country gentleman. He had his moustached lip curled in half a bemused sneer as he looked down at the girls. The woman was wearing breeches and rode like a man. Though Joy had never seen a woman in trousers before she had to admit the rider looked graceful and meticulously stylish. She regarded the girls with cold eyes.

"Goodness, they are girls," the woman said with disapproval as she took in the sight of Joy and Maisy. "Absolutely disgraceful."

Joy was taken aback for a moment and felt a pang of shame. Then she looked at the woman defiantly. She might be covered in mud and dust but she was still Joy of the Owlery. Glancing at the man again she recognised him now, it was Sir Mortimer Malheur, though she had never seen him up this close before. Another rider was approaching, an elderly but formidable lady riding side-saddle. That would be Priscilla Malheur, the Lady of the Wyrde Woods. A tall bulky man walked behind her, dressed in gamekeeper green with a rifle slung over his shoulder. The man bore an uncanny resemblance to Bill Hare, though it was not Bill's dad Silas.

"Some of the natives," Mortimer Malheur said with distaste in his voice, "are rustic to the extreme I am afraid, Miss Chesterton."

The sneer he produced along with the tone of voice contrasted his eyes which showed a curious interest.

"If you say so, My Lord, I would use the word 'savage' myself," the woman purred back at him. Her eyes came to rest on Joy. The girl felt a small shock when she discerned a look of utter contempt in the glance the woman gave her. There was a strong wave of negativity from the woman and Joy braced herself to withstand it.

"Lord?" Maisy whispered and nudged Joy.

"Lord Malheur of the Wyrde Woods," Mortimer Malheur said, "*My* Wyrde Woods, in which I find you on this day – and in this state – doing what, precisely?"

Joy sucked in her breath and threw a quick look at the approaching Groundskeeper. Truffles were not a trifle and gathering them could be interpreted as poaching depending on the whims of the law. Around here, the Malheurs owned the law. For a moment she considered making a run for it. She was covered in mud after all and not that recognizable. Joy was not sure, however, if Maisy would understand a signal to flee. Then there was Bacon as well, the pig was still back at the mud pool, along with Valkerie. Thallie would be fine but the ferret was stuck in the gasmask container. Joy glanced at her friend who was examining the riders with a semi-awed and semi-devil-may-care quirkiness.

"We were looking for the Amazons, Guv, in the woods like." Maisy said with a straight face. She performed a mixture between a bow and a curtsey, "Your Lordness Sir."

Joy nearly choked on a nervous giggle.

The elderly rider had reached the other two now and peered at the girls. She was in her late fifties with a face that seemed odd, jumping from posed blandness to keen curiosity and back again. She was large, but not in the way Sister Mary was; Lady Priscilla was simply formidable. She wore a sturdy outdoor dress and rode with a ladies saddle.

Lady Priscilla addressed Maisy: "Pray tell me child, the reason for this expedition to locate the Amazons?"

"To join them of course, Ma'am," Maisy answered. "To fight the Jerry bastards if they come here, even if they look like tram conductors, nuns or nurses. Or the vicar. And to take some prisoners, Ma'am. Proper handsome ones, innit?"

"Recommendable behaviour, splendid!" Lady Priscilla beamed and looked at Lord Malheur as if she had proven a point.

"Enough of this nonsense, Mother," he said curtly. "Mister Hare, could you come here please."

Joy shivered at the name, this would be John Hare then, Bill's uncle. The man had narrow eyes, a permanent suspicious sneer and seemed bigger than a bear as he lumbered over.

"Milord?" John Hare regarded the girls with ominous dislike.

"Can you identify these ragamuffins, Mister Hare?"

"Yes Milord," Hare answered. "*Disyer* lass is the Whitfield girl from the Owlery. The other is a Maskall evacuee."

Joy and Maisy glared at him. A sudden movement on the path to the mud-pool drew everyone's eyes.

"How?" Maisy hissed at the sight of Valkerie bounding down the path just below Thallie's flight path. The owl landed smoothly on Joy's shoulder and Valkerie clambered up Maisy's shoulder. The riders and gamekeeper were stunned into a moment of silence. So were Maisy and Joy for they had fully expected either Thallie or Valkyrie to devour the other one on sight.

Lord Malheur was the first to regain his composure. He spoke thoughtfully, "Maskall, you say…"

Joy felt comforted by Thallie's presence on her shoulder but the ground seemed to sink away beneath her feet when she heard thuds and familiar grunts on the path. Bacon was trotting to the rescue. The pig stopped the moment she reached the dirt road and perceived the riders. Bacon gave a small uncertain squeal. Joy's heart sank. Bacon was still wearing her truffle muzzle.

"A pig?!" Miss Chesterton's eyes grew wide. "Rustic indeed, Sir Mortimer."

"They were truffling, My Lord," John Hare stated with certainty. He reached for the rifle and Joy felt her legs turn into lead.

"There is no need for that Mister Hare," Lady Priscilla intervened. "The girls are truffling at my request, Mortimer."

"Your request, Mother?" Sir Mortimer did not take his eyes off Bacon. The pig had recovered from her surprise and having discovered the dry dirt road surface she proceeded to roll in the dust uttering little groans of delight, suddenly oblivious to being the centre of attention.

"Indeed Mortimer," Lady Priscilla answered. "You have been complaining that the import of French truffles has been inconvenienced by the war. It was my intention to surprise you with some fine English summer truffles and I asked the girls to procure them for us. You will find it an adequate substitute, I am sure."

"Why thank you," Lord Malheur answered drily though Joy reckoned he did not believe a word of it. He addressed the girls. "Carry on then and do pass my regards to Mister Maskall. I look forward to encountering him on one of his walks in my woods one day."

John Hare allowed himself a loud chuckle at that, then followed the first two riders down the dirt road. Lady Priscilla showed no intention of moving just yet.

"You are Sarah's lass, aren't you?" Lady Priscilla's eyes showed a mischievous glint.

"Sarah is my mother, Milady," Joy gave her a grateful smile. "Joy is my name."

"I'm Maisy," Maisy said. "A Robbins and a Maskall."

"And Fred Maskall a grandfather!" For a moment Lady Priscilla looked sad but then she smiled warmly. "Do pass my regards to both Sarah and Fred if you please. Betty too."

Joy nodded, wondering what connection the high-born lady had with their relatives.

"One more thing, Miss Whitfield," Lady Priscilla's smile melted away and she spoke strictly. "Your mother was never caught truffling. Some caution is required. I would have thought Sarah taught you that."

Joy nodded miserably as she looked at the ground in shame.

"Learn the lesson well," Lady Priscilla said. "Do remember to bring me a basket of truffles this week, you know where I live."

Joy nodded, "Yes, Milady."

"For the cover story innit?" Maisy asked and then added a quick: "Ma'am."

"Not entirely," Lady Priscilla shook her head. "I am rather fond of English summer truffles and believe I merit a reward for my quick inventions."

"Aye, Milady" Joy nodded. "You do, *bethanks*."

"A last piece of advice. You might both, perhaps, consider a wash before you visit Malheur Hall."

Maisy giggled and then the two girls, owl, ferret and pig watched Lady Priscilla ride away after the others.

§ § § § § § §

Joy led Maisy back to the Owlery after they had collected their things back by the mud pool. She was still somewhat shaken by the encounter with the Malheurs. She patiently answered Maisy's many questions though. Joy had no idea who the younger lady was. John Hare was Bill Hare's uncle. He had been appointed Groundskeeper of Malheur Hall by Sir Mortimer. Hare was responsible for all

Malheur land, including the greater part of the Wyrde Woods. A man to be avoided. Lady Priscilla was considered a local oddity. She was the daughter of Sir Oscar Malheur whose strange behaviour had earned him a reputation as a madman. One result of Oscar's follies had been the opening up of the Wyrde Woods for the few who cared to roam there. Tramping around in the woods would have been a bad idea a century ago when the woods were a private domain. Lady Priscilla had nurtured his legacy after her father's death but it was common knowledge that her only child, Sir Mortimer, sought to re-establish the Malheur grip on the woods. Servants at Malheur Hall gossiped of barely concealed warfare between mother and son.

"I like Lady Priscilla!" Maisy declared her allegiance.

"So do I," Joy nodded. Then she frowned. "Hush!"

They turned the last corner on the dirt road. The Owlery basked in the sunshine but that peaceful view was marred by disruption. There was an open carriage parked near the front gate, with a team of two patient horses and a coachman. Mum was standing at the gate, astride the path to the house, facing the familiar bulky shape of Wolfden's Vicar and two village women dressed in their Sunday finery.

Joy pulled Maisy into the shadows of the treeline and thus concealed moved cautiously closer till Joy could read her mother's face. It spoke of defiance.

§ § § § § § §

Sarah Whitfield had been tending her bee hives when her ears had perceived a novel addition to the lively birdsong in the trees and the occasional bleating of her goats. The gentle thud of horse hoofs on the dirt road and it was not accompanied by the tell-tale creaking and groaning sound of a farm waggon on the move.

Sarah walked to the front gate and saw it was Jasper Hornsby on the box of one of the open Malheur carriages. Jasper nodded a greeting as he eased his team of two horses to a halt but his face was grim. He climbed down from the box to pull out the foot steps and opened the coach door to assist the passengers out. Two women from Wolfden and Vicar Framsfield. Sarah's mouth grew as grim as Jasper Hornsby's as the vicar slowly lowered his obese body to the ground.

"I bid you a good day, Mrs Whitfield," the vicar greeted Sarah, his face red from the exertion of getting out of the carriage.

The two women said nothing, both giving Sarah triumphant looks as a greeting instead.

Sarah glanced at the carriage again. The Malheurs were the landlord of the Owlery and the presence of their carriage on whatever ill-conceaved mission the vicar and village women were on was an ominous signal. She had been wondering what the return of Mortimer Malheur might portend for the Owlery.

"A good day to you too, Vicar Framsfield," Sarah answered civilly, though she chose to ignore the women since they had remained mute themselves.

"It grieves me that I have yet to see you at Sunday service, Mrs Whitfield," Vicar Framsfield huffed and puffed. "I was hoping that we could…"

"…You would do well to take my absence as a given, Vicar Framsfield," Sarah said. "As you middling well know."

"Mrs Whitfield," Vicar Framsfield spoke, "you don't understand."

"Miss. I aint never married," Sarah said brazenly, then added. "As you well know."

The two women looked appropriately shocked. Little enough happened in Wolfden, Sarah reflected, if her own lack of marital status was still at the forefront of folks' mind. The Vicar fumbled with the buttons of his cassock but then continued.

"Miss Whitfield. There is genuine concern in the parish about your daughter."

"And who might it be, that is so concerned?" Sarah asked.

"The Wolfden Parish Christian Ladies Committee," one of the women said. Sarah knew her well enough, it was Alison Hare, wife of Silas Hare and sister-in-law to the new Malheur groundskeeper; John Hare. The woman was a rabid gossiper., the family a constant source of *moil*.

"That's quite a mouthful," Sarah nodded. "Middling impressive."

"Mrs Alison Hare has…" Vicar Framsfield began.

"The Wolfden Parish Christian Ladies Committee," Alison Hare interrupted him, "are keen to avoid disgraceful situations in Wolfden."

Disgraceful? Joy did not even know any of the members of this committee other than by face. What had she done wrong now? Joy squeezed Maisy's hand. Maisy squeezed back her astonishment.

"Disgraceful?" A dangerous edge crept into Mum's voice.

"We all agree that it's most un-Christian," the other woman piped up nervously.

"Just because you all chatter amongst yourselves like hens in a coop," Mum's eyes sparked with emerald fire. "Don't make anything the truth, *surelye*."

"Mrs...Miss Whitfield..." Vicar Framsfield raised a chubby hand.

"Besides," Mum challenged, "We *baint* Christians. We leave you be, you leave us be. That is custom."

"We feel..." Vicar Framsfield said, "...I feel that your daughter would benefit from church attendance...and Sunday School..."

"You want my Joy to attend your church?" Mum raised an eyebrow.

"And dress decently," Alison Hare added. "*Surelye* you agree that it *baint* fitting for a lass her age to walk around in the wanton manner that she does? Tis unaccountable."

"By Oak and Acorn!" Sarah Whitfield exclaimed. "The child is eleven years old!"

"She'll be...older soon," Vicar Framsfield offered. "Some people feel...a matter of public decency..."

"She should put on shoes," the other woman said. "And stockings."

Maisy uttered a low exasperated sigh and took a seat on Bacon's back. Joy raised an eyebrow but Bacon wagged her little tail and continued nibbling at the grass in the verge, totally unconcerned by Maisy's slender weight on her back. Valkerie's interest was aroused though and the ferret left her nest in Maisy's hair to clamber onto Bacon's head where she sniffed at Bacon's ears.

The coachman spotted the movement. He had a narrow face with a very thin pencil moustache; the perfectly straight whiskers protruding past the corners of his mouth by at least an inch. He wore a fine green felt hat with fancy display of pheasant feathers. He brightened when he spotted Joy and gave her a nod, grin and wink. Joy smiled back. Jasper Hornsby was one of the Malheur coachmen and member of the expansive clan which populated Hornsby Farm.

"Precisely, it's indecent," the second woman pitched in.

Jasper Hornsby raised his eyebrows, then his moustache and Joy stifled a giggle.

"Well, I'll be," Mum replied. "I've told Joy many a time that it's fine for her to run about the Wyrde Woods stark naked, but it's *bettermost* to *dight-up* and put on dress when she *gwoan* to Wolfden."

Maisy's hand flew to her mouth to supress a guffaw but she was too late and burst out into loud laughter.

§ § § § § § §

The three visitors by the gate turned in surprise. Sarah shook her head as Joy stepped out into the sunshine, Grace ambling behind her, bearing Maisy on her back and a white ferret perched on her head.

Joy approached the gate.

"How do? Vicar. Ladies," she said politely, though her face was impassive.

The visitors were speechless as they took in the sight of the newcomers and Sarah bit on her lip. The girls were quite a sight. The taller one disgracefully bare legged and covered from head to toe in dried mud and dust whilst the shorter girl was equally dishevelled and sat astride a pig which was coated in dirt and seemed to sport a spotless white ferret as headwear.

Sarah watched Joy glance at her friend. The ferret had become aware of the additional company and scurried to the safety of Maisy's mud-clotted hair from where it sniffed at the new people.

To Sarah's mind it had only been a short time since Joy had come home late one night to proudly announce that she had made a friend. Already though, the two seemed as inseparable as sisters and Sarah took pleasure in noting how Joy seemed to feel more confident and bolder in Maisy's company. The Maskall girl winked a greeting at Sarah. She seemed to be enjoying herself, not at all uncomfortable with the situation. There was much of Fred and Wilfred Maskall in her. Sarah gave the girl a brief smile. She liked the lass as it was and even more for the strength Maisy lent Joy.

"This..." Alison Hare was the first to recover and her thin dour face shone with vindictive triumph. "This is precisely what we mean. This *baint* proper English behaviour. Tis...tis savage."

"It's proper Sussex mud, *bettermost* mud in the country," Sarah said. The girls were filthy, to be sure, but what farm children were always spotless? "I see *naun* to be concerned about."

"Mrs...Miss Whitfield," Vicar Framsfield interjected. "Surely, when all the ladies in Wolfden..."

"There is but one Lady in the Wyrde Woods," Sarah retorted. "Lady Priscilla."

"We met Lady Priscilla in the woods, just a short while ago," Joy said. "She asked us to pass you her regards, Mum."

The vicar and the committee members showed disbelief on their faces. Sarah looked at Joy thoughtfully. So her daughter had encountered the Lady of the Wyrde Woods. Joy's time would soon come, Sarah reckoned, changes far more dangerous than the ones the vicar and his harpies seemed to fear.

"Tis true, Mum," Joy misread Sarah's moment of contemplation.

"I believe you," Sarah gave her a reassuring smile. Then she turned to Vicar Framsfield again. "Joy is free to choose. You may extend your invitation to her."

The vicar looked uncomfortable at having to address a *chavee*. "I was...we were..."

"You want me to attend church services," Joy said helpfully.

The vicar nodded gratefully.

"I'd like to," Joy said sweetly.

The vicar and his entourage looked astonished.

"If I can bring Grace?" Joy added.

Sarah chuckled.

"My child," the vicar began. "Grace is part of..."

"I meant my pig," Joy scratched Grace's head.

"Oink!" Grace added for good measure.

"But...," Vicar Framsfield shook his head. "You can't bring a pig to church!"

"Well, then I don't want to *gwoan* either," Joy shrugged. She walked past them towards Sarah who could not resist a chortle. Grace shuffled after her.

"Hullo," Maisy smiled brightly from Grace's back as she passed the people by the gate. "I am Maisy, innit? How do you do?"

Vicar Framsfield nodded, at loss for words.

"I didn't think there'd be much point in calling here," Alison Hare gave Sarah a hateful squint. "Beside it being our duty as Christian neighbours."

"There are some other farms left on our list," her companion said. "*Mayhap* we should leave now…"

"Then I bid you a good day," Sarah said, tired of the whole charade. "Come girls."

She led the little procession around to the back of the Owlery. By the time they reached the courtyard they could hear the carriage depart.

"Did we win?" Maisy asked. Joy looked at Sarah questioningly.

Sarah sadly shook her head. "There are *naun* winners in this game they are playing."

"Oh," Maisy said with some perplexion.

"As for the two of you," Sarah looked at them and shook her head. "You couldn't have made a *bettermost* display. You look alike Wodewoses, the both of you."

"We were playing…" Joy said.

"I can tell," Sarah said. "And that's fine. *Howsumdever*, if you think I'm *gwoan* to wash your clothes you've got another think coming, *surelye*. Best put them in a soak in the scullery, Joy. Then down to the stream to wash. I'll find something else for the both of you to wear for when you get back."

Joy nodded. "*Bethanks*, Mum."

"On you get then, and you'll be doing your own washing afterwards," Sarah smiled, then added: "Little savages of mine."

Joy and Maisy both grinned proudly.

8. Ambush

"Maisy, you young *scaddle!*" Gran placed her hands on her hips and sighed as she looked Maisy up and down.

Maisy looked surprised, she had just come down from the farmhouse loft and was not aware that she had been doing anything wrong. Other than starting the day too poorly to go to school and making a miraculous recovery by noon that was, but these things sometimes happened.

"Your clothes, lass," Gran tutted. "I just washed them for you *somewhen-the-other-day*. They're on ration now, you have to try and be more careful."

Maisy nodded, then looked down at herself. Not only was she covered in dry dust and cobwebs but some dubious dark stains had worked their way into her dress as well. She vaguely recalled accidentally knocking over some jars up in the loft's murkiness. There must have been something in them after all. She tried to recall when Gran had last done the washing. Was it two or three days ago that Maisy had helped to hang it all up on the washing lines? This was important because she was still looking for clues as to what *somewhen-the-other-day* meant. Was it the day before yesterday? The day before that? She was beginning to suspect the locals did not know either. Then she remembered the really important bit.

"Look what I found, Gran!" Maisy held out the treasures she had discovered.

"I suppose twere kind of you to clear the attic of clutter," Gran said.

"Clutter?" Maisy shook her head in denial. "Look, a hat! And a coat! Almost like a US Cavalry trooper outfit, innit?"

Gran looked at the old battered black felt hat with a broad rim and the dusty navy blue blazer in Maisy's hands. Then she suddenly looked sad and weary.

"Gran?" Maisy's voice filled with concern.

"They were George's," Gran answered softly.

"George?"

"Your *gaffer's* nephew," Gran explained. "George grew up on *disyer* farm with your mum. Like brother and sister they were. He moved to Brighton but passed away."

"Oh," Maisy looked at the hat and coat with new respect. It was difficult for her to conceive of Mum being a child and growing up on the farm. Let alone have the companionship of a brother. Who had such brilliant clothes. Did they play Westerns too?

"*Howsumdever*," Betty Maskall smiled. "I reckon George would've wanted you to play with his things. He used to love play. Put it all in the corner Maisy, and I'll see if I can clean them some."

Maisy beamed. "Thanks Gran!"

§ § § § § § §

When Maisy got back from school the next day she could not believe her eyes. Gran had not only cleaned and mended the blazer but she had gone through her button box and sewn on a number of shiny brass buttons in place of the old dull black ones. She had also transformed a roll of yellow ribbon into trimming on the sleeves, shoulders and collar. The hat had been dusted off and some of the yellow ribbon had been used to fashion a hat cord of sorts. Best of all was the shiny emblem which had been pinned to the front of the hat.

In the centre was a cross surrounded by a belt with a motto on it, around that was an eight-point star with a plume on top and a scroll below which read *The Royal Sussex Reg*.

"Where did you get this?" Maisy tentatively ran a finger along the surface of the badge.

"Used to be mine," Gramps said. "*Howsumdever*, your *gammer* confiscated it *disyer* morning and the pain of losing it has been hard to bear, I don't mind telling you. It's been causing an unaccountable ache."

"You'll scratch along, innit?" Maisy frowned as she tried to read the motto. "*Oni soit kwi...*"

"*Honi soit qui mal y pense*," Gramps said. "It means 'May he be shamed who thinks badly of it'. The official regimental motto."

"There's an unofficial one too?" Maisy asked. Now that she was a commissioned officer of the Royal Sussex Regiment it would be good to know about these things.

"Aye," Gramps nodded and grinned. "Nothing succeeds like Sussex."

"Nothing succeeds like Sussex," Maisy repeated happily. "I'll be a *leftenant*, I think."

"Well, are you *gwoan* to put it all on?" Gran asked.

"Wait!" Maisy ran upstairs and came back with her yellow handkerchief and cap gun. Then she rushed herself into the coat, let Gran tie the handkerchief around her neck and put on the hat. She picked up the cap gun and twirled round thrice.

"How do I look?" Maisy demanded to know when she came to a halt.

"Very unladylike," Gran shook her head.

"Like a proper *sodger*," Gramps answered.

"It's the best outfit ever! It's blooming cracking, innit?" Maisy enthused. "I'm going to show Spark!"

She straightened her back and saluted. Gramps saluted back gravely and then grinned as Maisy departed the kitchen in a whirlwind of excitement.

§ § § § § § §

Maisy had been patrolling the North Woods Lane on Spark, promptly saluting the postman, five carters, two lorry drivers and a single car driver as they passed her. At the Raven's Roost she felt a sudden urge to seek out Joy and show off her new outfit. She knew the way to the Owlery after all. She got off the pony and led Spark through the path in the Shims Copses, not sure how Spark would react to the morosity of this particular part of the woods. Spark neighed nervously once or twice but Maisy talked to the pony with assurance in her voice, just as she had heard Gramps speak to his horses, and that seemed to settle the matter for Spark. Once they reached the gate to the Forgotten Road Maisy mounted again and felt as free as an outlaw as Spark trotted down the road. It was an overcast day and Maisy took off her hat for a while to feel the breeze play with her hair. She laughed for the sheer joy of it.

When she reached the entry to the path which led to the Owlery Maisy put on her hat again and decided to ride straight on instead. She knew Roreford was not too far off and had been intrigued by the ruins which she had seen twice now but never really explored. She reckoned she would visit the remnants of the village first and then ride over to the Owlery.

When Maisy reached the last low ridge where the Forgotten Road plunged downwards into the ruined village she stopped. She felt just like *Leftenant* Blanchard on a scouting mission and decided that the deserted township down there posed imminent and doubly lethal danger.

She pulled the cap gun out of a blazer pocket and held it at the ready as she spurred Spark forwards to inspect the ruins. A few rolling tumbleweeds would not have been amiss as she rode into Roreford. Maisy cast an appreciative glance at the gaping mouth of Hood's Gorge. It looked just like a proper canyon and it was bound to be filled with Apaches who were even now being informed that the dreaded Royal Sussex Regiment had arrived.

Maisy rode past the huddle of roofless buildings clustered around the little church which was the most intact building there, though the roofless tower and nave seemed to be filled with nettles and brambles. Still a good place to hide treasure was her verdict but she decided to ride over to the smaller group of buildings by the bank of the Rore first. Spark would be thirsty as well.

As she crossed the open grassy space she thought she heard something and brought Spark to a halt.

It was then that the Apaches struck.

The enemy wariors emerged from the undergrowth and ruined buildings on all sides of her, whooping their terrible war cries and waving spears. They were of various sizes and all sported wild stocks of blonde hair but other than that oddity they were suitably daubed in war paint and adorned with a multitude of feathers.

Maisy wheeled Spark in a tight circle and waved her cap gun, though she was painfully aware that she had no ammo. The Apaches started circling her now and Maisy urged Spark forwards to the biggest gap she could see between the foes. The hostiles roared and Maisy whooped loudly as she made her getaway, thundering over the old bridge. They were running after her but Spark was fast outdistancing them.

Just then another Apache appeared from a side path on the other bank of the Rore; far larger than the others and riding a small dapple grey horse. He shrieked like a banshee and Maisy urged Spark into a canter, bending forwards with her knees hunched up and clutching Spark' mane though she barely had to hold them for support as she buoyed up and down in sync with the pony's rhythm.

It was like flying now and Maisy felt sheer exhilaration course through her. She was *Leftenant* Blanchard, fully uniformed and riding like Geronimo himself was on her tail. He probably was.

The moment passed and Maisy realised that her pursuer was slowly gaining on her. She looked back and envied his riding skills, he looked like he had been born in the simple leather saddle on his dappled grey. Maisy looked back in front of her as they sped down the Forgotten Road and then realised that Spark would probably run himself ragged if Maisy so desired but the grey was simply faster and Spark was tiring. She was not prepared to take unnecessary risks and she urged Spark to halt and wheel round.

Pointing her cap gun at her pursuer Maisy shouted: "BANG!"

He brought his horse to a halt too and showed his teeth in a wide grin. Behind all the war-paint and feathers he was just a boy, thirteen, maybe fourteen years old, though he towered over her on that horse of his.

"Who the *pize* might you be?" The boy asked. His hazel eyes laughed at her and he was handsome enough for the POW camp she and Joy wanted to establish in case they took lots of German prisoners.

Maisy felt an odd flutter in her belly but drew herself up proudly as she decided a field promotion was in order in honour of her gallant flight.

"Captain Maisy Robbins, Special Detachment, Royal Sussex Regiment."

In afterthought she added a salute, adding: "And who the heck are you?"

"That's a *bettermost* outfit," the boy smiled appreciatively, then held out his hand. "I've heard spoken of you Maisy Robbins. I'm Leon Hornsby, from the Hornsby Farm."

Maisy reached over to shake the outstretched hand. She had heard the Hornsby name mentioned a few times.

"And that lot in the village?" She asked curiously.

"Brother, sister and cousins," Leon answered. "There's a whole clan of us."

"A whole clan, huh?" Maisy's mind went into overtime and she smiled at the boy as endearingly as she could.

§ § § § § §

The sun was rising towards noon when Joy finished her day chores at the Owlery. She called a goodbye to Mum and set out for Roreford where she would meet Maisy.

It was a glorious day and there where the woods thinned into patches of wild meadow the air buzzed with the sound of busy bees and a kaleidoscope of butterflies danced over a sea of wild flowers. Two deer - a doe and a fawn - , crossed the path and after that Joy waited respectfully for a *Pook* laden with bundles to pass by; earning herself a little nod for her courtesy. She smelled a badger sett as the path started to descend to Roreford, running parallel to the Forgotten Road for the last few hundred yards until it merged with the road just before reaching the ruined village.

Joy was astonished when she entered the central clearing between Roreford's main cluster of ruins around the old church and the smaller huddle of jagged walls on the bank of the Rore. Maisy was there as they had agreed at school on Friday afternoon; wearing her new cavalry gear but there were a dozen other children and Joy tensed up, utterly confused for a moment. She equated any gang of *chavees* with persecution and to see Maisy with them - chattering to them like a *caffincher* - gave her a sinking feeling. Had Maisy been fooling her all along? Was this a trap of some sorts? Joy could not believe it, her heart told her Maisy could be trusted.

Joy was spotted and the group got very quiet, all but Maisy who glanced her way, smiled broadly, and then continued the animated conversation she had been engaged in. Joy knew about half the *chavees* from school in Wolfden, the other half looked vaguely familiar. They ranged from about eight to thirteen, she estimated.

Not sure what to do, Joy came to a standstill and stared back at the group. She uttered a low call and to her relief Thallie came flying to her shoulder. She could feel the owl's claws; they were blunted by the leather shoulderpiece she had fashioned but it was beginning to wear thin and would have to be replaced soon.

"Eeeeeeeeeeeechhhhhhhh!" Thallie screeched at the *chavees*, wary of such a large group of unfamiliar humans.

Joy walked forwards and some of the Wolfden children backed away. She grinned, they were frightened of her now. If they came to be bothersome they would soon learn to stay near the safety of Wolfden and not come wandering into her Wyrde Woods. She hooked the owl line to Thallie's leg none-the-less. The owl was nervous and might react with self-defensive agression which would result in lacerated faces and damaged eyeballs, not something that would meet much approval.

Maisy came striding over, her face beaming with pride.

"What are you playing at Maisy?" Joy asked shortly.

"They," Maisy gestured at the group and then pronounced grandly: "Have been waiting for you, innit?"

"Why?" Joy looked at them again and suddenly placed the vaguely familiar *chavees*. Maisy had drummed up the whole Hornsby Clan. Leon, the eldest and already tall for his thirteen years smiled broadly at Joy and she gave him a shy wave. Her anxiety evaporated.

"Can't be the Amazons no more, Joy. Need the boys to make up the numbers. We'll still be boss." Maisy's eyes shone. "We're the Wyrde Warriors now, innit?"

"You're a *chuckle-head*, Maisy Robbins," Joy began to smile.

Maisy turned around and made herself as big as possible.

"ATTENTION!" She roared.

The *chavees* made an attempt to form a double line and stand to attention, some of them grinning sheepishly at the tomfoolery of it.

Maisy smartly twirled around and gave Joy a formal military salute, her face transformed by the role she was playing. "TROOP READY FOR INSPECTION SI…MA'AM."

"Erm, stand-down," Joy told Maisy who promptly twirled around again.

"TROOP AT EASE," she roared and the children obediently slouched.

Maisy faced Joy again and saluted.

"Troop very much at ease Ma'am," she saluted again just in case Joy had not noticed the first time. "As per your orders Ma'am."

"Bethanks, Captain Robbins," Joy said formally, getting into the swing of it now. "Please address me as Colonel-in-Chief."

"Yes, Ma'am, Colonel-in-Chief, Ma'am!" Captain Robbins beamed.

"So, do I have a cunning plan, Captain?" The Colonel-in-Chief asked bemusedly, not quite knowing what to do with her new army and reasonably confident that Maisy would have prepared a dozen scenarios.

"Private Rye!" Captain Robbins shouted.

Katie Rye stepped forwards. Joy knew her from school, she was in a lower form, a year or two younger though she still towered over Maisy. The girl was lugging a satchel.

"You know my name is Katie," the girl frowned at Maisy.

"You're in the army now Private Rye, innit?" Maisy said grinning at her. "Tell the Colonel."

Katie Rye upended the satchel, shaking out a small pile of cloth arm bands. Maisy picked one up and handed it to Joy. She held the coarse material. The armband read: LDV.

"Where did you get these?" Joy was astonished.

"Katie here got them from her dad, didn't she? The LDV has been renamed. It's called the Home Guard now." Maisy explained.

"You can have these," Katie nodded. She seemed friendly enough, if somewhat embarassed.

"Private Hornsby!" Maisy shouted.

The lanky lad with a lopsided grin came striding over purposefully. Joy's eyes grew wide when she saw that Leon was holding a bow and six arrows. The bow was sleek, far better than the saplings she and Maisy had fashioned into bows in order to defend the hut they had built in a hidden hollow of Willikin's Drove. Though a ramshackle affair they had proudly dubbed it Fort Defiance and decided it would be their Amazon Headquarters.

"Leon, I mean Private Hornsby," the boy grinned. "This is for you Colonel-Sir."

"Ma'am," Maisy corrected him.

"Aye Captain," Leon handed Joy the bow and arrows.

"They're beautiful," Joy said, examining the arrows. They were properly fletched with grey goose feathers and even had steel points.

"My da makes them," Leon said proudly. "He said he could learn all of us how to make a proper bow. Learn us to shoot them as well."

Joy looked at the LDV armbands and then the bow and arrows in her hands. So they had uniforms and weapons.

"We'll need quivers too," she decided.

"I can show you how to make those," Katie suggested shyly. "Weave them from willow."

"That would be wonderful," Joy smiled and Katie looked proud.

"So what now?" Leon asked. "We'll need a plan."

Joy was at a loss for words, she could sense that Maisy was eager to say something but decided that if she were to be a Colonel that would require some occasional decision making. She was delighted with the gifts and reckoned they merited a reward.

"Well you two are promoted to *Leftenants* to begin with," Joy said.

Leon beamed and after a second of hesitation Kate smiled too, nodding her agreement.

"We'll need a Headquarters," Leon said.

"Well, Maisy and I know just the place," Joy nodded. "We'll need to expand our fort somewhat, but we can *gwoan* and start that today."

Maisy looked relieved, she had probably been hoping that Joy would not mind sharing Fort Defiance. It would make a perfect base for the Wyrde Warriors.

"Kleak-Kleak," Thallie agreed.

9. Secree of the Wirdewode

Maisy flicked a speck of dust from one of the polished brass buttons on her coat and self-consciously re-adjusted her cavalry hat. Joy was wearing a white dress as usual but her mum had washed and ironed it. The girls were on their way to Malheur Hall to deliver a small basket of truffles to Lady Priscilla.

Gran had walked Maisy to the Owlery in the morning and helped Missus Whitfield place a tin bathtub in the courtyard. They had filled it with hot steaming water and enticed the girls in. All enjoyment of a hot bath was ruined though by vigorous scrubbing with brushes that had stiff unforgiving bristles. Maisy and Joy had protested loudly but to no avail.

"It's one thing you insist on wearing your play clothes," Gran had chided Maisy. "*Howsumdever*, I'll *naun* have you calling on Malheur Hall all *dishabill* and coated in dirt."

"I'm clean already!" Maisy had wailed. "You're taking our blooming skins off, innit?"

It was true, both she and Joy had been turning brightly pink under the onslaught.

"*Oakum!*" Missus Whitfield had pronounced. "What kind of Sussex maid are you?"

Maisy had wanted to point out that she was *Sheere-folk,* as everyone usually seemed keen on reminding her, but decided not to when she realised she was kind of pleased to be identified as a Sussex maid.

"We're just delivering some truffles," Joy had protested when they had both been dried and the women produced combs and brushes and embarked on a furious mission to untangle and brush the girls' hair.

"You're calling on the Lady of the Wyrde Woods at Malheur Hall," her mother had answered. "Whatever else, you'll show that the Whitfields and Maskalls have *naun* to be ashamed of."

"Ouch!" Joy had cried when Missus Whitfield untangled a knot in her hair.

"And if you do cause trouble, then you'll find out what it's like to have your skin taken off," Gran had promised Maisy. "I'll flay you myself."

Released from the ordeal at last the girls had the sense to avoid the muddier parts of the Forgotten Road as they walked east. Both walked barefeet, carrying their newly shined shoes in their hands. Maisy had never seen Joy with shoes on and she was looking forwards to the experience. They passed through Roreford, then past the place where they had truffled and crossed a shallow river which Joy named as the Taunflow.

"It's like we've been invited to have a cuppa at Buckingham Palace," Maisy complained, concluding a long epistle about being cruelly tormented and tortured.

"I reckon so," Joy answered. "They're both in *gurt* awe of Lady Priscilla, aint it so?"

Maisy nodded; that awe had been tangible. "Joy? Have you been to the castle before?"

Joy shook her head.

"But you live near it!" Maisy protested.

"So how often do you drink tea with the King at the palace in *Lunnon*?" Joy winked.

"Just the once," Maisy answered. "Not really. Me dad took me to see the outside of Buckingham Palace once, innit? Then he got us a cuppa from a stand in the park."

"What's your father like?" Joy asked curiously.

Maisy locked her lips.

"Maisy?" There was concern in Joy's voice.

"I think he's fun, innit?" Maisy answered carefully, and then launched into a flood of words. "When he has money, he takes me places. Like the palace, but also the races and parks. Oh! And the fair. At night when it's all lit up like a proper Christmas tree. He'd give me some dosh and I'd go on rides and have a go fishing out a prize in those glass cabinets with little cranes, innit? When I was seven he took me to Sydenham Hill to watch the Crystal Palace burn down. I sat on his shoulders for hours and he never complained. There were more than 90 fire engines, hundreds of firemen. You should have seen it, I've never seen a finer fire."

"He took you all over *Lunnon*," Joy said wistfully.

"Yes," Maisy nodded. "But, Mum says he's irresponsible, innit? Dad spends all his money on fun when he has it. I don't mind, do I? But she has to work blooming hard to pay the rent and put grub on the table."

"You must miss them something terrible."

"I dunno what will happen now I'm gone, innit?" Maisy said sadly. "Mum'd be better off without the likes of Dad. But I wouldn't, would I?"

Joy nodded her understanding.

They passed a cottage. Joy told Maisy it was where the Groundskeeper lived and they kept quiet until they had passed it, though there was no sign of life.

They walked on amidst the stately oak columns until Joy stopped.

"Malheur Hall is *anigh*," she told Maisy. "We'd best put our shoes on."

They brushed their feet on some grass by the side of the path and balanced precariously as they slipped into the shoes, not wanting to sit down and risk stains on their clothes. Then they continued, Maisy grinning at Joy who was walking awkwardly, not used to wearing shoes at all.

They approached a gate similar to that which fronted the beginning of the Forgotten Road though this one was intact and well-maintained. An immaculate tall hedge rose on either side of the gate concealing what was beyond but the wrought iron gates offered a glimpse of neat gardens and a round corner tower at the far end of them. There were three people standing by the gate and Joy had a sinking feeling as she recognized them.

"Oh blast," Maisy said.

The Groundskeeper was at the gate and watched the girls approach with a frown on his forehead. He was flanked by a man who could have been his spitting image if he had been bulky rather than lanky. On John Hare's other side stood none other than Bill Hare. Bill went through his usual routine of looking bizarrely puzzled as he tried to make sense of something. When he had, he grinned evilly.

"Silas Hare, Bill's dad," Joy whispered to Maisy, referring to the Hare her friend had not met yet. Maisy nodded.

They both took a deep breath and then bravely marched towards the Hares.

"Well, well, well," John Hare said slowly, relishing the syllables. "What have we here? A Wodewose *chance-born* and a thief's granddaughter."

"My gramps aint a *Tea Leaf*," Maisy hissed. Joy put her hand on Maisy's arm.

"We've come *all-along-of* Lady Priscilla's invitation," Joy said as calmly as she could.

"An invitation," John Hare nodded and pretended to be impressed. "Well, let's see it then."

He held out his hand. Joy looked puzzled. Bill sniggered.

"When civilised folk issue an invitation," John Hare said haughtily, "they write it on paper, you *chuckle-headed* lass. The postman then brings it to your house."

"She asked us to bring her *disyer* basket," Joy said, holding up the small basket she carried. She was relieved that Mum had covered the truffles with a square of linen though John Hare could probably guess what was in there.

"Well, hand it over then," John Hare said. "I'll see that it *gwoan* get to her Ladyship."

Joy clutched the basket's handle tight. Truffles fetched high prices, she doubted that Lady Priscilla would ever receive the basket if she handed it over to the likes of Hare.

"Did you seriously think," the Groundskeeper grinned nastily, "that her Ladyship would receive you in her parlour for tea? Woodfolk?"

Silas Hare laughed sardonically.

"The likes of yourself *baint* welcome here, *chance-born draggle-tail*," Bill sneered.

"*Draggle-tail?*" Joy fumed and this time it was Maisy who restrained her friend.

Joy closed her eyes. This was not what she had expected. She had imagined knocking on some side door of the grand castle, perhaps catching a glance of Lady Priscilla long enough to offer her a smile.

"Make up your mind," John Hare growled. "Either you give the basket to me or else you take it back to that Wodewose mum of yours."

Joy opened her eyes. "*Naun*, I *gwoan* give it to Lady Priscilla, as she asked me to."

All three Hares laughed and Joy turned around and walked away, followed by Maisy. The girls were silent until they could no longer hear the laughter and taunts with which the Hares celebrated their victory. When they were out of sight Joy led them left onto a path which followed the contours of the great hedge which marked the castle grounds. After a while the path joined a far broader one which ran eastwards amidst oak woodlands, young and old.

"There's another entrance, innit?" Maisy guessed. "We'll trick the blooming *nickeys*, the whole *glocky* bunch of them."

"Aye, we're heading there now," Joy said. "*Howsumdever*, they'll reckon we'll do so and have word out at the other gate by the time we get there."

She turned to Maisy and shrugged.

"I just don't know what else to do, Maisy. I got to try, at least. I don't want to *gwoan* back to the Owlery - to Mum - and tell her I didn't manage to see Lady Priscilla. It seemed important to her."

Maisy nodded wholeheartedly. The detour would at least buy them some extra time to think of a solution. She did not want to go back to Gran either, to admit that Lady Priscilla had not had a chance to compliment the Maskalls on scrubbing Maisy's skin raw.

Despite their determination to see their mission through they walked in a defeated silence, the echoes of John Hare's mocking voice in their heads. Perhaps he had been right and their sort had no business calling at Malheur Hall.

§ § § § § § §

The path they were on followed the contours of low ridges which rose and fell like waves though the passage itself remained broad and even. They paused by an oak which was so huge in circumference and height that Maisy could hardly believe it was real.

"The Halfway Oak," Joy said.

"Made for climbing, innit?" Maisy's eyes shone longingly, then she remembered she was not to get dirty. She quickly added, "on another day."

"We're near Gallows Hill as well," Joy said.

"Gallows Hill? You said it was a bad place."

"Tis a place of blood and sacrifice," Joy answered gravely. "The most evil place in the Wyrde Woods I reckon."

"Is that why there is a Blood Stone?" Maisy was intrigued.

"Shhh," Joy answered and tilted her head as if she had heard something. Maisy listened too and soon discerned the approaching sound; the soft thud of multiple hooves on the sandy road surface.

Were the Hares following? The girls exchanged a worried look and drew towards the oak. Its great trunk had a considerable hollow and they half concealed themselves in its shadows.

Before too long a team of horses came into sight, they were hitched to an elegant open carriage which Maisy recognized as the same one they had seen outside the Owlery. The coachman was wearing that same fancy green hat, there was one passenger behind him, a woman.

"That ladies committee?" Maisy asked Joy softly.

"*Baint* their carriage, it's a Malheur Hall carriage. That's Jasper Hornsby on the box, a good man. Leon's uncle."

"It's Lady Priscilla!" Maisy cried when she got a better look at the passenger.

The girls edged out of the Halfway Oak's hollow into the light.

"Whoa!" The carriage came to a halt.

"Well met!" Lady Priscilla gave an elegant wave. She peered at them. "Joy Whitfield, Maisy Maskall and a basket of truffles, I have no doubt."

"Maisy Robbins, Ma'am," Maisy corrected her.

Joy nodded with a look of relief on her face.

"Heading for the front gate, Milady," Jasper Hornsby said.

"Indeed, the back gate would have saved you a long walk," Lady Priscilla looked at Joy questioningly.

"They said they wouldn't let us in, innit?" Maisy spoke up. "That it was a mistake for us to think…that we could…that woodfolk…"

She trailed off. To Maisy's surprise Lady Priscilla began to laugh heartily.

"Oh, you poor dears," Lady Priscilla said at last. "I do apologize, you've been caught up in the web of politics which surrounds Malheur Hall like a bad odour."

Maisy nodded her agreement; the Hares had not smelled very fresh.

"I could use a pair of Amazons to aid my cause," Lady Priscilla gave the girls a thoughtful look. "Would you be willing to offer me your assistance?"

Both Maisy and Joy nodded eagerly.

"Very well," Lady Priscilla smiled. "Jasper, would you mind…"

Jasper climbed down from the box. He walked to the side of the carriage and retracted a footstep after which he swung open the shiny lacquered door and held it open with one hand, extending his other hand in invitation.

Maisy and Joy exchanged a glance.

"Well, come on girls, get in," Lady Priscilla urged them.

They approached the carriage tentatively. The wheel spokes and rims were painted bright red, hardly touched by the dirt which clung stubbornly to the practical farm vehicles they were used to. The body had such a shine that it looked like it had just been painted. Jasper Hornsby assisted them up the footstep like proper ladies and before they knew it Maisy and Joy sank into soft velvet cushions opposite Lady Priscilla who beamed at them.

"The two of you look remarkably different today, compared to our last meeting. I must say I consider it an improvement."

Maisy nodded happily, committing the words to her memory so she would be able to repeat them to Gran who would undoubtedly be pleased.

The coachman had closed the door again, folded in the footstep and climbed back on the box.

"I would be grateful if you could take us home, Jasper," Lady Priscilla declared.

"Yes, Milady," came the reply after which he clucked softly and the horses obediently walked forwards.

Maisy stroked the soft velvet cushion; grinned at Lady Priscilla; turned to see Jasper handling the team impeccably; ran her finger along the smooth lacquered edge of the bodywork; and poked Joy in the side to make sure Joy was aware they were in a real Toff carriage like proper Toff princesses.

Joy's shining eyes told Maisy that she was enjoying the ride just as much.

"Pray tell me," Lady Priscilla addressed Maisy. "What rank do you hold?"

Maisy quickly took off her hat; she had forgotten that an officer would not keep it on in the presence of a lady.

"Captain Robbins, Ma'am," Maisy said earnestly.

"I see you are well armed," Lady Priscilla peered at the toy gun stuffed in the old belt Maisy wore above her blazer.

Jasper chuckled. "Begging your pardon Milady, but I have heard it said that Cap'n Robbins here patrols the Wyrde Woods on a fierce New Forest pony waving her pistol at bandits."

"Don't have any ammo, Milady, but don't tell anyone," Maisy laughed and took the gun from her belt to hand it over to Lady Priscilla who turned it around in her hand and seemed to admire it.

"It's a proper Hubley Cap Pistol," Maisy said proudly, "but you probably know that cause it's a right fancy toy, innit? It's the best toy I've got, Ma'am. My dad gave it to me, after the races, innit? But I used all me caps straightaway."

"You assume I am 'right fancy'," Lady Priscilla gave the gun back. "A flattering compliment."

Maisy stalled, unsure if she had said something she should not have, but then to her relief Lady Priscilla smiled again.

"What regiment are you in, Captain Robbins?"

"Special Detachment, Milady, Royal Sussex Regiment."

"The Royal Sussex! Impressive indeed, Captain," Lady Priscilla smiled.

"Nothing Succeeds like Sussex," Maisy said grandly.

"Honi soit qui mal y pense," Lady Priscilla answered.

"Shame on the blighter who thinks bad of us," Maisy said quickly.

Lady Priscilla laughed.

§ § § § § § §

The ride got better and better. The carriage emerged from the woods to continue along the formal tree lined drive and before long the girls could see towers and spires rising above the trees of the landscaped park which had replaced the woods.

An elderly man shuffled out of a small watchhouse to open a wrought iron gate and the carriage rolled through into the castle grounds; a bewildering complexity of neatly trimmed low hedges looping around bright flower beds, statues, fountains, manicured lawns and carefully laid out footpaths.

Joy looked at Malheur Hall in awe as its many towers, square and round, rose higher and higher as they approached. The walls were crenelated but instead of looking like forbidding obstacles they were given the elegance of a palace by two neat lines of high windows. As they approached the corner of the Hall, Joy could see a coachhouse to the left of the castle, separated from it by a row of gnarled chestnut trees. A wide moat now came into view and Jasper steered the carriage to the left - towards the bridge which spanned the moat. There was an impressive gate house with two small spired towers and an ornamental coat-of-arms depicting a rampant red griffin on a field of gold.

A man came walking from the opposite direction. It was John Hare who stopped and respectfully doffed his cap as the carriage made its turn onto the bridge. Bill and Silas walked behind him.

Lady Priscilla gave them a terse nod but the Hares did not notice for they had spotted the girls. Joy offered them a bright smile and Maisy waved enthusiastically. Three Hare mouths fell open.

The bridge was old and covered with paving slabs on which the carriage wheels rumbled like thunder. Jasper slowed gradually and the carriage was moving at a snail's pace by the time they were swallowed up by the open gate. Joy's eyes had to adjust as they drove through the shaded passage in the gatehouse and then again when they emerged in the sunlit cobblestoned courtyard. Windows rose two storeys high all around them and Joy smoothed her dress, suddenly pleased that she had been scrubbed and combed and tutted over. She eyed the rich fabric of the gown which Lady Priscilla wore and was suddenly conscious of her own simple appearance.

Maisy did not seem to have such worries; Joy's friend was beaming like a lighthouse, her eager eyes drinking in every detail of their surrounding.

"It's like a blee...a proper palace," Maisy said with awe in her voice.

"Indeed," Lady Priscilla smiled. "My ancestors had Malheur Hall built as a palace. The gatehouse, towers and moat were added as decorations more than defences."

Jasper brought the carriage to a halt and climbed down from the box. He gave Joy a reassuring smile when he helped her down to the ground but was then left behind as Lady Priscilla beckoned the girls to follow her towards the largest of the doors facing the courtyard. The door opened and an elderly man stepped out. He wore a black tail-coat and a dignified expression. He looked important so Maisy stood to attention and saluted him formally. Joy watched his face tremble with mirth for a fraction of a second before he pulled it back into set dignity. Two maids, dressed in grey dresses and wearing aprons with wide white ruffles came gliding out of the hall behind the door to line up behind the man.

Maisy stepped up to them and extended her hand. "Hullo, I am Maisy."

Both maids looked at the dignified man with consternation and his demeanor cracked again as he looked perplexed for a second; unsure what to do. Lady Priscilla gave the maids an encouraging nod and one by one they took Maisy's hand and mumbled their names.

Maisy shot Joy a look. *Don't be rude.*

Joy was getting very mixed signals and suspected that Maisy had done something unusual but she decided to stick by her friend and also stepped forwards to shake the maids' hands. For good measure she also offered her hand to the man, not having saluted him as Maisy had. The corner of his mouth twitched, in a nice way, as he shook it.

Then he turned to Lady Priscilla, "My Lady?"

"Cat's Chamber, I think, Jenkins," she said. "Refreshments for my guests would be much welcomed I suspect."

"Yes, My Lady," he turned towards Joy and Maisy, and gave them a kind smile. "May I be so bold as to recommend hot cocoa and scones to the young ladies?"

Maisy beat Joy to the answer: "Cor blimey!"

"That means 'aye' in *Lunnon*," Joy clarified.

"Miss Whitfield," Lady Priscilla said. "You have something for me, I do believe?"

Joy had almost forgotten and stepped forwards to hand Lady Priscilla the basket of truffles.

She handed it to Jenkins and said: "My compliments to Chef, and a gift of English summer truffles."

Joy watched in amazement as Jenkins handed the basket to the nearest maid who in turn handed it to the next maid who curtsied and then disappeared with the basket in her hand.

"Will there be anything else, My Lady?" Jenkins asked.

"No thank you, Jenkins," Lady Priscilla answered and Jenkins stood aside as she strode by. "Follow me girls."

Joy and Maisy stepped onto the marble floor of the reception hall to follow and the remaining maid preceded them to open a door. The girls looked around in wonder as they were led through chamber after chamber, each seemingly more grand than the previous one. Curtains which seemed to cascade down from great heights, decorated wood panels, furniture so polished it gleamed, sofas which could sleep a whole Edgelands family, lacquered desks and an abundance of accessories which seemed to serve no other purpose than to present an impressive sight.

"It's like a film set," Maisy whispered to Joy in awe.

At last they came to a corridor which had a stone floor and walls of hewn sandstone blocks. It ended at a large door made of aged oak planks and covered with long wrought iron hinges which extended this way and that in decorative loops and curls like tenacious brambles.

The maid opened the door and the girls followed Lady Priscilla in. Once in the room the girls looked around in pure marvel. Here too stone slabs formed the floor but unlike the low arched ceiling of the corridor there was a high rib vaulted ceiling supported by tall columns and arches. There where the ribs intersected were carved feline faces surrounded by wreaths of vines and leaves. Similar designs decorated the wood panels which ran alongside the outer wall below the line of clerestory windows; every single face depicted there in the Green Man style was feline. At the far end of the chamber was a small door. In the middle stood a stout table which could seat a score of people. Bookshelves protruded from the inner wall at regular intervals to form alcove upon alcove filled with books.

"The Cat's Chamber," Lady Priscilla said, seeming to admire it as much as the girls were. "The old chapel, but it has long since been converted into a library."

"So many books," Joy said, as she took in the regiments of book spines, bound in leather or painted cloth. "More than the library in Odesby has."

"And definitely more than school has!" Maisy added in wonder.

"Indeed, an army of books," Lady Priscilla answered. "However, there is one in particular which I have been meaning to show you, Miss Whitfield."

Maisy was puzzled, she thought that Joy and Lady Priscilla had met just the once but the Lady of the Wyrde Woods had spoken in a way that suggested they were more familiar.

The girls followed the woman into one of the alcoves where she stopped in front of a finely crafted mahogany book stand on which lay an open book. There was something odd about the letters, they were printed dark and clear within perfect straight margins but there was something irregular about them.

"That's been hand-written, innit?" Maisy's mouth dropped open.

"Tis old," Joy said with respect in her voice.

"Very old indeed," Lady Priscilla carefully shut the book and then took a step back so the girls could see better.

The book was bound with leather which still conveyed a faint trace of gloss on its dozen hues of brown. Finely filigreed brass trees and leafy branches formed a frame for the leather binding and a circle of vines and ivy surrounded the etched title.

Secree of the Wirdewode

Joy's eyes widened.

"I thought so," Lady Priscilla smiled, then turned to Maisy. "Your friend has heard of this book, it was written a long time ago by one of my ancestors. In medieval days."

"Robin Hood and Ivanhoe," Maisy's eyes shone as if she could hear the clash of sword blades and the swoosh and thud of arrows. She looked behind her into the old chapel as if expecting Errol Flynn to stride in.

"Precisely," Lady Priscilla smiled. "If you want to, Joy, you may study the book closely."

"Read it?" Joy asked with disbelief.

"Taking appropriate care," Lady Priscilla nodded. As if on cue the door creaked open and she smiled. "It is probably better not to combine the reading with the refreshments."

Jenkins supervised the laying out of one end of the great table. Maisy thought it was delightfully strange to sit with three at the far end of an otherwise empty table which seemed to stretch for half-a-mile towards the small door at the end of the chamber. She looked at the refreshments and suddenly felt shy. There were large porcelain cups on matching saucers filled with dark brown steaming hot cocoa and Maisy's mouth watered as the rich aroma of chocolate filled her nose. She had only ever had watered down powdered hot chocolate and that she had always considered a fine treat. Light traces of steam still rose from the hot scones, fresh out of the oven, and each plate was accompanied by a matching set of bowls containing fresh squares of butter, a selection of jams and succulent looking cream.

Maisy sat on her hands and held her arms stiff by her side, fighting her instinct to launch herself at the delicacies to conduct a voracious campaign of conquest. She remembered reading about Toff table manners but all she could recall was that they were dead important, she could not for the life of her remember anything practical. Joy was casting doubtful glances at her pristine white dress, probably thinking along the same lines.

"The scones won't bite you," Maisy could suddenly hear Jenkins say softly by her ear. "Just think about your movements, deliberate and slow. Mimic the Lady."

Maisy nodded gratefully as he used a silver contraption to place a scone on her plate.

"Thank you Jenkins. Some warm water and handcloths when we are done, if you please." Lady Priscilla smiled at Jenkins.

"Very well, Ma'am," Jenkins stepped back from Maisy. "Will there be anything else, My Lady?"

"Yes, assembly of the selection on the lawns afterwards," Lady Priscilla cast a glance at Maisy.

Jenkins inclined his head. "Very well, My Lady, I will see to it."

"Thank you Jenkins,"

Jenkins and his cohort of maids departed the room.

What followed was a curious mixture of dread and delight. Both Maisy and Joy cast surreptitious glances at Lady Priscilla and followed her cue in cutting the scones and then spreading them with butter, jam and cream. Maisy could not believe the liberal amounts she had been allocated in the bowls by her plate; enough for a whole family and there was a fine surge of anticipation as her generous helpings on her first scone left more than enough for the second. She was terrified that the butter, jam or cream would drip onto the fine white table cloth as she scooped it up from the bowls and made careful transferals in small doses. The scones tasted heavenly but were nothing compared to the hot chocolate, which was divine and Maisy only took very small sips to make it last as long as possible.

Maisy was sorry when the last crumb of scone and last sip of heavenly beverage passed her lips but also relieved that she had accomplished the daunting task of avoiding the deposit of chocolate, butter, jam or cream on her face, hands, hair, blazer, the tablecloth, floor and ceiling. Gran would be proud, Maisy was sure. She imitated Lady Priscilla in dabbing her lips with a serviette – though it seemed a shame to break its patterned fold - and said: "Cor blimey! That were cracking Milady!"

"*Bethanks*, Milady," Joy said. "It's the *bettermost* I've ever tasted, *surelye*."

"I am glad you enjoyed it," their host smiled graciously.

With perfect timing one of the maids wheeled in a trolley with two bowls of warm water, soap, handcloths and small towels and they all washed their hands.

§ § § § § § §

Lady Priscilla carried *Secree of the Wirdewode* to the other end of the table and gave Joy a pair of white gloves to wear for turning the pages. Joy was lost to them the moment she opened the book and Lady Priscilla then led Maisy into the furthest alcove where a small table held a map of the Wyrde Woods, its corners weighed down with wood paper weights carved with the likeness of the grinning cat which was present everywhere in Cat's Chamber. Perhaps it was the Cheshire Cat, that would be good, Maisy thought.

Her eyes sought and found familiar ground. Maskall Farm, the Raven's Roost and Mordrove along the North Woods Lane and then the long line which the Forgotten Road between the gateways at the edge of Shims Copses and Malheur Hall.

"Well, Captain Robbins," Lady Priscilla looked at Maisy with curiousity. "Tell me how your Amazons intend to defend the Wyrde Woods."

"It's no longer Amazons, Milady," Maisy answered.

"Oh?" Lady Priscilla raised an eyebrow.

"I've had to let boys in," Maisy nodded. "To make up the numbers, innit? So we're the Wyrde Warriors now."

"Very well. Sometimes these things can't be helped."

Maisy pointed at the map. "The Huns will come from the south, I reckon, from the coast."

"Parachutists tend to descend from the skies," Lady Priscilla said.

"Yes, but woods aint the best place for landing, are they," Maisy nodded. She pointed at Odesby. "That's what they'll want, bridges there and roads going every which way. Then they'll be looking to head north, innit? Towards London."

Lady Priscilla nodded. "Do you seriously intend to contest such passage north?"

Maisy shook her head. "I aint daft, am I, Milady?"

She reached into a blazer pocket and brought out a folded leaflet which had clearly seen much use. She unfolded it and showed it to her host.

"If the Invader Comes," Lady Priscilla read. "What to Do and How to Do it."

"Got me orders from the War Office, innit?" Maisy said proudly. "Personally delivered by the postman at Maskall Farm, Milady. Here, it says: Hitler's invasions of Poland, Holland and Belgium were greatly helped by the fact that the civilian population was taken by surprise…You must not be taken by surprise."

"So how would you avoid that surprise?"

"They stopped the ringing of church bells," Maisy declared. "So from now on if you hear churchbells ring it's a warning that Jerry is on his way. In that case the Wyrde Warriors assemble in the Wyrde Woods."

"Where?"

Maisy looked at Lady Priscilla and decided that she could be trusted.

"At the end of Hood's Gorge, there's a place there on top of the cliffs where you can see just about the whole of the Wyrde Woods. Joy showed me. It aint our HQ but it is our lookout point, innit?"

"And then what?" Lady Priscilla asked.

"Keep watch," Maisy answered immediately. "Just like the War Office Orders say, Milady. Anything we see, we'll go report it."

"To whom?"

"It says to be careful with army or police officers you don't know, innit? Cause they might be disguised Jerries. Just like nuns. Or tram conductors. But Gramps is in the Home Guard. They're at the Raven's Roost, so we'll send word to them. Including important details, like numbers, weapons, uniforms and where it was they were headed."

"It's large area," Lady Priscilla said thoughtfully.

"Yes," Maisy nodded. "See here: Remember that if parachustists come down near your home, they will not be feeling at all brave.

They will not know where they are, they will have no food, they will not know where their companions are."

"That would certainly apply to the Wyrde Woods."

"Innit just so?" Maisy confirmed. "They'll be looking for the way out and stuff to nick. So they might be headed for Wolfden, Mordrove or…"

"Malheur Hall," Lady Priscilla filled in. She read from the stencil: "Remember always that the best defence of Great Britain is the courage of her men and women."

She examined Maisy critically. "I've been wondering how much child's play is involved in your quest to take handsome prisoners of war."

Maisy recognized the reference to the Amazons and grinned.

The Lady of the Wyrde Woods grinned back. Her face changed as she did.

Maisy had already come to suspect that Lady Priscilla was far too casual for her station. Truffles were obviously a thing of class but even an East End chavvy knew that mere deliverers of the turd-shaped product were probably not usually treated to scones and hot chocolate in a private library. Lady Priscilla's eyes gleamed with gleeful anticipation of mischief. It was like looking in a mirror and seeing her own eyes, Maisy concluded happily. Before the tortoruous hot bath Maisy had anticipated that the visit would give a few impressions to feed her curiosity. She had not suspected that it would turn out to be a proper adventure.

"Have they told you I am considered mad?" Lady Priscilla enquired out of the blue.

"In the Wyrde Woods?" Maisy frowned. "They all think you're cracking, innit?"

"Cracking?" Lady Priscilla smiled. "A perfect double entendre if I ever heard one."

Maisy nodded somewhat confusedly, wondering if she had caused offence but Lady Priscilla remained perfectly friendly.

"Well, Captain Robbins," Lady Priscilla said formally. "Since you have had orders from the War Office and I have been woefully overseen it appears you outrank me."

Maisy looked at her questioningly. Lady Priscilla stood to attention and gave a formal salute.

"Captain 'Mad' Malheur, of the Malheur Marauders, at your service. Ma'am."

Maisy eyes widened but Lady Priscilla did not relapse in a smile; she stayed perfectly still, head held high, back straight and arms down by her sides at straight angles.

Maisy returned the salute. When she stood at ease Lady Priscilla did so too.

"The Malheur Marauders?" Maisy asked, and then added a tentative: "Captain?"

"Yes Ma'am," Captain 'Mad' Malheur nodded. "Ready for your inspection."

Maisy beamed.

§ § § § § § §

Joy was entirely oblivious to the exchange between Maisy and Lady Priscilla. She carefully turned the pages of *Secree of the Wirdewode*, marvelling at the texture of the parchment and in awe of the patience which the carefully handwritten words bore testimony to. The finely lined and colourful miniatures depicted scenes which sometimes seemed familiar. When they did she would read a few of the lines of the oddly spelled words until she established they were a variant of the tales she had grown up with. Some seemed unchanged though a few of these showed a new perspective or different interpretation.

Other tales were not known to her and the few she selected to read revealed the magnitude of the tapestry of myth and legend which shrouded the Wyrde Woods.

"Oi! Joy!" Maisy's voice penetrated Joy's consciousness. She looked up questioningly.

"I want to show your friend something," Lady Priscilla smiled. "In the garden. We shan't be long, my dear."

Joy nodded. Turning another page she was struck by the illustrations surrounding the first letter of the title:

The Faithful Speche of Fosterre

Figures had been drawn beneath the horizontal branch of the 'T' which had been formed in the shape of a tree; a dark green trunk and boughs with lighter green decorative leaves sprouting from the letter-tree. To one side of the 'T'was a lady dressed in a gown which was half blue and half red. Even though the artist had but a few lines to depict a tiny face he had managed to convey great beauty in her demeanor. To the other side was a hunched demon, dark and morose with red eyes and a grey beak. It seemed to wear a feathered coat of sorts.

> *In the olde dayes of ootherwordly legendes*
> *Al was this Wirdewode fulfild of fayerye.*
> *The elf-queene, with hir joly compaignye,*
> *Daunced ful ofte in many a grene mede.*
> *My leeve Mooder was one of hem*
> *Descended out of swich Briton gentilesse*
> *as served King Caradoc afore Arthour.*
> *I, Fosterre, speke of manye hundred yeres ago.*
> *and wol tell thee of how it cam to be*
> *that Nyade who walken this Wirdewode stille*
> *met dark Uleman of yvel entente*
> *and cam to lyven with the fayerye*
> *also how my Sire seeke and fighte*
> *a Worm of teethe and clawes and*
> *so cam to lyven with the fayerye.*

There followed a tale which was confusing for it had many strands which attempted to weave together the distances of centuries. Part of it Joy already knew, for it was oft told in the Wyrde Woods and one of her own favourites, but other parts were new to her and she was spellbound.

§ § § § § § §

The two Captains strolled out of the outer door. Looking around her Maisy could see that it was a partially concealed side entrance in the shadow of a large circular corner tower. Walking around the base of the tower they came to a small footbridge across the moat, which was at its most narrow at the back of Malheur Hall. There was a larger stone bridge further on for the official back entrance which was a smaller version of the gatehouse at the front. There were long lawns at the back, separated by a line of shaped hedges and flanked by flower gardens rich in colour as well as high ivy draped walls. Maisy's eye, however, was drawn to a small formation on the far end of the lawn. Helmeted figures bearing arms of sorts and being marched towards the Captains by a formidable woman in kitchen whites.

Lady Priscilla stopped and beamed her approval. Maisy stopped too and watched the squad approach. There were a score of them, all women, dressed in the maid's outfits she had seen before or more humble kitchen and grounds gear. They did all have a proper tin hat fastened by chin-straps, though what Maisy had first taken to be weapons turned out to be broomsticks and pitchforks.

"They're all women, innit?" Maisy grinned.

"MALHEUR MARAUDERS," the huge woman hollered. "HALT."

She was carrying a large wood rolling pin like it was a regimental standard.

"PRESENT!"

She raised the rolling pin. "ARMS!"

Rolling pin, broomsticks and pitchforks were duly presented.

"Thank you, Sergeant, at ease Marauders," Captain 'Mad' Malheur called out. Lady Priscilla then bent over Maisy's way and softly said: "Like the Amazons of old we keep a few men around for some of the more tedious tasks."

Footsteps approached behind them. Maisy turned.

"Lieutenant Jenkins," Lady Priscilla said and Jenkins was the first to salute formally this time. Maisy returned it, struggling to keep her face straight and not betray her pleasure. "And Sergeant Hornsby."

Jasper Hornsby gave a slovenly salute and smiled after which he said: "Logistics."

"Insolent but useful," Captain 'Mad' Malheur said pointedly.

"All the best soldiers are, Cap'n," Jasper grinned.

Lady Priscilla turned to the squad.

"This is Captain Maisy Robbins, tasked with the defence of the Wyrde Woods by the War Office itself. She has come to inspect our readiness!"

The squad cheered – raising their broomsticks and pitchforks – and Maisy was beside herself with disbelief and delight.

"Ready for inspection, Captain Robbins?" Captain 'Mad' Malheur smiled at Maisy.

"Cor blimey! You bet!" Maisy's smile seemed to spread from ear to ear before she remembered that she had to conduct herself like an officer from the Royal Sussex Regiment. She regained her composure and prepared for her first inspection parade of the Malheur Marauders.

§ § § § § § §

A boy tugged at Joy's sleeve repeatedly with an urgency which helped to draw her mind away from scenes of love and betrayal in centuries past.

"*Come,*" he whispered urgently, a sincere concern visible on his narrow triangular face framed by dark curls. He was about her own age and dressed in curious garments.

Joy frowned, trying to place him in the Cat's Chamber of Malheur Hall after her emergence from the Wyrde Woods of yore.

"*Come, we moot be faste,*" the boy insisted and Joy snapped out of her slow awakening and stood up. He took her hand and led her to the far corner of Cat's Chamber where the furthest bookshelf-lined alcove offered concealment.

Joy was about to ask who the boy was but he placed his index-finger on his lips and then she could hear the stout old oak door creak loudly as somebody opened it. She could hear footfalls on the stone floor.

"Why, Sir Mortimer, it's simply marvellous!" A woman's voice exclaimed and Joy held her breath. .

"It is indeed, Miss Chesterton," a suave voice confirmed. "Parts of Malheur Hall rest on the foundations of the old Norman castle which once served as my family's home. This is one of the few intact castle rooms left from that time. It's called the Cat's Chamber."

"Recently used by the looks of it," Miss Chesterton said. Joy realised she must have seen the cups and plates at the far end of the grand table as these had not been cleared away yet.

"Mother is enjoying the company of some ragamuffins," Mortimer Malheur said smoothly. "No doubt she hopes it will annoy me. I must apologize for my mother's behaviour, Miss Chesterton."

The voices continued to come closer and Joy and the boy retreated to the corner of the alcove.

"They're outside now," Sir Mortimer continued. "To inspect her rather awkward attempts at playing Boudicca. Which is why the maids haven't cleared up yet. I want to show you something, Cynthia. Something which may benefit your purpose."

"I was unaware you were that well acquainted with my purpose, Sir Mortimer." Miss Chesterton sounded guarded.

"I note your destinations in the Wyrde Woods and I know their history in detail." Sir Mortimer's voice was confident. "I rather doubt that Rudolf Hess is interested in the bluebells. You seek something dark, Miss Chesterton. That search, I might add, could be far more fruitful if you were to take me into your confidence."

"*They moot nat fynde it,*" the boy whispered into Joy's ear softly but insistently. "*They moot nat fynde it.*"

Joy nodded, trying to make sense of it all.

"I am not yet convinced," Miss Chesterton said.

"That's odd," Sir Mortimer said. He had stopped moving and Joy guessed that he was at the other end of the grand table now, right where she had been sitting. "Mother has been looking at the very book I wanted to show you."

There was a soft thud as the book was closed.

"*Secree of the Wirdewode,*" Miss Chesterton read. "This looks suitably old."

"So it is, a 13th century manuscript. The sole copy. Rather priceless."

Joy could hear the book opening again and the soft sound of pages being turned.

"Here, read this." Sir Mortimer suggested and then all Joy could hear was a low incoherent mumbling as the woman deciphered a number of sentences out loud.

"Well," Sir Mortimer continued when the mumbling ceased. "Is that not one of the things you seek?"

His companion didn't respond.

"So the key," Sir Mortimer said. "The key is the first step."

"*Releuen the stoon and thou shal fynde me,*" Miss Chesterton read again, but this time loud and clear. "*Cleuen the wode and I am ther.*"

"*They moot nat fynde it,*" the boy whispered into Joy's ear. She could feel his clean breath stir her hair. She looked at him questioningly, their faces very close. There was a desparate urgency in his eyes. Joy nodded, but uncertainly so. It was not clear to her what must not be found.

Suddenly there were muted voices outside, approaching the outer door.

"Quick," Sir Mortimer said and Joy heard the two make for the main door. They pulled it shut a fraction of a second before the outside door opened.

"What...?" Joy turned around to ask the boy for further clarification but there was no sign of him. She looked puzzled; bookshelves ran the length of all the three inner walls that formed the alcove, it was only at the far end of the main wall that the shelves stopped halfway up to reveal a segment of wall centred by a large portrait. There were no doors. Joy looked around again and then up at the portrait. She sucked in her breath.

§ § § § § § §

"Joy?" Maisy wanted to tell her friend all about the splendid allies she had recruited but Joy was nowhere to be seen when she dashed into the Cat's Chamber. The big old book she had been engrossed in still lay open on the table but the seat was empty.

"Joy?" Maisy looked around until her eye fell on the alcove. Walking towards it she saw Joy standing by the map table as if she had been nailed to the floor. Her friend's mouth had dropped open and she was staring at the painting which was hung high up on the wall. The painting seemed real old and was the portrait of a boy. The boy had a narrow face, hazel-green eyes which smiled and a cascade of dark curls which Maisy rather envied.

Maisy walked to her friend's side and gave her hand a concerned squeeze. Just at that moment Lady Priscilla, who had walked in behind Maisy, spoke up.

"The portrait is an old one," she said. "That youngster would not have recognized Malheur Hall as it is today. Just this old chapel and the few other parts of the old castle."

"Who is...was he?" Joy asked.

"Foster," Lady Priscilla answered. "Foster Malheur."

"Foster," Joy repeated. "Sir Richard's son."

Lady Priscilla inclined her head to look at Joy curiously.

"Mum teaches me," Joy clarified and Lady Priscilla smiled in reply.

"Yes indeed," she said. "Sir Richard Malheur of Farisee fame and his son Foster. Both of them Lord of the Wyrde Woods in the early 1300s."

"A long, long time ago," Maisy was impressed.

"But not all that far away," Joy said; mystifying Maisy though Lady Priscilla nodded thoughtfully.

§ § § § § § §

Jasper was requested to return the girls in the open carriage. He took a lane which led northwards to the North Woods Lane. They passed a field in which the Army was building barracks; a parade of half-cylindrical Nissen huts with skins of corrugated steel.

Joy was quiet and detached. She had been ever since she had lost herself in that book but Maisy did not mind. She had come to recognize the times when her friend drifted off into a dreamlike state and respected them by withdrawing into a silence of her own.

There were lots of things to think about anyhow; the visit to Malheur Hall had been eventful and she, Maisy Robbins of the East End had been received in a real palace like a proper princess. Moreover, she got to talk about the repulse of any Hun invasion of the Wyrde Woods and had been taken seriously.

In her mind's eye she saw the Forgotten Road stretch across the northern Wyrde Woods. Facing south, towards the Sussex coast, Maisy knew her right flank was covered by the Wolfden Home Guard based at the Raven's Roost. Captain 'Mad' Malheur's Marauders were on the left flank at Malheur Hall. The Special Detachment of the Royal Sussex Regiment would have to bear the brunt of it at the centre, but Maisy was fully confident that they would stand their ground. The war was practically won as far as she was concerned.

§ § § § § § §

Jasper turned left into the woods just before Mordrove and followed the dirt road to the Owlery where Goody Whitfield and Gran were waiting by the low gate. Maisy waved happily and both women raised their hands in reply.

"How do, Jasper?" Joy's mum asked as the carriage came to a halt. She grinned and added: "You bring more pleasant passengers *disyer* time."

"Last time it was Sir Mortimer who bid me to Vicar Framsfield's aid," Jasper shrugged. "Today I'm driving at the behest of the Lady of the Wyrde Woods."

"Bless her," Gran said.

Maisy nodded enthusiastically. Lady Priscilla was cracking.

10. Midsummer's Night

Gramps hitched a team to the light waggon and drove Gran and Maisy to Mordrove along the North Woods Lane.

Before, they would encounter a few waggons or a tractor on a jaunt along North Woods Lane. Sometimes there would be a lorry. Cars were less frequent though Maisy had seen the sleek black Malheur Rolls Royce pass one time. Since they had started to build the army barracks near Mordrove however, traffic had greatly increased. Army lorries rumbled over the road almost day and night. This time they were bringing the troops in.

Lorry after lorry passed the Maskall waggon to reveal the curious faces of soldiers trying to make sense of their new surroundings. They were greeted by the sight of a small blue-uniformed girl who stood on the box of a farm waggon, clutching an elderly farmer's shoulder for support with one hand and saluting them with the other. Most promptly saluted back; some with a grin on their face, others out of reflex.

Maisy was absolutely delighted. Her small Wyrde Woods defence force now had a strategic reserve of what appeared to be at least a thousand men. The Germans would find the Wyrde Woods a suitably tough nut to crack. She would have to devise a way to introduce herself to the commanding officer of her new reinforcements.

Gramps grinned throughout but Gran was not too pleased with the risk he was letting Maisy take. The endless column of trucks passing them made the team edgy. One lorry driver, possibly in a misguided greeting, sounded his horn right next to them. The jittery team lurched onto the grass verge. Gramps pulled Maisy down straight away with one of his strong arms, clutching her to his side as he used the other to control the team.

"Oh dear Gods!" Gran was shocked.

Gramps grinned and spoke to his horses, using his voice to calm them down. Maisy rested her head on her grandfather's chest for a moment, eyes shut and smiling. She felt safe with Gramps. She knew nothing could happen to her if he was around.

Everyone was relieved, though, when they left the North Woods Lane past Mordrove and drove into the Wyrde Woods. The roar of the lorries echoed in their ears for a while yet but at least the ground was not rumbling anymore. Moreover, saluting non-stop was tiring business, even for Captain Robbins.

Maisy was dropped off at the Owlery and Sarah Whitfield joined Betty Maskall on the improvised bench behind the waggon's box.

"Why don't they take us?" Maisy asked Joy after the elders had departed full of happy anticipation.

"Midsummer's Night. Tis a big celebration," Joy answered. "On top of Arthur's Fort, they'll get *tossicated* and there'll be plenty of *mucking about*."

"*Mucking about*?" Maisy frowned.

"You know…"

Maisy's eyes grew large. "They're *dabbing* it up?"

Joy grinned. "So I am told."

"Well, I'd rather be here with you, innit?" Maisy declared with conviction.

"We can have some fun too," Joy's eyes sparkled. She retrieved the key to the hidden door and disappeared in the cubicle beyond it to re-appear with a corked stone jug and a big leatherbound book.

"What's that?" Maisy asked curiously.

"Book," Joy answered.

"Really? Cor, I would've never guessed. How about the other stuff?"

"Mead."

"Mead?"

"Made from the *bettermost* honey." Joy had brought in two cups from the kitchen earlier and now poured amber liquid from the jug into them.

"I like honey!" Maisy took her cup and smelled the content, then looked up wondrously.

"It's alcohol," Joy smiled impishly.

Maisy grinned. "We're not supposed to…"

Joy shrugged and raised her cup, "Happy Midsummer to you, Maisy."

Maisy beamed and raised her own cup, feeling very grown-up all of a sudden, "Cheers, Joy."

She took a small sip; the initial sweet explosion of honey was replaced by an odd aftertaste which gave her a warm glow. She liked it.

They poured over the book which was printed in the old-fashioned way, some of the letters fading or replaced by odd symbols like ' ∫ '.

"Whatcha looking for?" Maisy asked.

"Something dark," Joy frowned as she tried to decipher a passage. "Something dark that *maun* be found."

"*Maun*?" Maisy asked.

"Must not," Joy clarified. "It must not be found."

"But you're looking for it? How does that make sense?"

Joy looked hesitant.

"We're mates," Maisy chided her. "You can tell me."

"You might think I am daft," Joy shrugged, shy like Katie all of a sudden.

"I think you want to tell me," Maisy said. "Cause you brought the book out, innit? You knew I'd ask questions. So cut to the chase."

"Cut to the chase?" Joy frowned.

"Skip the boring monologue and go on to the scene with the car chase," Maisy nodded. "It's from America, from the pictures."

"Car chase?"

"Never mind, I won't think you're daft. I promise," Maisy mustered all the sincerity she could.

Joy still hesitated.

Maisy stood up and laid her hand on her heart. Then she solemnly intoned:

Cross my heart and hope to die,
stick a needle in my eye,
a secret is a secret,
my word is forever,
I will tell no one,
Never-never-ever.

Joy was impressed.

"Do you remember coming back into the Cat's Chamber at Malheur Hall after your inspection of the Marauders?"

"Yes, you were staring at the painting."

"I was hiding," Joy said mysteriously.

"Hiding? Hiding from what?"

Joy told Maisy about the visit by Sir Mortimer and Miss Chesterton.

"So the painting talked to you?" Maisy asked breathlessly.

"*Naun* the painting. The boy came all the way to the table, to get me to hide. He seemed real enough, he touched my arm, held my hand. But then he was *gwoan*."

"Foster Malheur," Maisy sighed. "I wish I'd seen him."

"I think it was his *shim*, aye." Joy nodded.

"Of course it was," Maisy had no doubts. Castles were always filled with ghosts. It made perfect sense to her.

"*They moot nat fynde it*, they *maun* find it. He kept on saying that. It was really important to him."

"Find this dark thing? So you are trying to find it first, innit?"

Joy nodded. "It seemed important."

"Of course it is!" Maisy said. "If bloody Rudolf Hess is after it."

"I don't *ken* Rudolf Hess," Joy admitted.

"He's the Deputy *Führer*."

"*Führer*?" Joy recognised that word and her eyes widened.

"This Sir Mortimer and Miss Chesterton are German spies, innit?" Maisy said full of conviction.

Joy looked doubtful. So far Maisy had identified Sister Mary, nuns in general, the War-Ag Inspector, a gaggle of milk-maids, Vicar Framsfield, every member of the Wolfden Christian Ladies Committee, Bill Hare and the proprietor of Wolfden's Newsagent as potential German spies.

"Well, maybe not," Maisy conceded. "But they know something the Jerries are after, you don't get much higher than the Deputy *Führer*, Joy. Do you trust them?"

"*Naun*," Joy shook her head firmly. "*All-along-of* the fact that Foster don't trust them."

"He does have cracking hair, innit?" Maisy nodded. "*Luverly* eyes too."

Joy laughed and poked Maisy.

"Tis more than that, *Lunnon-girl*. It's like my heart and brain actually agree on something, *surelye*."

"Intuition," Maisy nodded. "Always trust it, innit? That means *we* are going to have to find it first."

To Maisy it was absolutely inconceivable that she would not be drawn into this plot. She wished she had a camera crew to film the adventure. *Maisy in the Woods*. She might even wear a posh dress at the premiere in London. She wanted something in the style of *The Cat and the Canary*. Maisy would be like Paulette Goddard and Joy would do absolutely fine as Gale Sondergaard's portrayal of the spooky Miss Lu. Leon could stand in for Chief Thundercloud.

"Maisy…" Joy looked unhappy.

Maisy looked at her guiltily. *Maisy and Joy in the Woods*. No, *Friends in the Woods*. That would be a better title. Then she realised Joy was not looking uncertain and pained because of the film's title but because of her uncertainty about Maisy's role in the picture.

"I aint afraid, am I?" Maisy said. "We wanted to stop the Jerries, any way we could. I'm dead serious, Joy. I want to fight them."

"I don't doubt that," Joy said. "*Howsumdever*, there are things in the Wyrde Woods…living creatures, but *naun* like us. You don't *ken* them."

Maisy thought about Foster Malheur's curly hair and bright green eyes which reminded her of Joy's. There'd be more ghostly reminders of the past and not all of them might be as friendly. Well, Maisy could be unfriendly too. She said: "I'll scratch along."

"There is something of everything and everything of something in the Wyrde Woods," Joy's eyes searched those of Maisy.

"Joy, I might not know them," Maisy maintained their eye contact. "But I know 'bad', even 'evil'. Not just because I watched *The Demon Barber of Fleet Street*, innit? The East End is a dodgy place. Tarzan would feel right at home there, it's full of hungry things with sharp teeth. Honest."

Joy tried to make sense of this and then nodded; relief on her face.

"I think I know the dark thing they are looking for. I read about it in *Secree of the Wirdewode*. Something called the '*Uleman of yvel entente*'. There is a legend in the Wyrde Woods about an Owl Man. I just never realised he was connected to Foster's story."

"Tell me about the Owl Man," Maisy's eyes gleamed.

"*Naun* at night," Joy answered, her face serious. "'Tis a tale for telling in bright daylight, *surelye*."

Maisy shrugged. "And they said finding the key was the first step?"

"*Releuen the stoon and thou shal fynde me. Cleuen the wode and I am ther.*" Joy took out a piece of paper and a pencil and wrote the words down.

"Bloody hell," Maisy took another sip of the mead and then another to make sure it really tasted that good. "I sometimes wished you Wyrde Woods folk spoke plain English, innit? All that Sussex is doing me head in."

"It's *naun* Sussex," Joy shook her head. "It's *Sheere-folk* English, but it very old. From Foster's time. I don't *ken* what all the words mean."

"*Releuen,*" Maisy rubbed her forehead. "*Releuen* the stone. Release the stone? So it's probably underneath a stone, innit?"

Joy nodded. "And *cleuen* the wood. It might mean cleave the wood, cut it in two."

"So there's a stone near some wood," Maisy was delighted. "You know these Wyrde Woods, Joy. Where could it be?"

"The Shy Maidens, the Guardians, the Blood Stone, the cliffs of Hood's Gorge and Willikin's Drove, Oscar's Folly…" Joy listed.

Maisy's face fell for a moment, then it lifted again. "We'll have our work cut out for us then, innit? It'll be like a proper adventure."

Joy smiled. So it was. They toasted to their adventure and made plans.

§ § § § § § §

"Joy!" Maisy whispered urgently but her friend remained deep in sleep. Maisy lit a candle and then began to gently shake Joy. "Wake up, Joy. *Nommus*! Wake up."

Joy opened her eyes and grunted. "Maisy, I was dreaming. A nice dream twere too."

A brief smile of recollection was followed by a frown as Joy peered at Maisy questioningly.

"There is an intruder, innit?" Maisy hissed. "A bloody *Tea Leaf.*"

"What?" Joy rose to prop herself on her elbows. "*Tea Leaf*?"

"A burglar! I can hear him! Downstairs he is. We should go whack him on the head, innit?"

"Maisy," Joy shook her head. "The owls…"

"Not the owls," Maisy shook her head. "Listen!"

Joy inclined her head and started hearing the sounds Maisy was referring to. Something was moving about downstairs; bumping into furniture and muttering when it did.

"Oh, that's just Master Dobbs," Joy shrugged. "If it were bad the owls would have made a *gurt* big stir, Maisy. You can count on that."

"Master who?" Maisy frowned. She had not realised the Owlery had another occupant. "A man?"

The intruder burped loudly.

Joy giggled. "Not quite a man."

They both tilted their heads when Maisy's intruder started singing boisterously.

Morning and evening
Maids heard the goblins cry:
Come buy our orchard fruits.
Come buy, come buy:
All ripe together
In summer weather,
Morns that pass by,
Fair elves that fly;
Come buy, come buy!

"Oak's Acorn! We left the mead out, didnt we?" Joy grinned.

"He's *lush*?" Maisy smirked.

"Only needs the one sip," Joy explained. "Master Dobbs aint used to much."

"Who the heck is Master Dobbs?"

"Master Dobbs is *Farisee*," Joy said. "He does chores for us at night."

"*Farisee*?" Maisy shook her head in confusion.

"A *Pook*. Faere Folk," Joy said patiently. "The Fae."

"You mean a faery?" Maisy was incredulous.

"They don't like that name," Joy shook her head. "You *maun* use it, Maisy."

"Are you telling me there's a blooming faery in your living room?" Maisy sounded outraged.

"You *maun* use that middling name," Joy insisted. "You don't want to upset them, *surelye*. I told you the woods were filled with critters of all sorts."

Maisy did remember but was not expecting a faer…a *Farisee* to be rummaging around in the Owlery. Something Joy was casual and matter-of-fact about.

"Back to sleep, Maisy," Joy smiled reassuringly and settled back down. "*Mayhap* I can still catch that dream."

Still speechless Maisy saw her friend close her eyes in total unconcern. Maisy pinched out the candle and settled on her back. She stared at the darkness above her listening to Master Dobbs continue to potter through the living room below.

Come buy, come buy:
Our grapes fresh from the vine,
Pomegranates full and fine,
Taste them and try:
Currants and gooseberries,
Bright-fire-like barberries,
Figs to fill your mouth,
Citrons from the South,
Sweet to tongue and sound to eye;
Come buy, come buy.

"Just a *Pook*," Maisy whispered to no one in particular and rolled her eyes.

§ § § § § § §

"Joy!" Maisy whispered urgently "Wake up, Joy, wake up."

"Huh!" Joy came to grumpily. "What's the matter this time?"

"The owls made a great big stir, innit?" Maisy said.

They had not just made a stir; it had been as if they had exploded into a frenzy. She did not need to explain that this had been followed by far more disturbing noises – for they could be heard clearly. Joy shuffled upwards, alerted.

There was an abundance of sound now, this time coming from outside where the girls could hear high pitched little shrieks, grunts and anxious calls piped in squeaky voices. Maisy's eyes widened in alarm when she registered that the sounds were approaching the Owlery.

Then, at some four or five places around the Owlery, they could hear loud eerie howls which sent the cacophony that was nearing the cottage into a frenzied discord. The owls in the living room added screeches of alarm. Maisy clutched Joy and held her tight.

"Boggerts," Joy whispered. "Boggerts a-hunting."

"Boggerts?"

"Bugbears, bogies." Joy answered calmly and Maisy felt her initial fright begin to diminish even though the names sounded ominous. She loosened her grasp on Joy but just by a little.

"They're squat critters, size of a calf with long shaggy hair and eyes like saucers, arms as long and strong as an oak branch. Meat eaters. Smell awful," Joy whispered.

Maisy's eyes widened and she tightened her grip on Joy again.

"Blimey! Sounds like a few East Enders I know. What do this lot do?"

"Hunt and eat the smaller *Farisees*," Joy listened to the intensity of the howls outside. "Sounds like a proper hunting party has been organised *disyer* night. Tis a rare thing for them to hunt in a group."

Maisy felt goose bumps all over as she listened to the squeals of alarm around the Owlery. The *Farisee* twitters and chitters had sent shivers down her spine when she first heard them but there was something oddly pathetic about them since the howls had begun. The poor *Pooks* were clearly frightened out of their wits.

"Should we go out and help them, or something?" Maisy proposed uncertainly. She started to release Joy from her tight embrace.

"*Naun*, oh *naun*," Maisy could feel Joy's head shake. "*All-along-of* boggerts also abducting *chavees*. They'd carry us off to their tunnels and that'd be the end of us. Boggerts like their prey to be squealing and squirming a bit when they start gnawing. *Naun* a pleasant way to go."

Something outside began to scream shrilly with piercing intensity.

"They got one," Joy said sadly as the screaming creature was torn apart.

Maisy increased her hold on Joy again; she was frightened and half hoped that she was having a bad dream. She had much rather dodge a few *bludgers* with *barkers* on a *bug hunt* in the Chapel. She'd even rather have had to search the local *lusheries* again; braving the leers and hoping that she'd find her father propped up on a stool somewhere staring into an empty glass so she could guide him home. That was all fairly run-of-the-mill stuff. This was just totally beyond her comprehension; surreal but the noises sounded real enough and now converged on the Owlery with some speed.

"They're coming to the house!" Maisy said with horror.

"Aye," Joy nodded.

They could suddenly hear the sound of the front door being opened.

"That'll be Master Dobbs," Joy said with evident relief in her voice though Maisy could not understand the relief for she could hear the sound of pattering feet approach; it sounded like the whole of the faery kingdom was making for the Owlery now. The noise increased as the *Farisees* stampeded into the house; some still squealing in fright but others beginning to jabber excitedly, right beneath Joy's room.

Maisy felt a sudden urge to wee.

The boggerts began to close in on the Owlery now as well, their ominous howls sounding much closer. Maisy gave a squeal of fright as did many of the *Farisees* who had gathered below them. A few owls squawked an irritated protest, presumably at the sudden overpopulation of the living room. It sounded like there were scores of *Farisees* in there. The front door banged shut again.

"Twill be fine, Maisy," Joy tried to reassure her friend.

"What if they come upstairs?" Maisy shuddered.

"The *Farisees*? *Naun*, they *ken* we're here. Tis *bettermost* if we don't *gwoan* down now and they won't come upstairs for the same reason."

"Not them," Maisy replied. "Those bleeding boggerts."

Before Joy could reply the howls reached a feverish apex and then ceased. There was an ominous hush downstairs as all awaited what would come next.

There was a curious loud humming sound that accompanied two or three creatures yelping in frightful pain. This was followed by ferocious barks and then more yelps as other boggerts launched themselves towards the cottage grounds only to be repulsed in hurtful confusion.

Silence followed. Silence in the attic, silence in the crowded living room of the Owlery and silence outside. It seemed to last forever till renewed barking and yapping outside broke it at last.

The former ferocity of the boggerts however, had been transformed into helpless frustration.

"What the blooming heck?"

"The Owlery is a sanctuary, Maisy," Joy explained. "Tis always been a safe place."

There were new sounds downstairs now. Someone was speaking to the others.

"Master Dobbs!" Maisy recognized the odd wheezy pitch. Joy nodded.

Master Dobbs must have conveyed the same information about the Owlery because a raucous cheer broke out below, loud enough to silence the frustrated boggerts outside. This was followed by happy shouts, cheeky taunts and then even spontaneous singing.

Rather than dying down the excitement below increased in pitch and intensity. Joy frowned. Master Dobbs picked up his song again, this time joined by two dozen others.

> *Down the glen tramp little men.*
> *One hauls a basket, one bears a plate,*
> *One lugs a golden dish of many pounds weight.*
> *How fair the vine must grow*
> *Whose grapes are so luscious;*
> *How warm the wind must blow*
> *Through those fruit bushes.*

Joy groaned. "They found the mead. We'll *naun* have sleep tonight."

More voices joined in the song below. Furniture was moved around and then the floorboards drummed to the feet of dancing *Farisees.* The owls screeched in protest but drew only laughter and imitation of their outrage whilst the singing continued unabated.

> *One had a cat's face, one whisk'd a tail,*
> *One tramp'd at a rat's pace, one crawl'd like a snail,*
> *One like a wombat prowl'd obtuse and furry,*
> *One like a ratel tumbled hurry skurry.*
> *She heard a voice like voice of doves cooing all together:*
> *They sounded kind and full of loves in the pleasant weather.*

One drop was enough, Joy had said and Maisy regretted they had not cleared up the jug earlier as she tried to sleep, her fingers plugged in her ears and her eyes pressed shut. She wanted to sleep. When she would wake all this would be over, leaving just the residue of a bad dream. The merriment, however, overpowered Maisy's improvised ear plugs.

> *Laugh'd every goblin*
> *When they spied her peeping:*
> *Came towards her hobbling,*
> *Flying, running, leaping,*
> *Puffing and blowing,*
> *Chuckling, clapping, crowing,*
> *Clucking and gobbling,*
> *Mopping and mowing.*

The dancing below seemed to reach new frenzies at every turn. The Owlery echoed to the sound of rumbling thunder as the *Farisees* began to dance as a collective; faster and faster they went, all the while adding laughter, whoops and jubilant cries to the song which went on and on.

> *Full of airs and graces,*
> *Pulling wry faces,*
> *Demure grimaces,*
> *Cat-like and rat-like,*
> *Ratel- and wombat-like,*
> *Snail-paced in a hurry,*
> *Parrot-voiced and whistler,*
> *Helter skelter, hurry skurry.*

"Cor blimey, Joy," Maisy assumed Judy Garland's breathless perplexity for the occasion. "I've a feeling we're not in Kansas anymore."

"*Quiddy?*" Joy replied. "Kansas?"

"Nevermind."

§ § § § § § §

The girls trooped into the living room groggily, having been summoned from their bed at dawn by impatient calls. The tumultuous celebration downstairs had stopped about an hour before dawn and blessed sleep had come at last – though far too short.

Maisy was too bleary-eyed to take in much more of the living room than the presence of her grandparents and Joy's mum.

"Morning, Maisy," Gramps greeted her. "Did you sleep well?"

Maisy grumbled an incoherent reply.

"Will you look at the state of the both of them?" Gran tutted.

"I'm *naun* surprised," Missus Whitfield said in a tone that made Maisy open her eyes wider to reassess the living room.

Furniture had been piled carelessly into the corners to clear space in the centre of the room though it was not empty for there was debris everywhere. Items that must have come from the opened cupboards and chests as well as an inexplicable amount of twigs and leaves. It was like a small miniature tornado had ravaged the room. Maisy turned to look at the adults again and was alarmed to see that Goody Whitfield was holding the jug of mead in her hands, upside down; it was empty. Maisy looked sideways at Joy. Joy was dazed and befuddled; slower in realising that things looked rather bleak for them.

"We had a cup each," Maisy declared, taking the lead. "That was all, I…"

"Be quiet," Gramps growled. "I don't mind your antics so much lass, but you *maun* lie to us."

"And you're far too young to get *tossicated*," Gran added disapprovingly. "Even on Midsummer's Night."

It was the first time that Maisy sensed disappointment in her grandparents and she cringed. She wanted to run to her grandfather and wrap her arms around him and swear that it was the faeries who had snuck in at night to complete the depletion of the bottle. She wanted him to pat her head and assure her no transgression had been made. Such a tale though, she realised with a sinking feeling, would probably just make it worse. Whoever would believe it?

"There was a boggert hunt last night," Joy stated, clearly of a different mind on this matter. "*Dunnamy*, half-a-dozen at least, *mayhap* more. A lot of *Farisees* sheltered in the Owlery and found the mead."

The adults shifted their focus to Joy.

"You mean to tell us the *Farisees* drank all the mead?" Gran asked sharply.

Maisy sighed deeply. *Here we go.*

"Aye, that they did," Joy nodded. "Apart from that cup Maisy mentioned."

"Who let the *Farisees* into the Owlery?" Missus Whitfield asked.

"Master Dobbs let them in," Joy answered.

"And who let the mead out of the closet?" Missus Whitfield asked.

"I did," Joy said, mixing guilt with defiance in her voice and expression. "To hail Midsummer's Night with my friend."

"Next time ask," Missus Whitfield said curtly.

"You'll say no," Joy shrugged.

"*Zackly* and *jes-so*," Sarah Whitfield nodded as she spoke those words and then suddenly spoke up much louder in a kinder tone. "Thank you Master Dobbs, for serving the Owlery in an hour of need once more. I am grateful for your help."

Maisy looked at her with wide disbelieving eyes. There had been no sarcasm in her voice, Joy's mum had sounded entirely sincere.

"Well..." Gramps looked uncomfortable. "I am middling sorry, Maisy, to have wronged you. Will you forgive me?"

Maisy nodded, quite flabbergasted. The adults seemed to accept the *Farisee* explanation without the slightest hesitation.

"You stayed out of their way?" Joy's mum looked at her daughter with concern.

"We didn't *gwoan* down," Joy nodded. "*Howsumdever*, we didn't sleep much."

"Poor *chavees*," Gran clucked like a mother hen. "You'd better get back upstairs, sleep it off. We'll clear up."

Fred Maskall and Sarah Whitfield nodded their accordance and Maisy shook her head in disbelief. She squeezed her eyes shut and for a moment she longed for the sanity of London, Luftwaffe bombs and all if need be.

11. Walking Tree

The soldiers moved cautiously. Forming two lines on each side of the road they walked some ten feet behind each other so as not to present a massed target. The Lieutenant walked in the middle of the road, more or less at the centre of the formation.

A tall lanky Sergeant walked some twenty yards ahead of him and an elderly Corporal twenty yards behind the Lieutenant. Most of the soldiers were in their forties and upwards though there was a scattering of youngsters who had only recently begun to shave. They had uniforms now, somewhat crudely cut and ill-fitting but they had been proud when the uniforms and Brodie helmets – tin hats as they called them – had arrived. It beat the previous LDV armbands as the only mark of their readiness to defend their community.

The troops were wary, most of them peering into the woods on either side of the road or scanning the edges of the clearings. These sometimes stretched into the woods like fingers revealing contours which kinked whimsically into erratic dips, gullies and mounds like a miniature mountain landscape – albeit one which had valleys deep enough to hide enemy soldiers in…or creatures of a worse nature.

A lot of the men were nervous. They were moving through Shims Copses. Many of them for the first time in their life as the dreary woodlands were an unaccountable area of the Wyrde Woods best left to its own devices. It was very early in the morning for they had set out at dawn and smoke-like wisps of mist meandered ominously between the pale birch trees. The soldiers' weapons drifted about in front of them as their hands moved in conjunction with their eyes; ready for danger.

"EEEE-EEEECCCCHHHH!" A sudden shriek pierced the morning.

"Bloody hell!" One of the soldiers cursed; a small wiry Wolfden man with a hooked nose dominating his narrow face.

"Now, now Private Rye," The Lieutenant said reprovingly. He was a beefy man in his fifties with old fashioned sideburns which were grey-streaked red like his mane of unkempt hair that struggled with his officer's peaked cap continuously as if seeking to escape. "Keep down the banter."

"Twere just a *scritch owl*, lads," the elderly Corporal told the men around him. The farmers grinned, the village men nodded, some uncertainly.

"I thought it were Goebbels with his knickers in a twist," Rye explained apologetically and many of the men laughed; some a little too loudly with an edge of relief in it. The Lieutenant noted that Rye had broken the tension of the moment and approved. He would still have to shut Rye up though.

"Private Rye," the Lieutenant spoke. "If you must daydream on the job, do spare us the sordid details if you please."

The men laughed and Rye beamed in his sudden popularity.

"Yes, *Leftenant* Mackellow," he said smartly.

"…eeeeeeeecccchhhhhhh."

The scritch owl sounded further away now but was answered by another and then a third. The men focused on their surroundings again. Many of them had spent a lifetime avoiding Shims Copses and the doom and gloom exuded by the woodlands helped their imagination conjure up the reasons why some parts of the Wyrde Woods were best left alone.

Or perhaps they were picking up subconscious signals that they were, indeed, being stalked.

§ § § § § § §

Walking Tree had come to be alone. He had sought a place where his own dark crown could brush those of the birch trees and where his mind could expand; wonder and wander at will to see what it may. This he considered to be part of his heritage and his mind fed on these moments of quiet meditation where he could be one with all around him. It was not to be this time though; the woods were stirring, restless even. Walking Tree stood firmly rooted to the ground for a moment; listening to the whispers of the breeze.

"Critters and tricksters," Walking Tree said slowly in his deep voice. "Many of them."

Despite his great size he moved off nimbly and was soon within sight of the dirt road which led into the woods. There were soldiers there; in patrol formation and moving carefully, almost hesitantly. Walking Tree could also hear the eerie calls of screeching owls which seemed to be protesting this armed intrusion into the woods. He did not fear the magic of owls as some did though and started following the patrol, deftly weaving between trees and dipping into depressions in the ground; moving four or five steps at a time before freezing on the spot. Then there would be subtle slow movement of his head as he examined his new perspective for a few breaths before moving on again.

§ § § § § § §

"EEEE-EEEE-EEEECCCCHHHH," Joy shrieked loudly from her vantage point at the end of one of the serpentine clearings.

"...eeee-eeee-eeee cccchhhh," Thallie answered almost immediately from a distance away and Joy smiled with satisfaction as she saw many of the soldiers shifting about nervously.

"Why don't you make ferret noises, Maisy?" Leon suggested innocently. "That'll put the fear of the Devil into them just as well. Sniff and squeak."

"Why don't you make sheep noises, farm boy," Maisy retorted. "Behehehé."

"More noises," Katie Rye contributed with a gleam in her eyes.

"Cccchhhhwwwwaaaa-aaaa!" A third call sounded nearby and Joy frowned, the unmistakable call of a scritch owl had not been Thallie's. Perhaps she could raise an army of scritch owls and have them descend upon the patrol in a dark cloud of beaks and claws, producing an otherworldly din that would send the soldiers scurrying back to the safety of Raven's Roost.

Joy smiled at the thought of such power and twirled around thrice, a movement made all the more dramatic by the long ribbons she had wound along her arms; ribbons that were festooned with owl feathers so that, as she twirled, it almost looked like she had wings. More owl feathers protruded from the headband she wore and she had daubed stripes on her face with the woad she had prepared earlier. The other three also had woad patterns on their faces and were similarly adorned with feathers and beads which they had fastened to their clothes or hung around their necks, ears and wrists. Maisy had stuck feathers in her cavalry hat. They all carried their bows and arrows and Leon had also fashioned a spear from a long straight branch which he had stripped of its bark and sharpened at its business end. The spear too was decorated with feathers.

Joy grinned fiercely, pleased with the little war band around her. She threw her head backwards after she came to a stop and screeched again: "CCCCHHHHWWWWAAAA-AAAA!"

"Cccchhhhwwwwaaaa-aaaa!" Thallie echoed her and for good measure the third owl added an "Eeee-eeeecccchhhh!"

"OW OW OW OW OW OW OW!" Maisy ululated.

"HUUUU-UUUU!!!! HUUUU-UUUU!!!!" Katie howled.

Leon joined in: "ARROOOO-OOOO! ARROOOO-OOOO!"

§ § § § § § §

Walking Tree stopped and turned his face towards the source of vocal mayhem. The tricksters might have sounded convincing to those not at home in the woods but these were no animal sounds that he knew of. Carefully keeping an eye out on the soldiers on the dirt road below Walking Tree began to make his way towards the source of these strange sounds.

§ § § § § § §

Lieutenant Mackellow noted that his formation began to break up as the woods erupted into a brief frenzied cacophony. Sergeant Silas Hare led the front section of the Wolfden Company and these men, all villagers, hastened their pace as Shims Copses lived up to its reputation. Many of them would have preferred to face a plane load of Jerry invaders rather than their own dark superstitions. The men at the back were farmers and they took their lead from Corporal Maskall who maintained his pace and failed to suppress an amused grin on his face.

Mackellow smiled inwardly, pleased with the sudden stress Shims Copses had lent his exercise, it was a good opportunity to observe his men under pressure. He put a scowl on his face and bellowed: "Sergeant Hare, slow your pace at once!"

Hare barked at his men and they reluctantly slowed down in order to re-establish the company's cohesion, casting anxious glances at the now menacingly phantasmal woods around them.

§ § § § § § §

The childrens' eyes gleamed with excitement as they moved forwards again to keep on shadowing the soldiers. Adrenaline lent them wings as they scampered forwards in a display of agility;

134

jumping over fallen tree trunks and gullies like warriors on the warpath.

"OW OW OW OW OW OW OW!" Maisy started up again and the rest joined in, howling to their heart's content.

§ § § § § § §

Walking Tree noted that the tricksters were heading straight towards him now. He descended into one of the deeper gullies where he decided to wait for their arrival. He stood rooted to the ground as if he himself grew from the moist soil and had his arms folded in front of him; a towering gentle giant exuding infinite patience.

§ § § § § § §

"COMPANY HALT!" Mackellow shouted. "Sergeant Hare and Corporal Maskall to me!"

The soldiers halted, instinctively turning outwards and pointing their weapons at the mass of pale birch stems of Shims Copses. The NCOs strode towards their commander; Hare's face a grim contrast to Fred Maskall's apparent bemusement.

"With all due respect *Leftenant*," Hare growled, squeezing his already narrow eyes further shut. "It *baint* a *gurt* idea to march through *disyer* unaccountable Shims Copses. There are plenty of other places in the Wyrde Woods for training."

"Some of the men say there is something of everything and everything of something in Shims Copses," Maskall added enigmatically, keeping a straight face though his eyes gleamed mischievously. "They also call it the Screaming Woods."

"We might as well pack up and go home if we're to be startled by noises, Corporal Maskall," Lieutenant Mackellow said crisply. "If the Jerries come, they won't visit just to have a picnic under the shade of an oak tree."

"*Baint* just animals *naun* more, Leftenant," Fred Maskall said. "There are other critters now, having a laugh at our expense I do reckon."

"Middling Shims Copses," Hare growled. "Tis an unaccountable place."

He glared at Fred as he finished his contribution: "A heathen place."

"Well enough is enough," Mackellow said thoughtfully. "The Wolfden Company is not to be trifled with. Sergeant Hare, take your section to the top of that clearing there. See if you can flush these critters out."

Hare hesitated.

"Well man?" Mackellow was incredulous. "Are you afraid?"

Silas Hare bristled at these words, even more so when he spotted the grin that twitched on Maskall's face. He turned and walked towards his section to organise them into a wedge that was to ascend to the top of the clearing Lieutenant Mackellow had indicated.

§ § § § § § §

The children did not spot the newcomer straight away despite his great height, so immobile stood he at the far end of the long gully they had just rushed into. Joy was the first to perceive that he actually was not part of the landscape and she came to a sudden halt, spreading her arms so that her wings warned the others something was afoot. They came to a halt, crowding just behind her outstretched wings and all of them stared at the unexpected apparition with open mouths.

"BLOODY HELL!" Maisy exclaimed on their collective behalf.

§ § § § § § §

Lieutenant Mackellow and Corporal Maskall watched with interest as Sergeant Hare led his men up the clearing. They were spread out and moving cautiously, once again holding their pitchforks, flails and scythes in front of them. These had been kindly lent to them by the men in Maskall's section, most of whom were armed with a variety of ancient hunting rifles, shotguns and even an old blunderbuss. Mackellow had given strict orders for these to remain unloaded though the farming men all carried their ammunition with them just in case Jerry decided to invade during a Wolfden Company exercise. The enemy were still clever bastards after all these years, that much they had gathered from the news of the new French campaign.

§ § § § § § §

Walking Tree took in the small war band with a great deal of curiosity. The girl with the white dress stood in front, her wings still stretched out protectively as her comrades crowded behind to get a good look at Walking Tree. Amidst the preponderance of owl feathers Walking Tree noticed the bows and arrows they carried and he looked at these with interest. Then he looked at their leader again…her face was somehow familiar.

§ § § § § § §

Maisy stared at the giant with awe. He was wearing what looked like regular issue army boots made of brown leather and khaki trousers but his upper torso was clad in a deerskin shirt with fringed sleeves. The top half of the shirt had been dyed blue and two strips of beads worked into colourful patterns flowed over the giant's shoulders to reach halfway down the shirt. Similar strips adorned his shoulders and upper arms all the way to his elbows. A red and green fringed neck tab completed the garment. The man had short dark brown hair and his light-brown face was adorned by a long lower jaw which seemed slightly out of proportion to the upper half of his face. He had striking chestnut coloured eyes which regarded Maisy and her friends inquisitively. Unlike the headbands which Joy and Katie wore with feathers sticking upwards the giant had two large eagle feathers hanging down the left side of his head, their quills fastened to his hair with red leather strips.

Maisy gasped, this beat the pictures anytime. Unable to stop herself she started yowling, flapping her hand in front of her mouth. "WHO-BOO-BOO-BOO, WHO-BOO-BOO-BOO!"

§ § § § § § §

Sergeant Hare grimaced when he heard the noise. His men were about two-thirds of the way up now and some stalled nervously.

"Keep going!" Hare barked. That damned Maskall had said somebody was having fun at his expense and the *leftenant* had given clear orders to flush these jokers out of their hiding place. Hare was determined to do just that. He half suspected the heathen woodfolk *chavees* were behind this and he hoped he would be able to give them a sound thrashing before Mackellow could intervene. Or Maskall for that matter, for that grand-brat of his from *Lunnon* had struck up a friendship with the little savages and might well be amongst them. His hands were fair itching to knock some sense into them.

§ § § § § § §

Walking Tree slowly shook his head at Maisy whose elated whoops died into a soft whimper. The three children behind their leader looked at him nervously, the winged girl was the only one who returned his gaze fearlessly. Out of the corner of his eye Walking Tree saw what the children could not see; soldiers making their way up the slope towards the gully.

"You are doing it wrong," Walking Tree told the children.

"He speaks English!" the short girl hissed.

"Better than you speak the language of war," Walking Tree said coolly, swallowing an edge of anger, "I am no savage."

He closed his eyes briefly. They were just children, he told himself, distorting his culture out of curiosity and fascination rather than treating it as something to ridicule. The soldiers were coming, he had a few minutes at the most.

Walking Tree opened his eyes again; the children looked at him with nervous anticipation, all but the winged girl in the white dress behind whom the rest huddled. She beheld him with a pride of her own that reminded him that while he might feel at home in woodlands there were those who considered these particular woods their home. She clearly had strong medicine and once again he was struck by the sense that he knew her. With sudden clarity he placed her. He had met her, he recalled. But that had been decades ago, on another continent.

"*He-ay-hee-ee!*" Walking Tree exclaimed, then added. "I will teach you."

Walking Tree turned towards the direction the soldiers were approaching from.

§ § § § § § §

Sergeant Hare looked left and right, his eyes catching those who were becoming increasingly jittery as they approached the treeline and he glared at them; willing them to continue their advance. When Hare was convinced that none would stall he looked ahead again; just half-a-dozen steps separated him from the woods now

and he fully intended to plunge in and discipline whatever culprits
he could lay his hands on.

§ § § § § § §

"This," the giant spoke. "Is how it is done."

§ § § § § § §

Sergeant Hare and all his men stopped instantly when the new
uncanny noise emerged from the woods. The sound started as a
keening hair-raising wail that rent the air to be followed by bloodcurdling high pitched prolonged yawps.

It stopped as suddenly as it started but none of the soldiers
dared to take another step forwards; to them, having never heard
these sounds before, there was a chilling quality to the whoops that
seemed unworldly as if vindictive spirits had risen as one to reap
vengeance upon the living.

§ § § § § § §

Joy was the first to imitate the shrill war-whoops and the giant
nodded approvingly.

"*Hecheto welo*," he said. "It is done well."

This encouraged Joy to try again and now the other children
joined in as well; shrieking at the top of their voices.

§ § § § § § §

Walking Tree grinned, the tricksters were not bad and their glee was
contagious. It was a good joke. He noted that the soldiers had frozen
in their tracks and Walking Tree decided to up the stakes. He
launched into the song that celebrated victory over Yellow Hair at
the place of Greasy Grass under the leadership of the great
Hunkpapa and mighty Oglala warriors whose names were still
uttered with reverence back home. He keened the words, stretching
each syllable into a triumphant ululation.

Kola tokile, kola tokile, kola ceyapelo.
Waziyata ki cizape.

The children continued to try out their new vocal arsenal as he intoned the syllables and Walking Tree nodded his approval as his feet and legs danced the beat of the victory war-song.

Kola tokile, kola tokile, kola ceyapelo.

§ § § § § § §

The first of the soldiers took a step backwards when the shrill yawps resumed in greater intensity and Sergeant Hare issued a growl but the man took two more steps backwards and to Hare's consternation others began to edge back as well.

"HOLD YOUR GROUND!!!" Hare bayed at them but they shook their heads.

"I signed up to fight Jerries, I'm *naun gwoan* to pick a fight with *Pooks*," one of them said. His statement was bolstered by others nodding their agreement.

"Christians don't muck about with the *Farisees*, Sergeant," another said loudly. "It *baint* middling healthy."

"It's witchcraft, *surelye*," a third man added.

Hare cursed but then the sounds from the forest were added to by what sounded like a hell-hound's keening and Hare soon found himself alone as one by one his men turned and legged it back to the road. Casting an uncertain glance at the woods which emitted such unbecoming noises Hare decided to beat an undignified retreat and he hurried after his fleeing section.

§ § § § § § §

"They are running now," the giant said with satisfaction and the children scrambled up the side of the gully to watch the soldiers' frantic rout. They began to grin broadly. Absorbed by the giant as they had been, they had not realised how close the soldiers had come in the first place; let alone that these would-be warriors had been given enough of a fright to opt for an inglorious retreat. The realizations prompted renewed triumphant yawping on their behalf and the retreating men seemed to speed up their flight in response.

§ § § § § § §

Lieutenant Mackellow was astonished as he watched the section halt just at the edge of the trees and then begin to edge backwards before beginning a panicked run back to the road. He strained to see what had frightened them but could only hear the distant unearthly hullaballoo.

Unlike the senior officer Fred Maskall was on the mark and wasted no time in contemplation.

"SECTION! FIND COVER ACROSS THE ROAD. COVER THE RETREAT!" He shouted and his men trotted across the dirt road to kneel down in dips or behind low mounds. They held their weapons at the ready, muzzles pointing upwards.

"Thank you Corporal," Mackellow caught on. "Should we have them load?"

"All of my lads are old sweats, sir," Fred said quietly. "*Naun* cold feet and they won't get *windy* and *funk* an accidental *plug*, sir."

Mackellow nodded, recognizing the trench slang immediately. Both his NCOs had selected their own sections from an abundance of volunteers and he was noticing the difference between Maskall's selection on basis of experience and Hare's village men who were either Hare's pub cronies or youngsters chosen to replace their fathers. Hare's own promotion had been political, his older brother was the Malheur Hall Groundskeeper and Sir Mortimer had pulled strings. Maskall had been elected at the Wolfden village parliament which some villagers and most farmers still attended.

"You think it's Hun *Z-Hour*, Corp?" Mackellow answered in trench slang as he watched Hare's section come streaming back down the hill. Both he and Maskall were scanning the treelines but they saw no movement nor anything else signalling an impending attack.

"*Naun* sir, we would have had a Code Cromwell and middling parachutists need aeroplanes which does make them somewhat noticeable I reckon, *bettermost* safe than sorry though."

"Very well, Corp. Proceed."

"LOAD YOUR WEAPONS LADS!" Fred shouted.

Mackellow was pleased with the speed Maskall's men showed in obeying this order. They were all ready by the time Sergeant Hare came racing through the gaps in the defensive line to find his men huddled in little groups gasping for breath. Silas Hare looked out of breath himself but made his way over to Mackellow and Maskall. The Sergeant had the grace to look embarrassed but Mackellow ignored him. The yowling from the forest ceased at last.

"A warning volley into the air, Corp?" Mackellow asked. "Be a good exercise and a message to whatever is up there?"

"Normal training procedure sir?" Fred asked, pleased that Mackellow had asked for his advice.

"Yes, conserve our resources Corp," Mackellow answered lightly, having decided there was not anything life threatening up there. "And if they are *Farisees* or *shims* there's no need to antagonize them further, is there, Sergeant Hare?"

"*Naun*, sir," Hare stammered. "Some of the men…they…"

"Yes I was fortunate enough to see their perfectly executed tactical withdrawal Sergeant," Mackellow said drily. "Carry on Corp."

"SECTION," Fred bellowed happily. "PREPARE TO SHOUT."

His men grinned at him.

"SHOUT!" Fred ordered.

"BANG!" they shouted in unison as they were wont to do in training for their ammunition was too limited to allow live fire exercises. They laughed at their effort as Hare and Mackellow formed the other section back into a line after which the Lieutenant ordered the patrol to march back to Wolfden. The morning's expedition had lasted long enough, Mackellow decided. He had got the measure of his men and there would be hot tea at the Raven's Roost. To be followed by a pint, of course.

Fred waited until the last of his section passed and then fell in step. He cast one more look at the treeline at the end of the clearing and shook his head as he saw a scritch owl glide towards it like a silent *shim*.

§ § § § § § §

"They're leaving!" Leon exclaimed needlessly as all of their eyes were trained on the road and everybody could see the Wolfden Company depart.

"Good," Joy said happily and turned around to examine their new acquaintance once again. The others gasped as they too turned and saw that the giant had disappeared.

"Blast!" Maisy whistled. "Was he for real? That was like watching *Stagecoach*."

"Or reading about the Wild West in *Boy's Own*," Leon agreed.

All of them had got used to Thallie now so no one even blinked when Joy spread out her arm to allow the Thallie to land as the owl swept into woods.

"Of course he was real," Katie said.

"But how?" Maisy protested. "This is England!"

"Sussex," Joy corrected her and - as if it explained everything - added: "And the Wyrde Woods."

Maisy shook her head. Castle ghosts, faeries, bogeymen and Red Indian warriors. She had clearly been missing out on things living in London.

12. Old Sodgers

"Tis a curious thing," Fred Maskall began to say.

"What's curious Gramps?" Maisy asked.

They had risen before dawn and after a simple breakfast Fred Maskall had whistled Hugin and Munin to him and headed for the Wyrde Woods with Maisy in tow. They had followed the Forgotten Road for a while but before they reached Roreford her grandfather had taken a right turn and led them southwards on a narrow trail. She had not been here before.

"*Disyer* Shims Copses. Most folk are *afeared* of these woods, *howsumdever*, you're striding along like you're taking a stroll in a *Lunnon* park."

Maisy looked around her. The sky in the east had become a deep blue but the day had not broken the darkness of the night yet. None-the-less the silver bark of the dense clumps of birches showed as a pale haze; a parade of endless ranks of ghostly soldiers. Maisy felt a cold shiver run down her spine.

"Well," she said with bravado. "Bunch of trees don't frighten me, do they? Even if they can dance."

She was lying through her teeth. The truth was that she felt safe in the Wyrde Woods if she was in the company of Gramps or Joy. Both seemed to know every nook and cranny of the woods and were in tune with the Wyrde Woods somehow. Maisy was unsure if they were aware of it themselves but they were both different here; so much at home that they seemed to be an actual part of the woods.

She did not mind traversing Shims Copses on her own during daylight for she knew the one path she needed to follow and the Forgotten Road had become so familiar that it already was like seeing an old friend. One the other hand Maisy was quite sure she would have gone raving mad if she had been at the Owlery on her own on Midsummer's Night, just as she would have been scared witless if she had been crossing this part of Shims Copses on her own in the darkness without Gramps.

Gramps carried a stout quarterstaff which looked to be a formidable weapon if so required. He also wore his ancient battered greatcoat and Maisy had decided he looked like Little John. That meant she would have to be Robin Hood but she had not minded a great deal; Erroll Flynn was one of her specialities. Maisy felt further reassured by the presence of Hugin and Munin. At the farm the dogs could frolick like pups but here they scouted the terrain with wary intent.

"Well, they ought to," Gramps said ominously. "*All-along-of* the *shims*."

"Really?" Maisy's curiosity was raised. "Why? What happened here?"

"Apparitions of old energies that *baint* realised their time has come and gone. *Disyer* part of the Wyrde Woods is said to be crawling with *shims*."

Maisy felt more shivers but these were thrilling, like at the pictures. Gramps and Joy told deliciously creepy stories about the woods and she was pleased at the prospect of another one.

"Oh, do tell," she pleaded. "Please, Gramps."

"Tis yet dark, lass. Tis a tale for daylight, *surelye*."

"I'm as blooming brave as a lad, Gramps. You know that, innit?"

Her grandfather did not answer but she could tell by his expression that he was mulling over her question. She liked it when he did that; the man always seemed to take her seriously – especially at moments like these.

"Just so, braver than most lads even," he said at last and looked at her pensively. "*Howsumdever*, do you *ken* when to stop, Maisy? Courage alone *baint* enough. A sense of caution – awareness; it counts for a great deal if you *gwoan* be a *sodger*. Take it from an old one."

Maisy glanced away to avoid his earnest look; instantaneously recalling the many moments when he had been most taciturn in response to her questions about his war experiences.

"What did old soldiers learn in the war, Gramps?" She changed tack.

"*Geemeny*," Gramps sighed. "You're a trickster like your mum and *gammer, surelye*."

Maisy pouted dramatically.

"*Howsumdever*, the both of them unaccountably rolled into one."

Maisy laughed.

"We learned…old *sodgers* learned…" Fred Maskall paused dramatically and Maisy held her breath. "…to be careful."

He looked at her pointedly.

Maisy rubbed her forehead and then said: "Joy told me it's bad luck to talk about the spirits at night, it draws them. But you talk about them, and it's still darkish; is Joy wrong?"

"*Naun*, your friend is right," Gramps answered. "I reckon you're thinking I am not being middling careful?"

He looked at her sharply.

"Well, yes," Maisy admitted hesitantly.

He grinned ruefully. "Your mind is as bright as a magpie's, lass."

"Well if I am the magpie you're the raven, innit Gramps?" Maisy said.

Gramps looked bemused; "A raven?"

"A raven called Grip," Maisy confirmed happily. "Rapping and tapping on windows and doors, innit?"

"You *have* been reading my books," Gramps scratched his head.

"Many a quaint and curious volume of forgotten lore, innit?" Maisy beamed. "Talking ravens everywhere, and you've named your dogs after some of them."

"Hugin and Munin," her grandfather said softly. The two lurchers stopped instantly and looked back to see if there were instructions.

"Gere and Freke would have made more sense," Maisy nodded wisely.

"Unaccountable!" Fred Maskall exclaimed. "Are you learning me the lore of Asgard now?"

"Teaching, innit?" Maisy beamed.

"Wait here a moment, Magpie," Gramps came to a halt and whistled softly. Hugin and Munin were at his side instantly.

"Hugin, stay," Gramps whispered. "Stay with Maisy. Munin, come."

Gramps took a few steps off the path and was swallowed up by the darkness.

The silence was sudden but not complete for Maisy began to hear other sounds in the woods. Soft rustling in the undergrowth, the hoots of an owl in the distance, her own breathing, Hugin panting softly by her side. She reached down to stroke the lurcher and Hugin wagged her tail but stayed alert.

"There, it'll be fine, Hugin. Nothing out there but Grip and Munin," Maisy said reassuringly though Hugin was not in the slightest nervous or fretful.

Maisy looked around her to perceive the pale forms of the birches anew. Their ranks had swelled since the eastern sky had begun to shade ever lighter hues of blue. She gritted her teeth. Gramps had admitted she was braver than most boys and the expedition was turning into a real adventure. He would not take her again if she started sniffling, she was sure of it. Besides, she would make a lousy Robin Hood if she could not stick it out in the Greenwoods. She could almost see Basil Rathbone's sneer if she was to flee the forest and present herself for arrest at Gisbourne's castle. Robin would only do that if it was a clever trick.

Still…thin tendrils of mist were beginning to form over the ground and started to twirl around the birch trunks in a manner which seemed to animate the trees into a slow sombre dance…

Fred Maskall stepped back onto the path; re-closing the ankle length greatcoat he wore. They continued on their way, Munin scouting ahead and Hugin trailing behind them.

"So why aren't you careful talking about *shims*?" Maisy asked. She had been much impressed by Joy's sincerity about the do's and don'ts of dealing with the *shims* and the *Farisees* in the Wyrde Woods. Taking it all seriously had not been difficult after Midsummer's Night.

"Just the *shims* of *disyer* area of Shims Copses," Gramps answered.

Maisy remembered something Joy had once mentioned about Shims Copses. "Is that because they were soldiers?"

"Aye, that they were; *sodgers*," Gramps nodded. "You're right about that, Magpie."

Maisy smiled.

"Go on then, Grip, tell us a war story," she pleaded.

Gramps looked at her sideways again, frowning at her persistence.

"So I can learn about being careful, innit?" Maisy implored. "You said it was important."

Her grandfather chuckled.

"Twere a long time ago," he began. "Afore **our folk arrived on the Sussex shores. Twere the Painted Ones who lived here then.**"

The Painted Ones Fred Maskall spoke of had their hall at Roreford and lived a relatively peaceful isolated life until the Romans came. Most of the warriors had gathered their arms and set off to challenge the Romans. None of them ever came back. With their warriors gone and columns of smoke marking advancing Roman army some of the folk followed their healer into hiding in Hood's Gorge. Some stayed behind, hoping for the best. The Romans spilled into the Wyrde Woods before too long and razed the hall at Roreford; slaying those who attempted to defend the huts which surrounded the hall. One of the healer's lookouts atop Hood's Gorge spotted the survivors being taken away in chains to be sold into slavery somewhere in that vast Empire the Romans had carved out with clever ploys and naked steel.

The soldiers themselves did not leave though; they built a watch tower at Roreford and oversaw the arrival of engineers and slaves to exploit the iron ore deposits in Shims Copses. The old woods there were steadily felled to fuel the furnaces of the bloomeries and the Forgotten Road had been busy with transport carts delivering supplies and taking away the wrought iron. The Rore had been wider and deeper then and they built a small port south of the Water Meadows to service the industry and thus Odesby was founded.

Maisy was enthralled as her grandfather filled the silent woodlands around them with wood choppers felling trees to deliver to the charcoal makers who in turn supplied the furnaces. There the iron ore was roasted at great heat and the strongest slaves assaulted the blooms with hammers to drive the molten slag out of it. Slowly but surely the old forest in Shims Copses – ancient woodlands – were replaced by unseemly slag heaps and the deforested area began to spread like a tenacious stain.

She was disappointed that Gramps stopped for another disappearance whilst she stayed on the path with Hugin. Poor Gramps did not have a very strong bladder, Maisy suspected as she peered at the ghostly birches encircled by the thickening mist. More owls hooted in the distance and Maisy heard a familiar screech amongst the hoots.

"Scritch owl," she told Hugin happily, pleased to recognize the distinctive call.

Her grandfather reappeared.

"The destruction of Shims Copses," he picked up his story. "Twere *naun* to the liking of the *Farisees*. They were used to respect from the Painted Ones but the Romans were *naun* alike any humans they had encountered before. Many a tree sprite perished here in Shims Copses, ancient revered *Farisees*."

"Did they fight back?" Maisy asked wide-eyed.

"Aye, that they did," Gramps answered. "The *Farisee*s visited at night and sabotaged what they could, as they are wont to do, *surelye*, whenever we start building in their domains."

"What did the Roman soldiers do?"

"They blamed the slaves at first and took harsh measures. The few Britons amongst the slaves tried to tell them twere *all-along-of* the *Farisees, howsumdever*, the Romans laughed that away; unaccountable *Sheere-folk* that they were."

"Those Briton slaves must have thought the Romans fools, innit?"

"They were crucified," Gramps said shortly. "Nailed to a tree and left to die."

"But…" Maisy stammered. "Just for telling about the *Farisees*?"

"For inciting trouble. The Romans wanted to set a middling example. They were hung up right in the middle of the biggest slave camp. Legionaries were posted to guard the crucified men and women. *Naun* of the other slaves slept *all-along-of* the the noises made by the dying. *Baint* a dignified death."

"Bastard legionaries!" Maisy fumed.

"*Sodgers* doing their duty," Gramps said grimly. "Blame those who led them."

Maisy nodded demurely; she had been hoping for a tale of heroic combat. This was unlike any war story she had ever heard.

"The *Farisees, howsumdever*," Gramps continued. "Didn't stop their sabotage and the Romans sought culprits and increased their patrols around the Wyrde Woods."

"The healer and his people!" Maisy exclaimed.

"Her; the healer was a woman. Niada was her name," Gramps said. "They were safe enough, for the upper reaches of Hood's Gorge were considered impassable. *Howsumdever*, one of the *chavees*, the son of one of the slain warriors, well…hiding in a tunnel like Old Brock *baint* to his liking."

"Old Brock?"

"A *bagga*," Gramps answered. "Badgers; *Sheere-folk* call them."

Maisy nodded but Gramps did not continue his story straight away. He organised another stop and while he was gone Maisy noticed that the sky was starting to grow lighter.

"What did that chavvy do?" Maisy pressed Gramps for a continuation of the story after he returned.

"Organised some of the other *chavees*," Gramps said slowly. "They started shadowing the patrols, prowling unseen in the woods alongside the tracks."

"Oh!" Maisy supressed a grin.

"Aye, *Howsumdever*…they pressed their luck. The first time the *chavees* made noises alike the *Farisees* the legionaries beat a hasty retreat. Twere unaccountable to their minds."

Maisy smelled trickery.

"Oi, is this story really about them Romans and Painted Ones?" She demanded, narrowing her eyes.

"Why wouldn't it be?" Gramps asked innocently and Maisy frowned.

"The chavvies weren't careful enough," she demurred.

"Aye, their game *baint* a bad idea. To have knowledge of your foe is a useful thing, Magpie," Gramps spoke.

Maisy smiled slyly.

"Howsumdever, their taunting revealed their positions and the next Roman patrol weren't so *timmersome*, some of them flanked the *chavees*."

"The chavvies were caught?"

"Aye, some of them," Gramps sounded very grim now. "They told the Romans about the hideout in Hood's Gorge."

"I would have never spoke a word!" Maisy declared bravely.

"Aye, you would have," Gramps countered. "Twere unspeakable what the Romans did to those *chavees*. No man or woman alive could withhold – the Romans were unaccountable experts at torture."

Maisy shuddered, wondering if the captured chavvies had been nailed to trees too.

"Did the Romans find the healer and her folk?"

"*Naun*, never." Gramps smiled. "Their hiding place is one of the gates to Pook Hall."

"Pook Hall?"

"The realm of the *Farisees*."

"The *Farisees* hid them!" Maisy was delighted.

"*Baint* that simple. The Healer and her folk were allowed to live amongst the *Farisees, howsumdever*, on condition that they never return from there."

"Oh."

"There is always a price to be paid for the use of magic, Magpie," Gramps shrugged. "An exception was made for the healer centuries later, *howsumdever*, a hefty price was paid for that as well."

"So there are humans living in…Pook Hall? And they live for centuries?"

"*Naun*, humans any more. They become *Farisees* themselves, we call them 'The Old Ones.' They are the youngest of the *Farisee* but the oldest of us."

Maisy nodded but her mind was probing the possibilities of living with the faeries in the tall halls of a magic castle for ever more. Gramps fell into a silence as she painted herself a lively image of the faery antics she would participate in and was thus happily occupied for a while.

By the time they got back to Maskall Farm Maisy had rehashed Gramps's stories a few times, injecting scenes with technicolour and the new-fangled multi-track sound system she had heard about and it was pretty clear to her that the Wyrde Warriors would have to become more careful.

13. Stone Square

Joy was in a wondrous state. She had been somewhat anxious about coming into Wolfden today, it broke with the low public profile she preferred to keep. Stone Square had transformed into a sea of faces and an ocean of prying eyes. The sheer number of people who had turned out created a deafening cacophony of chatter and laughter; something Joy was not used to and found unsettling. It seemed that every inhabitant of the Wyrde Woods' western Edgelands had come to Wolfden this day.

The general mood was inspiring though, people were in good cheer and though the war was on everybody's lips it was mostly in the spirit of defiance. Stone Square was festooned with bunting displaying both the Union Jack and England's St George flag. A huge Union Jack was draped from the top of the town hall and St Lewinna's Church flew England's red cross on a white field. The school displayed the stylised gold martlets of Sussex on a blue field and Joy thought all the bunting and flags made for a festive sight. There were a number of prominent citizens on the steps of the town hall, including Sir Mortimer and the Lady of the Wyrde Woods.

Joy smiled every time her eyes drifted to her left and she caught sight of Lady Priscilla. It was strange to think that she had been a guest in the Cat's Chamber not all that long ago. At first, upon entry into the imposing splendour of Malheur Hall, she had been in awe. She had only ever seen Malheur Hall from the other side of the boundary hedge before. Most often from the Halfway Oak where she had spent many an hour high up on the boughs of the ancient oak tree, looking dreamily at the crenallations, towers and spires which were visible. The rest of the castle was concealed from that vantage point by the row of great gnarled chestnuts. Lady Priscilla had told her that these trees had been planted when the hall had been built, in the days of Good Queen Bess. Although Maisy had repeatedly announced her full allegiance to Lady Priscilla, Joy was not entirely sure about her yet. The Lady of the Wyrde Woods was clever and kind and therefore eminently likable; but as an ally?

Joy had been left with two lasting impressions. The first was that she and Maisy were but a brief amusement, a break with the routine by adding some rustic flavour to a dull afternoon. Joy knew this was harsh but her wariness of people made her suspicious.

Everybody seemed to want something so it made sense to her to figure out what they wanted from the likes of Joy. She had enjoyed Lady Priscilla's hospitality but Joy was a proud girl, she did not want to be a rich lady's pet. The second impression, however, had been garnered when Lady Priscilla had said that there was a book she had been meaning to show Joy. There had been eye contact between them when the Lady of the Wyrde Woods spoke those words. How long, precisely, had she been meaning to show *Secree of the Wirdewode* to Sarah Whitfield's daughter, Joy wondered. It had suddenly seemed as if that moment in Cat's Chamber had been long overdue. If it was the *Wyrd* – fate at work – then Maisy might be correct in identifying the Lady of the Wyrde Woods as an ally.

Joy felt an uncomfortable sensation which drew her attention back to Stone Square. Somebody was directing hostility at her now and she soon located the source. Vicar Framsfield had taken position in front of St Lewinna's Church and the Wolfden Parish Christian Ladies Committee was out in force, surrounding him like bodyguards.

Alison Hare directed poisonous looks at Joy and made a show of pointing Joy out to her comrades, making sour comments as she did and those comments drew many a disapproving look. Elsewhere Bill Hare stood amidst his cronies and directed glowering looks at her which he occasionally exchanged for leering sneers. His mates, as always, took his cue and imitated him.

Joy returned the open hostility with a smile. Her smile was genuine for she had come to realise that something had changed. Before, she would have cringed under the force of negativity - mostly because she did not understand it, she had no idea why the Hares seemed to hate her.

She had been alone then.

Today she was in good company. Goody Maskall was close by, talking to some of the other women from nearby farms, all of whom had expressed their pleasure at seeing Sarah Whitfield's daughter in their midst. Maisy was there exuding her usual confidence which so intrigued Joy; her new friend was a powerhouse of spontaneous daft ideas and always held the utmost conviction that they could be carried out. Katie Rye and the other Wolfden members of the Wyrde Warriors had peeled themselves loose from their families to stand by Joy and Maisy. Katie's presence especially was remarkable though the girl was still *timmersome*. She stood between Joy and Maisy and clutched their hands tightly, eagerly lapping up their smiles and good spirit.

The crowd hushed as they could hear the parade approaching Stone Square. First came the Home Guard, led by *Leftenant* Mackellow, the Headmaster of the Wolfden School. All the *chavees* in the crowds cheered loudly for him, he had a reputation as a thoughtful and concerned teacher, the only one to avoid unneccesary punishment and he was sorely missed at school during the hours that he performed his duties as commanding officer of the local Home Guard.

The men who followed him looked proud, their simple uniforms clean and the newly received rifles lending them a more coherent and martial appearance. The first section of men was led by Sergeant Silas Hare and received cheers from some quarters and polite applause from others. It was the same for the second section led by the recently promoted Sergeant Fred Maskall. Goody Maskall and the farming wives whooped most unladylike and the Wyrde Warriors sounded loud appreciation whilst those led by Alison and Bill Hare could barely bring themselves to clap their hands.

The Home Guard marched towards the Town Hall where they smartly performed the drills required to stand to attention facing the way they had come. All cheered them on, there was not a single person in the crowd who had not witnessed the bumbling attempts at unit coherency during the first drills. More than one guardsman had been accidentally whacked by the broomsticks they had carried as their initial drill weapons. The local 'lads' had made considerable improvements.

The guardsmen beamed proudly, though a few faces betrayed relief that they had carried out their parade manoeuvre without making mistakes.

The crowd then hushed and heads turned towards the Roreford Road. The army barracks which had been built almost overnight outside of Mordrove housed troops from the Canadian First Division and the Canadians had accepted an invitation to reinforce Wolfden's Patriotic Parade. The Edgelands had been abuzz with rumours about the Canadian army camp for there had been no real interaction with the soldiers yet. The only local man who had ever met a Canadian, years before in Brighton, had been a welcome guest

in the Raven's Roost, the Earl's Barrel in Nickleby and the Carfax
Alus on the other side of the Wyrde Woods. Plied with pints at all
three pubs – and he tried to frequent all three every day out of a
sense of patriotic duty – his stories of the great wilderness in the
Dominion across the Atlantic grew by the pint and had evolved into
the stuff of legend.

The Canadian troops approaching Stone Square were rewarded
with instant popularity. Even before they could be seen their band
launched into the familiar tones of *Sussex by the Sea*. Wolfden roared
collective approval and then, as one, provided the words to the
martial music.

> *Now is the time for marching,*
> *Now let your hearts be gay,*
> *Hark to the merry bugle*
> *Sounding along our way.*
> *So let your voices ring, my boys,*
> *And take the time from me,*
> *And I'll sing you a song as we march along,*
> *Of Sussex by the Sea!*

There was movement by the town hall where Canada's Maple Leaf
now rose to flutter in the breeze next to the Union Jack and people
did not know whether to cheer themselves hoarse or keep on
singing about their beloved Sussex by the sea.

> *For we're the men from Sussex, Sussex by the Sea.*
> *We plough and sow and reap and mow,*
> *And useful men are we;*
> *And when you go to Sussex, whoever you may be,*
> *You may tell them all that we stand or fall*
> *For Sussex by the Sea!*

Joy grinned when she discerned Maisy's voice replacing every
'Sussex' with a loud 'LONDON!' though Goody Maskall, who had
also heard, frowned and shook her head in exasperation.

The singing faltered for a moment when the band came into
view. There were loud gasps and incredulous comments from the
crowd. There had been much speculation as to what a Canadian
looked like up close but none had expected this. The Canadian
soldiers had dressed in their ceremonial parade uniforms and as

their regiment was one with Caledonian roots that meant they were all wearing kilts, sporrans and other accessories of highland soldiers. The band played on indifferently and the crowd picked up the lyrics again when they got over the shock of seeing row upon row of bare hairy Canadian knees potruding below the rim of their kilts.

> *Sometimes your feet are weary,*
> *Sometimes the way is long,*
> *Sometimes the day is dreary,*
> *Sometimes the world goes wrong;*
> *But if you let your voices ring,*
> *Your care will fly away,*
> *So we'll sing a song as we march along,*
> *Of Sussex by the Sea.*

The band entered Stone Square and were now followed by rank upon rank of soldiers, all dressed in their highland finery and the sight of the multitude of firearms and ammunition pouches filled Wolfden with an unexpected sense of safety. Who would be able to stand up against these fine soldiers? Their renewed confidence sounded through in their singing which reached ebullient levels.

> *Oh Sussex, Sussex by the Sea!*
> *Good old Sussex by the Sea!*
> *You may tell them all we stand or fall,*
> *For Sussex by the Sea.*

The band had time for a rendition of *The Campbells are Coming* before all the participating soldiers had filed into Stone Square and now it was the soldiers who broke out into the *Sheere-folk* song.

> *Upon the Lomonds I lay, I lay,*
> *I lookit down to bonnie Lochleven*
> *And saw three perches play-hay-hay!*
> *The Great Argyll he goes before,*
> *He makes the cannons and guns to roar,*
> *With sound o'trumpet, pipe and drum,*
> *The Campbells are coming, Ho-Ro, Ho-Ro!*

There were speeches on the steps of the Town Hall by Wolfden dignitaries and Canadian officers but most of the crowd paid these little heed, their eyes drinking in the sight of the multitude of kilted men who stood to attention and grinned happily at the villagers.

"Maisy!" Joy exclaimed and pointed at one of the soldiers. The man was impossibly tall and dwarfed the soldiers around him. His brown face looked impassive and Joy and Maisy searched it and their memories.

"It's him!" Maisy decided and Katie nodded her agreement. When the last speech was done and the soldiers and the crowd slowly began to mingle the tall soldier stood alone; his appearance a barrier for most.

The girls hesitated and surprisingly enough it was Katie who pulled Joy and Maisy towards the soldier. "Come," she said simply and the other two followed obediently.

They lined up before the soldier. Even Joy, by far the tallest of the three girls, felt diminutive up close to the soldier. He turned his face down with a questioning smile.

"Hullo!" Maisy said. "We met in the woods, innit? You're wearing a skirt today."

"It's a kilt. I do like to go for walks in your woods," the soldier replied in a low deep voice. His accent was funny, but not distinct from the other Canadians they could hear talking around them. "So we may well have met."

"You don't remember us?" Katie sounded disappointed.

"We were playing redskins," Maisy exclaimed. "You're a real redskin, aintcha?"

The soldier's face fell.

"You don't like to be called that," Joy guessed.

He looked at them most seriously and nodded his affirmation. "It is not a nice name. It's kind of like being called a dwarf..." he looked at Maisy and then at Joy, "... or a witch."

The girls blushed.

"What is your name then?" Katie asked sensibly and the soldier smiled at her.

"Chunmaniye," he answered.

"Chunmaniye," they all replied, trying out the strange word.

"Is that another language?" Joy asked curiously.

Chunmaniye nodded, "It's Lakota."

"SIOUX!" Maisy shouted. Seeing his face fall again she quickly added, "I suppose you prefer Lakota, innit?"

He nodded gravely. "And your names?"

The girls introduced themselves and he repeated each name carefully. Maisy then proceeded to subject Chunmaniye to a barrage of questions. Most of them concerned her knowledge about Native Americans. This seemed to be based on the pictures Maisy was so fond of as well as adventure books but most of Chunmaniye's answers demolished her perceptions.

Joy smiled; feeling great love for Maisy as she watched the *Lunnon* girl's expression change rapidly from disappointment, interest, disbelief, enjoyment and insight. It was clear to Joy that Maisy's brain was working overtime again. Joy was sure that the encounter would result in another half-dozen audacious plans for the Special Detachment of the Royal Sussex Regiment.

Maisy wanted adventure but much more than that she craved companionship. Only now that Joy herself had such a friend did she realize how much of a missing element that had been before the *Lunnon* girl had entered her life. Joy could not even begin to imagine life without the Maskalls anymore. The elder Maskalls, she knew, wanted Maisy to be happy but they also seemed to delight in Joy's presence when she visited the farm. They clearly liked children and made them feel more than just welcome. They made them feel at home. Even Katie, on her first visit to Maskall Farm, had felt so comfortable that she had nearly outchatted Maisy around the kitchen table at tea time. For a while, there seemed to be nothing left of the *timmersome* girl whose ability to be invisible at school surpassed that of Joy's.

"Disgraceful," a sour voice marred Joy's warm happiness. Alison Hare was passing nearby with some of her flock and spoke just loud enough for Joy to hear.

Joy frowned. Why was the woman so keen to spoil a nice afternoon? Alison Hare seemed to Joy to be a spring of bitterness which she tried to alleviate by spreading her misery to others.

"Heathens," one of Alison Hare's companions spat. "One of them coloured too."

Joy took a deep breath, she was about to turn and spit fire at the waspish pests when Chunmaniye caught her eye. He was still patiently answering Maisy's questions and smiling at Katie but his eyes rested on Joy. Almost imperceptibly he shook his head, as if he knew what she was thinking. Joy's face broke into a slow smile as she looked back at him and nodded. It was uncanny, the exchange of a thousand words in a glance as if they had known each other for a long time.

Canadian officers began to stride about energetically, summoning their soldiers back into the ranks and the civilians began to retreat to the edges of Stone Square again.

"Will we see you again?" Maisy asked Chunmaniye eagerly.

"Time will tell," Chunmaniye answered. His eyes told Joy that they would and she smiled.

§ § § § § § §

"Cor blimey!" Maisy was not sure if she ought to be surprised that Joy seemed to be waiting for her on a grassy verge of the Forgotten Road when Maisy came riding by on Spark. Valkerie flicked her tail; she was draped around Maisy's shoulders as an exta addition to the Royal Sussex Regiment uniform.

"Were you waiting for me?" Maisy asked Joy. She had been on her way to the Owlery but that had been a spontaneous decision.

"The bees told me you were coming," Joy said mysteriously and Maisy shrugged. Joy said the oddest things sometimes but Maisy supposed if faeries could dance and sing in living rooms bees might as well talk. Maisy was not quite sure of anything anymore in the Wyrde Woods.

"I thought we might go looking for that key," Maisy said hopefully.

Joy nodded. "I was thinking the same. Wood and stone. The Guardians, *mayhap*?"

Maisy dismounted and grinned. "Lead the way!"

Joy led them to Roreford along the Forgotten Road, though she selected a much smaller path heading north-east before they got to the ruins. They crossed a wider path which Maisy thought she recognized as the passage between Roreford and the Owlery.

"So tell me about this legend of the Owl Man," Maisy demanded. "It's daylight now."

"The Owl Man is a sprite that has been seen in the Wyrde Woods at times." Joy answered.

"Like a ghost?"

"Not like a *shim*," Joy shook her head. "More of a spirit. *Naun* a nice spirit, a dark one."

Maisy nodded, the 'dark' made sense. Joy had told her that Sir Mortimer had spoken of a dark thing the Jerries were interested in.

"Man-sized, with red eyes and black wings and sharp claws," Joy continued. "Covered in black feathers all over. *Shrucks* and *skreels* like a stuck pig. Folk around here were *afeared* of him."

Maisy felt a shiver run down her spine and she looked at the trees around her, half expecting this Owl Man to be perched on a branch above them.

Joy laughed. "Tis been hundreds of years since the last sighting. He was most often seen around Tuckersham Church."

"Tuckersham?"

"Used to be a village, just the ruins of the church left now. It's south of the Guardians."

"Can we go there?" Maisy asked, intrigued by yet another abandoned settlement in the Wyrde Woods.

"Tis *naun* a happy place, just like Gallows Hill," Joy said softly. "I'd rather stay away; today, anyway."

Maisy nodded, recalling Joy's warning when she had tentatively revealed her Malheur Hall secrets to Maisy, as well as the howls of the Boggerts. Looking up again, in case this Tuckersham Owl Man decided to make an appearance anyway, Maisy perceived the bulk of a cliff looming over the forest.

"Hood's Gorge!" She exclaimed.

"Aye," Joy confirmed. "*Howsumdever*, the bottom end this time. We're taking a longer way, there's something I want to show you."

The trees started to thin and Maisy looked up to see the two pinnacles of stone that marked their lookout post high above. The area immediately below the cliff consisted of a broad grassy clearing that touched upon the Rore's bank where it emerged from the gorge and was centred by an oak tree with low limbs and boughs supporting the dome of its canopy. There were hundreds of ribbons and strips of fabric tied to the lower branches and twigs; some faded into pale representations of the colours they had once been, others still bright as if they had been tied on yesterday.

"Cracking!" Maisy looked at the tree with pleasure. It looked really festive.

"The Wishing Tree," Joy nodded.

She produced two blue strips of cotton. "If we tie these to it we can make a wish."

Maisy took one of the proferred strips and looked at the mass of ribbons swaying gently in the breeze like miniature banners. There was barely any space. Joy had wandered to the other side of the wishing tree with her ribbon. Maisy mounted Spark and spurred the pony to a gap amidst the lower limbs. Then she stood up on Spark's back, grinning as far more sparsely ribboned branches came into reach. Valkerie became lively around her neck, scanning the tree with interest as Maisy tied her ribbon to the branch. Maisy laughed as she fumbled with the strip of cloth for Valkerie's interest turned into delight and she was performing a joyful little dance on Maisy's shoulders.

"You're not helping, Valkerie," Maisy admonished.

Valkerie dooked softly; a ferret sound that was a bit like chirping.

"I wish…" Maisy rubbed her forehead. "I wish I had a proper horse, just like Leon does."

Spark neighed a protest and Maisy lowered herself on the pony's back again.

"I'd still keep you, silly bugger," she leant forwards to give Spark a reassuring rub on the neck. "To carry my provisions, innit? And Valkerie can ride Bacon."

Spark snorted and Maisy shrugged. "One that's less stubborn than this one," she told the tree. "Blimey!"

She could see Valkerie scurry along one of the larger boughs over her head. The ferret must have jumped onto the branches when Maisy had started to lower herself onto Spark's back.

"What's the matter Maisy?" Joy reappeared.

Maisy pointed at the branches above where Valkerie was now sniffing a piece of bark; slowly waving her tail to and fro like an explorer's flag.

"Bloody hell, Gramps is going to have me mucking out the stables for the next twenty years," Maisy bit her lip.

"Aye, I reckon he will," Joy agreed.

Maisy snorted and steered Spark back underneath the canopy. She stood up on the pony's back again and when she was within reach of a bough she took hold of it and hoisted herself up. She was two boughs over from Valkerie and moved a bough closer with slow movements. Maisy did not want to startle Valkerie. Gramps had told her ferrets were hunters who could be managed most of the time provided you knew what you were doing. Not always though.

"When instinct kicks back in..." he had told her in the long shed one evening. "By *Geemeny*, Maisy-mine, there *baint* a finer sight than a beast made for hunting running on instinct. *Howsumdever*, they don't snap out of it, *naun* just like that. If you ever see Valkerie do so, take care lass, even you might earn a nip from the little *scaddle*."

Maisy reckoned that was what Valkerie was doing now. The ferret seemed coiled up, all tense as she followed a scent. Maisy stifled a laugh when Valkerie suddenly stopped, seeming comically surprised by the sight of a large beetle. The beetle perceived a threat and squirted a jet of fluid at Valkerie, hitting the ferret square on the nose. Valkerie recoiled, twitching her face and seeming to pull up her nose as if the fluid smelled repulsive.

Maisy chuckled softly. Valkerie rubbed a forepaw along her face several times and then lurched forwards to snap the beetle up in her mouth. Maisy could hear the beetle's shell crack and took advantage of Valkerie's preoccupation with her prey to climb up onto the bough Valkerie was on.

When Valkerie finished the beetle she wagged her tail and made loud dooking noises. That told Maisy that the ferret was happy and approachable.

"Valkerie, Valkerie," Maisy cooed softly. Valkerie turned and sniffed her curiosity at Maisy.

"Come on, girl, come here Valkerie."

Out of the corner of her eye Maisy perceived that Joy had come to the base of the tree and was peering upwards. Fortunately her friend had the good sense not to call out.

"Come here girl," Maisy slowly stretched out her hand. To her relief Valkerie started forwards, her eyes on Maisy's hand. The girl had been worried that Valkerie might have opted for a game of chase – Valkerie loved to play chase even more than Maisy did but right now Maisy did not fancy wriggling along every bough and branch of the wishing tree in a vain attempt to keep up with the ferret.

Maisy smiled...then there was a red blur and angry screeching. The newcomer was a squirrel and streaked in from nowhere, placing itself on the other side of Valkerie. The ferret twisted herself backwards to face it.

The squirrel narrowed its eyes and brought its ears forwards. It raised its hackles and its tail hairs were standing on end making the squirrel seem far bigger than it was. The squirrel began flapping its tail, padding its hind feet and chattering its teeth.

Maisy's mouth dropped open. Surely the squirrel was aware that it was outnumbered two to one and yet the little animal took up a fighting posture, trying to intimidate them into departure. There was no way Maisy could intervene though. Valkerie had answered the squirrel's challenge by backing up slowly, with a bushed tail. She was hissing fiercely and Maisy knew better than to try and grab a hissing ferret, let alone from behind without warning. Valkerie would not have that on a good day, if it happened now she would respond as if attacked and turn on Maisy instantly, sinking those little teeth deep enough to puncture her skin. That prospect actually bothered Maisy less than the fear and panic Valkerie would undoubtedly be subjected to if the ferret perceived an unexpected second threat.

Maisy's interference was not needed though. Valkerie launched into her ferret battle dance; first arching her back as high as she could and then jumping up and twisting around in the air before landing again to feint a lunge forwards that was followed by a rapid retreat of some steps after which the ferret repeatedly hopped up and down on all fours, hissing all the while.

The squirrel's eyes widened and it flattened its ears. It began a high pitched growl and then abruptly squealed and beat a hasty retreat, scurrying along the bough before launching itself into the air to the safety of a higher branch. Fortunately Valkerie was in no mood to attempt a chase. Instead, the ferret twirled round once after her last hop and then dashed towards Maisy and clambered up onto the girl's shoulders.

"You're having all the fun," Maisy grumbled at Valkerie as she started to negotiate her way back down. "Letting me do the work."

Valkerie dooked again, quite taken by the sudden adventure.

"Sounded like quite a gathering up there," Joy commented when Maisy whistled Spark into position and lowered herself onto the pony's back.

"Squirrel," Maisy answered. "I reckon it had young, it was determined to *boat* me out of that tree."

Joy chortled. "Shall we carry on?"

Maisy nodded.

The girls followed the bank of the Rore south towards Roreford. The Wishing Tree was soon out of sight as the Rore's course made slight turns.

"Blooming heck!" Maisy suddenly exclaimed.

They had come to a grassy indentation between the river and the forest and there was a horse there, its neck bent down as it was grazing. It was a white gelding with a grey braided mane and tail. A beautiful high saddle of leather and wood rested on a green saddlecloth stitched with silver and gold thread at its rims. The reins were covered in similar cloth and the leather of the bridle was deep green.

Maisy looked around to see if there was any trace of a rider, but there was not. She spurred Spark forwards and then several things happened in quick succession.

First Valkerie dug her little claws in Maisy's shoulder. The ferret arched her back and hissed loudly.

Spark reared, neighed loudly and then refused to take another step forwards.

"Maisy, don't go near it," Joy said in alarm.

Maisy allowed Spark to turn and then circle back to Joy's side, a distance away from the white gelding. It had stopped grazing now and looked at them curiously. There was not any sign of the aggression or fear that warranted the reactions displayed by Spark and Valkerie.

"I don't understand," Maisy said.

"Tis a *kelpeye* horse," Joy said. "Whatever you do, stay away from it."

"It looks…," Maisy looked at the horse pensively, "…inviting."

"*Zackly*," Joy said. "The *Farisees ken* how to lure."

"It's *Farisee*?" Maisy shook her head. It looked like a perfectly normal horse to her. The very animal she had just wished for. Apart from the quaint saddle and bridling it had none of the attributes she assumed the mass of dancing and squealing *Farisees* in the Owlery's living room to have.

"*Naun* of a good kind," Joy frowned. "A *kelpeye* is a masterful disguiser. Anyone enticed to climb onto that horse's back…"

Joy shook her head. The horse did not respond to Joy's words at all, it just looked at Maisy and gently shook its head as if to deny the threat. Maisy felt the urge to go and pet it at least but then she recalled Valkerie and Spark. Those were animals she knew and trusted and their dislike of the horse was evident.

"What happens?" Maisy asked.

"The horse will plunge into the nearest body of water. The Rore *baint* a healthy river here, *atween* exiting Hood's Gorge and reaching the Farisee Bridge. The green jennies don't *gwoan* to Fey's Pool."

"Green jennies?"

"Once it's taken you into the river the *kelpeye* will show her true form as green jenny. Gnarled like an ancient yew tree and hair and garments like water weeds. Teeth as sharp as Valkerie's and with them she will feed on you."

Maisy shuddered. "I'm no *kelpeye* dinner."

"*Naun,*" Joy agreed. "Let's pass here quick."

Maisy felt somewhat nervous crossing the area between the horse and the Rore but the animal continued to just stand there, looking at Maisy with big sad eyes.

Maisy shook her head and looked away. She felt Valkerie and Spark relax as they put distance between them and the white horse. Maisy recalled Joy telling her that there were whole different worlds in the Wyrde Woods when she had first met her properly. She would have thought Joy right mad if the woodfolk girl had spoken of the *Farisees* back then. Now she doubted her own sanity, maybe Joy was contagious. That still did not explain Spark and Valkerie though and Maisy was convinced that they could not have been wrong.

They passed through Roreford where they crossed the Farisee Bridge and then followed the Forgotten Road east for a while until Joy led them onto a broad path to their right. Maisy dismounted and continued on foot, leading Spark and Valkerie who had settled on the saddle. They skirted a large pond which Joy called Lewinna's Pool. The water was crystal clear and Maisy could see the sunlight penetrating it deeply to touch the pond's bed. They stopped for a short while to let Spark drink and then they continued on their southern course till they reached a rectangular clearing.

"The Guardians," Joy said proudly, indicating the triple rows of standing stones, each some six foot high and broad in girth. They really did look like they were keeping a silent watch on the surrounding Wyrde Woods, Maisy thought.

She tethered Spark to a young ash trunk and then joined Joy in circling the standing stones, getting on their hands and knees to feel their way around the base of the stones just in case there might be a tell-tale cavity or another hint. Having found none, they stood by one of the stones, each girl deep in thought. Joy had her brow furrowed and Maisy rubbed her forehead.

"It would take all of the Maskall horses pulling at ropes in order to topple one of these blighters, I reckon," Maisy commented.

"Tis *bettermost* to *naun* topple sacred stones. The wood somehow gives access to what is below the stone, I think."

"The trees around here don't look that old," Maisy said. She had seen far older trees in the Wyrde Woods, the ones here were sturdy but did not yet seem full grown. Unless they were Maisy-trees and in no hurry to grow.

"Time can be a funny thing in the Wyrde Woods," Joy said pensively.

"Like a time-machine?" Maisy's eyes lit up.

"I don't think so," Joy shook her head. "It's not like jumping from one place in time to another. It's more, like the one briefly fuses with the other *somewhen*."

Maisy pursed her lips. "Time fuses?"

"Float towards each other and just mingle for a while," Joy nodded.

"We'd better check the trees then," Maisy decided.

They spent another hour examining the trees immediately around the clearing but found nothing remarkable. Heading back to the Forgotten Road they agreed to visit the stone circle called the Shy Maidens on their next expedition.

14. The Fight

Joy and Maisy sat next to each other during the mathematics lesson. Maisy was trying to contain the need to run and jump about; she was fair bursting with energy and could barely sit still. Joy seemed to have drifted off into her daydreams. It had been a long day already. There had been an unexpected air raid drill after lunch; the day disrupted by the scramble for gasmasks and then the journey to the cellars of the old school building and Town Hall. Workmen had recently finished the adjustments that were needed and they now served as air-raid shelters.

It was hard to get back into school stride after that and now the mathematics teacher, a frail bespectacled man who wheezed when he breathed, had drifted off into a cloud of his own confusion. Maisy had stopped trying to follow him, instead her eyes wandered around the interior of St.Lewinna's Church which they were using as classroom.

The walls of the church were whitewashed and just a tad uneven as the interior walls of rough stone were covered with a thick cover of loam. Aged wood supporting beams were set in the walls and far taller ones rose to the ceiling where a complex ribbed frame of arching beams supported the roof. There were a few decorations, a couple of small paintings depicting biblical scenes, memorial stones around the altar, stained-glass windows and crucifixes. Maisy and Joy were sitting on an uncomfortable church bench, their notebooks balanced on the very small ledge attached to the top end of the benches in front of them. Maisy's eye was repeatedly drawn to a statuette of St Lewinna, in an alcove just a few yards away.

St Lewinna, Maisy decided, was cracking. Rather than being a dull saint in long robes with a staff, lamb or howling baby – Maisy's main impression of saints – St Lewinna was depicted in a long chainmail coat. There was a broad belt around her waist and from that hung a scabbard with intricate decorations. The Saint held a long triangular shield. She wore no helmet or other headwear, instead the artist had depicted her long mane of hair as if a breeze were lifting it like a proud banner. Maisy did not know the first thing about chainmail but she suspected long loose hair and thousands of riveted steel circlets did not make a good combination.

None-the-less, the pose was dramatic and that Maisy could appreciate. The whole was completed by the depiction of a curled up dragon beneath the Saint's feet and an arm held high lifting a sword.

Maisy could barely keep her eyes off the Saint. Bugger Robin Hood and Ivanhoe, from now on play set in the Middle Ages would involve St Lewinna. Relunctantly she turned her attention to the teacher just in case he had started to make sense.

"So that is," he squeaked, "how you solve this problem…no wait…wait…"

He turned to the blackboard to examine his own spidery markings which apparently resembled words and numbers.

"Psst, Joy," Maisy nudged her neighbour. Joy looked at her questioningly.

"Why does Lewinna have a dragon below her feet?" Maisy whispered.

"*All-along-of* that she killed one, in the Wyrde Woods." Joy whispered back.

Maisy's eyes grew wide and she looked at the statuette again. A dragon-slayer even.

"Good Lord, I've got it all wrong," the teacher coughed, "You see class, you follow this approach halfway to the solution instead…using…using…"

Maisy looked to see if he was pointing anywhere that might clarify the approach he was talking about.

The teacher suddenly pounded an area of the board with great enthusiasm. "Yes! Yes! That is what you do here, then apply the answer there but instead of …no wait…YESTERDAY! Then you apply the sequence from yesterday…there…no here!"

The Master turned his back to the class and started sweeping the mobile blackboard with a rag which emitted clouds of chalk dust that enveloped him and caused him to lose himself in a coughing fit.

Most of the children stared at him in utter confusion. Maisy rolled her eyes at Joy who shrugged helplessly.

The teacher started scrawling new numbers and formulas on the blackboard, muttering an explanation which barely reached the first two rows of pupils.

Maisy looked at him pensively. She briefly wondered who on earth had decided that this man would do well in front of a classroom. Then she turned away again, it was bloody unfair really but she could not even be bothered to work herself into a state of indignation. She looked at St Lewinna again, the heroic pose appealed to her. She liked the contrast between the warlike aspects of chainmail, shield and sword and then that hair being lifted by the breeze and a clearly feminine face, almost dainty except for the grim determination set upon the Saint's lips.

Maisy started devising a complex plan to steal into the church at night, having secretly hitched the small farm cart and driven it to Wolfden, and rescueing the poor Saint from further mathematics lessons. She was quite sure Lewinna would much prefer to stay over in Maisy's room at Maskall Farm. Or maybe at Fort Defiance.

Maisy's eyes started wandering around the statuette to see if there were any doorways or trapdoors that might afford access. The main door would not do at all, as it faced Stone Square. Perhaps they could use the much smaller north door which Joy and a couple of other pupils always used when they entered the church for a class. Maisy looked at the stained-glass window behind the Saint though it would never enter her head to destroy such a work of beauty. The window depicted a bright sun rising over a clearing in a woods; brown branches and green foliage framing the sky from top to bottom. There were two scrolls with mottos, one above the sun and one below.

The lettering was clear and…

Maisy's mouth fell open. She gasped for breath.

"Maisy?" Joy whispered with concern in her voice.

Maisy stood up from her seat and walked a few feet towards the statuette and the window behind it.

"Ahem," the teacher coughed, "You there, what on earth are you doing? You there. Girl!"

"Joy!" Maisy called out. Joy rose and came to her side, laying a hand on Maisy's shoulder.

"Maisy, sit down, we *gwoan* get into *moil*." Joy threw an anxious glance at the teacher who was completely aghast.

"Both of you! Sit down at once!"

Maisy ignored him completely. Instead, she pointed at the window. "Joy, look!"

Joy's eyes followed Maisy's finger and when she saw what Maisy was pointing at the squawking teacher and sniggering pupils disappeared entirely, as did the church. All Joy saw was Lewinna's gentle face and flowing hair below a sun rising in the woods – and the words, of course.

Joy was barely aware of the teacher's footsteps on the stone slabs and only vaguely perceived that he closed one of his hands around her upper arm. She could only stare at the words.

RAISE THE STONE AND THOU SHALT FIND ME
CLEAVE THE WOOD AND I AM THERE

Joy felt delirious with triumph, even as the teacher took a firmer hold on both girls and pulled them backwards. He twisted them around and marched them out of the church towards the inn but Joy and Maisy were not impressed yet, instead they kept exchanging glances and grinning broadly.

It was only when they were pulled into the small hallway of the main school building and thrust on the wooden bench there that they began to comprehend they might be in a bit of trouble. There were four doors in the hallway. The two side ones led to the two large – and only – classrooms in the building and the door opposite the main entrance led into the Headmaster's small office. The teacher knocked on that door and entered, closing the door behind him.

They could hear snatches of conversation, a deep calm voice responding to high-pitched protestations.

"...little savages...disgraceful behaviour..."

The disgraceful savages giggled nervously.

"Cor blimey," Maisy said regretfully. "I done it now, innit? I never think properly do I?"

Joy shrugged. The discovery was much more important. *Raise the stone and thou shalt find me. Cleave the wood and I am there.*

"It'll be fine Maisy," Joy took Maisy's hand into her own and gave it a little squeeze.

Maisy still looked worried though. "I suppose we'll get thrashed proper now, innit?"

"Just a little," Joy said confidently. Mus Mackellow was known as a fair man; one of the few reasonable adults she knew.

They were called into the office and walked in holding hands. Mus Mackellow was twirling his fingers through his red side burns. His countenance was stern but his eyes sparkled with a cheerfulness which banished any lingering doubts Joy had as to the severity of their punishment. The Mathematics teacher stood by the side of the desk, arms folded and triumphant satisfaction on his face.

"Joy Whitfield," the Headmaster boomed. "And our London guest Maisy Robbins."

The girls nodded meekly and squeezed each other's hands.

"Mr. Hartfield tells me you caused a severe disruption in his class."

"It weren't so till…" Maisy began. "Ouch."

Joy had squeezed down hard on Maisy's hand.

"Twere a bad disruption Mus Mackellow," Joy agreed. "And we are both very ashamed *all-along-of* our behaviour."

Mr. Mackellow looked at them thoughtfully for a moment. "As I recall Miss Whitfield," he said at last. "You were always very quiet and withdrawn. Since your friendship with Miss Robbins started you have been sent to my office…?"

"This is the third time, Mus Mackellow," Joy admitted.

"And you Miss Robbins," Mr. Mackellow continued. "Ever since this alliance between the two of you has allowed you to feel at home here in Wolfden you seem to have become very…exuberant."

"Disgracefully so," the Mathematics teacher snorted.

Maisy shot him a look but Joy applied pressure to her hand again and her friend got the hint. Like Goody Maskall had said Maisy was clever enough, just very impulsive.

"Yes, sir," Maisy looked at the Headmaster again.

Joy squeezed again.

"Sorry Guv," Maisy added quickly.

"Well you need not be," Mr. Mackellow said.

"WHAT?" Joy, Maisy and the Mathematics Master chorused in unison.

"I think of your friendship as a positive thing," the Headmaster folded his hands in front of him and leaned forwards, looking from one girl to the other with disarming sincerity.

Joy and Maisy squeezed hands.

"Mr. Mackellow, I must protest!" The teacher fluttered.

"I wasn't finished yet, Mr. Hartfield." The Headmaster did not break eye contact with the girls and the teacher fell into a disapproving silence.

"The girls have admitted their misbehaviour and as such there must be punishment Mr. Hartfield. I do not approve of disrupted lessons." Mr. Mackellow held both girls' gazes with more intensity now and Joy nodded an acknowledgement of his earnestness. "However, in my school, I always think of the children too when I can Mr. Hartfield. In deciding the punishment I must also weigh up what is truly beneficial for them."

"But the girl was simply ignoring me," Mr. Hartfield protested. "Highly disrespectful."

Mr. Mackellow looked up at the teacher now.

"Yes it is," he said calmly. The Headmaster turned to the girls again. "This kind of behaviour has no place at this school, do you two understand?"

Joy nodded. Maisy said: "It won't happen again Guv, I promise."

"Now the most logical punishment I can think of to prevent further unfortunate disruptions to lessons," Mr. Mackellow continued sternly, "would *not* be beneficial to your friendship which is unfortunate since I am of mind that this fellowship of yours is beneficial for the both of you."

Joy nodded downcast, she had not considered not being allowed to sit next to Maisy in class anymore and suddenly the chasm of isolation beckoned again.

"Couldn't you just thrash us instead, please sir?" Maisy pleaded.

"Thrash?" Mr. Mackellow looked quizzical.

"Cane us Guv," Maisy nodded with some enthusiasm which was mirrored on the Mathematics teacher's face. Maisy raised her free hand as if she was holding a length of wood and brought it down to beat the Headmaster's desktop. "Whack! Whack! Twice oughta do, innit sir?"

The Mathematics teacher nodded his agreement.

The corners of Mr. Mackellow's mouth twitched as he looked at Maisy with bemusement which Maisy misread.

"Twice *each* of course, sir," she added hastily.

"I will tell you what I will do," Mr. Mackellow said. "If you value your friendship then you will make an effort to ensure that it doesn't disrupt any more lessons. Next time it does separation becomes inevitable. To ensure that you fully understand what such a separation would be like I have decided to give you a taste of it. For the next two months you will not sit together during the mathematics lessons. Do you understand why?"

Joy nodded. "So we know what it's like again *most-in-general*, if we aint more quiet Mus Mackellow."

"It's very clever, Guv," Maisy voiced her admiration and astonishment. "In London…"

"You are in Wolfden now, Miss Robbins," Mr. Mackellow looked at Mr. Hartfield. "Are you satisfied with this punishment Mr. Hartfield?"

"Why yes," the teacher looked puzzled. "It is very reasonable, Mr. Mackellow."

"Good," the Headmaster pronounced with satisfaction. "Back to class then. All of you."

§ § § § § § §

"You don't want to miss *disyer* sight, Bill." Tim Dagle announced from the upper end of the disused ditch which Bill Hare's gang used as their place to hang out. A score of wood planks – all different, a harvest of farm refuse - formed a rough roof at the end of the ditch, just where the bottom began to slope upwards to the higher ground around it. Bill was in the hut, sitting on a crude bench reading a Beano, as was his mate Syll who never really strayed far from Bill if he could help it and imitated him when he could. Tim had been posted as a lookout by Bill. This was not really necessary but Bill wanted to focus on the comic and Tim had not understood that weaselling his way into Bill's favour by incessant chatter was annoying. Syll and the four other boys remained respectfully silent except to chuckle whenever the comic made Bill laugh.

Bill sighed as he lowered the comic. He got up and walked out of the hut. Tim's narrow face betrayed excitement mixed with a little fear. Bill liked it that way and resolved to thump Tim if he was being called out again because some farmer was driving his waggon on the Roreford Road which ran along the lower end of the broad fields below the ditch fort.

Bill clambered up and looked over the fields. Tim eagerly pointed his finger at the small procession on the road but Bill had already seen them.

"What's there?" Syll asked in his slow dull voice, for he had followed Bill out of the hut like a faithful mongrel.

Bill ignored him. "Well done, Tim."

He patted the younger boy on the back and Tim beamed with pride.

Bill looked at the road again. It was the Whitfield witch but she was not alone, two younger chavees from school were following her, though one of them might have been that outlandish dwarf.

Bill narrowed his eyes.

"The witch has got herself a coven," Tim chuckled.

Bill lifted an arm, bringing his fist loosely in contact with Tim's jaw.

The boy yowled and rolled away in surprise at the sudden pain.

"What's a coven?" Syll asked, still focused on the road. The witch-child had stopped and was scanning the fields to her left. She must have heard something.

"Down!" Bill hissed at Syll and then added "Quiet!"

Bill and Syll ducked their heads low. Tim came scrambling back up and Bill gave him a glare.

"Tis *naun* funny, this coven business," Bill hissed. "*Naun* a joke."

"Sorry, Bill," Tim said meekly.

"Those are Wolfden *chavees* that witch is taking to Shims Copses," Bill bared his teeth as he spied on the road and saw the group of children walking on again.

"Rather them than us, aint it so?" Tim grimaced.

"Tis unchristian," Bill insisted. "Them Wodewoses taking our *chavees* to their middling woods in broad daylight."

"*All-along-o'* them will be *afeared* in Shims Copses?" Syll asked.

"*All-along-of* sinister rituals taking place out of sight, out of sight of God and out of sight of God-fearing folk," Bill quoted his mother who was scathing about the Wodewoses who lived in the woods and populated part of the Edgelands. "Unaccountable heathen rituals, with all the sins you could imagine; it's Evil. Pure Evil."

"Somebody ought to stop that, why haven't they?" Syll looked puzzled. If it was as bad as Bill had suggested the adults would have surely done something about it.

"Somebody will," a grin grew slowly on Bill's face.

"We save them Wolfden *chavees*, we'll be heroes." Tim caught on and grinned.

"Let's go," Bill gestured at the other boys.

They climbed up the other side of the trench. There was a narrow country lane there which ran parallel to the Roreford road until it took a sharp turn to the right to end at the Raven's Roost. Drunkard's Lane, the villagers called it for it was used by the men who did not want to be seen leaving the village for a pint at the Raven's Roost. The views of the Roreford road from the ditch fort and Drunkard's Lane had been much used by Bill's gang in harassing the farm children who walked back home from school along this route. The lane allowed them to shadow anyone on the road unseen and they had created small openings in the hedges which lined the fields so that they could intercept unwary passers at half-a-dozen points.

Bill set a quick pace and the others had to struggle to keep up with his determined strides. It paid off because they soon overtook the witch's coven.

"Syll, take the lads down," Bill pointed at one of their last secret paths to Roreford Road. "Just follow 'em."

"How about you Bill?" Tim asked.

"I'll go round the long way," Bill grinned at his own clever plan and they nodded their understanding.

As the others snuck through the hedge he started running. He stopped when he reached the back of the outbuildings of Raven's Roost. He walked around the pub, exchanging a nod with two of the carters walking towards the pub's main entrance, and stopped when he reached the corner of the Raven's Roost. Peering around the corner he saw that the witch and her friends – the dwarf was with them – had just reached the far side of the building and were mostly focused on backwards looks at Syll, Tim and the others who had formed a line across the road and were slowly following the three girls.

Good. Bill's dad had come home a while ago from a Home Guard patrol in the Wyrde Woods and he had been seething. Apparently the heathen *chavees* had made a mockery of Silas Hare and Bill's dad had taken out his anger on his son. He had kicked him into one of the sheds, taken his belt off and whipped Bill's backside black and blue, all the while shouting about Bill's savage classmates as if they were Bill's friends. It would be good, Bill reckoned, to even the score. He would have the *chance-born* little witch squealing for mercy. His mum had said she was asking for it anyway, the way she walked around without proper stockings.

When the girls were halfway along the Raven's Roost Bill stepped out of his concealment and barred their way. He grinned as he saw Tim lead two other boys to the far side of the road and Syll and the other pair closed up behind the girls. They had nowhere to run now.

Joy's reaction was disappointing though. She showed no surprise or fear when she saw that Bill barred her way. Neither did the dwarf, though the little Rye girl's eyes grew large and her lips began to tremble. It was a start, Bill supposed. He clenched his fists as he thought of the wickedness they undoubtedly got up to in those *shim*-filled woods.

§ § § § § § §

"Blooming heck! The Head is a good Guv, innit?"

Joy, Maisy and Katie were walking out of the village down the Roreford Road after school and Maisy was chattering away. If only half of what she said was true *Lunnon* schools in general had medieval torture machines at their disposal for dealing with transgressions.

Joy hissed. "Trouble."

She gestured behind them at Bill Hare's gang; the lads were emerging from a hedge by the roadside. They did not shout taunts, just started walking forwards, half-a-dozen of them.

"Should we make haste?" Katie asked somewhat nervously.

"*Naun*, we *baint afeared*, never be *afeared*," Joy said quietly.

They walked on in silence, the mood suddenly very tense. The lads behind them speeded up just a little to start closing the distance as the three approached the Raven's Roost.

They were halfway past the Raven's Roost when Bill Hare, who had been concealed around the corner, stepped in front of them, grinning contentedly. They stopped and he walked forwards slowly, lumbering over them like a giant.

"Hag-child," Bill greeted Joy triumphantly.

Joy noted that half the lads had crossed the Roreford Road to cut off their escape to the right. The other half were behind them. Joy turned momentarily to hiss at them and they kept a careful distance.

Sometimes her reputation at school was useful. Joy turned back to Bill.

"Bill Hare, please *gwoan* out of my way." She spoke with far more confidence than she felt. Joy's heart was pounding in her chest as she tried to keep track of what the boys around them were doing. Nothing as of yet, they had all come to a halt now. If it came to a fight, it would be seven to three. Two really. Katie would not have much of a chance and Joy did not even know if Maisy's beligerous manner extended to actual fighting, though she suspected it did.

"Your mum's a witch." Bill grinned nastily. "And a middling *draggle-tail, surelye*. So I reckon you're one too, so I do."

"Well you're lamentably *misagift* about the both of us," Joy answered, struggling to remain calm.

"*Naun*, I am not," Bill said with certainty. "Tis for you to decide if you want to keep these two..." he gave Katie and Maisy a dismissive glance "...*chavees* with you to watch as I teach you a lesson, or send them on their way."

Joy hesitated, it was a tempting offer and would see the others safe.

"We're not going anywhere, innit?" Maisy spoke defiantly.

"We stay with Joy," Katie said in a trembling voice.

Bill ignored them and sneered at Joy. "Your choice. *draggle-tail*. It'll be just you and me *all-along-of* the lads taking care of the *chavees* first anyway. *Howsumdever*, if you make me make them do that, *mayhap* I'll reward them with a handful of yourself after."

Joy stared at him furiously. She was beginning to perceive that Bill was intent on taking things to a whole new level.

"Over my dead body," Joy answered with all the conviction she could muster.

"I was hoping you would say that," Bill sneered again. "*Naun* much sense to be had in a witch's *chance-born* whelp."

He made to take a step forwards and Joy tensed. She formed her hands into fists and bared her teeth at the bully, growling at him like an angry dog. Bill paused, uncertain for a moment because he had not inspired the fear he had expected; he wanted the hag-child to whimper and beg for mercy.

Then Maisy stepped forwards.

"You look as daft as a *gobstopper*, innit?" she said calmly, looking entirely relaxed.

"Quiddy?" Bill shook his head, he had no idea what the Sheere-girl had just said.

"Picking on a lass half your bleeding size. I've a mind to plant my feet in your *cobblers,* hard like," Maisy looked Bill up and down. "But I'd be lucky to find your *knackers,* innit? Be the size of pigeon turds, I guess."

Joy laughed. She could not help it, there was something hilarious about seeing a wee sprite of a lass who looked like a pixie from Pook Hall confronting the big bully in such a fearless manner.

Bill was visibly taken aback and frowned. He was vaguely aware that the *Sheere-girl* seemed to be insulting his manhood and the other two were grinning at him as if he was the village idiot.

"Right," he growled. "I'll have the both of you, *naun* matter to me."

"I don't think so, you're just a *raspberry tart,* aintcha?" Maisy spat at Bill and her spittle hit him squarely on the chin.

Bill's face slowly turned into one of fury as his brains analysed the event. This gave Maisy a headstart as she darted towards the North Woods Lane. With a roar of anger Bill started his pursuit. Though he was slow to gather speed it was considerable when he reached full steam and it was obvious that he would catch up with Maisy soon enough.

Joy and Katie followed, they were not going to let Maisy face Bill's revenge alone. Looking over her shoulder Joy saw the other boys were coming forwards as well, but only at walking speed. They clearly assumed Bill would deal with the situation.

Maisy seemed to stumble and Joy held her breath as she fell. To Joy's amazement Maisy instantly rolled herself into a small ball on the road like a hedgehog and Bill – going at his full speed – was unable to stop in time.

He tripped over Maisy and went flying, sprawling onto the road with a thud. The *Lunnon* girl jumped up and turned to Joy and Katie.

"I guess the daft *nickey* just fell for me, innit?" Maisy grinned.

Joy stared at her with an open mouth; it had happened so fast and Maisy had known exactly what she was doing.

Bill got to his hands and knees and then rose unsteadily. His hands and face were badly scraped and bleeding and he looked dazed.

"Watch out!" Joy shouted as his bulk rose up behind her friend. Maisy grinned again, then turned around in a flash and kicked Bill in his groin with all her might. The bully's mouth flew open, for a moment he was unable to make any noise, then he bellowed like a bull at a slaughterhouse before crumpling to the ground where he squealed like a stuck pig.

Joy and Katie reached Maisy and looked at the pathetic bulk on the ground; clutching his groin with his bloodied hands and starting to cry like an infant now.

"Mum. I want Mum," he sobbed.

There was a shout behind them and they turned to see the other lads come forwards.

Maisy smiled at Joy and Katie, "Fancy a brawl?"

There was not much choice in the matter; the six lads who had slowly come forwards spread out and then rushed them.

Maisy did not wait for the boys to reach her, she ploughed straight into them. Joy saw that the boys were swinging their arms far and wide whilst Maisy settled for quick and short jabs straight in front of her. For every fist that landed on her she landed half-a-dozen. Joy threw herself into the huddle, hands formed into claws and making hissing noises which frightened her opponents. Then she raised a knee as if she were going to deliver a kick and her first opponent immediately dropped his guard, cupping his crotch with both hands to avoid Bill's fate. Joy grinned happily and started to pommel his face. Even Katie rushed in now; scratching, clawing, biting and hissing like a furious cat.

Their opponents' main advantage of numerical superiority crumbled fast as one after the other stumbled away from the fight, smarting, bleeding and bewildered. It was over in mere minutes and Bill was still whimpering on the ground. The danger had passed.

One of the boys looked behind him as he fled.

"You're all witches!" He shrieked a shrilly protest. "You don't fight fair."

Joy, Maisy and Katie looked at each other. Joy's nose was bleeding and her dress was ripped at the seam of her sleeve. Maisy had a split lower lip and the area around her left eye was already swelling; she'd have a black eye before too long. Katie had a cut across her cheek and when she touched it her fingers came away sticky with blood. It was a small price to pay for their epic victory though; the Battle of Raven's Roost had been convincingly won. The girls clutched each other and burst out into loud laughter, a combination of relief and triumph that seemed to follow the humiliated village lads all the way back to Wolfden.

15. Silver Bullets

Goody Maskall took issue with the dishevelled state of the children when they trooped into the Maskall Farm kitchen.

"By *Geemeny*!" Goody Maskall exclaimed. "Well just look at the three of you. All *dishabill*. Have you been fighting?"

Mus Maskall examined them critically. "I have little doubt they've been fighting."

Joy nodded.

"There was a bleeding bully," Maisy said.

"Twere Bill Hare," Joy added.

"And his mates, seven of them in total," Katie contributed proudly.

"Say something, Fred," Goody Maskall looked appalled. "A lass shouldn't be brawling like a *tossicated* ploughman at the Odesby Fayre. Tis *naun* proper."

"Young Hare is an outlander," Mus Maskall shook his head sadly. "*Sheere-folk* are *naun* much good except for *moil*. Tis unaccountable."

"I didn't know he was *Sheere-folk*," Joy said.

"Aye," Mus Maskall nodded. "His *gaffer* is a middling *furriner* from Surrey."

"Ah!" Joy exclaimed, "*Mayhap* that is why he's slow in the head?"

"*Mayhap*," Mus Maskall nodded. "*Sheere-folk* are an odd lot. Those from Surrey in particular."

"Oi, I'm '*Sheere-folk*' too," Maisy protested.

"Only a little," Mus Maskall smiled reassuringly. "Your mum was born and raised here *afore* she followed your dad to *Lunnon*."

"But," Maisy frowned. "If that blooming *nickey* is *Sheere-folk* on account of his *gaffer* then that leaves me…"

"Proper Sussex on account of your *gaffer* and *gammer*," Katie said, earning a grin from Mus Maskall. "It all adds up, *surelye*."

"*Asides* that, Maisy," Mus Maskall added. "Your dad is from Kent. They are *bettermost Sheere-folk* in Kent."

"Mus Maskall!" Maisy's grandmother protested. "You are meant to tell *disyer* girls how to behave, *surelye*. *Naun scorse* your opinions on *Sheere-folk*. Tis unaccountable!"

"*Zackly*, I was *abouten* to do so," Mus Maskall nodded and spoke to the children in a stern tone. "I do hope those lads are more *dishabill* than the three of you are?"

"Aye, Gramps. Bill were crying for his mum, weren't he?" Maisy nodded enthusiastically. "I kicked him in the *knackers*."

"Good, you did middling well then," Maisy's grandfather said approvingly.

"Oh dear Gods," Goody Maskall raised her eyes upwards. "Why'd you have to send me a *chuckle-head*?"

"By *Geemeny* woman!" Mus Maskall winked at the girls. "I did just as you told me, told them how to behave in a proper Sussex manner."

The children grinned and Goody Maskall turned to the sink to hide her smile.

"Best you come here so I can see to your war wounds," she said.

§ § § § § § §

The children were seated around the large table. Gran had made them all a cup of tea.

"The postman brought you something, Maisy," Gran said.

She handed Maisy a small rectangular package and a postcard.

"It's from me mum!" Maisy examined the postcard. Then her face fell.

"Maisy?" Joy asked. Maisy handed her the card. The front showed two childen, a boy and girl building a sandcastle on a beach with a lighthouse on a white cliff behind them and an aeroplane in the sky which had traced letters of white smoke that spelled 'Hello'. The text below was pre-printed and read:

How are You
My little EVACUEE?
I hope you are happy by the sea.
I love your letters.
Please do send another.
Love and Kisses from your MOTHER.

The back of the postcard bore the address of Maskall farm and a short scrawl: *Love, Mum*. There was not a word on how things were at home. Joy gave Maisy an understanding smile.

"I don't even live by the sea here, innit?" Maisy shrugged. Then she turned her attention to the small package. It was wrapped in brown paper and tightly bound with string. There was no sender's address.

"*Mayhap*, that's from your mum as well," Joy smiled.

Maisy untied the strings and carefully folded open the paper; she knew Gran would want to save it to be used again.

The package contained a small box coloured red, white and blue.

"Perforated roll caps!" Maisy looked incredulous.

"*Quiddy*?" Katie asked.

"For me cap gun! Look!" Maisy took out five rolls of red paper with evenly spaced perforations. "Two hundred and fifty shots!"

"There's a note," Katie pointed at a small folded note.

Maisy took the note and unfolded it. Gran, Joy and Katie leant closer to read it with her.

Save these for emergencies.
Silver bullets for a 'right fancy' cap gun.
Regards, Captain 'Mad' Malheur.

"A Captain?" Gran said. "You are keeping grand company, lass."

"Captain 'Mad' Malheur," Maisy said proudly. "It's Lady Priscilla, innit."

"The Lady of the Wyrde Woods sent you a gift?" Gran asked. "You must have made quite an impression on her."

"I scratch along, innit?" Maisy grinned. She picked up the roll caps again. Maisy would have been happy to take them outside and start shooting, but there was something about Lady Priscilla's words that made her put them back into the box.

"Emergencies," she explained to Joy and Katie and they nodded.

§ § § § § § §

"The church window..." Joy began to say. She had come along to the paddock where Maisy was now exercising Spark. Goody Maskall had taken Katie to her vegetable patch. Katie's father was a carter and her mum a washerwoman. They were not well off and the cottage in which they lived did not have much of a garden so

Goody Maskall had decided Katie should take home a basket laden with veggies and fruit.

"Raise the stone and thou shalt find me!" Maisy said with satisfaction for she was still thrilled by the discovery.

Joy watched Spark who was trudging in circles around the paddock looking thoroughly disgruntled. Even Joy, who saw beauty in all of the creations of the *Wyrd*, thought Spark might have been a mistake. She much admired Maisy for her total devotion to the beast though, and could see how Spark returned that devotion.

"…is less than a hundred years old. A replacement of an older one that was damaged in the storm." Joy concluded.

Maisy shrugged.

"*Secree of the Wirdewode* is more than six hundred years old," Joy said.

"Maybe they used the image and words from the older window?" Maisy asked.

"Naun, I asked your *gammer* and *gaffer* about that, they said that the old window showed a rising phoenix."

"Gran and Gramps?"

"Aye, they *ken* a lot about the Wyrde Woods," Joy nodded.

Maisy looked disappointed, "But then, it might mean nothing at all. Just a fluke."

"What does your heart tell you?" Joy asked.

Maisy shut her eyes and tried to overcome her logic which insisted that it was just an odd coincidence. She recalled being swept off her feet by the sense of revelation back in the church. Maisy visualised the statuette of St Lewinna with the window behind the Saint. She must have passed that window a hundred times outside, on Stone Square, without even noticing it before.

Maisy's eyes flew open.

"You've had an idea," Joy stated.

"Cor blimey, Joy!" Maisy gasped. She came over to the fence and drew a rough circle in the dirt with her foot. "This was us!"

She sketched another circle next to the first. "This is St Lewinna!"

A third circle was added to the line of circles. "This is the window. And this! This!" Maisy made a fourth circle a bit further out but still in alignment with the first three. Joy looked at it with wonder in her eyes.

"That would be…," Joy began to say slowly, "…the Cross Stone."

Maisy grinned. "The Guardians and such, cracking as they might be, are not the stones we're looking for."

"The key is under our noses," Joy smiled broadly. "Well done, Maisy, you have a *bettermost* mind."

"I scratch along, innit?" Maisy beamed. "Oh look!"

They looked up and watched a dozen fighter planes pass high over head, heading south towards the coast.

"Jerries have been hitting the channel convoys and ports, it was on the wireless news," Maisy said.

Joy watched the planes pass. She could hear the faint trace of their engines and marvelled there were people up there in the tiny specks which drifted across her horizon.

Interludes

29 July 1940
Maskall Farm
Wolfden, Sussex

Dear Mum,

Thank you for your postcard. I was very happy to hear from you. ~~I hope you will write a letter too sometime soon.~~ I have a very good friend now, her name is Joy and we have splendid proper adventures. ~~There is also a nice boy called~~ I have some other friends as well.

Gran and Gramps have really spoiled me, I have my own pony now. His name is Spark and he is a handsome New Forest and he's the most cracking pony in the world.

~~I ride Spark into the Wyrde Woods all on my own now! We had to run for our lives when we were ambushed by Apache warriors.~~

~~I am coping at school and have only got thrashed once.~~ I have met the Headmaster, Mister Mackellow. He is cracking and he was very kind ~~because he could also have thrashed me like the other teachers did. But that is okay, nothing to worry abo~~

How are things at home? I hope all is well. Maybe you can come and visit me some time soon? Gran and Gramps would really like that as well.

Your loving daughter,
Maisy Robbins

P.S. Tell Dad to write me please. ~~If you both write at once you can put the letters in one envelope and save on the stamp.~~

2 August 1940
Maskall Farm
Wolfden, Sussex

Dear Dad,

I am sure you are having a lot of adventures in London. Please do write me about them!

I have had lots of adventures. I joined the Army and am now a Captain of the Royal Sussex Regiment. I have to patrol the Wyrde Woods on my loyal steed (he's called Spark and he's right cracking). I nearly drowned in mud and I was nearly scalped ~~by a boy called Leon~~ and also nearly dragged into a tunnel by a monster who eats children but my mate Joy stopped them. It was funny afterwards because everybody was sure we were drunk but we weren't, ~~just a little~~, cross my heart and hope to die.

I also ~~liase~~ ~~lyase~~ ~~liaos~~ talk with the Wolfden Home Guard and Captain Malheur of the Marauders as well as a Canadian soldier I met in the woods. He is really cracking although he does sometimes wear a skirt. His knees aren't as hairy as some of the soldiers' knees I have seen though so that is okay. We talk about defending the Wyrde Woods against the Germans and I have had shooting lessons at ~~a boy's~~ farm and, (you won't believe this!) new ammo for my gun!!! I got into a fight and had a split lip and blue eye, but don't worry: I WON!!! I will become more careful though, Gramps sort of told me to after the Home Guard Patrol shot at us in the woods.

Your Captain Robbins

P.S. Better not tell Mum any of this
P.S.S. Please write

16. Chunmaniye

Chunmaniye had 24-hours leave and left the base at midnight to trek into the Wyrde Woods. The guards at the gate had chuckled good-naturedly; they preferred to spend their free time at the local pubs or a day in Odesby or Stancaster. They had known Chunmaniye for some time though. Some of the other men who hailed from the vast expanses of wilderness back home also often opted to spend their leave roaming the English countryside to seek temporary relief from the hustle and bustle of the Army. It was not that unusual.

Chunmaniye exchanged jokes with them and then set out. He went to the place which had been revealed to him on his first sojourn into the large expanse of woods just south of the base. That had been a memorable morning. Birds of two dozen plumages had joyously heralded his arrival at a shallow vale which angled down to the base of a sickle-shaped cliff. Within the grassy expanse embraced by the outstretched arms of the cliff stood a circle of six tall stones. These towered even over Chunmaniye but did not rise at straight angles, instead they gently curved upward giving them the illusion of movement. The location was clearly a Holy Place. To Chunmaniye the combination of sickle and full circle made it a place of Hanwi, she who travels the night skies in ever changing form and aspect.

Hanwi was out this night, in a bright half-circle brimming with silver light. When Chunmaniye reached the stones he sat down to take off his boots and socks. Then he took his holy shirt out of one a satchels he carried with him and put it on. He intended all thought and speech to be Lakota tonight. He had broken a few army regulations by bringing his shirt and feathers to Europe but he needed their reassurance to feel Lakota during his sparse free moments. It was the only time he could be true to himself.

He cast his eyes at the moon as he walked to the edge of the circle. Then he focused on the stones. He began to speak and the sound of the Lakota words did not seem out of place here. Chunmaniye had already concluded that the Wyrde Woods were full of convergences of energy which his own people marked as sacred and these standing stones demonstrated to him that the native population had deemed likewise.

"Wakan Tanka, Great Mystery, teach me how to trust my heart, my mind, the blessings of my spirit."

Chunmaniye stepped inside the circle and raised his eyes to Hanwi.

"Teach me to trust these things so that I may love beyond my fear and walk in balance with the passing of each glorious sun and each course of the moon."

Chunmaniye began to shuffle his feet as he started to chant softly.

Wanayan maniye
Wanayan maniye
Tatanka wan maniye
Ate heye lo, ate heye lo.

He began to shuffle forwards following the outer course of the circle. He continued to chant and each time he concluded a course he would move inwards to start on a slightly smaller circular trajectory.

Spiralling towards the within with the repetition of his chanting in his ears, moon and starshine in his eyes and soft grass beneath his bare feet allowed him clarity of thought with regard to the children he had encountered in the Wyrde Woods and Wolfden. Especially Owl Heart for he had met her before.

As a little boy Chunmaniye had grown up with his paternal grandfather on the Wood Mountain reservation in Saskatchewan. His grandfather had been present at both Greasy Grass and Wounded Knee and the great deeds of Hunkpapa warriors echoed in Chunmaniye's ears still. In particular those of Tatanka Iyotake, the most famous Hunkpapa of all, never afraid to act as he spoke and defiant to his death. Chunmaniye's mother was Oglala and she told him stories of their warriors and the great Oglala Tashunke Witke whose courage and bravery was legendary even here in the Old World.

It was his mother who insisted that he went south of the border to live with his other grandfather during his adolescent years; the Medicine Man Hehaka Sapa. When the young Chunmaniye had arrived there he was already fiercely intent on becoming a warrior like his great Hunkpapa and Oglala forebears but his grandfather had taught him there was another road that could be followed.

Hehaka Sapa was renowned for his visions and he had often spoken to his grandson about the mighty flowering tree of life which he had seen in a vision. The young Chunmaniye had experienced only one vision himself, though Hehaka Sapa had said it was a strong one. It had involved a search for Hehaka Sapa's tree of life in which Chunmaniye had been distracted from his purpose by a maiden who perceived *Wakan*, the life force, and was preparing to weave *Wakan* into patterns of her own. Her totem had been the owl and as always those of the owl walked a precarious path. There was no middle way for them; their path led always to a fork where they became *Heyoka*, their minds infected by chaos, and then veered to the extremes of either light or dark; good or evil. In his vision Chunmaniye had picked up his weapons to become a warrior to defend the *Heyoka* maiden as she came into her power.

Hehaka Sapa had chuckled and chortled when Chunmaniye sought him out to tell his grandfather of the vision.

"You are a new generation of our people," Hehaka Sapa had said. "And for a long time you will be torn between two paths, two worlds. Between Hunkpapa and Oglala. Between the Lakota and the *Wasichu* – the white man. Between your desire to be a warrior and your potential to to walk the path of a *Wicasa Wakan*, a Medicine Man."

"And the owl girl?" Chunmaniye had asked, eagerly then for he had been young and in his vision she had captured his heart.

"I cannot see this clearly," his grandfather had answered. "A distraction by tricksters to lead you off your chosen path, perhaps. Or else that which will finally allow you to feel whole. You will know when the time comes. Your heart will speak to you and when it does you must listen to it carefully."

That had been a long time ago though and over the years the vivid clarity of the vision had begun to fade. As a young man Chunmaniye had been envious of those braves who had fought in Canadian uniform during the Great War. They at least had been able to count coup and prove themselves as warrior, he himself had been too young to join. He had grown into manhood with a great deal of restlessness. Many of his generation had and that that restlessness had taken them into contact with the outside world; where some were so desperate to conduct themselves as warriors that they picked drunken fights in bars. Chunmaniye felt only shame when he would regard such a brawl; the wild swings – most of which missed – were a heart-twisting parody of the fighting skills once owned by the Hunkpapa and Oglala bands his grandfathers had ridden with. When the new war had begun Chunmaniye had enlisted immediately, hoping to honour the heritage of his forebears and also hoping that it would finally bring him into a place where he felt whole instead of torn.

Hundreds of others had enlisted too. Aboriginal soldiers, as they were called, were said to be adaptable and patient with good powers of observation, stamina and courage. They were much prized as snipers and scouts and there were many of them in the First Canadian Division, which was currently deployed all over southern England to defend the mother country against invasion while the British army reorganised after Dunkirk.

Chunmaniye had been content. His position as scout gave him a degree of independence and his tasks and responsibilities were clear to him. He was praised for his abilities and it had seemed to Chunmaniye that the doubt between paths to follow had ended at last. He was a warrior and he would soon count coup.

Then, out of nowhere, he had encountered Owl Heart in the woods and then had come the recognition that she was the one from his vision all those decades ago and new doubts had beset Chunmaniye.

"Wakan Tanka," Chunmaniye was approaching the centre of the circuitious pattern he had been following and he appealed to the Great Father again. "Teach me how to trust my heart and my mind."

Had he found his path only to encounter a distraction which he should ignore? Or was this part of his journey?

His heart and mind were at odds and the only answer he received, there in the moonlit stone circle, was a strong image of Hehaka Sapa's life tree.

The last time he had visited his grandfather and mentor had been a shock for Chunmaniye. The resolution with which the *Wicasa Wakan* had held on to his visions had wavered, he had begun to suspect that perhaps there was no life tree after all. Why then this vision here and now? Was the life tree in the Wyrde Woods? Suddenly Chunmaniye felt was that it might well be and he resolved to find it so he could tell Hehaka Sapa about it.

Chunmaniye left the stone circle with more questions than he had entered it with. The only thing he was absolutely sure of was that the Wyrde Woods had crossed his path for a reason, they were meant to be part of his journey and he would have to find out how and why.

17. Lewinna's Medley

The morning start-up at school lasted longer than usual. Two teachers were absent, Londoners badly affected by hay fever. One of them was the dour mathematics teacher scheduled to teach the girls's form the first lesson of the day.

"I am pleased to tell you," Mr Mackellow boomed at them when they were the last form still lined up on Stone Square. "That Vicar Framsfield has been found willing to teach you this morning, one of his Sunday School lessons."

There were soft groans all around but the Headmaster ignored these and beamed at them as if a small miracle had just happened.

"So, off to church you go," he chuckled and pointed at St Lewinna's Church where the door had opened and the bulk of Vicar Framsfield appeared to welcome the young congregation.

Maisy wrinkled her nose but made to walk to St Lewinna's Church anyway. To her surprise Joy did not move. She had dug her heels in the ground and had a stubborn look on her face.

"I *baint* going to his church lesson," Joy said fiercely.

Maisy looked at her friend helplessly. She glanced at Mr Mackellow who was slowly drifting in their direction. She was sure that an outright refusal to follow his instructions was not a mutiny he could afford to ignore. The prospect of losing Joy's companionship in class was a bleak one.

"Joy," Maisy brightened. "The church! We'll be in the church, innit? That's what we wanted, right?"

She could sense Joy's resistance waver. It would be the first time they could have another look in the church since their discovery.

"I suppose…" Joy began.

"Good!" Maisy sighed with relief and then smiled. She took her friend's hand to pull her towards St Lewinna's Church before Joy dug her heels in again.

"The north door!" Joy insisted.

Maisy rolled her eyes but pulled Joy to the north door.

They were some of the last ones to enter and were forced to move to the front to find empty seats, far away from St Lewinna's alcove, no matter how many longing looks Maisy cast in that direction.

There was an expectant buzz as Vicar Framsfield shut the main doors and walked towards the altar. Anything that deviated from the norm of school routine was interesting by very definition but Vicar Framsfield was visibly nervous. He turned by the altar and looked at the pupils helplessly, as if unsure where to begin. Maisy reckoned he was discarding his usual service openings as he tried to readjust to the new situation and she sensed an opportunity.

She raised her hand.

"Maisy, what the *pize* are you doing?" Joy hissed softly.

"Erm, yes, you girl, you have a question?" The vicar seemed relieved to have a cue.

"Can you tell us about St Lewinna, Guv?" Maisy asked as sweetly as she could. "I'd like to know more about her."

"Really? Splendid, splendid," Vicar Framsfield smiled at her. His smile froze for a brief instant when he recognized Joy but then he looked away again.

"Not bad, *Lunnon* Girl," Joy conceded softly and Maisy grinned.

"Saint Lewinna," Vicar Framsfield declared loudly, "didn't start life as a Saint, of course. She was a local girl who lived in one of the settlements in the Rore River valley. A farmer's daughter…"

Quite a few of the pupils cheered enthusiastically. Vicar Framsfield looked puzzled for a moment, not quite sure what to make of it. Then he smiled.

"Yes, just like many of you here. She grew up on a small farm, tending the chickens, geese, sheep, pigs and cows."

Maisy sensed that he had the general attention of his public now and Vicar Framsfield must have sensed it too because he began to speak with more confidence. Maisy decided that he was not all that bad when the Wolfden Parish Christian Ladies Committee were not present and she scrapped him off her Potential German Spies list. She would change that status in her new screenplay when she got home. *Jerries in the Wyrde Woods* was beginning to take shape quite nicely, Maisy thought.

"Lewinna's family were one of the few Christian families who lived here at that time, most of the others still following the misguided heathen ways of their ancestors."

Joy hissed soft disapproval as did a few others in the morning's congregation. Vicar Framsfield either did not hear or chose to ignore it.

"She was a pious girl; obedient to her parents, never spoke unless spoken to, did her work without complaining and avoided all temptation," the vicar continued.

There were looks of disbelief all around Maisy. They occasionally encountered these *chavees* in the storybooks Sister Mary selected for reading but no one had actually ever met such a *chavee*. It was hard to understand why adults in general persisted in believing in the existence of such creatures.

"However," Vicar Framsfield continued, "One day this virtuous Christian girl chose to disobey her parents."

His audience nodded their agreement, the story made sense again.

"Her parents wanted Lewinna to marry one of their neighbours but Lewinna told them that her heart belonged to Christ our Saviour and that she would give it to no other. And so Lewinna went to live at the priory in the Wyrde Woods, the remains of which we now call St Lewinna's Priory."

"More ruins?" Maisy whispered to Joy.

Joy nodded, "Good ones too."

"Cracking!"

"Lewinna was content to live a life of spiritual contemplation with the light of Our Lord in her heart. One day however…," Vicar Framsfield paused for a moment, "…the Devil sent one of his demons to the Wyrde Woods to drive the Christians out."

The audience shifted, collectively leaning forwards so as not to miss anything on the demon.

"The demon…," Vicar Framsfield declared, "…came in the form of a dragon.

Joy shook her head. "Twere a *wyrm,* not a *draca,*" she whispered to Maisy.

Maisy had already envisaged a great big scaly ferocious dragon in her mind's eye, one with weathered leather wings which spat fire and ate roast chavvies for breakfast, lunch and tea. She decided to quiz Joy on the '*wyrm*' later and stick to her own interpretation for now.

"The dragon came crawling out of the Devil's Tarn in the the Wyrde Woods and it started to become a nuisance; helping itself to sheep and cattle as it pleased."

There were dark looks from the local children. They had little sympathy for cattle and sheep rustlers.

"The Devil has a tarn in the Wyrde Woods?" Maisy whispered to Joy. "What's a tarn?"

Before Joy could respond Vicar Framsfield continued: "The villagers of Roreford and Mordrove, closest to the Devil's Tarn, organised themselves into an armed party and went to Devil's Tarn to confront the Devil's demon dragon. Alas, without the light of our Lord in their hearts they stood no chance and were decimated by the beast."

"It was then that Lewinna told her prioress that she had a dream about ridding the Wyrde Woods of darkness and the prioress took Lewinna to see the heathen chieftains. They asked for a mailshirt, shield and sword for Lewinna and in exchange she would rid the Wyrde Woods of the dragon. The heathen chieftains took a look at Lewinna, who was neither very large nor very strong, and then said girls had no business fighting like men and they just laughed and laughed."

There were mixed reactions. Many of the girls shook their head at the chieftains' stupidity while the boys nodded their agreement with the wisdom they perceived in the decision. Maisy rolled her eyes and resolved to insert a girl fighting a dragon in her new screenplay. That would give the Jerries something to think about for sure.

"They had little cause to laugh for long though," Vicar Framsfield continued. "For the dragon grew more and more daring, travelling all the way to the great road that ran from Wolfden to Malheur Hall in those days…"

"The Forgotten Road!" Maisy whispered to Joy who nodded.

"…and waylaid travellers there; his appetite expanding to disobedient children and passing farmers. He would eat the carter, horse and waggon and anything that was on it."

There were murmurs of disbelief in the congregation most of whom well knew that farm waggons were hard to eat.

"That bit is actually true," Joy whispered to Maisy.

"How did he know if chavvies were obedient or not?" Maisy whispered back.

Vicar Framsfield continued his story. Champions from all over the Kingdom of Sussex and beyond had come to challenge the dragon but none of them were Christians and all of them failed, many losing their lives in the process. Remembering Lewinna's offer the chieftains went to the priory with a chainmail coat, sword and shield and told her that they had reconsidered her offer. By this time they were so desperate that they were willing to try anything.

Lewinna, however, added a new condition. She told them that if she were to defeat the dragon in combat it would not be her strength but God's power that would be victorious. That it would be a miracle was something the chieftains could agree with. None refused Lewinna's requirement that they would all be baptised and accept Christ in their hearts if she defeated the monster which was staining the Wyrde Woods with blood.

"And so…" Vicar Framsfield spoke. "Saint Lewinna rode out on horseback wearing a chainmail coat and armed with a sword and shield. And with heavenly power in her arms and Christ in her heart she slew the wicked dragon."

He stopped speaking though everybody continued to stare at him, wanting to hear more.

"What was the fighting like, Guv?" Maisy blurted out, unable to contain herself any longer. There were nods of agreement around her.

"Oh," Vicar Framsfield replied. "No evil can withstand the power of God."

The children leant back with an audible buzz of disappointment. Maisy sighed, she had hoped for a vivid rendition of the clash of sword and claw but the vicar clearly did not consider that a dramatic highlight. He was a reasonable storyteller but had stopped telling at that magical moment where he could have swept them all away to faraway time of shining steel and a stout heart of Sussex oak.

§ § § § § § §

Joy was thoroughly disgruntled. Vicar Framsfield's tale was one she knew well but twisted it into something almost beyond her recognition. She perked up when he suggested they all had a closer look at the saint. The suggestion betrayed his lack of experience with a class of regular school *chavees* rather than a flock of Sunday School ones for the church immediately transformed into chaos as everybody jumped up and crowded closer to St Lewinna's statuette.

197

Though it was not to her liking Joy jostled for position in the crowd; examining the alcove around the statuette was the only reason she had allowed herself to be dragged into church in the first place. She bit her lip with disappointment when she realised she really was not going to get close enough. Mostly she just saw heads and arms and legs and all the while she was being bumped and accidentally poked and she became tense and anxious.

Then Joy laughed when she caught a glimpse of Maisy amidst the jumble of legs. The *Lunnon* girl had dropped to all fours and making the most of her small size was wriggling her way steadily forwards to the alcove. Once she reached the edge of the huddle of *chavees* she crawled on and disappeared behind the statuette's pedestal.

When Maisy came crawling back, an excited grin on her face, Joy saw something that made her heart stop beating for a moment. Bill Hare had jostled himself to the very front of the crowd. He showed little interest in St Lewinna but seemed rather pleased with himself for having squashed smaller children aside to become King of the Hill. His expression changed to one of characteristic bepuzzlement when he caught sight of Maisy wriggling past the pedestal but then that changed into a mean and vindictive sneer.

"Maisy!" Joy called out though her warning could not possibly be heard over all the excited chatter around her.

Maisy was caught totally by surprise when Bill brought his boot down on the outstretched fingers of her left hand. Maisy yelped in protest and looked up angrily only to stare straight into Bill Hare's eyes and he then proceeded to ground the heel of his boot on her fingers. Joy's friend screamed in pain.

Joy clawed her way forwards with fierce intensity and she reached Bill Hare at the same time that Vicar Framsfield did. The vicar pulled Bill Hare away whilst Joy helped Maisy up. The other *chavees* slowly edged up backwards and became quiet.

"Good Lord, William," the vicar was astonished. "What were you doing?"

"Just standing here, Vicar Framsfield," Bill said. "The *chavee* was crawling about on the floor, I didn't see her, honestly."

Joy hissed and Maisy groaned as she clutched her left hand.

"She was down on all fours," Syll, one of Bill's mates, told the vicar.

"Good Lord," the vicar shook his head and peered at Maisy. "What were you doing, girl?"

"I fell," Maisy said, clenching her teeth grimly.

"Well, you better go have that looked at," the vicar said, then frowned as he looked around at the audience which was becoming restless again. "The rest of you, back to your seats please."

Joy led Maisy out of St Lewinna's church and onto Stone Square.

"That *moil-maker* is why I don't like churches," Joy growled. "Standing there in his God's house and lying through his teeth."

"Doesn't matter, innit," Maisy examined her hand. "There's wood panelling behind the statuette, Joy. That's what we wanted to know."

"Can you move your fingers?" Joy asked, carefully taking Maisy's hurt hand in her own.

"It hurts if I try, innit?" Maisy looked pale and Joy was not surprised; her fingers were swelling and looked battered.

"You have to try," Joy insisted.

"BLAST!" Maisy flinched but managed to move all her fingers.

"Nothing broken then," Joy said. "I'm going to wrap some wet cloth around it and then take you to the Owlery so Mum can have a look."

"The Owlery?" Maisy looked up at her friend with a questioning look. "There's a day of school left."

Joy smiled. "I was sure I heard the vicar tell us to get it seen to, he didn't say where and *naun* will be surprised for the Owlery is the logical place for wounds and such."

Maisy started to grin through her pain. Bill Hare had inadvertently bought them a day off school.

§ § § § § §

"Tis badly bruised," Missus Whitfield was tending to Maisy's hand in the Owlery's kitchen while Joy was seeing to her chores outside.

"It hurt first, now it just throbs," Maisy said as she watched Missus Whitfield prepare a poultice.

"Joy was right to bring you here, Maisy Maskall."

"Robbins, innit?"

Missus Whitfield gave Maisy a smile. "I've never met a Robbins, and the Maskalls are near to my heart."

"I suppose there's Maskall in me," Maisy grinned.

"Suppose? By Oak's Acorn, lass. You're the spitting image of your *gaffer* when he was your age. As busy as a bee's hive and forever getting himself into *moil*. I don't recall a day when he wasn't off on some fool's errand devised by himself and his brother Wilfred."

"Really?" Maisy was impressed.

"Regular as clockwork," Missus Whitfield confirmed and gently applied her soothing poultice on Maisy's hand. "What were you two doing in the church anyway?"

"We use it as a classroom now, innit? And some teachers were sick and Vicar Framsfield came to teach us instead and he told us about Saint Lewinna."

"By *Geemeny*," Joy's mum shook her head. "Lewinna was no saint by their own definition, but I'm sure the vicar wouldn't have told you that."

"He said she was pious and Christian, didn't he?"

Missus Whitfield laughed. "Lewinna was the daughter of a chieftain who had his hall built in Wolfden. The first Christians had not even arrived in the Wyrde Woods yet. Lewinna was notorious for her disobedience to her parents. She was their only child, you see, and determined to become chieftain like her father. She knew she would not be if she married any of the many suitors her father proposed for they would usurp that role."

"She wanted to be ruler?" Maisy bumped St Lewinna even further up in her estimation.

"Aye, and that she became. That was why it was her task to fight the *draca*."

"Joy said it was a *wyrm*, something to do with a Devil's tarn."

"The Devil's Tarn is a pool of water in the northern Wyrde Woods," Missus Whitfield explained. "Smooth as a mirror and twice a *wyrm* slithered out and one of those was slain by Lewinna. But there were *draca* too."

"Oh," Maisy said, somewhat puzzled. The advantage of speaking proper English like she did was that she just called it a dragon. The hero fought and slew a dragon. That made sense and it was definitely a heroic task. Talk of disctinctions between *wyrms* and *draca* just muddled the story again making it less clear who slew what and when and how.

"So Lewinna wasn't a Christian?" Maisy asked.

Missus Whitfield sighed. "At the end of her long life she fell ill and was taken to a nearby priory which had been established by some of the first locals of that faith. They were skilled in healing, that much is true. But they were also skilled in falsehood."

"Falsehood? They lied?"

"Aye, lass. The nuns could see that Lewinna was close to her life's end and they dragged their delirious patient outside to baptise her and then voted her their new Abbess. Lewinna died three days later but they had made their claim and renamed their priory St Lewinna's Priory and pilgrims came from far and wide to worship at Lewinna's tomb."

"So they stole your story!" Maisy exclaimed.

Missus Whitfield nodded. "In a manner of speaking. Lewinna's heart belonged to the Old Gods. She was, in actual fact, one of the Guardians of the Wyrde Woods. A *Wudawyrde Weard*, the Saxons called it."

"A Guardian of the Wyrde Woods?" Maisy's mind shone with bright possibilities for her screenplay.

"There have always been Guardians of the Wyrde Woods," Missus Whitfield said, standing up. "Niada of the Painted Ones was one. So was Lewinna of Wolf's Denne Hall. Little Ellette as well, and Lisa Malone. Protectors, defenders and keepers of secrets the Guardians of the Wyrde Woods are."

"Are there Guardians of the Wyrde Woods now?" Maisy asked.

"There have always been Guardians of the Wyrde Woods," Missus Whitfield smiled. "And there always will be."

"Cracking!" Maisy decided that she would have to find out where these Guardians lived and talk to them. Then she frowned, thinking about the nuns at the priory, the sour committee women and Vicar Framsfield who had seemed likable today, albeit a bit foolish. "Are Christians bad then, Missus Whitfield?"

"By Merlin's Beard, no!" Missus Whitfield laughed. "Most Christians I know are decent folk, Maisy. They practise what they preach; generosity and forgiveness, they have love in their hearts. There's always a few rotten apples, dear. Never judge all of them based on those with envy or anger in their hearts."

Maisy nodded, that made sense.

"Maisy!" Joy ran in. "Mum! Come quick, they're fighting."

They went outside and Joy pointed at the sky. A formation of twin-engined planes was passing overhead and smaller single-engined fighters twirled and looped about it. They were flying low enough for Maisy to identify the planes.

"Messerschmitt 109s trying to protect Heinkel bombers," Maisy said as she peered up. "Those are RAF Hurricanes up there."

They heard the engines straining and the burst of machine-gun fire but before too long the whole aerial combat had moved inland and out of their view.

§ § § § § § §

Chunmaniye tried to follow the whispers of the breeze. At first they had brought him steadily north-west, past the ruins of Roreford and Hood's Gorge but then they started confusing him. Tugging at him to go north, east and south.

He realised that they were tricksters now, those who could only be seen when they wanted to be seen and could take the guise of birds or other animals; even the wind's whispers. If his mentor's tree of life was here it did not want to be found but Chunmaniye pressed on, heading in the only direction which did not lure him with hushed hints and enticing whispers. Whatever spirit was directing these defences would have to send something stronger in order to erode Chunmaniye's determination to seek out his grandfather's vision and it seemed to realise this for the tricksters faded away.

The trees started to change, the clarity of gloomy light amidst a legion of ghostly silver birch trees beginning to make way for copses of red barked and twisted young yew trees. From a distance they showed only as intensily dark patches as if there was an ominous nothingness there. Coming closer they revealed more, though still in deep shadow. Their angular branches spread like the forks of lightning creating an effective erratic barrier and thrice Chunmaniye had to backtrack as he simply could not proceed. He suspected that he was coming closer and when he did at last penetrate the yew forest deep enough the trees became older, taller in height and larger in girth. Most were multi-faced as their trunks curved and twisted into gnarled forms.

"Tis not very safe, to go further into the Whychwood," A girl's voice rang out unexpectedly.

Chunmaniye looked around but could not see anything. Then his eye was drawn upwards and he could see the red-haired girl he had named Owl Heart perched on a broad bough, her legs swinging in the air as she regarded him with light amusement.

"And why," Chunmaniye said as he returned her amusement with a smile, "would that be?"

He waited as Owl Heart clambered down the yew with the agility of a squirrel and skipped towards him.

"*Shims!*" Owl Heart pronounced in an ominous tone.

"*Shims?*" Chunmaniye frowned.

"Ghosts," The short dark-haired he had named Laughing Maiden came stalking around the base of the tree.

"Spirits from many centuries ago," Owl Heart nodded. "All around us even now."

Chunmaniye looked around. The gnarly shapes did seem to resemble faces with open screaming mouths and outstretched arms clawing at salvation.

"A whole army of them, then?"

Owl Heart nodded. "An army of *Draca*, dragons."

"Dragons even?" Chunmaniye studied the trees. From what he knew of dragons they seemed akin to the thunderbirds his people called *Wakinyan*.

"Men," Owl Heart shook her head. "Shiploads of them. Their longships were feared and the bows of their ships rose up into a carved dragon's head, the prow a depiction of its tail."

"These men intended no good?" Chunmaniye guessed, getting a mental impression of a band of Crow marauders much like the ones his ancestors had been at odds with.

Owl Heart looked sad. "*Naun* good at all. They came to take what wasn't theirs with sword and flame. *Naun* seemed able to stop them. After reducing Odesby to ashes they turned their eyes to the Wyrde Woods."

"What happened?"

"There was a young woman who was Chieftain of one of the settlements here, Wolf's Denne Hall." Owl Heart said. "Her people looked to her to defend them and that she did."

"A squaw took on these marauders?" Chunmaniye asked, full of interest.

"Lewinna, innit?" Laughing Maiden said. "Girls can fight."

"She was what we call a Wise Woman," Owl Heart explained. "My people believe in a life force, we call it the *Wyrd*. The *Wyrd* touches every living thing and invests that which doesn't live with spirit too."

"Something my people call *Wakan*," Chunmaniye was surprised at the similarities.

"Some are…in touch with that *Wyrd*, they can read it, attempt to weave it even. Those are the Wise Men and Wise Women," Owl Heart said. "Do you have those too?"

"They have powerful medicine," Chunmaniye said, slowly nodding his head. "We call them *Wicasa Wakan*, Medicine Men."

"*Wicasa Wakan*," Owl Heart smiled. "Our wise ones, the good ones, use their powers mostly for healing. Body and mind."

Chunmaniye smiled back. It began to dawn on him that his sensitivity to the Wyrde Woods might well be a result of this shared spiritual foundation. It was an eye-opener too, he had never suspected the *Saglasa Wasichu*, those called the English, to have roots in a belief that was akin to his own.

"How did your *Wicasa Wakan* Lewinna fight these *Draca*?"

Owl Heart's face changed into one that seemed much older and even contained a level of threat. "The *Wyrd* can be used for other matters aside from healing."

"Such as?" Chunmaniye asked.

"She called upon all creatures of the *Wyrd*," Owl Heart explained. "In all of their manifestations and raised an army such has seldom been seen in the Wyrde Woods."

"*Pooks* too," Laughing Maiden added.

Chunmaniye looked around at the multitude of anguished faces, frozen screams and twisted limbs. "A sorceress then?"

Owl Heart nodded. "She transformed every single *draca* warrior into a yew tree and here they yet stand, as a warning to would-be-invaders."

Chunmaniye wondered if the Wyrde Wood's reluctance to reveal its secrets to him meant that he too was marked as a would-be-invader. It seemed wiser to respect the local spirits, offending them was considered lunacy in his ancestral lands and *Wakan* was undeniably strong here.

"Perhaps this sorceress of yours would have known of the Tree of Life I seek."

Owl Heart narrowed her eyes slightly and he sensed that she became guarded. He suddenly realised that the Wyrde Woods had sent one of its most powerful weapons to stop his quest.

"I know the tree you speak of," Owl Heart answered. "We call it the Wishing Tree, I'll show you."

She pointed to the south-east and took a first few steps in that direction. Her friend did likewise.

Chunmaniye cast a last look at the yew intransigence ahead and concluded he was not meant to find whatever was there. Then he looked at Owl Heart. The child was looking at him expectantly with a mixture of childish innocence and knowing challenge. Her determination to lure him away was clear to him and he suspected that his respect for the *Wakan* present here was reason that the local spirits had sent a gentle nudge instead of something dark with claws, teeth and pitched madness.

"I will follow you," he told Owl Heart and then turned his back on the ranks of frozen marauders.

18. The Invocation

Mortimer Malheur stood on the grassy bank that bordered the huddle of Roreford's riverside ruins. The sound of the Falls was a distant and continuous rush though he could still hear the Rore chuckle as it flowed by. Mortimer cast a glance at the jagged promontories of the Hood's Gorge before turning to survey the open space between the two sets of ruined buildings.

Roreford was one of his favourite destinations in the Wyrde Woods. It had a strong connection with Malheur family history and he liked to come here to relive some of the scenes of the past. Mortimer sometimes believed he could hear the sobs, panic and screams as his forebears exercised their hereditary right to administer justice in the Wyrde Woods. At those times he was filled with a pleasurable giddiness and then anger that his grandfather had so willingly surrendered many of the family rights. The anger was sharp-edged and Mortimer appreciated the seething rage as much as the initial giddiness. It was why he ventured into the Wyrde Woods on his own now and again, seeking a catharsis of sorts; a way to sample pleasurable images and vent some steam.

He was about to stroll over to the middle of the common, where the whipping posts had been set up a long time ago, when he spotted movement at the far side of the clearing. Deftly he slipped into one of the river buildings. It was not much more than an empty shell but would conceal him from all but those who actually walked into cavity between the ivy covered ruined walls. Mortimer found a gap that had once been a window. It gave him a good a vantage of the entire clearing.

A small child riding a pony had reached the middle of the clearing and then waved a procession of other children out of the far forest edge. Mortimer brought a hand up to his chin and stroked it thoughtfully as he recognised some of the children.

§ § § § § §

Maisy rode Spark into the clearing at Roreford with her cap pistol drawn. Gramps had made a leather pouch for her belt in which she kept the five rolls of cap paper, wrapped in waxed paper which Gramps had said would protect them from the damp. She knew better than to give in to the temptation to load the cap pistol though.

The little cracking sounds a loaded cap pistol made were simply too irresistible and she would be through the roll in no time. There was no need anyway, Maisy concluded with a little disappointment. There were no Jerry paratroopers milling around the buildings, not even one.

She turned and gave an all-clear signal by waving her hat over her head.

A small procession entered the clearing, a score of children looking tired and dusty. Some of them carried tools. They had been building things at Fort Defiance for most of the afternoon. The column was closed by Leon riding his dappled grey. Maisy looked at them proudly. There were a dozen kids from Wolfden now; their number had doubled as village chavvies slowly perceived there was an alternative gang to Bill Hare's sorry lot. There was even a West Londoner in the Wyrde Warriors now.

The Wyrde Warriors said their goodbyes as Leon led the Hornsby's over the Farisee Bridge to follow the Forgotten Road eastwards.

"Katie," Maisy said. "You take the others down the road already. I'll catch up on Spark."

Katie looked worried.

"I'll be with you before you get to Shims Copses," Maisy promised. The Wolfden section was not quite up to traversing those feared woodlands by themselves yet; either Joy or Maisy had to escort them through it.

Katie gave a relieved smile, then shrugged apologetically.

"It's alright, innit?" Maisy grinned reassuringly.

"Fort Defiance is coming along nicely," Joy remarked as they watched the Wolfden chavvies follow the Forgotten Road westwards.

"Summer Holidays soon, innit?" Maisy said. "We'll have loads more time in the Wyrde Woods then."

The girls wandered over to the edge of the clearing. The ground rose here as it sloped upwards towards the ridge traversed by the Forgotten Road and the path to the Owlery. Much of the lower slope was open and teeming with the colour of wild flowers.

Maisy watched the butterflies, bees and other insects fly to and fro; hoping to catch the metallic glint of a dragonfly. The air seemed perfumed with the fragrance spread by the flowers and it made her feel mellow.

"We need to figure out how to get into St Lewinna's Church unseen," Maisy rubbed her forehead. She needed to focus, not drift away lured by bounty of a Wyrde Woods summer.

"Vicar Framsfield did invite me to attend church," Joy said thoughtfully.

Maisy closed her eyes and imagined the faces of the Wolfden Parish Christian Ladies Committee if she and Joy turned up one Sunday to attend service. They would have a fit, she was sure. Maisy laughed.

"No, the church will be full, innit? People standing up, mumbling, sitting down, mumbling some more, standing up, singing a hymn. Not much chance to do any exploring."

"Oh," Joy said with disappointment in her voice.

"We'll have to break in," Maisy decided.

"Break in? A church?"

"Well," Maisy shrugged. "It is for a good cause, innit? If we're right about the key being under the Cross Stone, then we wouldn't be taking anything from the church itself. We'd just be passing through, as it were. Though, honestly Joy, I think St Lewinna wants to come with us, she'd look cracking in Fort Defiance."

"I don't reckon it would be a good idea to *gwoan* break in," Joy shook her head. "If we'd get caught…we would be in middling trouble. Tis part of the school now too. Mus Mackellow would split us up for good. He's fair but also strict. He meant what he said."

"True," Maisy agreed. She rubbed her forehead some more but she was plain out of ideas.

Joy suddenly assumed a determined expression.

"Joy?" Maisy queried.

Joy did not answer. Instead, she started walking forwards, weaving around the wild flowers with the dexterity of a hind. Twenty yards in and she turned to face Maisy again, a reassuring smile on her lips. Then Joy shut her eyes and raised her arms; stretching her open hands sideways.

Maisy looked on speechlessly. Joy had her back towards the west. The sun's golden rays silhouetted her body's outline and turned her white dress into a radiant aura around her whilst setting Joy's red hair aflame. Maisy had never seen such ethereal beauty in her life and now it seemed to attract the attention of hundreds of butterflies which fluttered in a cloud around Joy whilst other insects zoomed in and out of this colourful dome around her friend.

"Hear me, please," Joy's voice suddenly rang out loud and clear. "Maisy of *Lunnon* and Joy of the Owlery have been assigned a task by Foster Malheur, one time Lord of the Wyrde Woods."

Maisy held her breath and at the same time – though it lasted just for a fraction of a second – the butterflies all seemed to stall in mid-flight.

"We need to get into St Lewinna's Church in Wolfden unseen, to get the key. Please help us, if you can." Joy continued.

Maisy waited for more but that seemed to be all. Joy lowered her arms and strode back towards Maisy, the insects scattered and the spell broken.

"You think asking the butterflies will help?" Maisy asked curiously. From what she had experienced of the Wyrde Woods so far it would not surprise her.

"*Naun*," Joy shook her heads. "I wasn't asking the butterflies. I was telling the bees."

"The bees?" Maisy recalled that Joy said some such thing before.

"Aye, the bees," Joy nodded, seemingly very pleased with herself.

"The bees will let us into the church?"

"*Naun, howsumdever,* they'll *scorse* our need with others," Joy answered.

"Others?" Maisy's eyes grew wide.

Joy nodded, a serene smile on her lips.

There was a low growl in the sky as, far overhead, a squadron of fighter planes crossed the sky over the Wyrde Woods.

"I thought it was clever to stay away from these 'others', innit?" Maisy pondered.

"Tis *bettermost* to leave them be." Joy nodded. "*Somewhen*, there is little choice."

Maisy shrugged. Anybody who would help them fight the Jerries or their spies were mates of hers.

They heard approaching hooves and turned to see Leon ride back over the Farisee Bridge. His endearing grin made clear that there was no cause for alarm but Maisy and Joy walked towards him curiously.

"I near forgot," Leon shook his head at his own foolishness as they met on the clearing. "Your mum is visiting our place, Joy. Dad said to bring you there for tea."

"Really?" Joy smiled.

Maisy frowned.

"Aye," Leon's eyes sparkled brightly. "As a *bethanks* also, for helping Mum get back on her feet. A proper feast."

Maisy felt her guts churn for a moment. She realised it was selfish but she did not like the idea of Joy going off on an adventure on her own. For a moment she contemplated inviting herself along, she doubted either Joy or Leon would object. Then Maisy recalled Katie's apologetic shrug, the innate fears the Wolfden chavvies had of traversing Shims Copses. Maisy might want to stay with her best friend but Captain Robbins of the Royal Sussex Regiment had a duty towards those who had already conquered some of their fears just to follow their Captain into the Wyrde Woods. She simply could not let them down.

"*Bettermost* you ride with me," Leon said, stretching out a hand to Joy. "We'll need to catch up with the rest."

Joy suddenly looked hesitant and gave Leon a coy smile. Then she looked up at Maisy, her eyes filled with happiness.

"I'll see you later, Maisy," Joy beamed.

Maisy answered with a curt nod. Tendrils of envy spouted within her as she watched Joy hop onto the dappled grey's back and fold her arms around Leon's middle. The woodlands chavvies said a last goodbye and then Leon spurred the horse into a trot towards the Farisee Bridge.

The London girl watched them go with mixed emotions. Pleased, because of Joy's evident pleasure. Forlorn, because she felt excluded. Most of all though, Maisy realised with a sinking feeling; envious. She just did not know whether to be jealous of Joy or of Leon. She had to admit they seemed made for each other; wild chavvies of the woodlands both, proper tall too. One handsome, the other beautiful, the one left behind a blooming freak. Maisy shook her head. It was all very confusing.

§ § § § § § §

The two girls who Mortimer had encountered on their dubious truffle expedition stayed behind when the other children left. They were not too far from his hiding place but speaking far too softly for him to overhear their conversation. Mortimer regretted that for they spoke with an intensity which made him curious as to what they were talking about. His mind was tempted to dismiss it as immature childish chatter but his intuition told him otherwise. His curiosity was satisfied shortly thereafter though.

The Whitfield girl had walked onto the flowered slope and assumed a position of power and Mortimer drew in his breath for she looked radiantly beautiful and he recognised what she was doing. He had always had suspicions about some of the people living in the Edgelands and the Wyrde Woods but this was the first time he saw these thoughts confirmed with his own eyes.

Then her voice rang out, loud enough for him to hear.

"Hear me, please. Maisy of *Lunnon* and Joy of the Owlery have been assigned a task by Foster Malheur, one time Lord of the Wyrde Woods."

Mortimer narrowed his eyes. Foster Malheur was one of his more colourful ancestors. He had been Lord of the Wyrde Woods in the 13th century and was long dead. None-the-less, Mortimer believed every word the girl spoke.

The girl's voice rang out again and when she was done a slow satisfied smile spread on Mortimer's face.

So that was where the keys were.

§ § § § § § §

Leon slowed the grey to a walk when they could see the gaggle of Hornsby's moving along the Forgotten Road ahead of them.

Joy felt sublimely happy. It had been a good day. Joy had meant it when she told Maisy that she would oppose any German *sodgers* attempting to invade the Wyrde Woods but she had not had a clue as to how such a thing could possibly be achieved. Surfing in Maisy's wake though, had been a splendid adventure as the *Lunnon* girl seemed capable of transforming the impossible into reality. Maisy had her own form of magic, that much was clear to Joy. They had a small army now and a defensible base that was growing each time they could spare the time to work on it.

Some of the free weekend days had been spent at the Hornsby farm where both Jasper and Jeremy Hornsby had proven to be enthusiastic teachers as they had helped all the Wyrde Warriors fashion their own bows and provided the materials to make proper arrows. Both men had longbows themselves, powerful ones, six foot long and made of yew. Joy had held one of them but could barely fit her slender hand around the grip, so thick was the bow stave. Maisy had been delighted, of course; seeing potential recruits in the Hornsby men and Joy had agreed. Jasper and Jeremy would be a reassuring presence in a fight. The brothers joked incessantly and when they were together did their best to outshine the other in being foolish and taking nothing at all very serious. When they picked up their yew longbows they still bantered and bickered good naturedly but physically they would assume a posture of calm confidence. Jeremy was the better shot, Joy had seen him knock an unripe green apple off a branch at a hundred yards during one of the shooting lessons the Hornsby men had given the Wyrde Warriors.

Fort Defiance was not quite complete yet but it had a well-stocked armoury and the whole gang had proven adept at acquiring basic archery skills, though the Hornsby *chavees* were by far the better archers.

More of the Wolfden *chavees* had joined them. Maisy had gained a reputation with her performance on the roof of Grumpy Row and their isolation at school was on the wane. Bill Hare and his chums had been keeping a relatively low profile since the fight by the Raven's Roost. That was good though Joy suspected they would want revenge after the sheer humiliation of their defeat. She doubted Bill Hare would be satisfied with the revenge he had taken on Maisy during Vicar Framsfield's lesson in St Lewinna's Church.

This was not the time to be worrying about that though. When Joy had stepped into the field of flowers at Roreford she had done so intuitively, almost sure that the Wyrde Woods would simply ignore her pathetic attempt to raise the *Wyrd*. She had never tried it before and Joy had been taken by surprise when she had simply felt the electricity of the *Wyrd* all around her – responding to her presence most strongly. The power of it had been a magnificent thrill, one that Joy had not tasted before and she was still filled with the heady exhilaration of it. She knew Mum had the gift and though Mum had been teaching Joy the lore of the woods and hinted at the invocation of the *Wyrd* she had never encouraged Joy to attempt such a thing.

But I did it anyway. I did it. I can do it.

To top the day off she was riding Leon's horse and felt the boy's back against her as she kept her arms wrapped around his middle. Yet another unknown experience and one that made her feel giddy, as if some of the butterflies at Roreford had been transferred to her belly.

She had known Leon since forever ago and Mum and the Hornsby adults always made jokes which referred to a future wedding between the two. Jokes the adults guffawed at but which Joy had found plain silly. It was one of those things, she felt, that would come in due time. Perhaps when she was old enough to attend the Beltane or Midsummer celebrations on Arthur's Fort in a few years' time. She had always assumed that when her time came she would jump over a fire holding Leon's hand in hers. It was like an unspoken understanding, though she had never asked Leon if he thought likewise; the question was simply too irrelevant.

This was the first time that she attempted to formulate some of those abstract feelings into coherent thoughts though, keenly aware as she was of Leon's presence. With a daring that surprised herself Joy laid her cheek against Leon's shoulder and let the weight of her head rest against him. The fluttering butterfly wings in her belly seemed to explode into a blossom of flowers like that of a healthy cherry tree in spring and Joy felt keenly alive.

"Your friend Maisy," Leon suddenly spoke. "She's *naun* as bad as I reckoned *Sheere-folk* to be."

Joy lifted her head and smiled at the sound of Maisy's name. Maisy was the best thing that had ever happened to her.

"She's a *bettermost* friend," Joy agreed.

"*Naun* bad for a girl either," Leon enthused. "She can play proper games like hunting and fighting and building forts. She has a proper cap pistol too."

"Hmm," Joy responded with a tiny spark of irritation as it dawned on her that Leon's mind was not on their proximity which so thrilled her. Instead, he was thinking about Maisy and the admiration in his voice marred the moment for her.

"Well," Leon tried to explain. "Most girls are into other things, aint it so? *Dighting* up, hair and dresses and that unaccountable *oakum*."

"I am a girl, Leon Hornsby," Joy said firmly. "In case you forgot."

Leon turned his head and dazzled her with his bright smile, his brown eyes bright. "You're different, Joy Whitfield. One of the woodfolk, like us. You're like family, you are."

The blossoms Joy had felt wilted in an instant. She suddenly realised she did not want to be considered as family by this boy with his suntanned skin, wild golden hair and handsome smile.

"Sounds to me like you fancy the *Lunnon* girl," Joy said with more bitterness in her voice than she intended.

Leon did not say anything but she could see he turned bright red before he turned his face away from her again – that was answer enough.

Joy felt a curious mix of emotions; temporarily pleased that she had put him in his place but also disappointed that he had turned his face away. She also felt guilty for her intonation when she had said '*Lunnon* girl' while at the same time there was a little sour stab when her mind's eye invoked Maisy's cheeky face.

Look back again, she pleaded silently. *Another one of those smiles – for me.*

Leon, however, remained silent until they caught up with his siblings and cousins and Joy felt the day's magic drain away.

There is always a price to be paid for using magic. It was a bitter realisation.

19. The Key Quest

There was an odd tension when Joy took her seat next to Maisy in class the next morning.

"How was it at the Hornsby farm?" Maisy asked, managing to insert a tone of careless disinterest into the question.

"Twere middling fine," Joy answered. Jenny Hornsby had exerted herself for the meal and the mood had been mellow. The adults had joked and laughed as they drank the cider that was brewed on the farm. It was said that Hornsby Cider was the best to be found in the Edgelands and Jeremy earned some extra income by selling most of it to his nearby local, the Carfax Alus. The *chavees* had, as always, been as lively as a nest of kittens, though both Joy and Leon had remained subdued for most of the evening.

"Twere a fine feast, a *bettermost* evening," Joy tried a smile to honour the Hornsby efforts.

"Well that's good," Maisy commented without enthusiasm.

Joy shot her friend a puzzled look. Something seemed to be bothering Maisy and she did not know what. Normally she would have asked but she was blockaded by a sense of unfairness. Joy believed she was the one who had the right to be bothered, even though she also realised it was hardly fair to hold Maisy responsible for Leon's telling blushes.

Their first lesson was a geography lesson which was one of Joy's favourite subjects because the teacher, a retired missionary, had lived all over the Empire and could easily be prompted to forget the curriculum and drift into long fascinating tales about Asia or Africa. At those times Joy would close her eyes and feel the hot red African soil beneath her feet as she evaded lions and crocodiles or else almost hear the hypnotical chanting in Hindu or Buddhist temples surrounded by the noisy chaos of thousands attending rituals.

Today's lesson concerned the Dominion of Canada and both Joy and Maisy paid it their full attention; curious as to where Chunmaniye hailed from.

The lesson was disrupted by the entry of one of the younger pupils, a boy who approached the teacher nervously to hand over a note. The teacher frowned behind her spectacles. She had been in full steam and though she was usually friendly everybody knew she had an intense dislike of being interrupted when she was transporting a classroom to far-flung places.

"Joy Whitfield, Maisy Robbins," the teacher read from the note. "You are to report to Mus Mackellow's office at once."

The girls looked at each other in surprise and then questioningly at their teacher.

"Well, hurry girls, I want to continue," the teacher said and Joy and Maisy quickly made their exit.

"What did we do?" Joy whispered to Maisy in the little hallway. The tension she had felt between them earlier had melted away and was replaced by apprehension.

"I dunno," Maisy shook her head in surprised consternation. Both girls had made a real effort to avoid being too noticeable since their last visit to Mus Mackellow's office.

"Mathematics is still ill. Probably Sister Mary," Maisy shrugged.

Joy agreed, Sister Mary had transferred some of her dislike for Maisy to Joy since the two had become friends and nothing they did or did not do could merit the teacher's approval.

The door to the Headmaster's office opened and it was indeed Sister Mary who stepped out.

"*Guten tag, Fräulein*," Maisy greeted the nun.

"WHAT did you say?" Sister Mary was temporarily taken aback. Joy was too; what was Maisy playing at now?

"I meant to say, good morning, Sister Mary," Maisy said quickly. "I got confused. I am so sorry."

Joy bit on her lip. Maisy had explained a theory she had that involved acting like the *chuckle-head* some folk assumed you to be.

"If you live up to their expectations," Maisy had said, "You can get away with murder half of the time, innit?"

Joy suspected Maisy was putting her theory into practice but the odds on not getting away with murder seemed steep to Joy. Sister Mary threw the girls a furious look and Joy resisted the urge to cringe. Those of the Wyrde Warriors who had witnessed Maisy's punishment after the girl's rooftop defiance had told Joy that Sister Mary had been especially voracious in administering pain. Joy reassured herself that whatever their transgression was it could hardly be on a par with a rooftop show involving a teacher's bloomers.

"Step inside," Sister Mary said curtly, dark thunder written all over her face.

Joy and Maisy grabbed each other's hand, simultaneously taking a deep breath to brace themselves for whatever they would encounter in the Headmaster's Office. Then they bravely marched in to face their fate.

Lady Priscilla!

"Joy Whitfield! Maisy Robbins!" Mus Mackellow beamed at them. "Intelligent pupils both, as you stated My Lady."

Lady Priscilla gave a small polite smile; only her eyes betrayed merriment.

Sister Mary gave a small snort as she followed the girls into the room and closed the door again.

"Milady," Joy said, creasing her brow as she tried to make sense of it all.

"Ma'am," Maisy said politely as her face betrayed a dozen thoughts at once.

"You do us great honour, My Lady," Mus Mackellow really was in high spirits. "A most generous offer beneficial to all our pupils."

Joy began to smile. She was keenly aware of Sister Mary's presence behind her, the nun simply radiated disapproval, but the Headmaster's cheer was genuine. Whatever the matter was it hardly seemed likely that she and Maisy were in trouble.

"As I mentioned, Mr Mackellow," Lady Priscilla was all dignified grace. "You have these two pupils to thank for it, it was they who alerted me to the situation."

Maisy grinned and nodded. She threw a quick sideways glance at Joy which told Joy that Maisy did not have the faintest idea what the whole visit was about but was beginning to enjoy it tremendously.

"I really do not think it appropriate," Sister Mary declared sternly, "that pupils of this school take it upon themselves to waylay their social betters and…"

"There was no such thing," Lady Priscilla lifted a hand to ward off Sister Mary's accusation and smiled. "The girls were my guests at Malheur Hall and I've never entertained more well-behaved company."

Mus Mackellow beamed approval.

"Your guests?" Sister Mary sounded flabbergasted and Joy desperately wished she could turn around to see the nun's face – but felt it would not do to antagonise the teacher. Maisy seemed of the same mind though her head twitched as rapidly as Valkerie's when the ferret tried to sniff at a situation.

"I don't entirely understand, *surelye*" Joy admitted hesitantly. It seemed impolite but she was dying to know why Lady Priscilla was at school and why Mus Mackellow seemed to be walking in the clouds.

"I'm in the dark too, innit?" Maisy confessed her ignorance in support and Joy felt grateful. The earlier brief tension between them seemed but a trifle now.

"Perhaps we might show them?" Mus Mackellow directed his question at Lady Priscilla who smiled her accordance and stood up.

Sister Mary opened the door and Lady Priscilla and Mus Mackellow led the way outside, followed by Maisy and Joy who made use of the opportunity to exchange a hundred thousand glances. Sister Mary closed the little procession which made out of the front door and stepped onto Stone Square.

There were a few dozen curious children without lessons to attend who had formed a curious semi-circle around a gleaming Rolls-Royce in black and red livery. A female driver wearing a peak cap and a uniform coat that was slightly too big for her stood at attention by the elegant lines of the motor vehicle. Joy noted the large chrome headlamps which fronted a shiny grill above which was the proud hood ornament which depicted a graceful woman leaning forwards as she trailed long wings behind her. She thought it was elegant and fitting. Priscilla Malheur did seem a bit like that.

"Cor blimey!" Maisy was full of appreciation. "Now that's a car!"

"A Phantom Sedanca Cabriolet," Lady Priscilla smiled. "I sat in the front for the back is filled."

"Filled to the boot," Mus Mackellow chuckled.

Joy and Maisy wandered closer to the car to look through the windows of the cab, behind the front seats which were out in the open, and saw that it was loaded with carton boxes.

"Indeed it is, Mr Mackellow," Lady Priscilla nodded. Then she turned to the girls. "It was very good of you to tell me your school was short of books for I recalled that we had surplus books at the Hall."

"Which Lady Priscilla has so very kindly donated to our school," Mus Mackellow expressed his delight.

"It's very thoughtful of you, My Lady," Sister Mary admitted politely.

"They are all suitable reading material," Lady Priscilla gave Sister Mary a smile.

"It's very kind of you, Ma'am," Sister Mary said, "But I am not sure we have the space to store them, the school is bursting out of its seams as it is."

"Nonsense," Mus Mackellow shook his head. "If needs be I'll store them in my office. With all the extra pupils we have been very short of materials indeed."

Maisy nodded wholeheartedly; four children to a book only worked if teachers got their intelligence assessment right, was her expert opinion.

Everyone looked up as a formation of fighters swept by to the west of Wolfden; intent on the interception of other planes no doubt. The skies were increasingly filled with aeroplanes flying to and fro these days and the wireless reported losses and kills on a daily basis now. Luftwaffe bombers were attempting to pound ports and airfields but the idea that Britain was now under a sustained attack was still surreal in the Wyrde Woods where mostly they just saw specks in the air.

"I do not think that will be necessary," Lady Priscilla remarked casually, bringing the focus back on the books. "As I recall, Mr Mackellow, there is a large vestry in St Lewinna's Church."

She suddenly looked straight at Joy and Maisy. "I did notice a whole wall in there with empty shelves not all that long ago."

Joy felt a light shock go through her. She heard Maisy's sharp intake of breath.

"That is quite right," Mr Mackellow bobbed his head up and down.

"If I may trouble you for a cup of tea in your office, Mr Mackellow," Lady Priscilla continued. "I did have an inventory made and would be delighted to walk through it with Sister…"

She looked at Sister Mary.

"Sister Mary, My Lady," the nun said. "I don't think that will be necessa…"

"Nonsense," Mus Mackellow decreed. "It would behove us, Sister Mary, to take an interest in such a generous gift and discuss how it is best put to use."

Sister Mary bowed her head in submission.

"As instigators of this sudden addition to your school," Lady Priscilla said to the Headmaster, "I feel the girls will be willing to carry the books into St Lewinna's Church, won't you girls?"

The Lady of the Wyrde Woods gave Joy and Maisy another short look. Joy tried to contain a wide smile and nodded her understanding.

"We'd be glad to, Milady," Joy said.

"Of course," Mus Mackellow agreed. "A splendid idea. Sister Mary would you see to the tea please? There's no class in the church at the moment, I'll unlock the door so Miss Whitfield and Miss Robbins can carry the books inside."

"Yes, Mister Mackellow," Sister Mary disappeared back into the school building. Just as she shut the door there was commotion on the Roreford Road. Joy looked to see Silas Hare march towards Stone Square at the head of his Home Guard section. They were still some way away but Joy could see that some of the men carried shovels, spades and pickaxes. Behind them, on horseback, rode Sir Mortimer.

"What on earth…?" Mus Mackellow voiced Joy's own question.

"Oh," Lady Priscilla said lightly. "Apparently Nazi sympathisers have buried a cache of weapons below the Cross Stone."

She indicated the standing stone in the centre of Stone Square. The girls' eyes widened.

"In the very heart of the village?" Mus Mackellow wondered. He frowned. "I am the commanding officer of the Wolfden Home Guard. I should have been told. What is Hare playing at?"

"Obeying my son's orders, no doubt Lieutenant Mackellow. Mortimer seems very sure of it," Lady Priscilla answered. "Though, personally, I suspect that they will not find anything."

"We'd better start unloading the books then, innit?" Maisy was quick to say as if this were a logical consequence. Mus Mackellow agreed and they all walked to the front door of the church. Lady

Priscilla's driver took her seat behind the steering wheel and drove the car right up to the church door. As Mus Mackellow escorted Lady Priscilla towards the school building the driver opened the rear door closest to the church. She was one of the Malheur Marauders.

"I'll lift the boxes out of the car and into the hallway," the driver told Joy and Maisy with a wink. "You can carry them further inside."

The driver cast a glance at the first Home Guard soldiers who had reached Stone Square. "You'd better hurry."

The girls nodded their understanding and entered the church.

"How the heck?" Maisy gave Joy a playful punch. "Your bees?"

"I don't *ken*," Joy shook her head.

"Sir Mortimer has come for the key, hasn't he? How did he find out?"

Joy shook her head again, she had been breaking her head over it but all she concluded was that they were caught up in a wider web of sorts.

The driver brought in the first boxes and they picked them up and started walking to the vestry door just past St Lewinna's alcove at the far end of the church.

"What was all that *fräulein* business with Sister Mary about?" Joy asked.

"Oh, I was just trying to draw her out, innit?"

"Draw her out of what?"

"Sometimes spies drop their cover, at something innocent like a 'thank you' or a 'good day'. Instinctively, like. So I was just testing Sister Mary but she's a bloody good spy I reckon."

"You seriously think Sister Mary is a Jerry spy?" Joy grinned.

"You should have seen those bloomers," Maisy nearly dropped the box she was holding when she wanted to spread out her arms as wide as she could. "Size of a parachute they were."

The route to the vestry took them past the alcove containing St Lewinna's statuette and they set down the boxes there. Joy looked at St Lewinna's determined face and smiled at the image of the saint and then gave the window a brief glance.

RAISE THE STONE AND THOU SHALT FIND ME
CLEAVE THE WOOD AND I AM THERE

Joy slipped past the statuette. There was not much space behind the pedestal. Maisy came round the other side.

"The wood panelling is only at this end bit," Maisy said thoughtfully.

"Cleave the wood," Joy mumbled.

"We can hardly chop through," Maisy shook her head. "Forgot to bring me axe to school this morning, innit?"

She knocked on the flat surface of the large centre of one of the panels. It did not sound hollow.

"Tis *naun* the lifting of stones or breaking of wood, *surelye*." Joy pursed her lips. "How about the frames?"

Joy studied the frames. Even from a short distance they looked like ordinary ornamental decoration but from up close she saw that the carvings were far more intricate; the carved flowers and ivy surrounding depictions of tradesmen carrying out their business. A farmer with a plough, a dairy maid with a bucket.

A sudden noise by the door cause Joy to look up and peek around the pedestal. She could briefly hear voices by the door and then the driver walked in on her own and set down another box of books.

How much time do we have?

"Cor blimey!" Maisy suddenly uttered. "Joy, look, it's a woodcutter!"

Joy came round to Maisy and saw that the depiction at the bottom of the inner frame showed a muscular man carrying a two-handed axe.

"Press it," Joy said with urgency in her voice.

Maisy applied light pressure and nothing happened. Then she pushed with all her might and there was a loud click as part of the lower panel suddenly sprung open.

Joy's eyes grew wide but her initial sense of triumph ebbed into pained disappointment almost instantly.

"Rotters," Maisy hissed.

§ § § § § § §

Mortimer walked into Barnaby Mackellow's office without knocking. Besides the Headmaster there was an astonishingly large nun in the room, as well as Mortimer's own mother.

Mortimer addressed the Headmaster, "Lieutenant Mackellow, I do apologize for not informing you sooner. I thought the matter of possible fifth column weaponry of great urgency."

The two men looked at each other. There was an immediate tension in the room. Mortimer had no right whatsoever to command the local Home Guard to do anything. At most he could only place a request for assistance with Mackellow. Both men knew this and inwardly Mortimer felt a great deal of satisfaction as he watched Mackellow struggle with his self-control. The man was angry but sensible enough not to risk Mortimer's ire. Though Malheur power was but a faint shadow of what it had once been Mackellow would find it hard to get much done in Wolfden if Mortimer were to oppose him. On the other hand Mackellow's acceptance of the situation as it was would set a precedent. Half the fellow's unit of civilian defenders - Silas Hare's men - , would no longer be under his effective command should Mortimer choose to override Mackellow.

"It would be so much better if you left these tasks up to veteran soldiers, Morty," His mother's voice. Of course it would be.

Mortimer swallowed. He hated his childhood's nickname and she used it to goad him when she disapproved of actions he took. Though he styled himself as Lord of the Wyrde Woods she had not yet relinquished her title to him in the old family ceremony that custom required. It was a Malheur thing and the damned woman had only become more obstinate about letting Mortimer assume his birth right after she had discovered Mortimer had no intention of honouring the memories of her father. It never ceased to amaze Mortimer how tightly his mother clung to the phantom of that madman. Although he would have preferred it otherwise she herself had a sound and sharp-edged mind.

She continued. "Lieutenant Mackellow served with distinction in the Great War, I do seem to recall. You, Morty, were galloping about on your hobby horse when it started."

"Thank you for that delightful memory, Mother," Mortimer bit back. "May I ask what brought you to Wolfden this morning? To the village school of all places?"

Mortimer cast a dismissive glance at Barnaby Mackellow; partly to remind the fellow of his proper station and partly because he knew it would irritate his mother.

"I have come to contribute to the war effort, Morty," she answered coolly.

"The War Effort? Indeed." Mortimer nodded as if very impressed.

"It may have escaped your notice, although it should not have, that the village school has had to house an extraordinary number of evacuee children. I have come to supplement their meagre stocks with our surplus children's books."

Mortimer nodded. When he had seen the Rolls parked near the old church he had been briefly worried that the interfering old woman had uncovered his plans in Stone Square. This, however, sounded like the typically misguided philanthropy she was fond of. Mortimer had no need or desire for these particular books but to gift them to these rural children was like throwing pearls before swine as far as he was concerned.

"Of course...," Lady Priscilla continued blithely, "...there is more that we can do, Mortimer. I am pleased you are here so that we can discuss this now."

In public with witnesses.

"Do tell, Mother," Mortimer smiled wryly.

"There is a desperate shortage of teaching staff," Lady Priscilla said. "Which we can alleviate by offering field trips to Malheur Hall. They can roam the grounds and I am sure some of the staff will be able to tell them all sorts of interesting things about the gardens."

"Oh my!" Barnaby Mackellow exclaimed. "That would be wonderful, truly wonderful."

Mortimer ground his teeth. It would be ungracious to refuse, though he would have done so if she had asked him in private.

"Perhaps even a picnic lunch, Mother?" He said, his voice dripping with sarcasm.

"A splendid idea, Morty!" Lady Priscilla nodded. She looked at the Headmaster who was still shaking his head with disbelief. "A score at a time, Mister Mackellow. I will provide lunch for the children and we will not stop until every one of your pupils has visited Malheur Hall."

Inwardly Mortimer groaned. It was bad enough that she had entertained the two woodfolk girls like they were visiting royalty without extending that invitation to all the rabble in the Edgelands. There was little he could do about it though. Better to focus on more important matters. Like those keys mentioned in *Secree of the Wirdewode*. Cynthia was waiting for him to bring them to her like a questing knight brings his favoured lady a trophy. That, however, was a minor boon compared to the real reward of finding both keys.

It was time to go back outside and check on Hare's men who had started digging a trench around the great standing stone that marked the centre of Wolfden.

§ § § § § §

"Blast," Maisy's shoulders sagged.

Joy nodded her agreement.

The section of panelling that had swung open was large enough to be promising but the actual tunnel entrance it had concealed was ten inches wide and ten inches high at most. It was constructed from blocks of sandstone and in remarkably good shape but looked more like a water channel than a tunnel designed to fit a human.

Maisy exchanged a sad glance with Joy. She had no doubt that the tunnel would lead to the Cross Stone but they could hear the dull thuds outside as Hare's men struck their spades into the ground around the stone. They were running out of time fast and Maisy tasted defeat, all the more bitter because they had come so near to completing their mission.

Just then the thunks outside were added to by a new noise, something gently rapping and tapping on the lid of Maisy's gasmask container.

"Valkerie!" Maisy and Joy called out in unison.

"Listen you two," Lady Priscilla's driver suddenly peered around the corner. "Your Headmaster, her Ladyship and Sir Mortimer have just come out of the school building again. You haven't shifted any of the boxes yet and I just don't know if someone is likely to walk in. I can't stop them."

"*Bethanks*," Joy nodded at the driver who disappeared again. Then she looked at Maisy. "Try Valkerie? I'll start shifting the boxes."

Maisy nodded. She crouched down by the tunnel entrance and opened the lid of her container a little bit. Valkerie wormed out and Maisy took her friend in her hands. She tickled Valkerie's tummy and spoke softly.

"There's a good girl, innit? The best vampire ferret in film history."

Valkerie dooked her agreement and then start twisting her head to examine her surroundings. Maisy turned Valkerie over in her hands and brought the ferret's snout close to the tunnel entrance. Maisy was nervous, there were so many unknowns. She had no idea how far Valkerie would fancy going into the tunnel and if she did how far she would venture or what she would find at the end. If the key was in any kind of container that would be the end of that. Even if it wasn't…

…Valkerie sniffed at the tunnel with great interest, turned her head to give Maisy a look with her bright little eyes, and then her body started tensing as the ferret struggled against the constraint of Maisy's hands.

"Blimey," Maisy whispered. Valkerie's instincts were kicking in, the ferret wanted to explore the tunnel. "Go on then, you little bugger."

Maisy released her grip on Valkerie and the ferret did not hesitate. She turned into a white streak and propelled herself into the tunnel until all sign of her faded in the tunnel's darkness.

Maisy bit her lip, and then imitated Stan Laurel's goofy voice as she repeated his words from *Way Out West*: "Now that you've got the mine, I'll bet you'll be swell gold digger."

§ § § § § § §

Mortimer surveyed the mounds of earth that marked the circular trench which now surrounded the Cross Stone. He took a few steps forwards. Mother and Mackellow stayed by the school door.

"Well?" Mortimer asked Silas Hare as the man approached nervously.

"About four feet in all around, Milord," Hare doffed his khaki Home Guard cap. "Nothing yet."

"Well, dig deeper," Mortimer shrugged. He noted with irritation that the operation was drawing quite a crowd as more and more villagers came to Stone Square to see what was going on.

"I beg your pardon, Milord," Hare said. "But we would weaken the earth that supports the stone. It could come toppling down on my men."

Mortimer regarded him coldly. He would have preferred to topple the standing stone to begin with. They could always raise it again after Mortimer had retrieved the keys which he was sure were beneath the stone. However, he knew the superstitions of the simple rurals well enough to know that he would be inviting a riot if he started toppling their standing stones.

"The stone, Mister Hare, is buried deep. It will not topple so easily. You will continue digging, and in the meanwhile send some of your men for posts long enough to prop the stone up, to put your mind at ease."

Silas Hare smirked uneasily.

"Well, get to it man," Mortimer snapped.

The Home Guard Sergeant nodded unhappily. "Yes, Milord."

"Surely, Morty, nobody could have dug such deep holes in the middle of the village without a single soul being alerted to the fact?"

There was concern in Mother's voice now. It was a warning to stop before Mortimer would make a fool of himself for this tale was one that would resound in the locals pubs for years to come. Much as Mortimer hated the notion of being labelled with his grandfather's madness he was too committed to call a halt.

What was Mother doing here anyway? A nagging doubt about her presence revived his suspicion. He gave her a calculating glance.

"While we wait," he suggested to Mackellow. "Perhaps I can have a look at the books which I have apparently donated to your school."

Mortimer was pleased to note a brief glance of discomfort on his mother's face.

"I really don't think that's..." she began to say.

"You scolded me for not being aware of the situation, Mother," Mortimer said slowly, savouring the words. "Now that I try to better my ways and show an interest you seem adverse to that."

Lady Priscilla had no answer.

"Ah, the fickle ways of the weaker sex," Mortimer looked bemused.

Mackellow gave Lady Priscilla a questioning look and she nodded. "You are quite right, Mortimer. I will come with you, duly flattered by your interest in my attempts to help our neighbours."

"Why, thank you, Mother," Mortimer said politely. He started to stride towards St Lewinna's Church, followed by Lady Priscilla and Mackellow. By the door he glanced into the empty Rolls-Royce and then strode into the church. He could hear voices through the open vestry door at the far side of the church and made towards the source.

§ § § § § § §

Maisy crouched into the corner and held her breath as she watched Sir Mortimer stride by St Lewinna's alcove but the man did not look left or right, intent only on the vestry. More footsteps followed; Lady Priscilla and the Headmaster but neither of them glanced into the alcove either. Sometimes it was useful being really small.

She heard voices in the vestry and bit on her lip as she looked at the open part of the panel. If someone did glance into the alcove they would see that oddity before they discerned Maisy...but to shut it...

Maisy shivered. Poor Valkerie.

Then she heard a strange noise come from the tunnel. A continuous scraping of sorts and as it grew louder Maisy's ears could also detect the pit patter of ferret paws.

Valkerie was on her way back. Somebody else was coming too though; new footsteps indicating another person had entered St Lewinna's Church.

§ § § § § § §

Mortimer strode into the vestry and came to a dignified halt. There were open cartons everywhere, as well as piles of books. One of the Malheur Hall servants was there. Mortimer had been exasperated when Mother had paid for the woman to receive driving lessons but now that his regular driver had joined the army he was secretly grateful for her foresight. The Whitfield girl was there as well. The two were sorting out the books and placing them on book shelves.

Mortimer narrowed his eyes. The girl was young but she had demonstrated considerable power the day before. An invocation to gain access to the very church he now found her in.

"Milord," the driver gave a respectful nod.

"Milord," the girl imitated the respectful nod but both continued to work through the piles of books.

"What is that girl doing here?" Mortimer asked nobody in particular.

"Miss Whitfield is one of our pupils," Mackellow answered. "We are using the town hall and church as extra classrooms."

"Hmm," Mortimer continued to scrutinise the girl. He could tell that she was pretending not to notice; she was a crafty one.

"Curiouser and curiouser," Lady Priscilla exclaimed suddenly with delight in her voice. She walked forwards to pick up a copy of *Alice in Wonderland*.

Mortimer clenched his teeth as she made a fool of herself; twirling round as if she was still a little girl.

"The time has come," Mother declared with a smile. "To talk of many things: Of shoes and ships…"

"…and sealing wax – of cabbages and kings." Mackellow finished with one of his foolish smiles. Mortimer was surprised that an educated man was playing along with the childish game.

"Did you know, Mr Mackellow, that we have themed gardens at Malheur Hall?" Lady Priscilla asked the Headmaster.

Mortimer sighed.

"I've heard it told, My Lady."

"Including a Shakespeare Garden and a Carroll Garden," Lady Priscilla nodded earnestly. "I shall make sure there's a croquet set out when the children visit."

Mortimer wanted to roll his eyes as Mackellow bobbed up and down with enthusiasm at the prospect of his hordes of untamed and unwashed farm children roaming the Hall grounds. It would make no difference for these children, why could Mother not see that? If they were lucky they would follow in their fathers' footsteps on farms and in workshops. If they were unlucky they would have no course but to drift to the slums of Stancaster, Brighton or London. Why show them what they could never have? It was a cruel kindness, as far as Mortimer was concerned.

"Milord!" Silas Hare suddenly appeared in the doorway.

"What is it?" Mortimer asked.

Silas Hare opened his mouth to speak but then looked down in surprise as a small girl slipped past him, her arms piled with books.

"That's the last of them," she sang out, seemingly oblivious to the presence of newcomers in the Vestry.

"Milord," Silas Hare grinned. "We struck something hard. Masonry, some sort of construction."

"Excellent," Mortimer breathed a quiet sigh of relief and then made towards the door, barely giving Silas Hare time to step aside.

§ § § § § § §

"Well?" Joy asked Maisy after Sir Mortimer and Hare had left.

Maisy cast a glance at Mus Mackellow, but the Headmaster had found a book to leaf through and seemed totally engrossed by it.

"Well?" Lady Priscilla directed an insistent glance at Maisy.

Maisy grinned from ear-to-ear and briefly rapped her fingers on her gasmask container which promptly tapped back.

"Got it," she said proudly.

Joy's hand flew to her mouth to stifle a cheer.

"Well done Captain," Lady Priscilla said softly and Maisy beamed.

"Milady," Joy addressed her. "How…?"

"This is not the time, Miss Whitfield," Lady Priscilla straightened her back, reassuming her more regal pose. "Get back to your lessons." Softly she added: "Guard it well."

As the girls walked out of the Vestry they could hear her say: "Mr Mackellow, I've dismissed your pupils, they looked tired after all their hard work. Would you mind help me sort the remainder of these books whilst we discuss ravens and writing-desks?"

"It would be an honour," the Headmaster assured her with pleasure in his voice. "I will have our tea brought here and Sister Mary can help us."

Joy smiled. Mus Mackellow was genuinely delighted by the generosity of the Lady of the Wyrde Woods. Joy cast a proud glance at Maisy who could scarce contain her excitement. Mus Mackellow was not the only one; the Lady of the Wyrde Woods had been most generous this day.

The north door was not locked and the girls slipped out of the church unnoticed. Everyone on Stone Square had their eyes on the small rectangular construction of mortared sandstone Hare's men had uncovered. The Home Guard soldiers were milling around it with sledgehammers and crowbars and Sir Mortimer could be seen nearby, hovering impatiently, as curious as the rest of them as to what would be found in the buried hiding place at the foot of the Cross Stone.

20. Fort Defiance

"Well?" Maisy enquired as Joy walked away from Tuckersham Church. To their surprise Valkerie had retrieved not one but two keys from the hiding place by the foot of Cross Stone and Joy had wanted to test the larger one.

Maisy had been posted as lookout while Joy entered the forlorn looking roofless church to try the large key in the lock of a door she said she had discovered.

The only intact part of the church seemed to be its short squat tower but Maisy relied on Joy's knowledge of the Wyrde Woods in this and was not altogether upset about staying on path. The path was separated from the church ground by a low wall and the other side was a wilderness of tall grass, brambles and gravestones; all jumbled and tumbled. The whole breathed an atmosphere of ominous threat and Maisy understood why Joy had described it as a bad place just like Gallows Hill where hundreds had been executed at the Blood Stone almost as if it were a place of sacrifice.

"It fits," Joy smiled and held out the key to Maisy. Valkerie had dragged both keys out by a fraying grey string they had been attached to and Maisy had replaced that with a ribbon she had borrowed from Gran. The larger key was an old fashioned ornate one with protruding teeth and covered in a fine layer of rust. The smaller key attached to the ribbon was far more delicate and when Maisy had rubbed its dark surface it had started to gleam silvery white.

"Did you try…unlocking the door?" Maisy's eyes were large.

"By Oak, Ash and Thorn, no!" Joy shook her head. "That's what they want."

Maisy nodded. It was very sensible if there was a dark Owl Man to be found behind that door but part of her was dead curious. She tucked the keys away in her ammunition pouch.

"*Naun* Valkerie's box?" Joy grinned.

"Blimey, no." Maisy shook her head. "Ferrets get very possessive about their hoard."

"Hoard?"

"Yes, they're worse than a *Tea Leaf*. Take anything that catches their fancy and hide it. They get very upset when you try to take it back, innit?"

Joy laughed. "We'll have to think of a good place to hide the key. Not at the Owlery or Maskall Farm."

Maisy nodded. That would be safer than carrying them around.

They started walking north to the Guardians and then the Forgotten Road where they would head west towards Roreford and then Fort Defiance. Some of the others were already there; beavering away at the fort and the Hornsby's were due later. The summer break had started and the Wyrde Warriors were out in the woods several days a week now, rather than the weekly half-day they had got in before.

"I am sorry about yesterday," Maisy blurted out suddenly.

"Me too," Joy nodded.

"It's just that…I was…" Maisy's words dried up.

"You were what?" Joy asked curiously.

Maisy pulled a series of faces. Then she turned red. "I was jealous."

"Jealous?" Joy's eyes grew wide as she tried to place this new information. "But, that means…"

"I don't fancy him or anything," Maisy sped into her sentence. "I just think he's nice and all, not like the other lads at school."

Joy laughed somewhat bitterly and Maisy looked at her questioningly.

"Then you've got a middling problem," Joy said. "Cause he fancies you, aint it. He said as much, *surelye*. You were all he wanted to talk about."

"He what?" Maisy was flabbergasted. "But I thought…the two of you…you and him…blooming heck…innit?"

"I thought so too," Joy said softly.

Maisy groaned as she understood the implication. Part of her wanted to skip down the path singing *Over the Rainbow*…

… part of her wanted to bombard Joy with questions as to what Leon had said and what intonation he had used and how he had looked as he said whatever he said including pauses and exclamations and…

…part of her told her not to be silly, Joy was having a laugh at her expense, it simply could not be…

…and part of her wanted to hug Joy and apologize because Maisy had a fair idea what her friend was going through.

"Bah!" Maisy summarised the medley that whirled inside her head in that one single word.

"*Zackly*," Joy agreed.

They walked on in silence until they came to the Forgotten Road and turned left.

"It gets complicated," Maisy emphasized her words by gesturing wildly.

"Middling complicated, *surelye*," Joy nodded unhappily.

"Well, we'll have to un-complicate things then, innit?" Maisy decided.

"How?"

"Well, you and I have to stay best mates, innit?" Maisy explained. "So we'll just Boycott boys."

"A Boycott…" Joy pondered.

"Yes, I even bet a girl invented that word. Keep boys in their cot, don't let them out till they learn how to behave," Maisy said. "We should listen to her, she probably went to a lot of trouble actually inventing a word for it and getting it in the dictionary, innit?"

"So we will Boycott boys," Joy cheered up. Then, in a doubtful voice, she added: "Do you think we can?"

Maisy frowned and then rubbed her forehead. She looked at the sky just in case the Jerries were invading then at the trees all around them. Then she said: "No."

Joy burst into laughter and Maisy joined her. It was not all that funny but the laughter got hold of them and whenever they managed to breathe in some air again they would glance at each other and start giggling uncontrollably until the peals starting ringing out loud and clear and they were blue in the face.

§ § § § § § §

By the time they crossed the Farisee Bridge Joy and Maisy were thoroughly exhausted and clutched at the bridge's stone parapet for support while they wheezed for breath.

"By *Geemeny*!" Joy exclaimed when they saw Roreford's clearing.

Maisy added a "Blimey" for good measure.

The Hornsby clan was in the middle of the clearing on the other side of the bridge; frolicking about as usual so that there seemed to be twice as many of them. In the middle of this haphazard revelry towered the unmistakable figure of Chunmaniye, dressed in his regular uniform this time. He had a rifle slung over his shoulder and wore ammunition pouches and a Brodie helmet.

"Hau mushkay," Chunmaniye greeted Joy and Maisy.

"Han khola," they responded in unison. Chunmaniye had taught them the greeting by the wishing tree.

"How do Joy? How do Maisy?" Leon smiled at them. He proudly added: "We ran into Chunmaniye on the way, he said he was scouting."

The boy looked slightly perplexed as both girls ignored him completely, an act made all the more obvious by the both of them looking away from each other. The look on his face was giggleworthy and that might set them off again.

"Have you been to Willikin's Drove, Chunmaniye?" Joy asked.

"We can show you our fort, innit?" Maisy looked delighted. Nobody objected. Fort Defiance Regulation Number Four stated quite clearly that bringing an adult to the fort would result in immediate execution of both adult and offender. They had unanimously agreed on the death penalty but somehow the Canadian giant did not quite fit into their understanding of a regular adult.

Chunmaniye readily agreed to come and they set off along the Acsa tributary of the Rore. Maisy, Joy and Leon walked next to Chunmaniye and the other Hornsby's trailed behind them.

"So what does Chunmaniye mean in English?" Maisy asked the soldier.

"Walking Tree," he rumbled.

The children all murmured their appreciation of the apt name.

"Does anybody call you Walking Tree?" Leon asked.

Chunmaniye nodded. "We are given our Lakota name and the reservation insists on a European name. But everybody in my unit calls me Walking Tree."

"What's your European name then?" Maisy asked.

"I will not tell you," Chunmaniye said. "Names are important but that name was made up by pen pushers for the benefit of paper stackers."

Maisy laughed.

"Do you mind if people call you Walking Tree?" Leon inquired.

"Not at all, some of my *Quebecois* buddies call me *Arbre-Qui-Marche*, that too is fine."

"I wish I was named after a tree, innit?" Maisy told nobody in particular.

"Kwebecwhat?" Leon pulled a funny face.

The girls ignored him.

"*Quebecois*," Chunmaniye answered. "French-speaking Canadians."

"Why would they want to speak French?" Leon looked confused.

Chunmaniye laughed. Maisy wanted to tell Leon about the French settlers they had learned about in geography but concluded reluctantly that a Boycott would have to include topographical information.

"So do you think in Lakota or English?" Maisy asked.

"In English when I am with my unit," Chunmaniye answered. "The second or two it takes to translate could make a big difference in combat. As a warrior my name is Walking Tree and I think and fight in English."

"Cor blimey," Maisy liked all the warrior talk. She would fight in English as well, she decided. Proper English, not that stuff Toffs spoke.

"But you think in Lakota at other times," Joy concluded.

"Lakota culture is based on being at one with the land around you," Chunmaniye answered slowly. "When I scout, on my own, as I do today, I find Lakota a better language for understanding what I see and how I can merge with it unseen. In the Wyrde Woods I think in Lakota and translate my thoughts to *Saglasa* words for you to understand."

"So when you think in Lakota," Maisy wanted to know. "Are we Maisy and Joy and…"

She stopped just in time and congratulated herself for remembering the Boycott. "Or do you translate our names into Lakota?"

Maisy was suddenly very keen on knowing the Lakota translation of her name. They could all use them as code names when they wanted to confuse all the Jerry spies in the Wyrde Woods.

Chunmaniye stopped walking and the three children followed suit. The rest of the Hornsby' kept a respectful distance apart from Leon's cousin Lizzie who drifted forwards to join them.

"I do not translate your names," Chunmaniye said.

"Oh," Maisy was disappointed.

"My thoughts have given you Lakota names instead," Chunmaniye said. "And that is how I think of you. Please do not think it rude, in my culture name-giving is considered a gift."

"Really?"

"Proper Lakota names?"

"What's mine?"

Maisy, Joy and Leon all spoke at once.

Chunmaniye chuckled. He laid a hand on Leon's shoulder. "You, my thoughts have named *Akichita Tashunka.*"

"Akichita Tashunka," Leon repeated slowly. "What does it mean?"

"Horse Warrior," Chunmaniye answered.

Leon began to beam and he smiled from ear to ear and secretly Maisy was pleased for him.

"And me?" Maisy asked eagerly.

"*Ehawee,*" Chunmaniye looked at her.

"Ehawee," Maisy repeated, savouring every syllable.

"It means 'laughing maiden," Chunmaniye explained.

Maisy smiled. She would have preferred it to mean Fighting Chief but Ehawee had a nice sound to it.

"How do I say thank you in Lakota, Chunmaniye?" Maisy asked.

"*Pilamaya,*" Chunmaniye answered.

"*Pilamaya,* Chunmaniye," Maisy put her hand on her heart and spoke solemnly.

"*Hohahe,* Ehawee," Chunmaniye mimicked her gesture. "You're welcome."

He looked at Joy who was regarding him with an expectant smile.

"You," Chunmaniye said, "my thoughts have called *Heechante*

"Heechante," Joy repeated slowly, tasting the words.

"It means 'Owl Heart'," Chumaniye explained.

At that moment Thallie chose to plummet through the foliage and then float serenely to Joy's shoulder, landing on the shoulder strap. Thallie swayed to and fro as she adjusted her footing and then almost comically rotated her head sideways to peer at Chunmaniye.

"*He-ay-hee-ee!*" Chunmaniye exclaimed. "The name was well-chosen."

"Kleak-kleak," Thallie agreed.

"*Pilamaya*," Joy smiled.

"I reckon you're a good Injun," Maisy beamed. Both Joy and Leon poked her in the side and Maisy yelped.

Chunmaniye laughed. "You watch too many movies, Ehawee."

"I'm sorry innit," Maisy was genuinely upset.

"It is said," Chunmaniye told her, "that there is a battle between two wolves inside of us all. One is Evil. It is anger, jealousy, greed, telling untruths and ego. The other is Good. It is joy, peace, love, hope, humility, kindness and searching for truth."

Maisy was intrigued by battling wolves. "Which wolf wins?"

Chunmaniye looked at her, smiled and then spoke: "The one you feed."

Maisy rubbed her forehead and then said: "*Pilamaya* Chunmaniye."

"So when you're in the Wyrde Woods,"Leon pondered. "We should call you Chunmaniye, and when you're outside of the Wyrde Woods we should call you Walking Tree?"

"I'd prefer it if you called me Chunmaniye," Chunmaniye looked at all of them earnestly. "It is what all my friends call me."

The children began to beam.

§ § § § § § §

The children did not just walk into Willikin's Drove, they insisted on stalking their way in, following an invisible foe who was making his way up the gorge along the river bed.

They said it would be a good exercise and Chunmaniye realised they were all looking at him expectantly because they were hoping to get instruction from him. He was happy to oblige, seeing it as a useful trade off. If it ever came to fighting in the Wyrde Woods his knowledge of the terrain could be crucial, the very reason the scouts were allowed solitary training exercises in the wider area around the base at Mordrove. These children seemed to know the woods inside out and were revealing its secrets to him.

Chunmaniye led the children along the animal tracks which skirted the gorge's steep forested banks and they carefully emulated his movements. The soldier had seen the entrance of the larger canyon from Roreford and marked it as a site to explore but he had no idea this smaller gorge was here though he had seen the small Acsa river marked on a map. His eyes drank in the scenery while his heart revelled in the song of the river. Sometimes it burbled contently but then it would rush by in a wash and or cascade into a constant din.

The party's progress slowed down as the sides of Willikin's Drove became steeper and reached higher, interspersed now and then with sandstone rock faces where they had to seek footholds on narrow ledges.

They came to an area where Willikin's Drove was all cliff-face and zigzagged in steep turns. They were forced to descend to the bottom of the gorge where they hopped from boulder to boulder until they came to a cluster of boulders which formed the shoulder of a small waterfall.

When they had climbed these they found themselves in a wide bowl on the other side of the falls. A third of this was made up by a wide crescent-shaped pool where the Acsa rested before plunging onwards. The loop within the crescent consisted of a steep shingle bank that led to a pine grove with an uncharacteristic amount of undergrowth. Puzzled, Chunmaniye examined the grove again.

"He-ay-hee-ee!" He called out appreciatively as he realised what he was looking at.

"Home of the Wyrde Warriors," Joy said proudly as they approached the grove. The undergrowth was in actual fact a curtain fence of interwoven sapling branches camouflaged with pine branches to break the line of the fence and suggest natural growth. There was a narrow opening in the fence, half-concealed by an extra length of wattle fencing. As they walked through Chunmaniye noted several well-concealed platforms of different sizes up in the pine-trees, good look-out points. Within the pine grove was a clearing and that was surrounded by an assembly of huts, some ramshackle affairs, others construed more solidly with branch roofs that had been covered with a layer of moss. At the centre of the clearing was a crude flagpole made from a slender birch stem. St George bunting had been wrapped around its top so that dozens of small red crosses on white fields swayed in the breeze. Behind the flagpole was a low rectangular shape. At first it looked like an oddly angular mound of grass which rose about four feet but then Chunmaniye noticed narrow horizontal slits at ground level, almost concealed by the grass that grew there. Walking around it he could see a stairway dug into the soil and leading down into an open space below. It was a bunker.

Various children started drifting into the clearing; some carried axes and spades or coils of ropes. A group of them carried bows and filled quivers.

"Well?" Maisy asked Chunmaniye expectantly as he came to a halt and surveyed the structures around the clearing. "What do you think of Fort Defiance?"

"I stand amazed," he answered truthfully, eyeing the bows and arrows with curiousity.

The children all grinned happily and Chunmaniye was reminded of what his grandfather Hehaka Sapa had said:

Grown men may learn from very little children, for the hearts of little children are pure, and, therefore, Wakan Tanka may show to them many things which older people miss.

"*Mayhap,* you can teach us more about archery?" Leon asked hopefully.

"Ey-hee!" Chunmaniye shook his head regretfully. "Alas, bows were discouraged on the reservations."

"Do you mean we have to teach you how to shoot a bow?" Maisy asked incredulously.

Chunmaniye grinned ruefully, he recognized the irony and thought it was a good joke.

"I would be much obliged," he admitted; eager to hold a bow and arrows in his hand.

"Well, you've come to the right place," Leon grinned happily.

Chunmaniye nodded solemnly. It occurred to him that he had indeed come to the place where he ought to be, led there by *Wakan Tanka* and his vision.

21. War Comes to the Wyrde Woods

"Me stockings itch." Maisy complained.

Her protest was ignored by both her grandparents. Fred and Betty Maskall were seated on the box of the small waggon. Maisy had been relegated to cargo bed. There was space enough for it was only half-laden. Maisy fretted and fidgeted as she watched the southern Wyrde Woods pass by. She had hoped to catch a glimpse of the three prominent hills she had seen now and then from locations along the Forgotten Road but the treeline blocked any wider view of the Wyrde Woods along this stretch of the North Woods Lane.

"I don't know why I have to wear my hair in a braid and a ribbon on me head," Maisy frowned. Gran had braided her hair and she could feel it tug at her scalp when she moved too fast.

"I think I have problems breathing cause of it, innit?…oh!"

Maisy swooned dramatically. "No air! I can't breathe, can I? Help me!"

"That'll be *enow* of your antics, lass," Gramps said in a friendly tone.

Maisy screwed up her face, it was one of her best performances of Vivien Leigh's interpretation of Scarlett O'Hara ever. If they were going to dress her up like a girl she knew how to play the part. It was a shame nobody around here went to the pictures much or else they would appreciate such a feat a bit more.

Maisy looked at the huddle of houses around a church as they passed. This was the village of Nickleby where the North Woods Lane ended as it met the main road leading east to the town of Odesby. They were bound for the market and Maisy was looking forwards to seeing Odesby as it was her first visit.

"But this is plain torture, innit?" Maisy decided to resume her protest to fill the time. The stockings did itch and the braid did pull at her scalp and the starched Sunday dress was uncomfortable and the ribbon was just plain awkward. She would have preferred to ride into Odesby on Spark in her day dress, with bare legs and her Royal Sussex Regiment blazer and hat on. She was Captain Robbins and Chieftess Ehawee, defender of the Wyrde Woods, not a prettified doll. She plucked at her braid, gave the ribbon a tug, scratched her itchy legs and picked at the stiff fabric of the dress.

"Enow," Gramps growled. *"*You're free to get off the waggon and walk back to the farm, Maisy. It's just as far from here as your school walk, *surelye."*

"I'm sorry." Maisy bowed her head. "I'd like to see Odesby, innit?"

"Townsfolk look down upon us," Betty explained. "They think we're little better than savages. We're proud of you and want to show you off a little, lass. It *baint* often we ask that of you."

"Zackly," Gramps nodded. "Just because we're lamentably tolerant to you swanning about the Wyrde Woods like a Wodewose, don't mean you can't look like a little lady every now and then."

"Little?" Maisy huffed indignantly.

Gramps brought his team to a halt, with a firm hold on the reins he turned around and looked Maisy straight in the eye. She shrunk and felt guilty before he even opened his mouth.

"You *ken* middling well what I meant, *surelye."* Gramps said, frowning.

Maisy nodded, feeling miserable. She had mouthed herself into trouble again. This time she had done a proper job of it though, risking her grandparents' esteem. She recognized she had been unfair in this and resolved instantly to never speak again; instead she would nod and shake her head and get by with non-verbal communication. It would be dead easy if she focused on it and help her avoid all kinds of trouble.

"Do you understand?" Gramps looked at her sharply.

Maisy nodded to show she fully understood.

"No more *moil* from you?"

Maisy shook her head. No more *moil*.

"Well that is a good thing, surelye," Gramps turned around and clucked at his team.

Maisy nodded her agreement. She thought the vow of silence was working rather well so far.

"Should we tell her?" Gran asked Fred Maskall as the waggon rumbled back into movement.

Maisy rubbed her forehead. *Tell her what?*

"Twould be akin to bribery," Gramps answered. "Maisy is old enough to know how to behave proper when needs be. Without us having to middling bribe her, *surelye."*

Bribe? Maisy's eyes grew wide. She nodded. Bribery sounded good.

"By *Geemeny*, you *maun* start suggesting I am the lenient one, Mus Maskall," Gran declared. "You're the one who lets the *chavee* get away with murder *dunnamy* times a day."

Maisy nodded sagely, Gran was quite right.

"*Jes-so*," Gramps said. "*Howsumdever*, I am about to start mending my ways."

Maisy shook her head. She did not think that was a good idea at all.

Gran turned her head to throw an apologetic glance at Maisy.

"I'm sorry, lass," she said regretfully. "Your *gaffer* can be as stubborn as a mule. Unaccountably stolid in his convictions, refusing to see the error of his ways."

Maisy pouted.

"Like a proper angel," Gran beamed approvingly and then turned her eyes front again.

Maisy nodded.

"Angel?" Gramps grunted. "She's as mischievous as a Pook making folk *afeared* in Shims Copses. Tis unaccountable. There's far too much of her *gammer* in the lass."

Maisy narrowed her eyes. Grip knew far too much.

"True," Gran nodded. "And as fond of dirt as the *Dobie* called Brownie-clod, I do reckon. She's like as *naun* to start pelting innocent Edgelanders with handfuls of mud just like that *Pook* does, *surelye*. She's turning into a middling *scaddle* just alike her *gaffer*."

The urge to steer the conversation into a more rewarding direction overcame Maisy's solemn vow. "I can behave, innit? Honest, Gramps. Honest, Gran. I'll be a good girl. A *bettermost chavee*, innit? I'll scratch along looking proper for a day. Cross me heart and hope to die."

Gramps reached into his pocket and took something out which he flicked at Maisy who clutched it in her fist mid-air. She opened her hand and grinned as she saw the shiny new tuppence.

"The reason your *gammer* wanted you to *dight-up*," Gramps said. Is *all-along-of* her wish to have you somewhat respectable on your visit to the sweet shop on the High Street."

"SWEET SHOP?! Cor blimey! Cracking! Smashing! Bloody brilliant!"

Both her grandparents chuckled and Maisy was suddenly lost in a world where she was surrounded by big glass jars filled to the brim with all the colours of the rainbow. She had not even known Odesby had a sweet shop or else she would have visited earlier. What would they sell? Jelly beans? Gobstoppers? Maisy made a list of her other favourites: Acid drops, mint humbugs, black jack chews, aniseed balls, pear drops, bull's eyes, brandy balls and chocolate drops.

Tuppence should buy her a fair selection. Two bags if they sold penny portions, but maybe four if they had ha'penny portions. Four would be good because she wanted to share some sweets with Joy too. She could finish half-a-bag in Odesby, a quarter-of-a-bag on the way back to Maskall farm and half-a-bag at Maskall farm. That left her quarter-of-a-bag as rations for the journey to the Owlery and…

Maisy frowned as she tried to keep track of the halved and quartered parts of ha'penny portions by counting her fingers. She definitely wanted to share some with Joy but there were the Wyrde Warriors to consider as well. Emergency rations as it were. Maybe Chunmaniye would like some sweets too, she was not sure if they had sweets in Canada, it might be an eye-opener for him. By the end of her calculations she had worked out that if she split four ha'penny portions into quarter parts each and limited herself to just one of those quarter parts for the combined time in Odesby and the return journey she might just have enough…Maisy frowned again, suspecting she had lost track of some of the sixteen quarter portions. She would have to label the bags just to be on the safe side. It was not inconceivable that she would arrive at the Owlery only to hand Joy an empty paper bag and that would not do at all.

To her left Maisy caught a glimpse of the broad Water Meadows and the surrounding Wyrde Woods, including the far away buffs of Hood's Gorge. Then her attention was drawn to her right; by sound rather than sight at first. The Nickleby Road ran parallel to a railway line and Maisy could hear the mechanical rhythm of a train engine chugging closer fast. She smiled as she saw the puffs of smoke ejected by the machine appear over a small copse of trees. The black engine appeared as the Maskall waggon was halfway across the road bridge over the Rore and the train thundered past on the parallel rail bridge. The engineer blew the whistle a few times as he crossed the bridge and Maisy loved the shrill wails. To her they were an epic soundtrack for the scene in which an intrepid explorer of unknown hinterlands returned to the civilised world. Perhaps she had travelled into the far corners of Africa to rescue Tarzan the Apeman. It was a shame about the Boycott for Leon would have made a real good Johnny Weissmuller. Maisy was sure she could pull off Maureen O'Sullivan's Jane.

"I wish you'd knock before you enter my boudoir," Maisy said in her best Toff English.

"Quiddy?" Gramps asked.

"A boo-what?" Gran asked.

"Sorry, I was thinking out loud, innit?" Maisy said quickly, determined to *bettermost* her way into that sweet shop.

She could see the rooftops and church spires of Odesby to her right now and warned herself to be ready for festive crowds celebrating her return. She practiced a ladylike wave, like the one Lady Priscilla had given Joy and Maisy by the Halfway Oak.

Traffic increased, there were lorries, a number of cars and a lot of farm waggons on the road. Maisy continued waving regally at all the drivers and carters, practising polite smiles. Gramps steered them past the railway station where the train they had just seen had come to a halt, its black engine now hissing like a landed dragon and its mechanical music just a slow thumping beat. It seemed like a living thing and exuded a power that fascinated Maisy and she stopped waving to stretch her neck to watch the machine as long as she could.

Gramps took a right past the railway station and they crossed the tracks and then rolled into a neighbourhood of small terraced houses, street after street of them, and Maisy was happy because it reminded her of London. Turning left they came to an imposing building draped with Union Jacks next to a pub called the Neverland Arms.

A number of large fields faced the Neverland Arms for the pub was on the very edge of Odesby and the Maskall waggon became one of many farm vehicles to pull onto the fields. It was as busy as one of Gran's bee hives; waggons pulling in, carters unhitching their teams and watering the horses, families unloading the goods they had brought in and then displaying them on broad wood planks resting on trestles.

Maisy helped Gran to unload the waggon while Gramps saw to the horses. Gran gave strict instructions as to what could be on display and what was to be kept back. The baskets of eggs and cuts of pork were to be picked up by designated shopkeepers during the course of the day. Like all farms Maskall Farm had significantly reduced their number of chickens and livestock. The Ministry of Agriculture and the Ministry of Food had ordered this because of the shortages of animal feed and a War-Ag Inspector came by once a month to inspect Maskall farm. Eggs and bacon were strictly rationed and their sale was regulated.

Gramps had chosen to keep as many pigs as he was allowed at the expense of his dairy herd, keeping just a few of his milk cows. Gran had joined a so-called pig club and this allowed for two extra porkers on the farm, though half of their product had to be yielded to the government at slaughter time. Two Maskall pigs now also resided at the Owlery as part of a Pig Club initiative, one ostensibly belonging to Sarah Whitfield and the other to the Rye family. The Maskalls would not see a lot of product from those pigs; half was owed to the government and half of what was left to the hosts. The Whitfields and Ryes would benefit though, and that, Gramps had explained to Maisy, made it worthwhile.

Sausages had not been rationed yet though many of those for sale had very little meat in them. The Maskalls made their own sausages to sell on market days and Gran told Maisy they would probably be sold out within an hour, for Maskall sausages were appreciated for their high meat content.

"Your *gaffer* is considered a magician *all-along-of* his ability to procure a *gurt* deal of meat for our sausages," Gran said with a wink Maisy could not place.

"How about these?" Maisy pointed at a few mystery packages left in the corner of the waggon.

"*Bettermost naun* draw attention to them," Gran answered. "Help me with these onions, instead."

The Maskall vegetables were Gran's responsibility and made up the greater part of the goods which the Maskalls were allowed to sell on the market. Gran had tripled the size of her vegetable patch and had appropriated a small field for growing onions. Maisy often helped Gran weed the vegetable patch and had also helped with the onion field. She had been surprised at how quick onions grew and amused at the pride Gran took in them. Maisy knew Gran had been clever. Before the war most onions were imported so cheaply that few were grown in Britain anymore but the imports had ceased altogether and onions had become unbelievably scarce. Gran chuckled with satisfaction as she predicted her onions would be sold out sooner than Gramps' magical sausages.

"As sweet and crispy as you could wish for," she said.

Many townsfolk came to the market early and Maisy was in her element, standing atop a crate as she loudly praised the quality of Maskall goods in proper English.

"All right me old *china*? No *godforsaken* or *borrow and beg* today, but we got *mae bangers* and *luverly* onions on the *apples*. Come have a *butchers*!"

"I do reckon your lass is running a fever," one of the buyers told Gran.

"She's from *Lunnon*," Gran explained.

"Ah! That's why she's speaking *oakum*. There's something of everything and everything of something in *Lunnon*, aint it so?" the buyer gave Gran a sympathetic smile.

Maisy could not care less, Gran and Gramps seemed happy to let her bang on and draw attention to their stall.

"We're *three stops down from Plaistow today*, practically giving it away! I aint taking the mickey, Guv, it's *plain brass. Luverly Robin veg! Luverly bangers!*"

Gran had been right, the Maskalls sold their entire stock of onions and sausages within the hour and the onions were the fastest to dwindle into depletion. Within two hours the crowd seemed to dissipate until there were but a few shoppers left and the next phase of the market day started: *scorsing* pleasantries.

Farmers and their wives took turns in attending their stall so the other was free to go for a wander and exchange greetings and news with fellows from all over the Edgelands. Maisy gathered that the Edgelands extended all around the Wyrde Woods, not just the western edge along the North Woods Lane. Gran was the first to go for such a walkabout.

"How do, Fred?" A deep voice asked behind Gramps and Maisy as they rearranged the remnants of their goods by the front of their display.

"Oh, he's scratching along," Maisy answered on Gramps' behalf as she turned.

She smiled when she discerned Jasper Hornsby's dapper frame and proud pencil-moustache. He was not wearing his coachman's hat this time and his thin dark hair had been oiled and combed to perfection. Next to him stood a much taller man, with a broad girth and a ready smile on his face. Unlike most of the farmers, who had all seemed to have made a point of dressing up for the occasion, he wore old green overalls and wellies. He had a mane of blonde-grey hair which was uncombed and looked a bit like a bird's nest. Maisy had met him before, he was Leon's father; Jeremy Hornsby.

"Jer, Jasper. How do?" Gramps eyes twinkled.

"Scratching along," both men answered in chorus. Maisy knew they were brothers but she marvelled at this because they seemed so unlike one another.

The three men launched into seemingly interminable farm chatter. Maisy stood by exerting all her energy into being a *bettermost chavee*; smiling sweetly and trying to pretend she found all the jabber interesting.

The Hornsby's spoke of Jenny Hornsby's recovery and the new paraffin range cooker in their kitchen as well as their portable petrol-powered generator which had allowed for the installation of electric lighting in their outbuildings so they could work late into the evenings. Gramps told them about his plans to generate silage using sugar beet tops and nettles as the basis.

"Where will you store it?" Jeremy Hornsby asked.

"Building two small silos with corrugated steel," Gramps answered.

"I thought you worked for Malheur Hall, Mus Hornsby?" Maisy asked Jasper.

"Four days a week," Jasper answered and then started telling Gramps about the new Percheron draught horses he had acquired. They were a *bettermost* team and if Gramps wanted any ploughing done Jasper would be happy to ride them over for a day. Gramps nodded gratefully. Jeremy then spoke of their efforts to fire their own roof tiles. They had been ordered to make the derelict buildings of the old Hornsby farm habitable once again to house evacuees.

"I've got my own evacuee," Gramps smiled and tried to ruffle Maisy's hair, apparently forgetting about the braid and ribbon.

"Oi, me ribbon!" Maisy protested.

"Sorry lass," Gramps chuckled.

"Twere a hard job keeping that kiln burning at a constant heat for two days and two nights," Jeremy said. "Needed non-stop attention, so it did."

"As did the little distillery," Jasper grinned. "The kiln had its benefits. I brewed a little hooch, Fred. I'll make sure you get a bottle or two of it."

Two children appeared on either side of the pair of Hornsby's. At first Maisy did not recognize them in their Sunday best and neatly combed hair. Her mouth nearly fell open when she realised it was Leon and Lizzie Hornsby, the eldest Hornsby chavvies.

"How do, Mus Maskall," Leon said. "Hullo, Maisy."

Maisy grinned awkwardly. The Boycott would be hard to maintain and she quickly decided that Odesby would have to be neutral territory. That still left a problem; what on earth do you say to a boy who was said to fancy you? She decided silence might be the best way to go. Officially she disapproved of his interest but she did not want to discourage him by being too much of a mouth.

"Leon, Lizzie," Gramps smiled at them. Then he looked at Jeremy and Jasper. "I forget which one belongs to whom."

"So do we," Jasper winked. "We stopped keeping track. There's only half-a-dozen of them but they make *enow* noise and *moil* to equal a score of Wodewoses, *surelye*."

"Tis unaccountable," Jeremy growled.

"As does Maisy-mine here. A score by herself alone, *surelye*," Gramps nodded.

Maisy did not bother denying it.

Gran came back and greeted the Hornsby's. This was occasion for an extension of *scorsing* pleasantries but less dull this time because Leon and Lizzie gathered around Maisy.

"I got tuppence for the sweet shop, innit?" Maisy said and beamed because she had found a good fancy-free subject to talk about.

"We got thruppence," Lizzie said, showing Maisy the twelve-sided coin.

"Howsumdever," Leon said. "Tis for all six of us."

"Do they sell ha'penny bags?" Maisy asked and was relieved the two Hornsby chavvies nodded.

"So that's ten ha'penny bags altogether," Maisy's eyes sparkled.

"Ten different kinds of sweets," Leon grinned. "We'll need to plan this *bettermost*. Swop some of ours for some of yours?"

Maisy started to outline her plans to divide each ha'penny portion into quarters and then they worked out how to divide the forty quarter parts between them.

"Tis a reversed miracle that you don't do well in middling mathematics at school, Maisy." Gran walked over to the children as they finished their calculations.

"This is important, Gran," Maisy said. "Triangles and missing numbers aren't, are they?"

"I *maun* prolong your sweet shop visit much longer, I can tell," Gran smiled. "There is one more chore, lass. *Bettermost* we do it now, so your *gaffer* has some time for a pint at the *alus*."

Maisy looked at the three men and saw that their eyes were increasingly focused on the farmers making their way to the Neverland Arms. She nodded her agreement.

"Can we help you, Goody Maskall?" Lizzie asked and Gran nodded.

Gran and Maisy gathered the mystery packages from the waggon and deposited them in baskets. Gran then led the three children, each carrying two baskets, down the road which ran past the Neverland Arms and the estate of small terraced cottages. The road crossed a canal and then they found themselves on Odesby's busy High Street. Maisy was in her element. Wolfden had a few shops scattered on the three main streets that led to Stone Square but to be on a busy street full of shops again was just wonderful. If she shut her eyes and listened to the crowd buzz and the sound of lorries and cars driving by it was almost as if she were back in London.

Gran led them into an alley right past a fancy restaurant and then through a gate so they stepped out in the backlot of the restaurant. Empty crates and piles of bottles were stacked up against the fences. Gran indicated a small table and the children put their baskets on them. Soon enough a harried looking bald man in kitchen whites stepped out.

"Goody Maskall, what have you for us today?" He inquired.

"Spring onions, sweet and crisp," Gran answered. "A smoked Maskall ham and the usual special delivery. Oh, and a basket of Whitfield summer truffles."

The man peered into the baskets and looked up happily. "A fine offer, shall we conclude the deal over a cup of tea in the kitchen?"

Gran nodded and turned towards Maisy. "I'll make my own way back to the market, Maisy. I'll need you to be back in two hours, no longer."

"Two hours," Maisy promised, trying to sound solemn. Sweet shop time at last!

Released from duty the three children chattered happily on their way to the sweet shop. It was a relief not to be Boycotting for a while, Maisy thought. Standing in front of the sweet shop they were suddenly quite happy to prolong sweet anticipation by studying the jars in the display window and reworking their master plan three times until they all agreed it attained perfection. Then slowly, almost reverently, they entered the shop, hearts lifted by the chiming bells on the shop door and the bounty of colour all around them. They stocked up and then Maisy proceeded to thoroughly confuse the shopkeeper with a long explanation of ten ha'penny portions divided into forty quarter portions to be divided into a 2:3 ratio. In the end the shopkeeper simply handed them a pile of extra bags and they left the sweetshop to squat down on the pavement and re-divide their accumulated spoils.

"Is it true that your dads don't know who belongs to who?" Maisy wanted to know.

"Of course not," Leon said. "I'm Jer's and Lizzie here is Jasper's."

"My mum passed away," Lizzie clarified. "So dad moved in with Uncle Jeremy and Aunt Jen. Aunt Jen treats us all like her own."

They were just finished when they noted that people were stopping all around them to look skywards.

Maisy, Leon and Lizzie stood up and walked towards the kerb of the pavement to see what had drawn everybody's attention.

"It's a Spit!" Leon exclaimed and Maisy nodded as the Supermarine Spitfire made its way over Odesby. It was high up, they could only hear a faint grumble. Then two specks appeared from the cloud cover high above the Spit and hurled towards the British plane. Maisy thought her heart would stop.

"Jerries!" She shouted at the RAF pilot but he had seen them and started a dive of his own to evade the enemy fighters which Maisy made out to be Messerschmitt 109E fighters. All three planes descended rapidly and it was clear the Messerschmitts had the edge over the Spitfire in this manoeuvre, they saw tiny flashes along the Messerschmitt wings and then heard the crackle of machine gun fire. The Spitfire shuddered as it was hit and then levelled out to head north, trailing a plume of black smoke.

Maisy's face fell and it was oddly quiet on the High Street as people watched the wounded Spit limp away. Then she frowned. The Messerschmitts made no attempt to pursue their damaged quarry, instead they hurled further downwards and the noise of their engines became louder and louder. The planes pulled up at the last possible moment and before Maisy could even comprehend what her eyes told her they were level with the top of the ruins of Odesby castle at the far end of the High Street. The machine guns sounded much louder now and were interspersed with louder bangs as the Luftwaffe pilots used their cannons too as they thundered over the High Street. Maisy could see the impact of bullets and cannon shells; multiple trails of miniature fountains of debris and dust. The crowds scattered, seeking cover.

The children dived into an alley and turned immediately to watch the planes roar by over their temporary patch of High Street. They were stunned but then Maisy's eye was drawn towards a shiny object on the street. It was a cannon shell and she ran out of the alley to claim her prize.

"Maisy, be careful," Leon shouted after her but the planes had reached the end of the High Street already and seemed to be pulling up.

Maisy squatted by the shell and tentatively brought a fingertip close to it to establish if there was any heat.

"Maisy!" Lizzie shouted, but Maisy ignored her, transfixed by the gleaming shell. Then the rumble of engines sounded closer again and Maisy looked up to see that the Messerschmitts had turned and were coming in for another run, single file this time. Already the first pilot was firing his machine guns and cannon. Maisy's mouth fell open. She could see the pilot's head in the cockpit and it seemed to her that he was looking right at her as he squeezed his triggers and tell-tale plumes burst from the road surface, ever so quickly racing towards Maisy in the middle of the road.

Then she felt two arms seize her and roughly drag her to the other end of the street. There she was thrown down behind a parked car and both Maisy and Leon – for it was he who had dashed out of the safety of the alley to grab her – contracted, making themselves as small as possible. Maisy felt the draft of the first Messerschmitt as it passed in a tumultuous roar. She edged backwards against Leon and he threw an arm around her. Then the second Messerschmitt hit the fuel tank of a car some twenty feet away and there was a loud swoosh as the car was enveloped in a blaze. Maisy could feel the hot blast of air but kept her eyes shut for a trail of bullets now shattered shop windows on their side of the street and a rain of glass fragments showered upon the two children.

The second strafing run was over in seconds though these seemed to last forever. None-the-less, Maisy and Leon remained where they were, just in case the planes returned for another pass.

"Well this is cosy, innit?" Maisy remarked. It was a scene fit for the pictures really and she had never been this close to a boy before. She was fairly sure that she had broken all rules of a Boycott – even one that was temporarily suspended – and then regretted the words for Leon pulled his arm away and scrambled upwards, blushing with embarrassment. The engines of the Messerschmitts faded as the pilots headed south for the Channel and Maisy stood up as well. People slowly started emerging from shops or scrambling up from the pavement and road. They seemed dazed and confused as they took in the columns of smoke rising from vehicles that had been hit and heard the crunch of glass beneath their feet.

Lizzie ran across the street to hug Leon. Maisy growled at a townie who scurried towards the cannon shell she intended to claim as her prize. She made to move towards him but was driven back by a plume of filthy foul-smelling smoke from the nearest burning car.

"Drat and double-drat," Maisy grimaced.

"Are you alright?" Lizzie asked with concern in her voice.

"Yes," Maisy smiled. She would not have minded a third strafing run, really, just to savour the fleeting intimacy with Leon a bit longer and she surprised herself with the thought. "I suppose that was very silly of me, thank you Leon."

"It was silly, *surelye*." Lizzie scolded Maisy. "Twere unaccountable."

Leon just shrugged like it did not matter and assumed an expression of disinterest.

The children collected their sweets from the alley where they had set their bags down and started making their way back to the market along the dishevelled High Street. They remained silent, still stunned by the sudden course of events. War had come to the Wyrde Woods at long last, just as everybody had started to think there was not all that much to be worried about after all.

"Will you look at the middling state of us?" Leon grumbled. Maisy looked down and was horrified to discover that her dress and stockings were torn, stained with dirt and darkened by smoke. She had managed to lose her ribbon too, somewhere in the fury of the Luftwaffe attack. Both she and Leon were also covered in scratches made by flying glass. Maisy bit on her lip and felt her belly sink at the thought of the disappointment on the faces of Gran and Gramp. She had been utterly sincere in her determination to be a *bettermost chavee* but forgotten it all in the excitement about the sweet shop and the suspended boycott and had clearly failed miserably. Nor had she been particularly heroic in this first encounter with the Jerries. She shuddered when she recalled the face of the Luftwaffe pilot, it had seemed so…personal. As if he had been specifically intending to mow Maisy Robbins down. They must have heard about the Royal Sussex Regiment Special Detachment in Berlin.

She looked up to see Gramps and the Hornsby men pounding down the street; frantic worry on their faces.

Fred Maskall came to a halt just in front of Maisy, staring at her as he shook his head in disbelief.

"I'm sorry, Gramps," Maisy squeaked as he took in her dishevelled state. There was little left of the *bettermost chavee* he had lifted onto the waggon that morning. "I didn't mean…"

Gramps swept her into his arms.

"Maisy," he said, his voice choked with emotion. "I thought…I was…Oh my sweet girl, my little girl."

Maisy could barely breathe because he held her so tightly and then she clasped him back with all her might and, feeling safe at last, began to cry.

22. Betrayed

"Let's *gwoan* swimming," somebody suggested.

It was a hot sweltering day and everyone was tired after a ruthless drill exercise concocted by Captain Robbins. It had started with an inspection parade by Colonel-in-Chief Whitfield and then a division in two teams to practice Urban Combat in the ruins of Roreford. That had generated into an all-out brawl with impromptu sword-fighting using sticks and wrestling matches after the sticks had been reduced to tatters.

The Wyrde Warriors looked at Joy expectantly. The Colonel let her eyes wander, noting the green and brown smudges on clothes, cuts and scrapes on knees and elbows and damp evidence of perspiration. She decided it was far too hot for the Germans to invade and some recreation time was in order.

"To the Fey's Pool," she ordered.

The Wyrde Warriors cheered loudly and embarked on an immediate disorderly march towards the Fey's Pool by the Falls. They chattered happily though Maisy was remarkably silent and her eyes conveyed worry.

They reached a place where the path forked, left leading up and right leading down. The Fey's Pool was close now, the Falls already a steady roar in their ears and Leon waved his arms over his head.

"Who's for the dive point?" He hollered happily and the elder and more daring children cheered and followed him as he took the left path. Joy led the younger ones to the right and Maisy followed. This path circled down until they came to the south bank of the Fey Pool, a large forest lake into which the Rore crashed and rested before continuing its journey south to the sea.

To Maisy's surprise the younger kids stripped entirely and ran into the water screaming with delight. Joy was in less of a hurry, pulling her dress over her head slowly.

"What about bathing suits?" Maisy asked.

Joy dropped her dress on the ground and looked amused.

"Bathing what?"

"Clothes for swimming in, innit?"

"Clothes to swim in?" Joy laughed. "Are they waterproof?"

There were loud whoops from the point of the sand-stone cliff where it was safe to jump into a deep part of the Fey's Pool, about fifteen feet below the point where Leon and others now appeared, stark naked like the rest, and launched themselves into the air, legs and arms clawing at the air till they disappeared in mighty splashes.

"No, they get wet," Maisy shrugged.

"Then what is the point?" Joy shook her head at the *Sheere-folk* foolery and waded into the water. Maisy made no attempt to follow and Joy turned when she was knee-deep into the water to give her a quizzical look.

Maisy returned it with an awkward shrug.

"Are you *timmersome*, Maisy?" Joy asked.

"Yes. No." Maisy answered. "I..."

Joy waded back to the shore. "We're friends, right? That means you can tell me, aint it so?"

"I can't swim," Maisy looked at the ground with embarassment.

"But you said you lived near the Thames, in *Lunnon*?"

"You'd be a right *nickey*...I mean *chuckle-headed* to swim in the Thames," Maisy laughed.

"But...tis a river, aint it?" Joy was surprised.

"Maybe upstream," Maisy said. "At the Isle of Dogs it's brown and murky; floating mud with turds in it and a lot of other things besides."

Joy shook her head at this new *Lunnon* oddity. "Well, it *baint* a problem, Maise, I can learn you how to swim."

"Really?" Maisy asked in disbelief. She looked longingly at the surface of the Fey's Pool which was filled with splashing and gleeful children. It looked like a great deal of fun.

"You'll be swimming like a fish afore the hour's up," Joy promised.

Maisy grinned happily.

§ § § § § § §

They practically had to drag Maisy out of the water for she refused to leave it even after the others had grown tired and waded ashore to collapse on the soft grassy bank opposite the Falls and bask in the sun. When Maisy had joined them with extreme reluctance they dressed and formed a circle to hold council.

"We're missing some of the Wolfden chavvies," Joy opened the meeting.

"On account of those rat-arse-faces, innit?" Maisy said with vehement outrage.

The Hornbsy's looked puzzled at that. Joy explained: "The Wolfden Parish Christian Ladies Committee has been making house calls."

"That turd Bill Hare told them," Maisy supplied.

"I don't understand," Leon frowned. "What's this with a committee?"

"Gossips in Wolfden," Joy said. "Been worried about proper Christian morals and manners. Say we don't have them."

"They have been visiting the homes of Wyrde Warriors in Wolfden and our part of the Edgelands," Maisy said.

"Preaching at parents. Some have told their *chavees* they can't play with us *naun* more. Katie told us, she was there when they came," Joy added.

"Is that why Katie aint here?" Lizzie Hornsby asked. She was just a year older than Katie and the two had struck a chord and became friends.

"*Naun*," Joy shook her head. "Katie told us she would still come. I don't know where she is now. Her mum and dad think the world of Mus and Goody Maskall in any case, they didn't have much time for the committee. But other parents…"

There were downcast eyes at that and a surly mood pervaded the moot.

"Well, I think it's downright unaccountable that this Bill Hare has gone and told grown-ups," Leon suddenly said angrily.

Everybody nodded, Bill had broken an unspoken code. You never told adults; never. The only possible outcome was that adults would spoil the fun. All the Wolfden *chavees* knew Bill had a gang and a fort somewhere and it was typical of the bully to deny others the same, that they had expected. For him to inform his mum and have her interfere…

There were looks of anger around the circle.

Just then Katie came dashing from the path to Roreford. She was running as fast as she could and she sprawled onto the grass just before the gathering, gasping for breath.

Lizzie beat Maisy to Katie's side and helped her sit up. Katie was still heaving as she sought to find her breath.

When she did, she panted: "They're coming!"

A dozen questions were asked at once. Joy jumped to her feet.

"Quiet!" She ordered, and then looked down at Katie. "Who's coming Katie?"

"Bill Hare, and his dad, and his uncle," Katie spoke urgently. "And a bunch of their mates. And Lord Malheur on a horse."

"Coming here?" Maisy asked concerned.

Katie shook her head. "Geoff is there too!"

There were looks of dawning horror. Geoff was the West Londoner who had joined the Wyrde Warriors.

"They're heading for Fort Defiance," Katie added and then relapsed into silence.

Maisy, Joy and Leon looked at each other.

"If they follow the gorge we can beat them to the fort," Joy said.

"We'll use the bows and pepper them with arrows," Maisy declared fiercely.

"Don't be daft," Leon shook his head. "Shooting at Jerries is one thing, we can't go killing Englishmen."

Maisy shrugged, she supposed not.

"The bows and arrows!" Joy suddenly said.

They all felt their blood drain from their faces. Their complete arsenal was at Fort Defiance, and the bows and arrows would not be easy to replace.

"Leon, Joy, Lizzie," Maisy named the eldest and strongest of them. "Let's go. The rest of you, get home, as quick as you can. They're might be all over the woods after they're done at Willikin's Drove."

She gave Katie a worried glance.

"I'll take them through Shims Copses," Katie nodded, she had begun to lose her inherant fear of that part of the woods.

The four children pounded up the path to Roreford at dizzying speed. They turned left before they reached the ruined village, following deer trails which led steadily upwards south of the Acsa. Geoff had only ever been to Fort Defiance by way of the gorge and that route was slow going, preferred by the *chavees* for the very reason that it was an adventure in itself. The deer trails were boring in comparison, offering little challenge besides a few steep bits and leading through dense forest where there was little to see.

Right now it gave them hope though, hope that they would reach Fort Defiance before the invaders did and when they arrived at the bluff overlooking the bowl where the Acsa looped around Fort Defiance there was no sign of unwelcome visitors yet. They scrambled down the steep slope of the bluff and then waded across the Acsa. Just as they walked through the entrance they could hear voices in the gorge behind them.

"Quick!" Leon hissed and they dashed to the corner hut where they had stocked their arsenal. Leon was in first and started handing the bows and filled quivers out. There were loud calls from the boulders by the small waterfall as men started scrambling up and the children quickly divided the bows and quivers amongst them and then ran to the much smaller gateway at the far end of Fort Defiance. There they scrambled through the undergrowth until they reached a small track which zigzagged up the steep face of Willikin's Drove. Though they were concealed from view now by the canopies of trees which grew there they still hunched over making themselves as small as possible. A crow alighted from his tree croaking a protest at the strange view of four hunched creatures intruding his territory looking for all the world like strange hedgehogs with bow staves and arrows portruding from their backs and arms in all possible directions.

Once they had reached the top of Willikin's Drove they ran into the forest for a few hundred yards until they reached the hidden empty weapons cache which Leon had built there and which only the four officers of the Wyrde Warriors had known about. It was not much more than a hole in the ground with oiled canvas sheets inside and a camouflaged trapdoor made of laced branches but once the bows and arrows were placed inside and covered with sheets and the door was shut and given an extra covering of loose leaves it was impossible to see there was anything out of the ordinary there.

The four children carefully made their way back to Willikin's Drove and found a hidden vantage point from where they could look down at Fort Defiance.

§ § § § § § §

Sir Mortimer's men were busy pulling at the bunker roof which was beginning to to shift in response to their efforts. Bill Hare and some of his friends were kicking or pulling the last of the smaller huts apart. The flagpole had already been toppled and the St George's flags had been trampled into the ground.

The men had brought shovels and spades and at Sir Mortimer's direction began to dig into the earth around the bunker and the sturdier huts which had proved harder to pull down.

"Oh, *naun*," Joy groaned as she saw all their work undone; Fort Defiance demolished. She was overcome with misery and reached out to the nearest person, who happened to be Leon. He responded by putting his arm around her shoulder and pulled her closer. Joy turned her head towards him and rested it on his shoulder. She let out a sob of despair.

"They're looking for the keys, Joy, innit?" Maisy said in a somber tone. Then she looked sideways to see Joy leaning against Leon and her face turned to thunder.

"Wait a minute," Leon pushed Joy away. "What keys are you on about?"

Joy swallowed. She and Maisy had debated telling Katie, Leon and Lizzie about the keys and Sir Mortimer and his mysterious guest. They had decided that those three needed to know but had not yet found the time needed to paint a picture of the convoluted interests and participants involved. There had been the Boycott to complicate matters as well.

"They are looking for something specific, aint it?" Leon looked angry. "Something you two know about?"

"There's are some keys, innit?" Maisy kicked angrily at some dirt. "Sir Mortimer and his German spy wanted it, but we got it instead."

"We were going to tell you," Joy told Leon.

"What the *pize* are you two playing at?" Leon demanded. "Risking all our efforts for one of your games? Do you know how long it takes to get here and back from the farm?"

Joy felt guilty, she had not thought about it from that perspective before. "It's not a game, Leon," she tried to assure him.

"If you want a gang, your own bloody little army, you've got to tell us this stuff," Leon's eyes blazed. "What if we had been in the fort when they arrived? What would they have done?"

Maisy shrugged. A painful thrashing would probably have been in order.

"Instead you have all your little secrets," Leon spat on the ground. "And then spend days ignoring me like I don't bloody well exist."

Joy was shocked at his vehemence, the Boycott had mostly been a giggle she thought.

"You did," Lizzie took her cousin's side and looked at Maisy and Joy accusingly.

"I'm out," Leon shook his head. "I've got other things to do."

He turned and strode away, Lizzie hurrying to catch up with him.

Joy felt miserable and looked at Maisy for support.

"You bloody cow," Maisy hissed at her.

"Maisy?" Joy was perplexed at the sudden ferocity.

"We had a Boycott, innit?" Maisy lip trembled. "And then I don't look for a minute and you're all over him. Cow."

"Maisy," Joy pleaded. "You don't…"

"Oh yes I do," Maisy turned her eyes skywards and placed the back of one of her hands on her forehead and said dramatically. "Oh, Leon, I'm swooning. Oh Leon, hold me!"

Joy flared up. "Is that all you can think about, Maisy? Look down there. Look at our fort."

They both looked down. The men not digging were dragging the branches and logs of the huts towards the exit and the steep shingle beach. There was already smoke rising from two fires there.

"A bloody waste of time, innit?" Maisy said bitterly.

"We'll build a new fort," Joy suggested with hopeful desperation in her voice. "A *bettermost* one that *naun* can find."

Joy saw a tear well up in Maisy's eye and was about to step forwards to her when the *Lunnon* girl turned around and walked away.

"Maisy?" Joy called softly.

Maisy did not answer, she found a course heading towards the North Woods Lane and kept walking, leaving Joy alone.

Alone in the Wyrde Woods like she had always been.

Joy kept her head raised to salvage some pride and started to make her own way home, much of it by familiarity for she could barely see through the haze of tears that filled her eyes.

Everything had come undone.

23. Powwow

"What's been bothering that lass?" Fred Maskall frowned as he watched Maisy ride off on Spark. "She's been hanging around the farm moping like a little storm cloud. I aint seen Sarah's *chavee* around for some time either. Have they fallen out?"

"Tis *naun* a thing for you to be middling worried about, Fred." Betty stood by his side.

Fred assumed a dubious expression. "I thought I had reached her, Betty. I was hoping she'd come and tell me if there were *moil*."

"Aye, and she'll come to you when there's *oakum* in the Wyrde Woods to be discussed," Betty said. There was a tone of satisfaction in her voice which made Fred look at enquiringly. "And to others when she needs a woman's advice."

"A woman's advice? You spoke to her?"

"She spoke to me, when she was lending a helping hand in the vegetable patch *disyer* morning," Betty chuckled. "The lasses don't see eye to eye about a lad, that's all."

"A lad?" Fred spoke sharply. "Is it that Hornsby? Tis always a Hornsby, aint it so? I'll *gwoan* have a word with the lad."

"You'll do *naun* such thing, Fred Maskall," Betty retorted. "Do you *naun* remember the last time, with Liz? You traversing the Wyrde Woods to bellow like a *scrowse* at the lad's farm in the dead of night? Challenging him to a duel? A duel of all things, Fred Maskall! You scared that poor lad half to death and Liz wouldn't speak to you for weeks on end, she were that furious with you."

Fred scratched his head.

"My recollection of that is hazy," he said. "I remember poor Liz was heartbroken."

"*Oakum!* Liz was being dramatic about it," Betty shook her head. "Twere just a dance at the harvest fair and then the lad chose to dance with another. Twould have been forgotten in a day or two if you hadn't barged in baying for the lad's blood."

Fred shrugged, "Maisy seemed happy being friends with Sarah's lass."

Betty laughed. "Closer than sisters they are and you can't break those apart. Tis all child's play, Fred. Who likes who though Maisy swears she doesn't like him but just doesn't want Joy to like him or him to like Joy though she don't mind him liking her. I don't even think the poor lad had anything to do with it."

"She's all unhappy and looking as *tessy* as that pony of hers," Fred protested.

"These are things they need to discover and solve for themselves," Betty tutted. "All you can do is give advice if they happen to ask for it."

"And what did you advise her?"

"That menfolk are foolish and useless," Betty answered. "Most definitely not worth losing friends over."

Fred nodded. "Well spoken. You're right as always, my nightingale."

"And you," Betty nudged him. "After all these years you're still surprised to find that I am right. Tis unaccountable. You ought to know better by now."

Fred smiled. He did but he was not going to tell Betty that just yet.

§ § § § § § §

After more than a week of self-imposed exile at Maskall Farm Maisy decided that there was no reason to hide herself away. After all, it was hardly her fault that Joy was wrong and Maisy was right. There had been a dogfight between two fighters over Maskall Farm that morning, the planes twisting and turning to get a shot at each other before they had roared away over the horizon. It had been a reminder that an invasion was imminent and Maisy had not been on patrol for ages.

As she rode up the North Woods Lane she decided it would be best to patrol the Forgotten Road to Roreford as well. She had sworn a solemn oath to defend the Wyrde Woods after all. She would just have to do it by herself if the others insisted on being unpatriotic rotters. She would definitely not go up to the Owlery. She was not looking for Joy. It would be different if she ran into Joy along the Forgotten Road, of course. In that case it would be mighty uncivil not to give Joy a chance to apologise even though Joy should have really come to Maskall Farm to apologise already.

The Wyrde Woods were indifferent and devoid of visible human life. It was the first time Maisy did not enjoy one of her patrols as her mood sank deeper into misery. The sight of Roreford filled her with more gloom as happy memories flitted by. Traversing the Farisee Bridge on her way to adventures with Joy. Being ambushed by Apaches and that marvellous chase scene that followed with Leon.

"I'm not lonely, cause I got you Spark," she said to break the silence. "It's still fun here, innit?"

Spark snorted.

"You're right," Maisy pouted. She set course for Willikin's Drove to go to the bluff where she had last seen the others. There was no sign of life there either and the pine grove below looked a mess; cratered by churned earth and littered with the smaller hut materials which had not made it to the bonfires on the beach.

It was bloody unfair, Maisy reflected. It was not just the huts because those could be rebuilt nor was it all the time they had invested in building Fort Defiance. What was lost was more abstract. Their activities had whirled them into a vortex of energy, a collective feeling that they were part of something larger than themselves and a sense of companionship.

Maisy grunted with disgust at herself as she felt a tear well up and quickly wiped it with the blue sleeve of her cavalry blazer. Then, without giving the demolished remnants of Fort Defiance another look, she urged Spark back to Maskall Farm.

§ § § § § § §

"How do, Maisy-mine?" Fred had emerged from one of the stables with a wheelbarrow full of fouled straw to see his granddaughter ride into the farmyard. "Did you have a good time with Joy?"

"Couldn't find her, could I?" Maisy said, clearly still in a surly mood.

"Well, that's a shame, so tis," Fred shook his head in sympathy.

"No it aint," Maisy said with exaggerated conviction. "I don't want to speak to her, innit?"

"Well," Fred was puzzled. "Then it was good you didn't find her, I suppose."

"Yes. Maybe. No," Maisy was all desperation – showing a young vulnerability which made Fred's heart ache for her. She was about to speak, then shook her head. "It don't matter, Gramps, it's complicated, innit? You wouldn't understand."

Fred raised his eyebrows. The child was already using that haughty dismissive tone womanfolk reserved for telling men they did not understand female *moils*. In his experience that mainly meant he would not understand what all the fuss was about, so Maisy was probably right. He sighed, why were *chavees* forever in a hurry to grow up? It was not all it was made out to be; for one the memories of a magical summer in the woods would start to fade until it was but a distant recollection.

"I suppose so, Miss Robbins," Fred said. "You'd best see to Spark afore your *gammer* rings the bell for tea."

"Thank you, Gramps," Maisy answered with a sudden dignity that was partially spoiled by a particularly foul expression which Spark directed at Fred.

He shook his head again and picked up his wheelbarrow.

§ § § § § § §

Joy had withdrawn into herself and when her mum had started to make enqueries she had hidden herself in the Owlery books. She replaced the sudden emptiness which left her feeling devastated with the determination to carry on the quest she had once shared with Maisy. She had been sure that Sir Mortimer had been after the Owl Man but she started to encounter other shadowy hints about dark things in the Wyrde Woods which made her question that notion. Joy started writing down everything she remembered from her reading of *Secree of the Wirdewode* and cross-checked that with the information in the Owlery books. It left her feeling distinctly uncomfortable and that was enhanced by the realisation that struck her again and again. She would have to face it alone. Alone again.

It was a gut-wrenching shock that would send her tumbling down an endless pit in a free-fall. She fought the howling emptiness and focused on her notes and books again. She was glad it was summer holidays which meant she could postpone returning to school to see Maisy chatting and laughing with the new friends the *Lunnon* girl would undoubtedly make. It was not something Joy felt she could do as readily. For now though, there was work to be done.

Joy decided that she would visit Tuckersham Church to see if the location would shed any hints as to the secrets it held. She would go that very night. She surprised herself somewhat when she felt no apprehension at the prospect of visiting Tuckersham Church on her own in the dark. The fears which ate at her resolve all involved Maisy and the Wyrde Warriors.

There was a sense of loss which almost drove her to Maskall Farm to seek out Maisy but it was countered by a sense of pride which told her Maisy would have to come to the Owlery first.

"Kleak-kleak," Thallie shook her head.

§ § § § § § §

Chunmaniye sat with his back against one of the Guardians, the triple row of standing stone sentinels which seemed to form the ritual passage between north and south in the Wyrde Woods. He had chosen one of the outer stones which marked the north entrance as was befitting for a Hunkpapa and lit a small fire. It barely gave off any warmth but that was not the point and Chunmaniye had wrapped a blanket around himself as he stared into the flames and thought about the vision he'd had as a young boy. After all those years the time had come. Chunmaniye had no doubt as to who would soon come gliding by in the midst of the night, moving as lightly as an owl feather.

Now, as he studied the flames, Chunmaniye's last doubts melted away.

Sharing the secrets Hehaka Sapa had taught him with outsiders was something that had bothered him. On the one hand Chunmaniye was Canadian and that meant a special bond with the *Saglasa*. To think of England as a motherland had always seemed surreal and abstract to Chunmaniye but it was part of being Canadian so he accepted it. Sensing the connections in these Wyrde Woods had been a revelation to him and made that acceptance easier. Chunmaniye was also Lakota. His own motherland had disintegrated and was fragmented in reservations on two sides of an artificial boundary pencilled in on a map. However, from what Heechante had told him the *Saglasa* had more in common with the Lakota than Chunmaniye could have possibly imagined. Those *Saglasa* who were aware of *Wakan* at any rate. It would be good to speak to Hehaka Sapa about this. Right now though, Chunmaniye was certain that his grandfather and spiritual mentor would assure him that following his vision was the right thing to do.

A small sound brought Chunmaniye out of his thoughts and he lifted his head. He could be mistaken, misled by the rustling of a small animal in the woods behind him or an *iktomi*, one of the trickster spirits which he sensed populated these woods in abundance. He knew he was not mistaken though and marvelled at the stealth that was being used as somebody tried to creep past the Guardians some twenty feet into the woods. Chunmaniye nodded approval; she was curious otherwise she could have simply doubled her distance and passed by unnoticed. She was also alert, she had not just strolled up the path from the former holy place which fascinated her so which meant she had spotted the fire and taken precautions. The soft rustling ceased. When it resumed her pace was far slower, stalking Chunmaniye's Guardian with very slow careful movements. Had there been a breeze strong enough to rustle leaves and twigs he would not have heard her approach the dim red glow of his fire and he was impressed.

"*Hau mushkay*, Heechante," Chunmaniye said loudly.

He grinned as the noise stopped, all sound as the girl even seemed to hold her breath for a moment. Then, dropping all stealth, she made her way out of the forest fringe and stepped into the dim glow; barefoot, in her white dress with her owl wings attached. She had painted a circular pattern on each cheek with blue paint and this intrigued him for she was not engaged in the child's play she had been when he had first encountered her outside his dreams.

"*Han kholá*, Chunmaniye," Heechante said. "How did you *ken* I was there?"

"You may move as silently as warrior on the warpath but not quite as silent as an owl on the prowl," Chunmaniye answered. "And I have the ears of a *tokalu*, a fox. You wear face paint?"

"Woad, from a local plant. It has…certain qualities," Heechante answered and then in a slightly suspicious tone asked: "How did you *ken* it were me?"

"You do not know, Heechante?" Chunmaniye was surprised until he recalled Heechante, for all her strong medicine, was a child who had only just begun to walk her path.

Thallie appeared in his vision as a blurry pale streak behind Heechante. When the owl reached their dome of light she slowed above the girl and adjusted her wings rapidly as they beat up and down to perfect Thallie's landing on the girl's shoulder. Thallie folded her wings and closed her eyes instantly, her white oval face patch thus appearing like the faceless countenance of a spirit.

266

"*He-ay-hee-ee!*" Chunmaniye exclaimed, impressed once again by the companionship of the two.

"I don't *ken*," Heechante shook her head but her suspicion was waning as fast as her curiosity was waxing.

"The *Wakan Tanka*, the Great Spirit sent me," Chunmaniye said earnestly. "I have been waiting for you, young Heechante."

"The *Wyrd*," Heechante answered with awe, beginning to understand.

"*Ai*, the Lakota *Wakan* and the *Saglasa Wyrd* are much the same," Chunmaniye nodded. He gestured at the ground opposite him where a blanket lay waiting for his guest. "Will you share the light of the fire with me? *Oo-oohey*, it is time. We have much to speak of."

Heechante lowered herself down, folded the blanket around her back so as not to disturb Thallie and then looked at him expectantly. "What do you want to talk of, Chunmaniye?"

"Darkness," he held her eyes with his so he could read her response in the light of the small beacon he had lit.

Heechante narrowed her eyes as if to scrutinise him anew.

"You sense darkness?" She asked carefully.

Chunmaniye stopped himself from saying that right at that moment he sensed it in her heart even. He had hoped that the child would have been granted some years to grow stronger in spirit before her strength would be tested but it was clear as daylight to him now that this fledgling had already spread her wings; sampling her abilities to weave the *Wakan* to designs of her own. Just as she had in his vision.

"I sense a lot of things," he said softly. "I just wanted to be a warrior, but..."

"I understand," Heechante said and Chunmaniye believed that she did.

"We believe that we follow a journey in our lives," Chunmaniye began to speak. "Though we may stray from it, or be distracted from it or forget our purpose along the way."

"We believe in such a journey too," Heechante nodded. "The Norns, the three sisters of fate, weave our possible paths below a tree..."

Chunmaniye looked up. *The tree of life?*

"The tree is called Yggdrasil, and sometimes the Heart Tree," Heechante seemed to have read his mind. "Those who *ken* the *Wyrd* will recognise when they arrive at a crossroads and have the power to determine the direction of their path. Others are swept along."

"One must be strong, in body and in spirit, to use the *Wakan* in such a manner," Chunmaniye said. "Our *Wicasa Wakan*, the wise ones, are that but we believe that even an accidental brush with the *Wakan* make a person *Heyoka*, infected with the Spirit of Chaos."

"*Heyoka*," Heechante repeated the word carefully.

"*Ai*, they say that even dreaming of the *Wakinyan*, the great feathered thunderbird, is enough to make someone *Heyoka*."

"Great feathered thunderbird," Heechante whispered. "I have dreamt of such a one."

"I was afraid you had," Chunmaniye said.

"Why afraid?" Heechante looked at him sharply with challenge in her eyes.

"*Heyoka* is two-faced, double-edged. We believe that those with the owl totem are especially at risk. Most people find a balance between *Anp* and *Han;* light and dark. Owl People do not. They veer to the one or the other."

"What can happen?" Heechante asked intently.

Chunmaniye wondered why she was not being instructed by local *Wicasa Wakan* who must have sensed her potential. He had not met any yet but he was aware of their presence in the Wyrde Woods. Or was the girl forging ahead, too impatient for a slower journey? Probably the latter, he decided. He could not influence that decision for it was one she had already taken.

"The weak have their minds altered and we say they live life inside out and upside down. Laughing when they are sad, crying when they are happy, always moving backwards in their mannerisms and often caught in a journey which they repeat again and again but never complete. Lost in relooping the past."

Heechante nodded, "and the strong?"

"Some will revel in dark shadows and reach high. Their Medicine is strong but they often overreach. Anog Ite, mother of the four winds, is such a one. She tried to replace Hanwi, the night sun..." Chunmaniye pointed at the moon which had appeared over the tree tops. "...she who guards her people during the night by piercing darkness and revealing the shadows of the night. Anog Ite was punished for her ambitions and condemned to bear two faces. One of great beauty but the other of hideous deformation and her heart grew dark and bitter."

Heechante shivered.

"Those who choose the path of light can become influential wise men and women. Healers of body and mind like my teacher Hehaka Sapa. He told me of his vision of a great tree of life the branches of which offer shelter to the children of all men and women, regardless of race or creed."

Heechante's guarded look reaffirmed Chunmaniye's suspicion that she knew of this tree and even knew where it was to be found. He closed his eyes. Hehaka Sapa's words about the lessons that can be learned from a child echoed in his head. It was ironic that he was instructing her in the ways of his *Wakan* whilst she had possibly decided that he, many times her years, was not yet ready for all of the *Wyrd* as she knew it. Chunmaniye set that thought aside, this was not about him.

"And some," he continued, "become so strong that they can make the impossible possible, like Tasunke Witko or Tatanka Iyotake. Though their brilliance can shine so bright their own people extinguish their light."

"Risks and rewards," Heechante said softly.

"And always," Chunmaniye warned. "A dark abyss right next to your path, ready to swallow you whole."

"I do not seek my great feathered thunderbird…" Heechante began.

Chunmaniye felt a shard of pain pierce his mind as he got the image of an ancient dark menacing presence.

"…for my own betterment. Others, with darkness in their hearts for sure, seek the creature."

"Yet you search for it," Chunmaniye pointed out. "Are you ready for a confrontation with such a being?"

Chunmaniye's instinct told him just how vulnerable the girl was, she was yet on the threshold of a path of power, seeking to grasp that which she not yet fully understood. His intuition was to bundle her over his shoulder and deliver her where she would be safe. However, he also understood that nothing but death could turn her from her journey now and in that they must be equals.

"I think," Heechante gathered her words slowly. "That this creature and I are like Maisy – Ehawee - and Spark."

There was a sudden sadness there which Chunmaniye could not place as he thought of Ehawee's pony which truly did look like a representation of Anog Ite's hideousness.

"Nobody understands what Ehawee sees in the pony," Heechante continued. "I don't think any who know of the Wyrde Wood's thunderbird, *Waki*…?"

"*Wakinyan.*"

"*Wakinyan*; understand it properly. Those who seek it want to harness its darkness, I *ken naun* why. It has something to do with the Germans. The others…," she paused.

Chunmaniye was certain now that these others were the local *Wicasa Wakan* and realised this was the reason she was unguided on her journey; she was defying the wisdom of her own elders. He felt uneasy about aiding her in such a situation but then decided it must be part of her journey. The girl had a sharpness of mind which reminded him that age does not always bring wisdom and lack of experience meant fresh perspectives. Thus the young reinvented the world. So it should be for it would be theirs to pass on to a new generation one day.

Heechante shrugged. "The others only see the darkness."

Chunmaniye took a deep breath. The girl was on a far more dangerous path than he had even imagined yet he doubted not that she must see her journey through to the end or forever wander in a mind's warren of confusion.

His own journey, as foreshadowed by his vision, was to aid her. The air was positively laden with recognition for Chunmaniye, what the *Saglasa* called Déjà vu.

"You seek to protect the *Wakinyan*?" He asked.

"Aye, from all who intend to harm him."

Him, not 'it'.

Heechante looked at Chunmaniye with that challenge in her eyes again and he realised he was being tested. Would he try to talk her out of it? Forbid it even? Or accept her will?

He bowed his head. When he raised it he widened his eyes and sought hers.

"I will tell you all I know of Owl People and the *Wakinyan*," he said. "In the hope the knowledge will make you stronger."

She smiled.

"The first thing," Chunmaniye looked at her sharply. "Is to bear light in your heart, anything other will be a weakness which the Spirits of Chaos will exploit. Their minds are ancient and full of clever tricks for which you are no match yet."

Heechante nodded her acceptance of this and he truly hoped she did perceive her own limitations. Lose sight of those…he felt a shiver run along his spine. Heechante could still easily turn to embrace darkness.

"Is your heart clear of anything but light now?" Chunmaniye asked as casually as he could.

This was his test.

He knew her heart was not for some reason, if the girl lied to him he could not possibly trust her with the power he could gift her.

Heechante looked down and then shook her head. "No, it is troubled," she admitted

Chunmaniye felt relief and smiled at her. "Then you know that you must clear it of trouble before you do anything else. Have I told you about my vision? The one I had twenty years ago."

She shook her head.

"You were in it," Chunmaniye said.

Heechante did not seem to think this strange. She said: "*Wyrd bid ful araed.* Our paths are chosen for us and I think now that we were meant to meet."

Chunmaniye nodded. "Then let's talk of the great feathered ones. I need to know about your *Saglasa* thunderbird, and I will tell you about the Lakota *Wakinyan.*"

"To begin with," Heechante said with a smile. "My thunderbird is *naun Saglasa*, he is older than that."

"Kleak-kleak," Thallie opened her eyes for a moment and looked around as if surprised to find herself in a clearing in the woods surrounded by the stolid Guardians.

Heechante smiled and then began to tell her story of the Owl Man of the Wyrde Woods.

§ § § § § § §

"Bloody hell!" Maisy exclaimed angrily. "But this is plain trickery, innit?"

She could tell by the looks on their faces that Joy and Leon thought so too and were just as unhappy about it as Maisy was.

Katie had shown up at Maskall Farm earlier and insisted that Maisy come to the Wyrde Woods with her. Ostensibly because a number of the Wolfden chavvies wanted to continue the gang and had asked for Maisy to provide direction.

It was a measure, Maisy thought, of how well Katie had come to know Maisy already. She must have counted on Maisy's inability to resist curiousity at such a request. Katie had led Maisy to the Guardians and to Maisy's initial surprise all of the Wyrde Warriors had been there, barring the traitor Geoff. Her first reaction had been delight. Then she had seen Joy and Leon sitting unhappily in the midst of the Guardians.

"What are you playing at?" Maisy looked at Katie suspiciously.

Lizzie had come to stand by Katie and both girls conveyed far too much satisfaction for Maisy's liking. They both took one of Maisy's hands and led her to Joy and Leon. The rest of the Wyrde Warriors now drifted into a wide circle around them.

"I was tricked into coming here," Maisy announced to Joy and Leon, just to be sure they did not think Maisy had wanted to see either one of them again. Ever. It was good to see Joy though, just a little bit. Even Leon. Just a little bit.

Both Joy and Leon nodded to indicate they had been tricked as well.

"Sit down," Katie ordered and Maisy was so surprised by the forceful imperative that she sat down without further protest.

"I don't *ken* what you two hope to achieve," Joy told Katie and Lizzie sullenly.

Maisy looked up at the two girls who were beginning to walk around their little circle of unhappy captives. They lived a Wyrde Woods apart but had managed to co-ordinate a complex operation none-the-less. It was something to be admired. She snuck a glance at Joy just as Joy did the same. It had become a habit, those glances. Both quickly looked away.

"It's a waste of time, innit?" Maisy said, gesturing. "These two..."

"SHUT UP," Katie shouted.

Maisy's mouth dropped open as far as it could. Katie seemed dead angry.

"Lizzie," Leon directed a plea at his cousin. "Couldn't we just…"

"You shut up too, Leon," Lizzie folded her arms in front of her. "We're with Katie in this."

Their were 'ayes' and murmurs of confirmation from all the other Hornsby's. Leon was genuinely shocked, Maisy knew his leadership of the clan had never been contested. He looked at Joy and Maisy helplessly.

Joy shrugged. Maisy rolled her eyes a few times. Joy giggled at that but stopped when Maisy immediately sought eye contact at that familiar sound. They looked away from each other again.

"If it were just the three of you…," Lizzie said. "Then you could mope and sulk like toddlers all you wanted."

"Toddlers?!" Maisy, Joy and Leon protested as one.

"There's *naun* doubt about that," Katie said placing her hands on her hips. "*Howsumdever*, have any of you thought about the rest of us?"

Leon looked at one of the Guardians, Joy looked up at the sky and Maisy examined the grass by her feet. It was the kind of green that looked tasty, she thought. She would have to try some one day. Spark seemed to like it.

"We didn't think so," Lizzie snorted.

"You start all of this up," Katie's eyes were spitting anger as she swept her arms in a wide circle. "For some of us, that's made a big *gurt* difference. If you've been minding us at all, you would know about that."

Maisy bit her lip. They had made a world of difference for Katie, she knew that.

"They…" Leon began

"She…" Maisy and Joy started together.

"STOP IT." This time it was Lizzie who vented fury. "All three of you."

"You made a middling difference," Katie continued. "And then all three of you just walk away? Take it all away again from the rest of us?"

"That's cruel, that is," Lizzie added.

"You're right," Maisy mumbled, feeling horrible. "I'm sorry."

"Aye," Joy wiped an eye.

"*Mayhap*," Leon wavered.

"You're meant to be angry at Bill Hare, not each other," Katie said. She squeaked the last of those words and then her anger was spent. Maisy saw how she gave Lizzie a glance and shrug as if to say: *I've done all I could.* She could not recall the two of them becoming such good friends, she realised. Looking at them interact reminded her of…

"Maisy," Joy said hesitantly. "She's right about Bill Hare, I think."

Maisy stared at Joy and wanted to smile and laugh and beam. She grinned instead and then looked at Leon.

"I think we should learn that *scrowse* a middling lesson he won't forget," Leon growled.

"We'll need a plan," Maisy's mind began to race. The Wyrde Warriors closed in on the little circle till the groups fused and the rest of the afternoon was business as usual.

§ § § § § § §

At the look-out point on the top of Hood's Gorge Sir Mortimer lowered his binoculars. The group of children had appeared on the Roreford clearing after emerging from the path that led to the Falls and Fey's Pool. After forming a brief huddle on the clearing they had split up; drifting east and west along the Forgotten Road or, in the case of the Whitfield girl, heading north to the Owlery. They were all out of sight now.

Cynthia lowered her binoculars too.

"You are certain?" Cynthia asked coldly.

"Yes," Sir Mortimer said curtly. It had been tense between them since he had returned to Wolfden to report the discovery of an empty chamber at the foot of Cross Stone. He continued:

"There was a crack of sorts, in the chamber. Possibly a hidden door. There were too many villagers out and about to explore it. I believe there's a tunnel to the church and questioned the Rolls driver. She said Mother only entered the church in my presence."

"And the children?" Cynthia asked.

"Were in there on their own for a good hour," Sir Mortimer said darkly. "The day after the Whitfield girl mentioned both St Lewinna's Church and 'a' key."

"She just happened to mention this, within your earshot?" Cynthia raised an eyebrow.

"The girl was…" Sir Mortimer hesitated. "She was calling on the spirits of the Wyrde Woods."

Cynthia looked at him for some time and he looked back without blinking. She was seeking dark legends – myths even – on behalf of a task master who had a known interest in the other worlds. If she dismissed Sir Mortimer's observation she was the wrong person for this mission.

"Did you find that surprising?" Cynthia asked at last.

"No," there was no hesitation from Sir Mortimer this time. "There are many entities who call the Wyrde Woods their home. My ancestors have known this for a long time."

"Is your Mother involved?"

"I suspect so but have no evidence." Sir Mortimer grimaced. Her latest interest had been in the hunting rifles, ammunition, stored petrol and all maps at Malheur Hall. Mother had told him – not asked him but told him – she intended to have anything that might be of use to German invaders secured and hidden away.

"If she is…there will be loyalty issue."

"There will be no loyalty issue," Sir Mortimer promised. "When the Wehrmacht arrive at Malheur Hall I intend to welcome them and she will not be there to interfere."

"Securing you a position in the new liberated Britain," Cynthia said mockingly.

"Yes," Sir Mortimer admitted without hesitation. There would be unimaginable rewards for the handful of loyal servants of the *Reich*, of that he was sure. Power and wealth restored to Malheur Hall.

"And in the meantime?" Cynthia narrowed her eyes. "If she interferes with my mission?"

"Our mission. There will be no loyalty issue regarding Mother. You have seen how it is."

"And the girls?"

"How do you mean?"

"It may be necessary to dispose of one or the both of them," Cynthia said coolly. "Permanently so."

"I have given thought to that," Sir Mortimer put his binoculars in their leather case.

"And?"

"In my scenario," Sir Mortimer smiled, "That will be an essential requirement. I shall not flinch Miss Chesterton, there will be no hesitation on my part."

"Good."

24. Submission

The witch-child reached the North Woods Lane and stopped in the middle of the road to usher the three children – a girl and two boys – across the road. The dwarf was not with them which was good. The witch looked around her, seeming to stare straight at Bill for a moment. There was a low overgrown mound next to the outbuildings of the Raven's Roost and it overlooked the old carfax but Bill and his lads were crouching low in the undergrowth and well concealed. None-the-less, a little knowing smile rested smugly on her lips and it infuriated Bill. Despite the destruction of their pathetic little clubhouse the witch-child just kept at it; once again taking Wolfden *chavees* to those woods of hers.

Naun this time. After the witch-child had followed the children into the almost overgrown opening of the footpath into Shims Copses Bill beckoned Syll and Tim, the only lads present in the ditch fort when the *chavees* had been spotted walking down Roreford Road. They followed him as he crossed the carfax.

Syll and Tim hesitated when they reached the beginning of the footpath. Neither of them had ever set foot in Shims Copses before. If they had to be in the Wyrde Woods they took the long way around past Mordrove or the twin hills on the road to Nickleby.

"Bill," Tim said nervously. "We could wait here, they got to come back *somewhen.*"

"*Zackly,*" Syll nodded.

Bill grinned. That was what the witch-child would expect, she would reckon herself safe now. He felt rising excitement at the prospect of the alarm and then horror on her face if he were to follow her into the woods and catch her by surprise. He answered the other two by plunging into the murky narrow passage into Shims Copses. They looked at each other and then shrugged; following Bill with an uncertain tread.

Bill moved slowly; he could hear the distant chatter of the children ahead of him somewhere and he did not want to catch up to them while the path remained narrow. He recalled that it widened into a dirt road about half mile ahead and the open space there would be good for a quick charge that would allow them to draw abreast with the witch-child and the *chuckle-headed* village *chavees* who so blithely followed her into the woods.

The path twisted and turned as it followed a zigzag course within the bounds of the old road which had once been here. Bill knew that the irregularity of the path was far more consistent than it seemed but Tim and Syll were unnerved by it. They stared at the slender trees which did not rise straight up but seemed to writhe upwards in serpentine patterns. Lichen cascaded down between the foliage like the trailing tentacles of a sea creature and there was a taste of mouldy rot in the air. The ground was dark and moist and seemed to be crawling with insects and worms yet there was no birdsong in this rich feeding area, just the hoarse calls of rooks which seemed to be mocking the boys.

Bill managed to supress the eerie forlornness which sought to take control of him by focusing on his target and intended fun. They seemed to be slowing down; the voices drifting along the path suggested they were but six or seven turns of the path ahead. Bill adjusted his own speed accordingly. He wished they would speed up. Bill could sense the growing uncertainty of his friends and knew that they would feel more confident again in the open space offered by the dirt road and its patches of broad grassy verges. With their prey in sight and panic to instil they would regain their sense of purpose but the longer it took to get there the stronger their fear of Shims Copses would become.

"You're *bettermost sodgers*, lads," Bill turned to give them a crooked smile and he flashed his thumb up. Syll nodded grimly and Tim smiled weakly; their nerves highly strung by the menace exuded by the woods.

Bill frowned. The chatter ahead had abruptly ceased. He cocked his head to make sure but there was nothing to be heard apart from the sardonic croaking of the rooks. He started to speed up, afraid that his prey would evade him after all. Syll and Tim followed him and Bill broke into a jog which he maintained till Shims Copses spat him out through the forlorn gate onto the Forgotten Road. Bill came to a sudden halt and Syll and Tim bumped into his back.

The Forgotten Road stretched out before Bill and looked empty. Then he spotted movement at the very end of it where it bent out of sight into the woods about half a mile ahead. He could make out the witch's distinctive white dress and the other chavees just before they disappeared from view.

He shook his head. He had been sure that they had only been just ahead of him a few minutes ago. He felt an icy fear grip his heart when he realised the Wodewose bitch might have used her magic to gain the sudden extra distance.

"We run," Bill scowled and started immediately, pounding down the Forgotten Road with all the speed he could muster, followed by Syll and Tim who recovered their confidence now that they were out of the opressive enclosure of Shims Copses.

They were about two-thirds of the way to the bend when Tim shouted: "Bill!"

Bill turned his head angrily but when he saw what Tim was pointing at he skidded to a confused halt. He double-checked but there was no doubt about it, some fifty yards behind them they could see the girl in the white dress and her entourage leaving the Forgotten Road and enter a path which led northwards back into Shims Copses. Bill looked back at the deserted bend, then back at the path. Tim and Syll looked bewildered, they too had seen the small party they pursued in front of them before they had suddenly reappeared behind them. Bill's blood turned cold, the little witch was using her magic for sure. The realisation that she was probably laughing at him now made him furious. He growled and snorted and then sped back up the Forgotten Road. They were closer now and he might yet catch up with them.

The path led them into an area of Shims Copses that was dominated by coniferous trees and below their crowns which seemed to block every sliver of light all was dank and murky. Tim and Syll became hesitant again; oppressed by the gloom they started to trail behind their leader.

"Bill...you've *gwoan*...and left...the path," Syll barely had the breath to utter the words.

"Never mind. Faster," Bill snapped. The lack of significant undergrowth allowed him to see that white dress weaving in and out of the trees ahead and he scraped together all his reserves for a last burst of speed. He was not going to allow the little witch out of his sight again; this time she would be his, squirming beneath his hands and terrified as he throttled out whatever Evil possessed her. With the Owlery girl out of the way he could go after that dwarf. Knowing now that the diminutive *sheere-girl* could fight like the devil he would make sure she was on her own during that encounter, facing every Wolfden lad Bill could summon.

He would have to catch the witch first though.

Bill cursed as his quarry left the darkness of the needle-carpeted shadows to enter a clearing where the sunfall's bright light merged with the distinctive dress.

"Spread out!" He ordered, hoping that Syll or Tim might catch a glimpse of movement if the witch tried to scurry to the left or right.

The lads did so reluctantly and Bill urged them to cast a wider net; the fury in his voice overriding their fear of Shims Copses. They reached the crescent shaped clearing in a state that was a far cry from the fearsome effect Bill had counted on. The sudden emergence into the warmth of the sun and the dazzling bright light brought them to a halt. Both Tim and Syll, a good fifteen yards to either side of Bill, bent over with their hands on their knees as they tried to catch their breath. Bill's chest was heaving too, his physical power momentarily spent by the running he had done since first emerging onto the Forgotten Road.

Bill squinted into the shimmering brightness trying to concentrate on the lighter woodlands beyond the clearing. This was why Joy Whitfield appeared wholly out of focus at first.

Bill's head reeled as his eyes readjusted. Joy was reclined on a small tumuli a mere twelve feet away. She was propped up on an elbow and offered him a sweet smile.

"How do, Bill Hare?" she asked with a total lack of concern.

Bill gasped for air.

Joy's smile changed into smirk as she slowly rose to her feet, her hair aflame and surrounded by a halo of golden sunlight.

"Witch…" Bill managed to utter. Tim and Syll had seen Joy rise and edged towards Bill cautiously.

Joy's eyes sparkled and she spread her arms, her palms out as if warding off the other two lads.

"Stay, don't come *naun* closer!" Joy snarled and the lads froze in their tracks. Bill warily edged backwards a step…he was entirely unsure of the situation and bereft of confidence.

Joy rolled her eyes dramatically and began to intone: "*Sitte ge, sigewif, sigað tō eorðan!*"

"Stop it!" Syll yelled fearfully.

"Næfre ge wilde tō wuda fleogan!" Joy continued with a gleam in her eyes which seemed to burrow straight into Bill's soul. She dropped one hand and made a fist with the other. Punching the air with it she shouted: *"WUDAWOSE! TŌ WUDAWYRDE FLEOGAN!!"*

This was followed by keen high-pitched ululations from the forest behind her and a distant rumbling. Bill took three more steps backwards, looking left and right anxiously. Syll and Tim took this as cues to edge even further backwards; so far back they could feel the needles of the pines behind them prick their backs.

"WUDAWOSE!" Joy shouted again and looked at Bill while a little laugh danced on her lips.

Bill snarled and took a step forwards, he was frightened but he was not going to let the little witch get away with her cheap tricks and laugh at him to boot.

Just then the riders came crashing out of the forest on either side of Joy. Both mounts and riders were of different shapes and sizes. It was hard to see where the one started and the other ended for they were adorned with leaves and feathers and their flanks and torsos were daubed in woad patterns. They did not stop, just uttered fiercesome demonish shrieks when they spotted Joy's foes and sped straight at them.

Tim shrieked and ran into the darkness of the coniferous copse. Syll did likewise on Bill's other side.

Bill held his ground a second longer, glaring at Joy for all he was worth.

"EEEE-EEEE-EEEE-CCCC-HHHH!" A feathered pale ghost descended from the air and swooped towards Bill, sharp claws outstretched.

Bill whimpered and turned to run. The riders followed the lads into the woods, still howling the promise of devilish wrath.

Bill ran. Faster and faster. He soon discovered that the riders chasing him could not follow him into the places where fallen pine trunks and boughs were grouped together and he crashed through these barriers forcing them to ride around. The branches whipped him furiously for his violent passing and their needles stung him in scores of places.

He emerged only to find himself faced with one of the smaller riders who brandished a small axe in each hand and raised these whilst cackling madly. The mount, a foul-faced pony, snarled at Bill.

Bill fled back into the dubious protection of the fallen pines and this time it seemed that the branches formed skeletal arms reaching out for him; clutching at him, ripping his clothes, pricking him and scratching him. He lost his orientation and when he emerged there were more riders charging him and driving him in a direction of their choosing as if he were a deer panicked by beaters.

His vision started to spin; flashes of sky, glimpses of hateful painted faces, the ground passing beneath his feet, branches and twigs sweeping in to score more hits. He was out of breath and in complete panic when he emerged back in the clearing where he let himself fall to the ground.

The riders chasing him ceased their screeching immediately and did not emerge onto the clearing. Much further away now Bill could hear distant commotion as Tim and Syll were pursued further into Shims Copses.

He heard light footsteps and tried to scramble up on his elbows but Joy was faster and gave him a well-placed kick that forced Bill to roll onto his back. He tried to gasp but the sound was choked when Joy placed a foot on his throat and applied light pressure.

Bill froze.

"Thallie," Joy commanded and suddenly the feathered demon was back, hovering a few feet over Bill's face. He could feel the air move when its wings flapped down and kept his eyes on its claws apprehensively.

"I don't rightly *ken* where to begin," Joy said menacingly. "Your eyes, surelye, but *mayhap* you'd like to watch your privates torn to shreds first?"

"Please...no..." Bill began to cry.

§ § § § § §

Joy felt like she was soaring on the sense of power and it filled her with a giddiness she had never before experienced; a strange fluttering emptyness in her belly, an impression of weightlessness and the glory of triumph in her head. It was far stronger than the time she had called upon the Wyrd at Roreford. Far more satisfying. She watched Bill squirm and bawl and beg beneath her foot and was tempted to bid Thallie to leave a permanent mark of her power on the bully in exchange for all the spite he had directed at her in the past.

She spread her arms again and hissed: *"Wudawose. Wudawose."*

All around the clearing tendrils of mist started to rise and then converge to form writhing shapes which began to hover into the clearing. Faces formed, gaping holes where eyes should have been and jagged rents which continued to grow and form soundless screams.

Joy smiled. She could do far more than leave an owl's mark on Bill's face.

She could break his mind.

He would never intimidate or hurt another *chavee* in the Wyrde Woods. Instead he'd shuffle around mindlessly, as harmless as a vole.

"No please, please Joy, please," Bill whimpered as he noted the expression on her face.

"So much hatred for me," Joy sneered insidiously. *"WUDAWOSE!"*

The whispering whisps of Shims Copses sped forwards at her command to hover in a circle around the two.

"Eeee-eeee-cccc-hhh," Thallie screamed at Bill who cringed. Joy raised a hand and the whispering whisps shuddered as they awaited her command. Joy felt the glory of supremacy coursing through her every vein and she revelled in it.

"Heechante!" The words rang out over the clearing. Joy looked up.

Maisy came riding into the clearing on Spark followed by Leon astride his dappled grey. Both were unrecognizable; daubed in woad and hung with feathers they looked quite feroscious. That impression was further strenghtened by Leon's spear and Maisy's axes.

"Heechante," Leon took his cue from Maisy and Joy very slowly lowered her arm. The whispering whisps writhed and hissed audibly; eager to be fed and irritated at the delay.

"I said I'd deal with Bill," Joy said angrily.

"Cracking special effects, innit?" Maisy quipped, nodding towards the whispering whisps.

"You've dealt with him, by the looks of it, Joy of the Owlery," Leon looked at the whimpering heap of misery on the ground.

"Feels mighty fine, innit?" Maisy said lightly. "This kind of triumph must be what Bill feels, dontcha reckon, Heechante? When he bullies a chavvy in Wolfden? Like nothing can stop him?"

Joy felt nauseous as she realised the glowing sensation of power she felt was probably the very stimulent which drove Bill to exert his strength over the *chavees* in Wolfden. She tried to banish it and her every sinew seemed to shriek a protest. *More, naun less, more!*

"Please…anything…" Bill slobbered.

"Thallie, be *gwoan*," Joy said curtly and took three deep breaths.

The owl ascended and perched on a high branched from which she regarded the scene below impassively. The whispering whisps started to lose their forms and their loosened strands drifted back into Shims Copses.

"You will leave my folk at school alone," Joy ordered. She was not enjoying it anymore, she wanted it over and done with now. "Those from the farms and Wolfden."

Bill nodded.

"*Naun* more taunting, it ends, do you understand?"

"I understand," Bill squeaked.

"And *naun* telling adults. Anything." Joy pressed her foot down very lightly: "I will find you, Bill Hare, don't be doubting that."

Bill could only wheeze incomprehensibly in reply but Joy could read in his eyes that he believed her.

She stepped back. He stood up very slowly, shaking and holding his hand to his throat. When he had risen to his full height he towered over her but Joy did not step backwards, just regarded him very coolly without a hint of fear.

Bill started to say something.

"Kleak-kleak," Thallie announced her nearby presence.

Bill cast a frightened look up at the owl, then, throwing one more defeated glance at Joy, he turned and scurried into the dark shadows.

Maisy jumped from Spark and thrust her axes in her belt. She walked to Joy and laid a hand on Joy's forearm.

"How do, Joy?"

Joy sighed, "Scratching along, *bethanks* Maisy."

"That's what mates are for, innit?" Maisy grinned.

By and by the others returned to the clearing. Leon greeted them with loud whoops and Maisy joined him. Lizzie, wearing one of Joy's white dresses, led her entourage of the youngest Hornsby's in. They were grinning at the success of their ruse and the younger *chavees* laughed as they recalled the Wolfden bullies running to and fro in confusion as to where Joy and the Wolfden *chavees* were. The last riders came in to report that Tim and Syll were legging it back to Wolfden in tears and renewed happy chattering broke out.

Joy did not join in and strayed to the edge of the huddle, troubled still by what had just happened. It would have been so easy. She would have to learn to be wary of it.

When her name was called Joy braced herself and turned around with a graceful smile. They had done an amazing thing today, they had shaken off a yoke around their necks and they deserved to be praised. Her smile turned to a broad grin and she flashed them Winston Churchill's victory sign. All of them cheered loudly at that; shaking their fists in the air and roaring like the victorious warriors they were.

Fort Defiance had been avenged.

25. The Double Sunset

Joy, Maisy, Leon, Lizzie and Katie were at the look-out post at the end of Hood's Gorge. They had been debating the location of a new HQ for the Wyrde Warriors and the view over pretty much all of the Wyrde Woods had helped in their deliberations. They had decided to establish a new outpost deep in the Wyrde Woods, east of St Lewinna's Pool and the Guardians because there were no landmark features there nor any main paths. It was closer to Hornsby Farm as well; a recognition of the Hornsby contribution to the Wyrde Warriors.

It had taken some time to reach a decision though and it was both too late and too hot to make a start. Instead Maisy was teaching them how to sing *Run, Rabbit, Run!* to celebrate when they heard the familiar distant throb of aeroplane engines. They got to their feet and looked north. Far beyond Folly Hill were tiny specks sparkling in the day's glorious sunshine. Joy frowned, there seemed to be a lot of them.

"Cor blimey!" Maisy seemed to think so too. Formation after formation appeared in the sky over distant Kent until the entire northern horizon seemed to be filled with a thousand planes or more. They were flying westwards.

They had seen a few large formations over Kent and Sussex before but those tended to diverge into different directions. This air fleet droned steadily onwards in the same direction, seemingly unstoppable in their mechanical might.

"London," Maisy realised. "They're heading for London, innit?"

"*Mayhap* the London airfields?" Leon suggested. "The Luftwaffe has been targeting the RAF airfields."

Maisy shook her head. "No, this is bigger, this is the invasion, innit? The Jerries are coming for sure."

Joy smiled. So far the few planes they had seen pass close by, German bombers pursued by fighters or fighters embroiled in dogfights, had elicited the same response from Maisy.

"I'm serious, Joy." Maisy frowned. "This is big."

"Shhh," Katie said.

"Listen!" Lizzie added.

Joy closed her eyes. Her ears picked up a sound that was both familiar and unfamiliar.

"What?" Maisy asked. "BLOODY HELL!"

It was just the one at first but as it started to gather momentum another one joined in and then more. They could hear Wolfden and Mordrove quite clearly whilst Nickleby and Odesby were more faint.

All the church bells were ringing, their continuous tolling fusing with the persistent drone of the Luftwaffe attack force. The Germans were coming.

§ § § § § § §

When Hugin and Munin started barking Fred came out of the long shed behind the barn and walked onto the farmyard just as Betty wandered out of the farm house where she'd been fixing tea. They were expecting both the War-Ag inspector and the vetinary surgeon to visit some time soon and both were important visitors, though it seemed far too late in the day for a visit. Fred noticed the dull drone of a mass of aeroplane engines to the north as he stepped outside.

Then he focused on the sight of Tony Rye speeding towards them on a bicycle. He was wearing his Home Guard uniform and Brodie helmet. He stopped in front of Fred, sweating and panting from the exertion. He must have ridden from Wolfden fast and it was a remarkably hot day.

"Rye?" Fred asked. "What's the matter?"

"Code Cromwell," Rye said between breaths. "Mackellow told me…to pass the word."

Fred paled. "Code Cromwell? Are you sure?"

"Yes, Code Cromwell from London, from The War Office. There's bombers and fighters all over Kent." Rye swept the northern horizon with his arms. "Hundreds, thousands of them, Fred. The Jerries are up to something. I have to go to the next farm."

Fred nodded. "I'll see you at the Raven's Roost."

Rye turned his bicycle and peddled away again. Fred turned to Betty.

"Code Cromwell?" She asked.

Fred nodded grimly. "It's a signal that invasion is imminent, Betty. The Germans are coming."

§ § § § § § §

Chunmaniye looked up in surprise. He was seated on his stretcher bed in the Nissen hut he shared with his squad, reading a letter from his sister who lived on the Wood Mountain reservation. Lieutenant Levesque walked in unannounced. He was Chunmaniye's immediate superior and Chunmaniye liked him. As a *Quebecois* Levesque understood that it was possible to be fiercely loyal to Canada without surrendering other identities and loyalties.

"Attention," Chunmaniye told the others and rose from the bed to stand to attention at the end of it.

"*Merci*, at ease, *mes amis*." Lieutenant Levesque said. "I have some important news."

The Lieutenant held a piece of paper up. The men gathered around him.

"The Luftwaffe is targeting London today, using every aeroplane at their disposal, it seems," the officer told them. "The War Office has sent the following message."

Lieutenant Levesque read from the paper: "Message to all UK units: codeword CROMWELL. Home Defence forces to highest degree of readiness. Invasion of mainland UK expected at any time."

Chunmaniye drew in his breath.

"Hot damn!" one of the others exclaimed. "Is this for real?"

"The War Office seems to think so," Lieutenant Levesque lowered the piece of paper and looked around him.

"Gentlemen, you are all to report at the Quartermaster's in full kit and draw five days of ammunition and supplies. After that the entire battalion will deploy according to the local home defence scenario we have practised."

The men looked at each other.

"Well, what are you waiting for, *vite, vite,* you're not paid to stand around gaping like goldfish. Get a move on."

The Lieutenant left again and Chunmaniye and his bunkmates rushed about to select the equipment they would need and put on their webbing.

The churchbells of nearby Mordrove started to toll, hesitant at first, as if they were shy after inaction for so long, but then more urgently. The Germans were coming.

§ § § § § §

Fred had gone into the house to change into his uniform and get his rifle and ammunition. Then he saddled one of the horses so he could get to the Raven's Roost as quickly as he could.

Betty came outside with packed sandwiches and a flask of tea.

They both looked up as the Wolfden and Nickleby churchbells started to toll insistently, calling out their dire warning as they did in the days of old.

They both looked at the northern sky. The specks were tiny up there but even so they could see there were countless planes; waves of attack formations heading steadily in the direction of London. Were they carrying bombs or German parachutists?

"Is Maisy still at the Owlery?" Fred asked.

Betty nodded.

"Good, safest place in the Wyrde Woods," Fred said with relief. "*Mayhap*, Betty, you'd *bettermost* go there as well. We're too close to the North Woods Lane. The farm might be crawling with Germans tomorrow. *Mayhap* sooner if there are parachutists."

Betty laughed. "Just because you're wearing a uniform don't give you no right to order me about. I aint leaving the farm…," she indicated the farmyard all around her, "…all we've worked for, all we are. Asides, there are the animals, I aint leaving them on their own."

Fred nodded.

"Maisy might head this direction," Betty added.

"By Merlin's Beard," Fred grumbled. "I hope the lass is sensible enough to stay put where she is. The roads will be dangerous tonight. A lot of anxious half-trained men with guns peering into the darkness."

"I suspect she'll be itching to fight," Betty shrugged. "*Howsumdever*, I will rely on the common sense of Sarah Whitfield."

Fred nodded. "We'll hope for the best."

He was ready to go and looked at Betty helplessly. They had been through this before but he had been far younger then and far more optimistic about his chances of survival. Though he was proud of his section and reckoned they would be able to put up a fight he was also well aware that German parachutists were counted as elite troops – well-trained and supremely fit young men recently battle-hardened in combat. It had been a while since Fred's veterans had experienced the adrenaline of combat.

"Don't get sentimental on me," Betty winked at him. "I'll save your tea, though it'll probably be cold by the time you get home."

Fred grinned and shared a brief hug with his wife and life companion. Then he mounted his horse and rode off to war.

§ § § § § § §

The children descended down into the Wyrde Wood to retrieve part of the arsenal of bows and arrows from the hiding place and then chattered their way back to Roreford. They had a greater view of the sky there after coming out of the thickly canopied woodlands around Willikin's Drove and to their surprise there were still attack waves of Luftwaffe planes heading in the general direction of London. Other formations were coming back, heading towards Kent or flying over Sussex. At long last they could discern the tell-tale signs of dogfights; smaller aircraft weaving amidst the bombers, the occasional flashes of machine-gun fire and struck planes diverging from their formations. Some of the latter went into a steady descent, trailing smoke. Others spun crazily before plummeting down with the grace of a brick. The RAF was fighting back now and Maisy hoped they would get as many of the Jerry murderers as possible. She tried not to think of London – of parachutes floating over the rooftops or sticks of bombs screaming down towards the streets. She told herself Mum and Dad would be perfectly safe. Who on earth would want to invade the Isle of Dogs?

A much louder growling sound started to override the continuous hum in the sky and the pealing of the church bells.

"Better find cover," Leon suggested, looking around as he tried to ascertain where the noise was coming from. They went into one of the ruined buildings near the river, peering through every possible gap in the torn walls until a formation of Luftwaffe bombers appeared over the treetops. Flying low they barrelled towards London filling the air with a deafening roar, already pulling up over Roreford to pass over the heights of Hood's Gorge.

Maisy recognised the bulbed shaped heads immediately. When the sound started to fade she said: "Dorniers. Flying Pencils. They like to fly low."

Higher up further formations were flying in from the south.

"How many planes do the Jerries have?" Katie asked in amazement.

Nobody answered. The wireless had been listing the daily tallies and most of the time the Luftwaffe losses were said to considerably exceed RAF losses. Folk had become hopeful that the Nazis might not be able to sustain their aerial assault indefinitely. This evening though, the Germans seemed to mock those hopes by the overwhelming forces they sent across the English Channel. More than ever their military seemed like a merciless machine – mindlessly set to wreak havoc.

The children slowly emerged from their shelter but did not stray far from it. The Dorniers, so close they had seen the heads of some of the crew through its windows, had made an impression. Maisy had vivid memories of the strafing attack on the Odesby High Street. She glanced at Leon; would he be thinking back of that? Lizzie had paled and clutched Katie's hand.

Maisy was continually scanning the sky now. An invasion would be preceded by parachutists, scores of little silk clouds drifting steadily downwards. How many would be in a unit, she wondered. She patted her new leather pouch; Gramps had made a bunch of them for everyone to keep their bowstrings in. They only strung their bows when they used them to prevent the staves from losing their power and she wondered how soon they would have to prepare them for use this evening.

§ § § § § § §

Fred Maskall had cantered some of the way up the North Woods Lane, slowing to a walk when six army lorries filled with soldiers passed by heading for Nickleby. The sight filled him with confidence. There was a whole battalion of Canadians in the area, the local Home Guard units would not have to bear the brunt of any attack alone.

His renewed confidence popped like a soap bubble when he arrived at the Raven's Roost.

"Halt!" Someone shouted. The Home Guard had set up roadblocks, barring much of the road on all three of the approaches to the Raven's Carfax. Some men were rolling out barbed wire between the concrete anti-tank barriers which had been installed on the road verges.

"Who goes there?"

Fred brought his horse to a halt. He shouted back: "Sergeant Maskall, Wolfden Home Guard."

A shot rang out, unexpected, and Fred shrunk instinctively. The bullet passed overhead close enough for him to hear it passing.

"What the *PIZE!*"

"*Chuckle-head!*"

Angry voices rang out from the roadblock and one of the younger lads started saying 'sorry' over and over again.

Fred shook his head. He spurred his horse forward and hoped Maisy had the sense to lay low at the Owlery. The villages around the Wyrde Woods would all have their Home Guard out by now. Nervous men ready to be startled by the slightest rustle in the trees or movement on the road. Fred suspected the Canadians would send soldiers into the Wyrde Woods as well, enough to provide a thin screen of skirmishers on the higher hills and river crossings.

He reached the centre of the crossways where Lieutenant Mackellow was giving Sergeant Hare a hard time.

"Who the Devil told you to have the men load their guns?" Mackellow voice was not raised or angry but dripped with fury.

"I thought...I thought..." Silas Hare stammered.

"You were under clear orders, were you not?" The Lieutenant asked. "To keep all guns unloaded unless specifically instructed to load them by myself."

"Yes Lieutenant," Silas Hare gave Fred a look that suggested it was all Fred's fault.

Mackellow sighed. "Both of you, check all your men, and those who'll still be coming in. No loaded guns. We will load if there's actual evidence of Jerries heading this way, not before."

Silas Hare was glad to create distance between himself and the Lieutenant.

"Are you alright, Sergeant Maskall?" Mackellow gave Fred a concerned look.

"A poor shot, he missed me by several yards," Fred said. While he did so he threw an inquiring look at his superior and tapped his fingers against his rifle stock. Mackellow nodded and tapped his sidearm in reply. The two of them, at least, would have loaded weapons just in case, as they had agreed. They looked up as the sound of low flying bombers suddenly passed by from the Wyrde Woods.

"Heading north, sir," Fred said. Mackellow nodded.

"It will be a night to remember, Sergeant," he said.

Fred frowed, that was exactly what he was afraid of.

§ § § § § § §

Lieutenant Levesque talked incessantly as he led his men off the base and onto the North Woods Lane. The troops which were being sent to Nickleby and Odesby rumbled by in lorries whilst those assigned positions in the Edgelands and Wyrde Woods left on foot.

"We're the lucky ones, *mes amis*. We'll sit on a hilltop and watch the show, eh?"

"What if their airborne units drop right on top of us, Lieutenant?" One of the men asked.

"Oh, but that would be *fantastique*!" Levesque enthused. "Right over the forest, *n'est-ce pas*? They'll be hanging from the branches like ripe fruits ready for picking. It is a dream scenario, eh?"

The men laughed.

"It is true," Levesque continued. "That their airborne forces are the biggest threat to us. They will not have uncontested access to the Sussex beaches. We'll hear it, with our very own ears, if there are landings on the coast, and have *beaucoup* warning before the *Wehrmacht* shows up on our doorstep. Parachutists; they're another matter, *non*?"

"But they won't come to the woods?" Someone asked.

"Not for the landing. That would be suicide, *n'est-ce pas*? If their *Fallschirmjagers* come here the *Boche* will converge on Odesby. There are many roads and a railway line there. The woods...," Levesque shrugged, "...if they are driven out of Odesby they will head our way. Not to fight but to hide."

Chunmaniye grinned. Levesque was clever, talking courage into his men whilst at the same time reminding them of the larger picture. He and the other scouts had identified the hilltops, river crossings and crossways of the main paths in the woods and soon enough the men would be in far smaller groups; keeping a watchful eye on the Wyrde Woods from the positions selected for them by the scouts. In case of contact the scattered pickets would slowly fall back towards the base; a fighting withdrawal to slow down any German advance giving Allied reserve units time to bolster the thin line.

"Let them come," one of the soldiers said full of bravado.

Another one, Lakota like Chunmaniye but from another reservation, shouted: *"Hoka Hey!"*

It was Tasunke Witko's battle cry. *It is a good day to die.*

Some of the officers in the battalion actively discouraged any language other than English and looked down on any other cultural expression. Lieutenant Levesque was not like that and had been much taken with the Lakota battle cry. Mostly, Chunmaniye thought, because Levesque knew it irritated some of the Anglophile officers, the same reason why Chunmaniye suspected Levesque took care to use French expressions in his speech whenever he could. He grinned happily, Levesque could be deadly serious but he had a sense of humour which Chunmaniye appreciated.

"Oui!" Levesque replied to the shout. *"Hoka Hey!"*

It had become a unit thing and they all replied as loud as they could: *"HOKA HEY!"*

It was a good day to die.

§ § § § § § §

The driver started to slow down and Sir Mortimer leaned forwards to see why the Rolls was easing to a halt.

"Roadblock," he frowned.

"Oh dear," Cynthia Chesterton said. Her papers were in order but as any scrutiny of them might involve a background check it was something she preferred to avoid.

Sir Mortimer rolled open his window when the Rolls came to a stop at the Home Guard roadblock by the Raven's Roost. There were several uniformed men milling about, all of them armed. One of them approached the car.

"What's the meaning of this?" Sir Mortimer demanded to know. Cynthia sat back, half-concealed by her host who was leaning forwards.

"Roadblock, Milord," the man answered. "We'll need to see your identification, sir."

The man shifted a little to peer past Sir Mortimer. "Everyone's identification, sir."

"Fred Maskall, isn't it?" An icy tone crept into Sir Mortimer's voice.

"Sergeant Maskall, Milord," came the reply. Cynthia told herself there was nothing to be worried about. The soldier was just one of the dull locals, a farmer or carter by day, they might as well have given these men pitchforks for all the good they would do against the *Wehrmacht*.

"This is outrageous, Maskall," Sir Mortimer told the man. There was anger in his voice now. "You know damn well who I am, man."

"There's a war on, sir," the man persisted. "I will need to see your identification."

"Is there a problem?" Another Home Guard soldier approached the car. Cynthia vaguely recognized him.

"Sergeant Hare," Sir Mortimer said. "This man demands to see our papers, it's preposterous. My Rolls is well known and we're heading for Malheur Hall."

"Regulations, Milord," Silas Hare mumbled.

"You will let us pass unhindered and do so now," Sir Mortimer leaned back into his seat to indicate the discussion was over.

"Very well, Milord," Silas Hare shrugged.

The other soldier started to speak.

"I still outrank you, Maskall," Hare snapped at him. "Let them through."

Cynthia smiled serenely as they were waved through the road block and the car picked up speed again. Mortimer knew how to handle the local countryfolk well enough. Farmfolk had no business stopping their betters and demanding this, that and the other.

§ § § § § §

Levesque's men had left the North Woods Lane to walk down a narrow dirt road which led into the Wyrde Woods. After a while the road passed a small cottage which Chunmaniye had noted before. There was a woman by the gate.

"*Bonsoir Madame*," Levesque greeted her.

"First the church bells, now *sodgers* strolling by my home," the woman answered. She had a striking mane of dark red hair and bright green eyes which reminded Chunmaniye of Heechante. "I'd be obliged, sir, if you could tell me what is happening."

Levesque stopped and smiled. The whole unit came to a halt behind him.

"*Madame*, we have received orders to anticipate possible enemy actions."

"The Germans are invading?"

"Not yet," Levesque said resassuringly. "It is a matter of precaution right now. But, I'd like to suggest you stay inside your home for the meantime, eh?"

The woman shook her head. "My daughter is out in the woods, along with other *chavees*. Five that I know of. I'm going to find them first."

Levesque looked at her thoughtfully. "I agree that it would not be wise for these children to be playing in the woods right now."

"That's right," the woman said. "*Naun* if you lot are *gwoan* to be out there looking for German *sodgers*."

"Excuse me, Lieutenant." Chunmaniye stepped forwards. "I think I know these children. They have a fort beyond the ruined village."

"Aye, they've been building something out in the woods," the woman nodded.

"Very well," Levesque sighed. "The woods will be dangerous tonight. Chunmaniye, you know where this fort is."

"Yes sir," Chunmaniye answered without hesitation. The betrayal of their trust was worth their lives.

"Go find them, bring them back here, then join us at Arthur's Fort." Levesque ordered. "With all the haste you can manage, *mon ami*."

Chunmaniye stood to attention and saluted. "Yes sir."

§ § § § § § §

"Wait!" Chunmaniye stopped and turned to see the woman with the red hair following him.

"Ma'am?" Chunmaniye inquired.

"Call me Sarah please," she answered. "I left a note on the kitchen table, in case the *chavees* show up."

"Sarah," Chunmaniye smiled. "It might be better for you to wait at home."

"*Oakum*," Sarah dismissed that idea. "Tis my daughter Joy out there."

Chunmaniye nodded. The chances of enemy soldiers winding up in the woods on this night was small and he suspected that if he did not accept her company then she would head out into the woods anyway.

"My name is Chunmaniye," he said. "We'd better get a move on."

As they walked she looked up at him and he waited for the inevitable comment about his height. Whenever he met new people they seemed to find it important to remind him of it, just in case he had somehow managed to get this far in life without noticing.

Instead she said: "You've met my Joy."

It was not a question but a statement and Chunmaniye nodded.

"She is a remarkable child," he said.

Sarah nodded. "She told me about you. You have been teaching her your ways, she has been lecturing me on your *Wakan*."

"She has been eager to learn." Chunmaniye was wary. The *Saglasa* were often contemptuous with regard to what they called 'heathen' superstitions. He had never, in all this, contemplated the rights and wrongs of teaching Heechante. It had seemed so much a part of both their journeys that he had, perhaps foolishly, taken his interactions with the child for granted, essentially overruling a parent's authority.

"Well," Sarah smiled. "I am much obliged to you, Chunmaniye, much obliged."

"Really?"

"It's been…solitary, for the *chavee* to grow up in the woods. I chose that life, she had no such choice. Meeting her friend Maisy from *Lunnon*, hearing your lessons, *naun* having a dad to learn from…it gives her a broader horizon."

"Ehawee," Chunmaniye laughed, partially with relief that Sarah did not doubt his intentions.

"*Quiddy?*"

"Ehawee, it means 'laughing maiden'," Chunmaniye explained. "The Lakota name I have given Maisy from London."

"It's very apt," Sarah said. "Have you given Joy a name?"

"Heechante, it means 'Owl Heart'."

Sarah smiled at that. "Tis *bettermost*. So how serious is the threat tonight? Your Lieutenant seemed rather concerned."

"London expects invasion to be imminent," Chunmaniye answered truthfully. "Though it would probably be a day or two before this area would come under threat. The children will be safe. The danger, once night falls, is that there will be a lot of nervous sentries in the woods."

They came to one of the flower meadows which patched the woodlands here and still being higher up could see the Wyrde Woods roll southwards.

Three fighters suddenly seemed to fall out of the sky, their sudden roar startling Chunmaniye and Sarah. The first plane, a Messerschmitt 109e, pulled up and barelled southwards over the treetops. The two RAF aircraft in pursuit, Hawker Hurricanes, were slightly slower in levelling but then hurled after their quarry. The harsh bark of machine gun fire sounded loud and thumped in Chunmaniye's heart.

He gave Sarah an apologetic glance. "Though there are some risks."

Just then they heard a thunderous blast which seemed to freeze time for a fraction of a second after which sounded a series of loud thumps and they saw an orange ball of fire blossom to the south. It was followed by another explosion, and then another.

Chunmaniye froze. The bright flashes of detonations came from the direction of Odesby.

§ § § § § § §

"Cover!" Maisy shouted and they all ran into the ruined building again as machine-driven uproar rushed towards Roreford from the north.

A Messerschmitt appeared over the ridge to the west of Roreford and thundered down towards the village. There were two Hawker Hurricanes on its tail and Maisy watched awestruck as their wings seemed to spit fire. The rapid bursts of gun fire were deafening as the Messerschmitt made a sharp turn right over Roreford and then sped westwards. The Hurricane engines bellowed a protest as their pilots forced their aircraft into sharp turns and the two RAF planes howled after their prey.

The echoes of the thudding machine guns were still in Maisy's ears when the first explosion rumbled through the air. At first she thought the Hurricanes must have taken the Jerry plane down, but then she realised the new sound was coming from another direction. She ran out of the ruined building just as further explosions sounded and then stood open-mouthed as she watched orange flames and dark smoke billow up to the south.

"Odesby," Leon came to stand next to her. "Maisy, do you think we should stay out here?"

Maisy turned to look behind her. Katie and Lizzie emerged from the building now, clutching each other's hand and huddled close together. Joy appeared behind them, looking concerned. Joy wrapped her arms around the younger girls and gave Maisy a quizzical look to ask the same question Leon had just asked.

Maisy threw another glance towards Odesby which had just been racked by explosions whilst her ears still rang from the machine gun fire. Katie and Lizzie were clearly scared and Joy was focusing her energy on the girls now. That left just Maisy and Leon.

The words of Gramps suddenly echoed in her ears. *…old sodgers learned to be careful…* She also remembered what he had told her about the Painted Ones chavvies who had thought they could outwit professional soldiers. Then there was that moment of her own carelessness on Odesby High Street.

"We're just meant to be observing and reporting, innit?" Maisy said loudly. "We won't see much when it get's dark. Time to find shelter, I reckon. The Owlery is the closest…we shouldn't split up now."

Everybody nodded their agreement.

"Good decision, Cap'n," Leon said in a low voice and Maisy gave him a grateful smile. Then they headed towards the ridge.

§ § § § § § §

The men at the roadblock looked up when the sounds of explosions rocked the air.

"Odebsy," Mackellow looked at Fred who nodded grimly. He had not expected this.

"Might be an air strike, sir," Fred suggested. "*Bettermost naun* take any chances though."

"Have the men load their weapons, your section only," Mackellow said. "Deploy them around the roadblock, Sarge. And for God's sake, tell them to think twice before pulling any trigger."

Fred began to nod but then the Wyrde Woods seemed to roar and they glanced to their left to see a Messerschmitt hurl from the treetops, trailing flames and drawing fire from two pursuing Hurricanes. The Messerschmitt engine sputtered and then stalled and the airplane ploughed into the field on the south side of Raven's

Roost. The Hurricanes immediately pulled up and soared to greater height before disappearing.

"Maskall, with me!" Mackellow started running towards the field and Fred followed, as did some of the others.

They hopped over the fence and saw that the German plane had made a belly landing, its propellors twisted and a small field of debris littering the gouged up earth behind it.

Mackellow drew his sidearm and slowed down. The pilot of the Messerschmitt forced open his canopy and started climbing out. He was clearly shaken and Fred saw blood running down one of his legs. None-the-less, at this moment he was still an enemy to be wary of.

Fred raised his rifle and trained it on the pilot as the man turned to face them.

"*Hände hoch oder ich schiesse!*" Mackellow shouted, pointing his gun at the pilot too.

"*Nicht schiessen! Nicht schiessen!*" The pilot shouted and raised his arms in the air.

Fred sighed a breath of relief. The Wolfden Home Guard had just taken its first Prisoner of War. He threw a glance at the columns of smoke rising from Odesby. It might not be as easy the next time if the explosions there were a sign of the dreaded Jerry parachutists.

§ § § § § § §

Chunmaniye had sighed a breath of relief when they had run into the children who were making their way to the Owlery.

"I will bring you back," he told Sarah after greeting the children who were cheered to see him.

"*Naun* need," she shook her head and looked pointedly at the smoke that was rising from Odesby. "We're close enough, you'd better join your Lieutenant, I suspect he has need of you."

Chunmaniye nodded. It was beginning to get dark now and if there was enemy activity at Odesby then he had a job to do. He said his goodbyes and departed.

§ § § § § § §

Fred Maskall joined Lieutenant Mackellow for a cup of tea in the Raven's Roost. The men in there were clustered around the wireless.

The BBC spoke of a Luftwaffe raid on London that was of an unprecedented scale. Hundreds had been killed and many more injured. The Ministry of Home Security had released a communiqué: *Our defences have actively engaged the enemy at all points. The civil defence services are responding admirably to all calls that are being made upon them.*

Fred had a sinking feeling when the BBC reported that the raids were concentrated on the docklands in the East End. Some three hundred bombers had attacked that area for over an hour and a half and there were hundreds of fires.

Tom Chalmers reported from the top of Portland House, Fred could hear bombs falling even as the reporter spoke.

I'm standing on top of a very tall building from where I can see practically the whole of London spread round me. And if this weren't so appalling I'd think it would be one of the most wonderful sights I've ever seen. The whole of the skyline to the south is lit up with a ruddy glow, almost like a sunrise or sunset.

A messenger boy came running into the pub. He was about sixteen and proudly wore a Brodie helmet with an 'M' painted on it for 'messager'.

"Yes?" Lieutenant Mackellow enquired.

"Nickleby Home Guard sir," the boy saluted with the enthusiasm which reminded Fred of Maisy.

"You have news on the explosions in Odesby?" Mackellow asked. Suddenly the wireless was forgotten and the boy became the centre of attention.

"Yes sir," the lad nodded. "Twere the Odesby Home Guard, sir. Somebody panicked and blew the charges on the Rore bridges when they saw a Canadian convoy drive towards them. *Naun* hurt, sir, just Odesby pride."

There was a roar of laughter at that, much of it in relief.

Fred shook his head. So far the local Home Guard had put on a poor show. He hoped nobody would start shooting at the Canadians.

His ear picked up the radio broadcast again. It spoke of shattered buildings, ferocious dogfights over the Thames and a sea of flames.

Worried about his daughter who was somewhere in that cauldron of fire he stepped outside with his cup in his hand to scan the horizon. The sun, so fiercely present on this hot day, had begun to withdraw, darkness loomed on the eastern horizon whilst the sun sank into warm hues to the north…Fred frowned…looked again and nearly dropped his cup.

§ § § § § § §

"We can go home, Goody Whitfield," Leon suggested as they approached the Owlery.

"Stop speaking *oakum*," Sarah responded. "The woods are crawling with Canadian soldiers already, all of them with loaded guns, your Canadian friend told me. We don't know what is happening at Odesby either, it might be that German parachutists landed there and there might be fighting in the Wyrde Woods tonight. Tis *naun* a good time to go wandering about in the woods."

"Dad and the rest will be worried," Lizzie said.

"Gramps and Gran will be worried too," Maisy said.

Sarah stopped. "All your folks *ken* you're visiting the Owlery *disyer* day?"

Maisy, Leon, Lizzie and Katie all nodded.

"Well then, they know where you are and will trust me to keep you safe," Sarah said. "I'll fix you all something to eat and find you a place to sleep tonight."

She started to walk again.

"Where is everybody *gwoan* to sleep?" Joy wondered.

Sarah sighed. "I'll sleep in your room tonight, lass. Just this once. My bed is large enough for all you girls and Leon can sleep on the couch."

"It'll be like a party, innit?" Maisy brightened.

"We could play *Snakes and Ladders*, or *Sorry*," Joy suggested, naming all the board games the Owlery possessed. They had been birthday presents from Mum and sometimes the two of them would play.

"*Snakes and Ladders*!" Katie voted and Lizzie nodded. It was the first time the two girls showed some cheer since the first fly-over at Roreford.

They came to one of the flower meadows and for a moment had a clear view of the horizon. There was an oddity which took a fraction of a second to register. Instead of one sunset there were two. The sun was sinking into a bed of rosy clouds to the west but there was another one to the north, glowing brightly: yellow, orange and red. It owned a considerable part of the northern horizon and pulsated and glowed intensily in some places; first here, then there and after that in several places.

Maisy stopped dead in her tracks, lead in her belly.

Joy came to a halt next to her, Leon came to stand on Maisy's other side.

"Is that *Lunnon*?" Maisy vaguely heard Leon say.

"Aye," Joy answered.

"Maisy?" Leon again, concern in his voice but Maisy was far away, on the Isle of Dogs.

"Her mum and dad are there," Joy said softly.

Maisy began to sing, with a quavering voice.

London's burning, London's burning.
Fetch the engines, fetch the engines,
Fire fire, fire…

She choked on a sob. She felt Joy take her hand in hers, and then Leon's hand closed around her other. They both squeezed and then Katie and Lizzie came to stand behind Maisy and put their hands on her shoulders.

Maisy drew strength from that as the children stood there and watched the reality of war as London burned.

The city would burn all night.

26. The Stolen Child

It was a long night. Hare was upset that his men were not allowed loaded weapons whilst Fred's veterans were and he withdrew into the Raven's Roost where he proceeded to get drunk.

Mackellow gave Fred a look of angry helplessness when he heard.

"Malheur?" Fred asked and the Lieutenant nodded miserably.

They reorganised the entire unit on the spot; pairing one of Hare's men with one of Fred's. Some of Hare's men were sullen about it but most found it a comfort. Not knowing how long the situation was going to last Mackellow divided the new unit into two sections. One was to stand down and rest while the other maintained guard.

"I am not invoking rank, Sergeant," Mackellow told Fred as the first group drifted off to the Raven's Roost to find a corner to curl up in for some sleep. "But Sergeant Hare is quite obviously on his rest time now and I think it best if he and I supervised a section together. So I shall sleep first. You're in command."

"Yes, sir," Fred was genuinely enthusiastic. Now that Hare had pulled rank on him with Sir Mortimer it would happen again and again. Having his own command was far more to Fred's liking and he appreciated Mackellow's trust.

As the long night wore on the veterans were gradually shedding their civvy skins and slipping back into a past long gone. When Fred did his hourly round around the various rifle pits they had dug near the roadblock and behind the hedges further along the road he was greeted with confident grins.

"Just like old times, aint it, Corp?"

"Sergeant Maskall to you, Jim," Fred had joked.

"Not back in Arras and Vimy, Corp."

The men were alert and Fred was proud of them. He could also see their presence inspired confidence in Hare's men. It was a good thing too, for lorries ferried up and down North Woods Lane all night, between the army base at Mordrove and the damaged bridges at Odesby. Nervous sentries could have resulted in groups of men firing upon each other; the confusion worsened by the dark.

Shortly after dawn Mackellow was heard bellowing in the Raven's Roost and the other section made a groggy appearance on the dirt terrace in front of the pub. There was no sign of Hare.

"Anything to report?" Mackellow seemed fresh and crisp as he approached Fred.

"Army traffic all night, all friendlies. The men held up well, sir," Fred answered.

"Good work," Mackellow beamed. "Go get some sleep, Sarge."

"Sir?"

"Yes, Sarge?"

"I'd like permission to fetch my granddaughter, she was at the Owlery last night, or so I hope."

"Good Lord, you need sleep man."

"Sir," Fred said as sincerely as he could. "I'll catch three hours of sleep, I promise. But I need to get her home."

"Maisy, isn't it?" Mackellow's eyes lit up. "A very spirited lass."

Fred smiled.

"Go, but if you don't get that promised sleep, I'll have you digging latrines."

"Thank you, sir." Fred snapped to attention and saluted Lieutenant Mackellow who started a grin but then stood to attention to return the salute.

Fred saddled his horse and rode into the Wyrde Woods.

§ § § § § § §

Sarah was up early. She went downstairs and slowly pushed open the living room door to sneak inside. The owls, fortunately, were dozy and none of them greeted Sarah. Leon was curled up on the couch, snuggled into a blanket. Only his unruly mop of straw-coloured hair showed. Sarah smiled and took a few more steps into the living room.

The girls were coiled up every which way and apart from their faces, angelic in sleep, there was a confusion of arms and legs protruding from the pile of blankets on the bed. Though she considered herself a practical woman, not easily given over to emotion, Sarah felt her heart melt at the sight. She had never had qualms about letting Joy grow up semi-feral in the Wyrde Woods. As far as Sarah was concerned a woman needed to know how to put up a fight in order to be independent and keep her head held high.

Even that simple dignity was denied by society unless you were audacious enough to seize it for yourself. Joy's solitude, however, had been a source of worry for Sarah. It no longer was; the very tenderness of the image she was looking at symbolised a collective strength.

Sarah crept out of the room again and shut the door. She went into the kitchen, revived the fire in the oven and put the kettle on it. She would make tea and then see to the animals.

Stepping out of the kitchen door to see what the sunrise had brought this day she saw Fred Maskall ride around the cottage on one of his great big draught horses.

He looked haggard and weary beneath the rim of his Brodie helmet. He was wearing his long leather coat over his Home Guard uniform and had a rifle slung over his shoulder. The horse stopped on its own account and for a moment Fred sat there motionless, every inch the statue of some long forgotten soldier.

Sarah walked towards him.

"Maisy?" He asked tensely.

"Inside, safe, all the *chavees* are here."

Fred slumped, tension leaving him along with his strength. Sarah helped him off his horse.

"Did you get any sleep, *disyer* night?" She asked with concern.

"*Naun*, I'm off-duty now, *howsumdever*…Maisy."

Sarah nodded. She helped him into the kitchen and sat him down by the table while she poured him a cup of tea.

"Feeling the age kick in a bit," Fred confessed, sipping at his tea.

"Betty will have a right go at you," Sarah answered. "You *baint* eighteen no more, Fred Maskall."

"She's mentioned it several times, aye."

"I'm *naun* sending you back to her, without you getting some sleep first," Sarah said in a tone that invited no protest. "*Otherwhile* you'll fall off that horse and break your neck."

Fred nodded. "A corner to kip would be greatly appreciated. Three hours at most though, Sarah."

She frowned but nodded her agreement.

The kitchen door opened and a very sleepy Maisy wandered in. She was wearing one of Joy's old nightgowns which was far too large for her and her hair looked like a crow's nest.

"I thought I heard you, Grip…" Maisy stated groggily and started climbing Fred's lap. He reached for her and settled her in his arms.

"Magpie," he said. "I am mighty pleased to see you, lass."

"We were in the woods Grip, the planes were coming over low…machine guns pounding away…big explosions at Odesby."

"What did you do, Captain Robbins?" Fred asked.

"I'm a *sodger*, innit?" Maisy rested her head on his chest. "We're careful, we are. I ordered a retreat."

Fred looked at Sarah who nodded her confirmation

"You're a *bettermost* lass, Magpie."

Maisy shook her head sadly. "Truth is, Gramps, I were scared, weren't I?"

"You're the bravest grandchild any Sussex man could wish for, Maisy-mine, and a proper Maskall," Fred planted a kiss on his granddaughter's forehead. "I've come to take you back to the farm, Magpie."

"It aint the farm, is it?" Maisy said sleepily.

"*Naun?*"

"Tis home, innit?" Maisy said.

Tired as he was Fred managed to beam.

Sarah smiled. It was time to muck out the pig styes, she reckoned. There only so much sugary sweetness she could handle this early in the morning and she had fair had an overdose since waking.

"Take your *gaffer* upstairs, Maisy," she told the girl. "The bed is empty, he needs some sleep."

Maisy nodded and scrambled off Fred's lap. Turning around to look at him she sounded a bit more awake. "Cor, you don't half look like a proper soldier, innit?"

Fred grinned weakly and then let himself be led out of the kitchen.

"Three hours," he told Sarah in passing.

"Three hours," she promised.

§ § § § § § §

Three hours later the Owlery's kitchen was filled with hungry *chavees*. The previous evening's ordeals seemed forgotten as they chattered happily. Fred and Maisy came down, Fred looking a whole lot better, though immediately deserted by his granddaughter who flocked to the others around the kitchen table.

Fred joined Sarah by the sink where she was cutting up a loaf of bread. She poured him a cup of tea.

"*Bethanks*, Goody Whitfield."

"What news then?" Sarah asked quietly. "The blasts at Odesby?"

"Our own side, blowing bridges."

"Already? How close are the Germans?"

"They've *naun* landed as far as I know," Fred answered. "*Naun* yet, anyway."

"We saw…London, last night, all aglow."

Fred nodded. "The wireless…London was hit very bad."

"Any word from Liz?"

Fred shook his head. "It might be a while, there was much destroyed and they'll focus on putting out the fires and pulling folk out of bombed buildings first."

Sarah grimaced. "Twill be a hard few days, then."

Fred nodded.

§ § § § § § §

Not much later Mus Maskall rode away from the Owlery towards the Forgotten Road followed by Joy and the other *chavees*.

Joy was proud of Maisy. Just as she had done the previous evening, after arrival at the Owlery, Maisy kept up a brave face though in forgotten moments Joy could read the worry on her face. Joy could not even begin to imagine what it was like to see the horizon lit up by a burning city, knowing your parents were somewhere in that inferno.

She sensed Maisy did not want to talk about it but held her friend's hand until they reached the Forgotten Road where Leon and Lizzie set out towards the east and Mus Maskall, Maisy and Katie headed west.

"There's a crashed Messerschmitt in the field next to Raven's Roost," she heard Mus Maskall say.

"Really? Blimey! Can we have a look at it? A Messerschmitt! Who shot it down? What happened to the pilot?"

"Lieutenant Mackellow took him prisoner."

"The Headmaster?" Katie asked and then the voices started to die away.

Joy was in a *bettermost* mood as she started walking back to the Owlery. To begin with she had the Foster's keys tied around her neck with a ribbon. She had told Maisy that she had discovered the perfect hiding place and Maisy had surrendered them to her immediately. The metal felt cold against Joy's chest but reminded her of their joint accomplishment so she did not mind. Much better though, Joy had greatly enjoyed the stayover imposed by circumstance. Having Maisy over occasionally had been grand but Mum had really done her best to turn last night into something of a party. It had taken their minds off the uncertainty of the moment and Joy rejoiced as she once again heard the chatter and laughter of her friends in the Owlery. She smiled and closed her eyes to savour the memory.

It was for that reason that she did not perceive the man who suddenly appeared on the path just behind her. She was not aware of him until he suddenly hooked one arm around her neck and pressed a moist rag against her mouth and nose. It smelled strongly of chemicals.

Joy's eyes widened as she struggled fiercely, kicking backwards, clawing at the arm around her neck. She slowed down her resistance when she was overcome by a strange wooziness. She could barely keep her eyes open…everything around her seemed…

…far away…reaching her with…

…odd delays in…time and…

…the last thing she was aware of was being bundled over her abductors's shoulder and then being carried away into the Wyrde Woods.

27. Mobilisation

The postman stopped to greet Hugin and Munin. He stepped off his bicycle and petted the dogs. Then he turned to stand at attention and return Maisy's salute. She was wearing her Royal Sussex Regiment uniform and though she was dying to know if there was word from Mum, Maisy was also a firm believer in observing correct military etiquette. The postman wore a peak shako hat and a jacket with piping and shiny buttons, it looked almost as important as her own uniform. He had become a familiar sight on Maisy's North Woods Lane patrols and had always promptly saluted back, sometimes five or six times an hour as their paths crossed and re-crossed on their mutual rounds.

Maisy rushed away after the salutes and dashed into the kitchen.

"Gran! The postman!" Maisy shouted and rushed out again.

The postman was walking towards the kitchen door where Gran had appeared, wiping her hands dry on her apron. Maisy followed him. It had been three days since she had returned home from the Owlery. Gramps had left again shortly after bringing her back. The Wolfden Home Guard was to remain out in force for the time being. The BBC said there were troop concentrations at ports in occupied France, Belgium and Holland where the Jerries had been gathering vessels for a channel crossing and London had been pounded by the Luftwaffe night after terrible night. The Canadians, though, had been returning to their base at Mordrove in large numbers, leaving only a few units on standby at Odesby.

"Telegram for you, Goody Maskall," the postman said.

Gran paled and Maisy froze. A telegram could mean one of two things…

"From your daughter," the postman added quickly.

"MUM!" Maisy dashed to Gran's side.

Gran kept her face composed as she reached out for the rectangular slip of paper but Maisy could see her hand tremble as she read the telegram. She handed it to Maisy when she was done.

Maisy saw that Mum had stuck to the minimum of nine words to keep the postal charge at sixpence.

Maskall Farm
Wolfden PO

There must have been some dirt that blew into her eyes because Maisy had to wipe them clean.

"Goody Maskall," the postman said. "We've had a whip-round at the Post Office. *All-along-of* what your Fred is doing for the Home Guard and all. The Post Master said there's enough for you to send a telegram back, free of charge. You don't even need to *gwoan* to the Post Office, I've brought the form."

"Oh my," Gran's sudden smile was beautiful.

The postman took the form and a pencil from his satchel and held them out.

"Try to keep it short, though," he smiled apologetically.

"Maisy?" Gran asked and Maisy took the form and pencil.

She dropped down to the doorstep and started to think rapidly. Short was terrible. She really needed about eleven or twelve telegrams to respond properly but she would have to do with this one. She saw that someone had already filled in the return address and subtracted those words from her total of nine. A penny for each extra word added up fast. She had five words left to convey an ocean of feeling. *Thank you for the telegram* left no room for other words but Mum had to know they received the telegram, otherwise she would be left guessing if it was a response to her own or not. Mum was the type of person who could have a sleepless night over something like that.

Maisy pencilled in the words *Received* and *Relieved*. She thought that was rather clever. Then she pondered the last three words. At last she wrote them down.

She stood up and handed the pencil to the postman. He gave her a quizzical look which she did not understand.

"You may keep the pencil," he said grinning.

Maisy looked at the pencil and saw that she had chewed the end of it into a ragged mess.

"Oh," Maisy said, crestfallen.

The postman laughed at her expression.

"*Gwoan* fetch one of your own pencils, Maisy," Gran chided her. "To replace that one."

"That's really *naun* necessary…" The postman shook his head.

"It is and she will."

Maisy nodded, handed Gran the telegram form and ran inside, raced to her room, collected half a dozen pencils from here there and everywhere and raced back down.

She held out her pencils for the postman to pick one.

"The middle one is only nibbled a little bit," she suggested helpfully.

The postman smiled and took the pencil which was still intact though it had numerous teeth marks impressed in it.

"Does Gramps know?" Maisy asked, looking at the chewed ends of her other pencils with some wonder.

"I didn't see him at the Raven's Roost when I passed, only Hare and I didn't want to *scorse* with him," the postman shook his head. "I can pass the word on my way back?"

"I can ride over and tell him, I can saddle Spark and go now, Gran, please?" Maisy implored.

Gran cast a look at the far-off vapour trails in the sky. "If there's *moil*...," she started saying.

"I'll take cover and hide," Maisy promised. "Did you like my message to Mum?"

Gran bit on her lips and her eyes grew moist. Then she nodded: "Aye, you speak for all of us, Maisy dear."

Maisy beamed and let her eyes wander along the pencilled words one last time before it was entrusted to the Royal Mail.

Received Relieved Please come HOME

§ § § § § § §

Despite her intention to stay clear of Jerry *moil* Maisy decided that she had better bring her bow and quiver of arrows along with her cap gun. The Jerries might decide to impose their *moil* on her forcefully and properly armed she would teach them a lesson that would send them scurrying back to Berlin.

She brushed some dirt off her hat, ran her fingers along the owl feathers stuck in the hatband, straightened the yellow handkerchief around her neck, buttoned up her blazer, patted her ammo and bowstring pouches, looped her bow stave with a string so she could carry it on her back along with her filled quiver and stuck the cap gun in her belt. Then she mounted Spark.

The ride to the Raven's Roost was enjoyable. Maisy felt profound relief at the knowledge that her parents were alive, the sun was shining and Gran had said it was okay for her to ride on to the Owlery. She could share the good news with Joy and ask Joy where she had hidden the keys. Gran had said she had to be home before dark so there might even be time for a small adventure.

"HALT!" Somebody shouted as she approached the Home Guard roadblock. "Who goes there?"

Spark snorted as Maisy urged him to stop and shouted back: "Captain Robbins, Special Detachment, Royal Sussex Regiment."

There was sudden laughter from the hedge by the roadside and Maisy peered in but could not see anything remarkable, other than a hedge.

"Good on you, Cap'n," the hedge told her and she saluted it respectfully just in case it was a high-ranking hedge.

"Come forwards, have your Identity Card ready for inspection."

Maisy spurred Spark forwards while she dug her National Registration Identity Card for under sixteen year olds out of her blazer's pocket. The lad who took it looked to be about seventeen or eighteen.

She handed it over rather proudly. Nobody had ever asked to see it before and it seemed proper that somebody finally took a look at the authorised endorsement stamps in it because they looked dead important.

The Home Guard soldier studied the document. "There *baint* anything in here about officer's rank or the Royal Sussex, be there now?"

"I am on a Top Secret Special Covert Mission, innit Private?" Maisy retorted. "I have an important secret message for Sergeant Maskall. Dispatch from London and all."

"My daughter says *disyer* officer is a Captain of the Royal Sussex, Private Twyner," one of the older men wandered over. It was Katie's dad. "That's good enough for me. I'll take the officer in."

The lad grinned and handed back the Identity Card. "Very well, Cap'n. You may pass."

Maisy saluted him and rode past the roadblock to Private Rye who helped her off Spark and then tethered the pony to a post.

"Private Rye? What's all this?"

Maisy turned round to see the Headmaster in his Home Guard uniform. He had a shiny leather holster for his side-arm, she noticed. It was not new but carefully waxed though the brown leather had discoloured patches here and there.

"Erm," she said. It was one thing to be haughty to youngsters not much older than herself, the Headmaster of her school was another proposition.

"Captain Robbins of the Royal Sussex Regiment, Special Detachment, sir," Private Rye said. "On a top secret special mission to bring Sergeant Maskall dispatches from *Lunnon*."

"London?" Mackellow looked at Maisy intently. "Is it good news?"

Maisy nodded with a shy smile.

"Excellent. Best take her to the Sergeant, Private Rye," Mackellow instructed. "He's been meaning to speak to her on account of the Whitfield girl, I do believe."

"Come along, lass," Private Rye said and Maisy followed him towards the Raven's Roost. On the way to the pub's door she noticed that the Messerschmitt was still in the field. Two members of the Home Guard were positioned by the machine and a number of villagers leant on the fence looking at the crashed plane and discussing it at length.

"Here? What's this about Joy?" Maisy asked Katie's dad as they walked into the pub. She had never been inside before. Her main impression was that the inside of the Raven's Roost looked even older than the outside; a warren of timbered niches and alcoves and passageways to further hidden lairs. Men in Home Guard uniforms formed the only clientele. Some of them were *scorsing* pleasantries, others playing cards or fast asleep on the floor beneath thin blankets.

"Fred will tell you," Katie's dad answered. He led her into one of the passageways and they came to a little nook. "You have a visitor, Sarge."

Rye stopped and gently nudged Maisy into the nook after which he departed.

Fred Maskall rose from his seat. His face seemed worn, lined with worry.

"Grip! It's Mum, she sent a telegram, they're safe!" Maisy burst out. "Mum's safe, and the post people had a whip-round and

Mum's safe and we sent a telegram back and I wrote it and all. Dad is safe as well. So is Mum!'"

She looked at Gramps expectantly. He nodded and tried a smile but it was more of a grimace.

"Aren't you pleased?"

"I am, Magpie. Middling pleased, *surelye*," Gramps said. "There's another problem. It's your friend, Joy."

"Joy?"

"Aye," a woman's voice said. Maisy half-turned to peer into the corner of the nook which she had not seen yet. Sarah Whitfield was there, looking exhausted and distressed.

"She's missing," Gramps said. "Joy's disappeared."

§ § § § § § §

The first thing Joy became aware of was the foul chemical taste in her mouth. Her tongue was dry and she was greedily thirsty. Her memory was a complete blank. For a short frightening moment she did not even know who she was. The air was chilly and had a moist earthy smell like it did in the cellar of the Owlery. How did she get here though?

She discovered that somebody had bound a blindfold around her head and that was frightening. Even more so when she realised she was lying on her side on a lumpy straw mattress with her hands tied behind her back. She tried to shake her hands but did not have very much control over her limbs yet. Where was she? Was this to do with the war? She had a faint impression of mechanical monsters roaring over the Wyrde Woods pumping death into the air around her.

Joy tried to swallow but her mouth was too dry.

"Water," she whispered hoarsely but not loud enough for anybody to hear. She could hear them though; people moving around overhead. Footfalls moving from one space to another; sometimes right overhead. Who were they? Why had they taken her? Where was she?

§ § § § § § §

When Joy had not come back to the Owlery after leaving with Fred and the *chavees* Sarah had presumed that she had accompanied Maisy to Maskall Farm and would stay the night there, as she sometimes did. Though there had been no tolling bells that evening the skies had been alive with planes as another assault on London took place and Sarah told herself that the Maskalls might have decided it would be safer for Joy to stay with them for the duration of another uncertain night.

When her daughter still did not show the next day Sarah had become angry first and then anxious. The bees had nothing to tell and she had wrapped her shawl around her shoulders and walked as far as the Forgotten Road and back. Focusing on her daughter she had a gnawing feeling all was not well though she was not sure if this was her intuition speaking to her or her heart's anxiety. She had barely slept that night and in the morning had decided to set out for Maskall Farm.

Sarah had encountered Fred at the Raven's Roost roadblock. When she had learned that Joy had set course back to the Owlery after saying her goodbyes at the Forgotten Road her world collapsed. Fred had led her into the Raven's Roost for a cup of tea and consultation. Maisy was led in by Private Rye not long after that.

§ § § § § § §

"The keys!" Maisy blurted out

"What keys?" Gramps looked at her sharply.

Maisy shrugged and wrinkled her nose. To tell was TREASON.

"Maisy," Missus Whitfield looked at Maisy intently. "Don't look away lass. Anything you may know that could help us find Joy, any mischief the two of you got into…we need to know."

"Whatever game you were playing," Gramps said slowly. "The rules have changed now, Magpie. New inning, new rules. Do you understand, lass?"

Maisy nodded. She recalled how they had reacted on that morning after Midsummer's Night. They believed in faeries, even though they were grown-up. She could tell them everything.

She told them everything she could think of. Fast and breathlessly. How it started with *Secree of the Wirdewode* and Joy's subsequent encounter with Foster at Malheur Hall. The conversation her friend had overheard between Sir Mortimer and his guest about Rudolf Hess and his interest in something that was hidden in the Wyrde Woods. Foster's insistence that he should not find it. How

Joy had been convinced they were after the Owl Man and had perused the books from the Owlery's secret closet. Then the discovery of the words at St Lewinna's church and Valkerie's recovery of the key right under Sir Mortimer's feet. How Fort Defiance had been destroyed.

"Joy had the keys last. I am sorry," Maisy said at the end of her waterfall of words.

"Don't blame yourself, Maisy," Missus Whitfield said and Maisy was grateful for the words.

"Joy is not to blame though, innit?" she asked.

"*Naun* if Foster is involved," Gramps said. "A request like that…" He shrugged.

"Lady Priscilla helped us too," Maisy said but they ignored that.

"Mortimer Malheur," Gramps said darkly. He looked at Missus Whitfield. "We cannot confront him publicly."

Missus Whitfield nodded.

"But he's a crook, innit?" Maisy frowned. "Do you think he took Joy?"

"There is *naun* evidence that would be credited," Missus Whitfield shook her head.

"But if we find where he's keeping Joy, then we can go get her, innit?" Maisy said.

The two adults exchanged a glance.

"I suspect he has her well-hidden," Gramps said.

"We know where he will take her to, though," Missus Whitfield said grimly. "*Bethanks* to your information, Maisy."

Maisy wanted to ask where but she could see both Gramps and Missus Whitfield were thinking hard and she kept her mouth shut.

"If we don't make an effort searching…," Gramps supplied at last.

"…then he will suspect we *ken* what he is up to," Missus Whitfield nodded.

The Headmaster strode into the nook. "Fred, Sarah. Do we know more?"

He sat down and Maisy looked at him curiously.

"Aye, Barnaby, that we do," Gramps answered.

Barnaby? Maisy was thoroughly confused for a moment. Even on the Isle of Dogs, where she had seen her teachers out of school often enough, it was always strange to realise teachers had another job being ordinary people. Especially when someone as dead important as a Headmaster addressed her grandfather with genuine respect in his voice.

They did not tell him everything though.

"We believe Joy is in the Wyrde Woods somewhere, held against her will," Gramps said.

"Then a search is essential," the Headmaster declared immediately. "I cannot spare many men, though. Ten at most. We're still on full alert."

Gramps nodded gratefully, "Ten would be grand, Barnaby."

The Headmaster hesitated, looking from Gramps to Missus Whitfield and back. Then he asked: "Is this *Pook* business?"

"A part of it might be," Gramps nodded.

"Then you'll know best which men to pick," the Headmaster said. "I'll go and ask Clerky to draw up your orders."

"Bethanks, Barnaby," Missus Whitfield said. When the Headmaster was gone she turned to Fred. "Will ten be enough?"

"More would have been better," Gramps shrugged. "To convince Malheur that we don't *ken bettermost* than to search the Wyrde Woods."

"I can ride to Hornsby Farm?" Maisy suggested.

"On your own?" Missus Whitfield shook her head. "Tis far too dangerous lass, Mortimer will assume you *ken* far more than he would like."

"Meaning she's *naun* safe here either, place is crawling with Hare's men, nor safe to ride back to Maskall Farm." Gramps said thoughtfully. "Jasper and Jeremy will need to know."

"You cannot send the *chavee* off to Hornsby Farm on her own," Missus Whitfield frowned.

"Oh *naun*, on her own would be inviting *moil*," Gramps admitted and Maisy's face fell.

§ § § § § § §

Time became an obsession for Joy. The passing of it became interminable; seconds stretched into minutes which seemed like long hours. Snatches of sleep seemed far too short but she had no way of knowing how long she had slept when she woke again. She discovered that she could shift into a sitting position on the mattress and would sit up to lean against a rough brick wall, its texture coarse to the touch of her fingers where her bound hands, mattress and wall met.

There was nothing to look at but darkness due to the blindfold but Joy would keep her head upright and sometimes shift it slightly to the left or right as she used her ears to pick up any sounds she could hear. She kept telling herself not to panic for she could perceive a tidal wave of fear looming nearby, ready to overwhelm her with madness.

Joy tried to take stock of her situation. Her ears told her that there were two distinct patterns of footfalls in the building. One thundered; heavy practical thuds which brought the owner from one place to another with impatient determination. The other shuffled, barely taking his or her feet off the floor, sweeping the floor in slow unhurried movements. One of them was a man, the other a woman for Joy could hear occasional voices. Never distinct enough to hear what they said but clear enough to differentiate between a man's low baritone and the woman's higher contralto.

Joy felt weak, her thirst was raging continuously now and she was faint with hunger. It must have been some time since she had last eaten or drunk and she wondered if she was being deliberately weakened. That brought her back to the purpose of her incarceration and struggling with her fears which tried to impress upon her horrible lurid images of her intended fate.

§ § § § § § §

Maisy rode Spark north along the North Woods Lane. The pair were dwarfed by Privates Rye and Twyner who rode behind her on great big draught horses, the chin straps of their Brodie helmets fastened and their rifles slung over their shoulders. They had strict orders to escort Maisy to the Hornsby Farm and then bring any men they could muster in the eastern Edgelands to Roreford where they would meet with the rest of Sergeant Maskall's chosen men. If Maisy had not been fraught with worry about Joy she would have thought the escort rather cracking.

The three riders slowed down and drew towards the verge when a small convoy of army lorries passed. Maisy stared at them dully until an idea started to form in her head.

§ § § § § § §

The sounds of the combined footfalls changed, they came from a new location and Joy realised that they were coming down a stairway. The door of the cellar opened with a loud creak and Joy instinctively looked that way. She was rewarded by a dim perception of a light source.

Joy took a deep breath as she heard both distinctive foot patterns up close now, they had both come down into the cellar. She felt vulnerable, unable to see them and sensing that they were both observing her.

"Water, please," she whispered.

There was a loud metallic click which shut Joy up immediately. Someone had bolted a rifle or a shotgun.

"*Naun moil* from you, do you understand?" A man's voice said. It sounded vaguely familiar as if Joy had heard it before one or two times. She nodded her understanding.

"I'll untie your hands," the woman said. There was nothing familiar about her voice other than the broad Sussex accent. "So you can drink and eat. If you so much as touch the blindfold I'll take the middling food away."

Joy nodded again and shifted her back towards the voice to allow easy access to the rope which bound her hands. Causing *moil* was the last thing on her mind; all she could think about was the promised food and drink. The woman shuffled forwards and untied Joy after which she handed her a chunk of bread and a tin tankard filled with water. Joy drank from the tankard with relief, the water was cold and fresh and she had never tasted a finer beverage in her life.

"Who are you? Why am I here?" She asked when she was done and her hands were tied behind her back again.

The only answer was a grunt after which Thunderer and Shuffler departed again, leaving Joy alone in her prison cell.

§ § § § § § §

Chunmaniye was in Lieutenant Levesque's office helping to tally the use of provisions during the three days that they had remained at their battle stations in the Wyrde Woods. There was a tentative knock on the door.

"Come in," Levesque hollered as he frowned at a stack of forms in front of him.

A young Private entered. "Sir, there's somebody at the gate wishing to speak to Walking Tree's commanding officer."

Levesque and Chunmaniye exchanged a puzzled glance.

"Well, that would be me, *n'est-ce pas*?" Levesque shrugged. "Does this person have a pass, eh?"

"Nope, sir," the soldier shook his head. "It's…well the duty officer at the gate suggested you come have a look sir, you'll understand then."

Levesque seemed glad to let the paperwork be and gestured at Chunmaniye to follow him out of the Nissen Hut which served as his office and sleeping quarters.

When they got to the gate they were greeted by quite a sight.

Ehawee was there on her pony, dressed in her uniform and adorned with her bow and arrows. Behind her were two men dressed in Home Guard uniforms. They towered over Ehawee on large horses and were armed with rifles. Ehawee gave Chunmaniye a little grin but he could sense something was amiss.

Levesque walked towards them. "What's the meaning of this?"

"Captain Robbins, Special Detachment, Royal Sussex Regiment," Ehawee saluted.

Levesque looked puzzled for a moment, then he grinned and saluted back. "Lieutenant Levesque, at your service, Captain."

"I wish to parlay, *Leftenant*" Ehawee told him.

"*Parlais*?" Levesque smiled. "Very well, Captain."

He motioned at the guards to open the gate and stepped outside, followed by Chunmaniye.

They withdrew to the other side of the road and Ehawee told them that a local girl had gone missing. Chunmaniye felt a cold dread when he understood it was Heechante.

"My men and I," Ehawee indicated her escort, "are raising a search party. Now I reckon, Leftenant, that this would be a cracking exercise for your men, innit? Be seen to help in local matters for one, scouting the woods like proper soldiers for two, and helping us save Joy for three."

Ehawee had said all this in complete earnesty and when she finished she looked at Levesque expectantly.

"*Mon Dieu*," Levesque shook his head. "And you thought to recruit the Canadian Army for your purpose, eh?"

"A local officer, sir, sent by our superior at the Home Guard HQ," the elder of the two Home Guard Privates spoke up. "Requesting your assistance, sir."

Levesque shook his head again. *"Mon Dieu, les Anglais!* The *Boche* would be crazy to invade this island."

§ § § § § § §

As time passed Joy learned to use the noises she could hear to re-define time. There were times when both the people were in the house and times when only Shuffler was at home. There was also a time when the noise produced by both Thunderer and Shuffler ceased altogether to be replaced by the sound of the occasional rat scuttling around the cellar. Those were tense moments for Joy because the rats were curious and came to explore the mattress. She would draw herself against the wall and use her legs and feet to kick out in the directions where she perceived the scratching of rat's paws to be. There would be little sleep for her until the occupiers of the house roused again to amble to and fro above; a signal for the rats to make themselves scarce again.

Exhausted, Joy would succumb to sleep at last but never a long peaceful one, desperate snatches at most till a loud noise would startle her back into that miserable cellar wondering again and again where she was and why. A range of scenarios passed through her mind but as time passed Joy began to suspect that it might well have to do with the keys and Tuckersham Church. Why else would somebody lock a girl into a basement?

§ § § § § § §

Fred, Sarah and eight of Fred's picked men reached Roreford to find it deserted. Fred asked for two volunteers for sentry duty and told the rest to stand down. To Sarah's surprise they more or less immediately dropped down in the shade of a chestnut at the edge of the clearing and seemed to fall asleep instantly.

"Old campaigners," Fred told Sarah. "Sleep and eat whenever you can. We should try and catch a nap too, twill be a long day."

Sarah was reluctant to sit down in the shade of the tree, convinced she was far too anxious to relax but she nodded off soon enough, exhausted as she already was.

She had no idea for how long she had slept…five minutes or hours…when she was drawn out of her sleep by a voice. She was slow in coming to and realising where she was and why.

"Sarge, Sergeant Maskall!" The voice was insistent. "Sarge, you're *naun gwoan* believe this."

Sarah saw that Fred too was slow to return from his slumber. He grumbled and scrambled up after which he helped Sarah to her feet. All around them the other soldiers stirred and began to stand.

The sentry who had woken them pointed, needlessly, towards the Farisee Bridge.

"By Merlin's beard!" Fred shook his head.

Fred's granddaughter led the procession which was crossing the Farisee Bridge, flanked by her Home Guard escort and Leon Hornsby on his dappled grey. Behind her Jasper drove the Malheur carriage which was filled with Hornsby *chavees* and their bows and arrows. Behind the carriage strode Jeremy Hornsby at the head of half-a-dozen farmers and carters armed with pitchforks. These were followed by Lady Priscilla marching at the head of a squad of women dressed as maids, stable hands or groundkeepers. They all carried broomsticks over their shoulders apart from the formidable cook who wielded a wood rolling pin. The reinforcements were completed by a Canadian Lieutenant at the head of a platoon of fully armed soldiers marching in disciplined order.

"Oak's Acorn," Sarah shook her head. "That's some Maskall you're raising there, Fred."

Fred nodded slowly, "There's something of everything and everything of something in that lass."

Maisy could contain herself no longer and spurred Spark forwards until she reached them as the procession behind her filled the clearing.

"I brought some help, innit?" she said. "Now we can go find Joy."

§ § § § § § §

Joy woke and immediately perceived a difference in the cellar. There was a dim glow which suggested a light source had been brought in. She remained motionless as she tried to verify the change in circumstance using her hearing and smell. A cold chill closed around her heart when she honed in on the new sound and identified it. It was the sound of somebody breathing. Someone was in the cellar with her and she had a strong sense that the person was looking at her.

Somebody other than the two prison keepers she had come to know. This new person's breathing was different. Thunderer drew irregular shallow breaths, Shuffler huffed and puffed as if every effort was one too many. This breathing was soft and measured in a disciplined rhythm.

Joy struggled upright, seeking the support of the brick wall as she stared blindly into the cellar.

"Who are you?" She asked.

There was no answer, just that sustained breathing which did not change in its pattern at all.

Joy suddenly felt terribly vulnerable, more so than with the exposure when Thunderer came to stand guard as Shuffler allowed Joy brief freedom to eat, drink and use the smelly bucket in the far corner of the cellar.

"Why am I here?" Joy demanded to know, trying to avoid fear creeping into her voice. Never show fear, she had learned. Doing so was the fuel that fed their longing for more. "I know you are there."

The breathing continued steadily; neither denying nor confirming the presence.

Joy could almost feel the eyes which were probing her and she shivered, getting goose bumps all over. Blind and bound she was at a terrible disadvantage.

"Who are you?" She asked again, this time directing her words not to the cellar in general but at the source of energy which she perceived to be close by.

Her nose picked up a fancy scent; cologne.

"Is this about the keys?" Joy asked. She thought there was a very brief cessation in the rhythm of breathing and pressed her case. *"Releuen the stoon and thou shal fynde me. Cleuen the wode and I am ther."*

She could detect a very light change in the breathing, it seemed just a bit more forceful. Joy was suddenly certain that it was Sir Mortimer. That realisation struck home hard for it answered all sorts of questions about her imprisonment. He had dropped hints, that afternoon in the Cat's Chamber, about certain interests he had concerning the Wyrde Woods. His determined efforts to obtain the keys betrayed an intensity of ambition which now made her wonder how much he knew and what he was after.

§ § § § § § §

Gramps spoke to Jasper, Jeremy and the Canadian Lieutenant while Missus Whitfield went to have a word with Lady Priscilla. Maisy dismounted Spark and surveyed the Roreford clearing with some pride.

Priscilla left soon after, leading her Marauders back into the direction of Malheur Hall. There was thunder on her face.

"Is Lady Priscilla angry?" Maisy asked Joy's mum when she came over to Maisy.

"Aye, but *naun* at us," Missus Whitfield answered. "Her folk are *gwoan* search Malheur Hall and the castle grounds."

"Oh, good," Maisy said.

Gramps split those who stayed behind up into several search parties, mixing the Canadians and Home Guard with those who knew their way around the Wyrde Woods. The Hornsby's had brought horns to blow and a signal system was agreed on. Each party was assigned a part of the Wyrde Woods to search, mostly in the northern Wyrde Woods, and would blow intermittent single notes on the horns which Joy might be able to hear, wherever she was.

Gramps walked up to Missus Whitfield and Maisy.

"Sarah, I want you to *gwoan* home to the Owlery."

"*Naun*," Missus Whitfield shook her head.

"Joy might show up there, Missus Whitfield," Maisy suggested.

"Maisy-mine is right. *Asides* that, if we find her, we'll send for you, straight away," Gramps said. "*Howsumdever*, Sarah, the real test will be tonight. We need you strong and rested."

Missus Whitfield uttered an angry groan which left unclear if she agreed or not.

"And you," Gramps turned to Maisy. "You've done a *bettermost* job today, Captain Robbins. What role did you see yourself play in this afternoon's search?"

Maisy had quite a few in mind. She let her eyes pass the assembling search parties. Leon was there, and Chunmaniye, Gramps of course, the Hornsby's and a proper Canadian Lieutenant.

325

All would be interesting to accompany. What would Joy have chosen? Maisy glanced at Missus Whitfield.

"Sergeant," she declared. "I shall escort Missus Whitfield to the Owlery and stand guard as she rests."

Gramps was taken aback, he had not been expecting that answer, Maisy reckoned. Then he smiled.

"You never cease to amaze me, Magpie, tis a *bettermost* choice."

"I shall be glad for the company," Missus Whitfield said softly. *"Bethanks*, Maisy."

"Leave Spark with me," Gramps added. "I'll take him home when I fetch your *gammer* to drive her to the Owlery tonight."

§ § § § § § §

Maisy and Missus Whitfield started walking to the Owlery.

"Why tonight?" Maisy asked.

"*All-along-of* all the folk looking for Joy now," Missus Whitfield replied. "Tis bound to make holding her till the next full moon more risky. We're forcing their hand."

"Oh, is that clever?"

"Tis a gamble, but *bettermost* now, with all the folk what showed up," Missus Whitfield replied. "Two or three days from now those numbers will fall rapidly. There's a war on, folk have other tasks to attend."

"And you think they'll take her to Tuckersham Church?"

"I said *naun* such thing, *chavee*," Missus Whitfield looked at Maisy sharply. "Neither did your *gaffer*."

"Well," Maisy shrugged. "That's where the Owl Man lives, innit? Joy said the big key fits a door in the church somewhere."

"A door in Tuckersham Church?" Missus Whitfield frowned. "I aint never seen that, did she tell you where the door was?"

Maisy shook her head.

"I'm *naun* sure how much of a living tis, for Ufmanna," Missus Whitfield shook her head.

"Ufmanna?"

"That's what our folk have called the Owl Man from the days of old. When *disyer* Sussex were the Kingdom of Suth Seaxna Lond. Your kin too."

"Kingdom? This is England, innit?"

"Tis now, afore the Angles had their Kingdom in Anglia, the West Saxons had their Kingdom of Wessex and us South Saxons had Suth Seaxna Lond. Twere a Kingdom for nigh on four hundred years, though twas more than a thousand years ago."

"And Ufmanna is from back then?" Maisy's eyes grew wide.

"*Naun*, he had a different name afore us Saxon folk arrived, he's much older. For a long time, I recollects, he'd give folk a fright, raid their chickens and take the occasional sheep. Then him were drawn to the village and his mischief took a dark turn."

"Was he the one who destroyed Tuckersham?"

"Naun, in the end it were the villagers themselves who did that," Missus Whitfield shook her head sadly. "By murdering one of the Guardians of the Wyrde Woods who helped us bind Ufmanna. One of her own, she was. Lisa Malone They hung her from a tree."

Maisy felt a shiver pass along her back.

"Bind?" She had images of rope, lots of rope.

"Bound by spells," Missus Whitfield answered. "Spells to keep the creature bound to its lair, so it could *naun* more terrorise the Wyrde Woods."

"Bloody hell!" Maisy exclaimed. "And the Nazis want it released to cause trouble for the troops?"

"I suspect so," Joy's mum answered. "That's why they needed that key. It's the first step to breaking the spells, battering the door down will *naun* do."

"Has anybody tried before?"

"Aye," Missus Whitfield said grimly. "Mostly out of curiosity, but Ufmanna is guarded and we thought the keys well hidden."

"The Guardians of the Wyrde Woods!"

"That's right, Maisy."

"You're one of them, aren't you, Missus Whitfield?"

"Indeed I am."

"And what's the next step? To break the spells?"

Missus Whitfield stopped walking. Maisy did too and saw how Joy's mum looked sad and weary all of a sudden. Most of the time she looked strong, but sometimes that strength seemed to seep out of her. She looked at Maisy, seeming to appraise her.

"I would like to know," Maisy said. "Joy's my friend, innit?"

"Aye, that she is," Missus Whitfield smiled warmly for a moment. Then she looked Maisy straight in the eye and said: "The next step they will need to take is to make a blood sacrifice."

Maisy felt faint when the implication of those words struck her like a hammer blow.

§ § § § § § §

Joy remained silent and so did the visitor who continued his steady breathing but made no other sound, not even the smallest movement. Joy did move, shifting about uncomfortably under the gaze she still felt. What did Sir Mortimer – for she felt sure it was him now – want from her? She was astutely aware of the cold weight of the keys on her chest.

She froze again when she suddenly heard the visitor shift; walking closer to her now. Joy pressed her back against the wall as hard as she could.

"The Guardians will stop you," Joy cried out in half a panic.

The visitor stopped walking and began laughing; the noise unexpectedly loud in the underground space.

"The Guardians know nothing," the man spoke vehemently. Joy was puzzled. The voice was partially what she had expected but there was an undercurrent of energy to it that frightened her. If this was Sir Mortimer he was acting very differently from the other occasions where she had heard or seen him. There was naked aggression and cold confidence in his voice.

"The Guardians have unwittingly aided me, even." Amusement too this time and then the man stalked closer to Joy. She could feel the mattress shift slightly as he knelt down on it in front of her and every one of her senses seemed to scream his proximity at her.

"I needed more than the keys," the visitor chuckled. "I needed…"

Suddenly his hand rested on her temple and she shuddered and wanted to whimper. Slowly he brushed his hand downwards along her cheek – making her skin crawl – and then grasped her chin and held it firmly, raising her face upwards a little.

"You," he whispered.

Joy did whimper when he rested his other hand on her shoulder and shifted her dress aside to bare a shoulder. She was trembling now, though she fought to try and get it under control. His breathing quickened. He let go of her chin and laid both hands around the back of her neck. He brought his face forwards for she could suddenly feel his breath hot in her ear and on her neck.

"Your blood is mine," he hissed. Then he slowly pulled his thumbs back till they pressed against her throat. "There we are."

The pressure of his hands was lifted off her neck and throat and she felt him slip the ribbon around her neck up; the keys lifting off her chest.

"We'll start with this," the visitor sounded well satisfied and rose to his feet. "You I will see later, young Joy Whitfield."

He departed, leaving Joy in the cellar, slumped on the mattress and shivering violently.

§ § § § § § §

Katie Rye hovered around the roadblock at Raven's Roost with great uncertainty in her mind and fear in her heart. The fear was twofold. Earlier that day she had been seized by a sudden conviction that her friends were in danger. Joy, Maisy, Leon and Lizzie; especially Lizzie for Katie had come to love her new friend more than anybody else in the world. Joy and Maisy were kind and granted her courage but they were often wrapped up in the dynamics of their own friendship, something Katie both envied and admired. Then she had met Lizzie who seemed to understand Katie's every thought, hope and fear. It was that friendship which had given Katie the courage to confront Maisy and Joy about their behaviour, something a hundred thousand miles outside of her comfort zone.

The unformed fear had simmered in Katie all day long and when her father had come back home briefly from his Home Guard duties and told her he had searched the Wyrde Woods for Joy those fears had erupted into a cascade of dire intuition. Katie had followed her father back to the Raven's Roost unseen and slipped across the road where she stalled by the entrance to Shims Copses.

Katie had already begun to traverse the somber and sullen forest here without Maisy or Joy but that had been in daylight and it was dark now and she was near paralyzed by fear of entering the haunted woods on her own.

Her conviction that all was not well in the Wyrde Woods was stronger in the end and Katie made her way into Shims Copses with trembling limbs and goose bumps all over. In a way the darkness made it easier for she could not feel but only sense the doom and gloom there but there were a few times when she nearly screamed because of unseen branches brushing her arms or legs.

Katie did scream, loudly, when the darkness turned into a sudden sea of bright light which blinded her.

"Well, well, what have we here?" A man's voice enquired and Katie realised the light came from a torch. The man lowered it and she recognized him.

Sighing a breath of relief and offering a tentative smile Katie answered: "I am on my way to the Owlery."

"On your own? In the dark?" The man shook his head. "I am heading in that direction myself, walk with me."

Katie nodded eagerly and followed him deeper into Shims Copses.

28. Grounded

Sir Mortimer had been unusually smug during the evening. A small predatory smile played on his lips when he lost himself in thought and Cynthia thought it was endearing. He reminded her of a tom-cat in his prime; confidently stalking fledgling birds in a garden. There was a savage undercurrent to Sir Mortimer which appealed to her. It was usually hidden deep beneath the veneer of social etiquette; a game Sir Mortimer played to perfection, but she had detected it closer to the surface at times, especially on their rides through the Wyrde Woods. She had been startled this evening when she realised just how close it came to spilling over the edges tonight; something had set his blood boiling.

She smiled at him with a smugness of her own. Had she been a fledgling bird she would have been nervous and keen on being elsewhere. Cynthia was quietly confident about her position vis-à-vis this particular tom-cat though; any fledgling unfortunate enough to be hooked onto his claws would be dragged, dead or alive, to her and he would offer her the choice bits first.

Cynthia knew the old Lady Priscilla kept a far sharper eye on goings on in Malheur Hall and the Wyrde Woods than she pretended to and Cynthia suspected that Sir Mortimer's mother believed that Cynthia was having a love affair with her son. There had been ample opportunity for discreet encounters and Sir Mortimer had hinted that he was willing. At times Cynthia found it hard to restrain herself; they were matched in elegance, intelligence and ambition and he was a handsome specimen.

Two things had stopped her. The first was private, she wanted to be more than a temporary mistress this time, she had seen an opportunity here to gain far more once her mission was completed. Priscilla Malheur would contest it no doubt, but Cynthia had set her eyes on Malheur Hall itself. It was not unrealistic. Sir Mortimer was an elegant bachelor but the years were beginning to press on him and he had a duty to produce offspring. She was from a respectable family; a wealthy one with all the right connections. Any child she might bear him though, would have to be legitimate, so she did not encourage his advances but ensured that he knew she was not discouraging him either. She gave him just enough hope to continue his pursuit and knew that made the prospect of her conquest all the more enticing for him. He was an intelligent man and knew what game she played but went along with it willingly, no doubt assuming he was the one in control as they circled one another in a dance of words which was slowly drawing them inexorably into a tighter orbit.

This was advantageous for the second reason she was learning to play him. Most men in his situation would feel an instinctive desire to show their prowess; display their might in order to prove they were the most compatible and advantageous partner. The longer she held him off the more he would want to prove himself. This was why Cynthia believed she was the one in control. Clever as he was, Sir Mortimer was driven by a man's instinct and his willingness to prove himself useful would stand her in good stead in the completion of her mission here in the Wyrde Woods.

"If I did not feel it would be too forward," Sir Mortimer broke her reverie, "I would venture to observe that you seem very much at ease this evening."

She looked at him. She was; a situation helped by Priscilla Malheur's earlier departure which entailed that she shared the dining table with Sir Mortimer alone this evening.

"Almost...," he studied her with a light smile on his face, "...feline and I do apologize if that comparison offends you, Cynthia."

She allowed a slow smile to spread on her face, taking the coincidence of her own similar comparison as a pleasant reminder that their minds were much alike.

"I shall take it as a compliment, Sir Mortimer," she purred and, almost imperceptibly, straightened her back some in a slow subtle and languid manner which could not fail to beguile a man alert to such signals. "I am indeed complacent and will have to divide the blame equally between the ambience of your home, the excellent food and the pleasure of good company."

"*Mea Culpa*, although I would have hoped to merit more than a third of the blame," he said with a twinkle in his eyes.

"Then you shall have to earn it, Sir Mortimer," she smiled sweetly. "You are, after all, Lord and Master of both the Hall and its larder. Surely it is within your capacity to exceed them?"

She saw a tiny spark of anger in his eyes though his face betrayed nothing.

"I am Master of more than that, Cynthia," he said with a dangerous edge in his voice.

Cynthia smiled, he was trying to impress her now and that was precisely what she wanted – needed for her mission. She decided that the time had come to see how he would react to a breach of etiquette. Instead of formulating a flowery reply Cynthia simply said: "Show me."

§ § § § § § §

Maskall Farm was fading into an awkward dusk. As usual the sounds were plentiful; chickens squawking, geese honking outrage, sheep bleating, pigs *scorsing* guttural pleasantries and flurries of whinnies and neighs. There was no sound from the farmhouse itself though. Not even the mice were stirring.

The *scritch* owl came gliding in as coolly as the unseasonally chill evening air. It forewent the usual precautionary recons and went straight for the fence post of one of the paddocks. It screeched loud fury at the lock mechanism and then tackled it with its claws, causing a ruckus which raised a cacophony of alarm from the other Maskall Farm animals.

The paddock fence swung open and a foul faced New Forest pony trotted out and followed the owl to a long shed behind the main barn. The pony turned tightly by the door allowing its rearward kicks the best distance for the impact of its hooves. Three were enough to force the elderly wood to yield, the fourth kick swung the door wide open to the chittering consternation of its occupants. More squeaks of alarm followed when the owl flew into the shed and made straight for one of the back cages where it unlatched the door and then hovered higher. A sleek white ferret came out first. It paid no attention to the owl whatsoever and that was a signal for some eleven companions to follow their leader out of the cage –

<blockquote>out of the shed –

off the farmyard –

down the dirt access road –

into the Wyrde Woods.</blockquote>

§ § § § § § §

Mortimer smiled at Cynthia. He had been enjoying their exchanges, loaded with subtle entendres and hidden meanings. Well conducted courtship was an art to begin with but there was far more to it with this young woman. Her mission to begin with. Mortimer had come to admire her drive and tenacity. There was his own agenda as well; though it had much overlap with hers his own ambitions reached far further than this delightful creature could possibly anticipate. Now that she had challenged him he would start to reveal to her just who her ally in the Wyrde Woods was.

The double doors of the dining room were flung open and inwardly Mortimer groaned as his mother came striding in; thunder on her face.

"Miss Chesterton," Mother barely managed a tone of civility in her voice. "I desire to have words with my son and would appreciate a moment alone with him."

"Mother, can this not wait until after desert?" Mortimer frowned.

"I shall oblige, My Lady," Cynthia said and rose from her seat.

"There is no need," Mortimer said, looking at his mother coldly. "I have no secrets to be kept from Miss Chesterton."

Cynthia looked pleased, a little smile playing on her lips, but Mortimer's mother shook her head.

"You may not, Morty," she decreed. "But I do. Miss Chesterton, if you please?"

Cynthia nodded and left the dining room.

§ § § § § § §

"Dad, you can't be serious." Leon, surrounded by siblings and cousins, glared at his father.

Jeremy, Jasper and Jenny were making preparations for their departure in front of the thatched farmhouse. All of the other children looked at their fathers angrily as well. They had been told they were to stay put at Hornsby Farm shortly after returning from the afternoon and early evening's fruitless search of the Wyrde Woods.

"*Naun* joke," Jeremy growled. "You'll be staying at the farm as I told you."

"Joy is our friend!" Lizzie said angrily.

"We have *naun* idea what we're dealing with, Liz," Jasper said.

"Most likely to be Guardian business," Jenny added.

"Do you not recollect the Tale of Tuckersham?" Jeremy asked Leon.

"That was centuries ago, times were different," Leon frowned.

"Guardian business," Jasper said grimly, "*baint* always pretty."

"Nor good for your health," Jeremy said with finality in his voice. "You stay put and you mind the other *chavees*, that's the end of it."

Leon looked down at the ground in surrender and the rest of the tribe drooped.

§ § § § § § §

"Sergeant," one of the Home Guard veterans approached Silas Hare who was trying to enjoy a pint in the Raven's Roost. Lieutenant Mackellow had leave and Sergeant Hare was the senior officer at the road block.

Hare frowned in reply to the veteran. The men ought to know their duties well enough without having to bother him every other minute.

"Something mighty odd at the Carfax just now, Sarge," the veteran said. "A pony came trotting up the North Woods Lane and took a turn up the old Wolfden Road."

Hare shrugged.

"There were about a dozen ferrets on the pony's back and an owl flying over its head," the veteran added.

Hare laughed. Ferrets riding a pony were amusing. Then he frowned. The animals were heading for the Wyrde Woods. He stood up.

"The telephone," he barked. "I need to make a call."

Ten minutes later the veteran soldier who had approached Hare earlier saw the Sergeant come out of the Raven's Roost with a handful of his loyal followers.

Sergeant Hare made to stride right through the roadblock.

"Sarge?" The veteran asked.

"I have an assignment, we'll be back later."

"But," the veteran looked puzzled. "You're the officer on watch, Sarge."

"Which means I get to do what I like without having the likes of you question me," Hare sneered. He marched off with his men, heading for the path which was all that was left of a long forgotten road.

"Mother I must protest," Mortimer shook his head. "This is not how I care to treat guests in Malheur Hall."

"You will release the child at once and bring her to me," Priscilla Malheur was clearly in no mood for games.

"I do not know what you mean," Mortimer replied.

His mother looked at him, her eyes conveying a mixture of anger and sadness.

"I was afraid you would make that denial," she said sharply, and then continued with weary resignation. "I was hoping that your interest in certain aspects of the Wyrde Woods was on a par with your other interests in managing Malheur Hall and the estates, Mortimer. Curiosity and knowledge, to take it any further is dangerous."

"It is precisely that, no more, no less," Mortimer insisted, though he knew it was in vain.

Mother turned to him, her eyes softer now.

"We both know better than that, Mortimer," she paused and Mortimer was surprised to see genuine concern on her face. "There is a reason some things were hidden," she continued. "Their lure is strong but they are rotten to the core, Mortimer. Do not be tempted to believe you can master them."

"Or else?" Mortimer bristled. Mother's level of awareness gave him cause for concern – how much opposition to his plans could she muster? How much did she actually know?

"You'll get hurt," the softness left her face and Mortimer experienced a brief flash of sadness but then he stiffened his resolve.

"Quite frankly, Mother, I do not know what you are talking about."

She responded with another weary look and then departed without a further word. Jenkins came in soon after.

"Sir Mortimer," the butler said. "There's a telephone call for you, from the Home Guard at Raven's Roost."

"Thank you Jenkins, I'll take it in my study."

Mortimer pondered the conversation with his mother as he made his way to the study. He also recalled the fragment of *Secree of the Wirdewode* he had shown Cynthia, the text just below the image of a small ornate box which contained what he sought.

> *No swerd or spere may do what I can*
> *For I keep derk myght noon moot hath*
> *The derknesse moot dwelle unbidden,*
> *Kept sauf and cursed, I its secree holde*
> *Releuen the stoon and thou shal fynde me*
> *Cleuen the wode and I am ther.*

It was time to set into motion that which would bring Mortimer the dark might which so frightened his mother. He had the keys and he knew where the box could be found. Unlike his mother he did not fear what was in the box and he wanted the rewards which would be his if he could slip the Blood Ruby on his finger.

§ § § § § § §

"You might as well have sent me back to Maskall Farm, with Spark," Maisy tried to contain her anger.

Gran, Gramps and Missus Whitfield looked at her with collective resolve. It made Maisy feel helpless.

"Joy is me mate, innit?" Maisy could not avoid something of a plaintive whine and disliked herself for it. She wanted control; wanted desperately to communicate her absolute conviction that she was needed in the Wyrde Woods tonight.

"There will be strange critters abroad tonight, Magpie," Gramps turned into Grip. Sergeant Grip. Maisy's most reliable and experienced NCO. "Twill be dangerous. Even for us, twill be desperately dangerous."

"The Owlery is safer than Maskall Farm tonight, dear," Betty added. "You recollect Midsummer's Night?"

Maisy's face drooped as she nodded. Howls and screams. Smelly boggerts with sharp appetites.

"Is this a special night then? An old feast night?" Maisy asked, she could not recall any mention of it.

"*Naun*, it *baint*," Gran shook her head.

"*Howsumdever*," Gramps said, "somebody has called upon the Wyrde Woods to weaken the boundaries *atween wurrelds*, almost as if twere Samhain."

Missus Whitfield stepped forwards and then knelt down in front of Maisy so that they were eye to eye. Maisy liked that. Joy's mum laid her hands on Maisy's shoulders.

"I love you dearly, Maisy Maskall. Joy could not have asked for a more loyal friend. She would want you to be safe tonight. You'll be safe at the Owlery."

Maisy nodded miserably.

29. The Summonings

The door of the cellar opened.

"Tis time," Thunderer grunted. "And your time be up, lass." He chuckled at his own joke.

Joy felt an involuntary shudder spread from her spine. Despite the blindfold she squeezed her eyes tightly shut as she heard heavy footfalls approach her straw mattress. She held her breath as she waited for rough hands to seize her and take her to Sir Mortimer.

§ § § § § § §

Chunmaniye arrived at the circle of standing stones. He had asked Levesque for permission to continue the search when darkness had come and the Canadian contribution to the search party made to return to the Mordrove base.

Levesque had hesitated. "I suspect, *mon ami*, that when they warn about local attachments it is matters like these that cause more concern than trying to steal a barmaid's kiss in the local pub, eh?"

Chunmaniye had nodded. It was not to be denied.

"Very well," the Lieutenant had shrugged. "You have my permission, I want you back at the base in the morning. If trouble comes from it, however, I cannot shield you, *n'est-ce-pas*?"

"*Merci beaucoup*, Lieutenant Levesque."

"*Merde!* I do not approve, Chunmaniye, eh?" Levesque had shrugged again. "I suspect however that if I don't give my permission you will go anyway and I will have to court-martial my best soldier."

Chunmaniye had shrugged, unsure if he would have disobeyed Levesque.

"Clear the matter up," Levesque had said briskly. "I want you back tomorrow, fully focused on defeating the *boche*. We have a war to fight."

"I look forward to counting coup with you, Lieutenant," Chunmaniye had saluted him and taken leave of the soldiers.

He had been carrying his holy shirt in his pack all day and when he arrived at the stone circle he put it on.

Chunmaniye took place at the edge of the circle. He needed guidance.

"WAKAN TANKA!" He called. "Please hear me, I have need of…"

"Kleak-kleak," Heechante's owl uttered calmly as it appeared from nowhere and hovered in front of him.

"*He-ay-hee-ee!*" Chunmaniye exclaimed. He had imagined conflict to involve outfighting the German soldiers and chasing them back to Berlin. *Wasichu* business. Instead he found himself in the midst of his Lakota journey and seeing Thallie brought him absolute certainty as to why Wakan Tanka had brought him here, far from Chunmaniye's own world yet near it. Tonight his journey and that of Heechante would converge, both would become *Heyoka*.

"Kleak-kleak," Thallie repeated.

"*Hecheto welo*," Chunmaniye answered her. "It is well done."

§ § § § § § §

Maisy sat on a rocking chair by the fire, rocking steadily to the beat of her impatience. Every now and then she would jump up and pace around the Owlery's living room.

She frowned when she paced to the hallway door and spun around to walk to the far wall again. Feeling helplessly inactive was not something she took to with grace and it was certainly not improving her mood.

She spotted a pile of Joy's books and picked one up. Maybe she could read to take her mind off things, though she doubted it very much. The book was a copy of *Through the Looking Glass*, one of Maisy's favourites. Maisy leafed through a few pages before choosing a random passage.

> *'Twas brillig, and the slithy toves*
> *Did gyre and gimble in the wabe:*
> *All mimsy were the borogoves,*
> *And the mome raths outgrabe.*

Maisy read the words aloud to an empty room, for even the owls were gone. Her eyes were drawn to the small spidery letters in the margins. Joy's handwriting.

UFMANNA – HEOLSTOR & DREFAN
All bound, ALL unbound by blood.

Maisy narrowed her eyes. There was more than one bad guy? She read the next words.

There is only ONE place for
blood sacrifice in the Wyrde Woods.
ONLY ONE! ONLY ONE!! ONLY ONE!

"Bugger!" Maisy nearly let the book fall out of her hands. She knew that Grip, Gran and Missus Whitfield were heading for Tuckersham Church.

It was the wrong destination. Joy would not be taken there.

§ § § § § § §

Fred, Betty and Sarah made their way to the Guardians with a firm stride. Hugin and Munin circled them. Fred carried his quarterstaff, the women were unarmed. Little barred their way although the green jennies fretted restlessly in the water as they crossed the Farisee Bridge at Roreford. By the time they reached Lewinna's Pool the air was becoming heavy with menace. Both dogs raised their hackles and would occasionally bare their teeth at the shadows.

Though the full moon was bright enough to cast shadows much of the Wyrde Woods around them remained inscrutably dark. There were noises though. Ominous ones. They were being followed now but the creatures did not yet dare attack the three Guardians.

"The Guardians," Sarah said when they reached the standing stones. "We'll wait here for the other four."

She and Betty were drawn to the silent contemplation of the centre stone but Fred paced up and down the two avenues between the stones impatiently whilst Hugin and Munin prowled around the edges.

"There!" Fred pointed at the cavernous mouth of the path to Tuckersham as it was swallowed up by the woodlands at the southern edge of the clearing. He stood by the furthest stones and was much closer but Sarah and Betty could see well enough a dark robed shadow stride by the edge of the clearing towards the path entrance. The shadow carried an elongated white bundle over his shoulder and seemed to look in their direction before moving towards the path and then disappearing into the darkness beyond.

"He's got her!" Fred hissed loud enough for Sarah and Betty to hear for they had come his way.

"My Joy!" Sarah said and made to go after the menacing figure.

"Sarah, wait!" Betty called out but it was too late, Sarah had already broken into a sprint. Betty turned to Fred, "We should wait for the others."

"That might leave it too late for Joy," Fred shook his head and whistled Hugin and Munin to him. "And Sarah for that matter."

Betty nodded grimly and the Maskalls headed for the path entrance at a trot to follow Sarah Whitfield.

§ § § § § § §

The Lady of the Wyrde Woods approached the Shy Maidens with reverence. Her archers stayed behind to prowl the forest around the periphery of the clearing dominated by the standing stones and the reflection of the moon on the exposed crescent of sandstone.

Priscilla lowered her hood and opened the cape she was wearing far enough to expose the pendant which hung from a slender silver chain around her neck. The pendant depicted a stylised swimming swan with river reeds rising around the creature and it glittered bright in the moonshine. Priscilla moved to the centre of the circle and knelt down there, raising her arms in supplication. She tried to banish her anger. It was anger that was aimed at herself for Priscilla realised that she had been blinded by her feelings for Mortimer. Although his character and ambitions often seemed totally alien to her he was still her son. The abduction of the Whitfield girl though, the pure base depravation of such an act, had opened her eyes at last.

The Lady of the Wyrde Woods had no doubt that if it had been anyone else delving into the darker secrets of the Wyrde Woods she would have taken note and appropriate actions well before such a dark risk grew into a threat. With Mortimer however, she had closed her eyes to tell-tale warnings which hindsight now reminded her of. Blinded by her refusal to believe that her own son could be capable of such dark desires. Alarm bells had started ringing when Fred Maskall had told her Maisy and Joy had found two keys; not one as Priscilla had expected. She knew, however, what lock the second key could open and the realisation had struck her like a hammer blow.

She perceived in the Wyrde Woods this night that the fabric of her own world was unravelling to mix with others and that alone told her that Mortimer's powers far exceeded her worst fears. It would have taken all of the Seven together to accomplish such a feat.

The worst of it was that it would not be Priscilla who paid the price for her mistake; others would and they would pay with their lives.

Priscilla closed her eyes and forced her doubts away. Berating herself was a luxury for later. As Head of the Seven she needed to concentrate on what, at best, would be a damage limitation exercise. She swallowed and then submitted to a bitter novelty; thinking not the best but the worst of her son. Sarah had told her that Maisy had confessed to having uncovered Mortimer's interest in Ufmanna, something Priscilla had already begun to suspect. Charged with the safekeeping of the Tuckersham key Priscilla had allied herself with the girls to snatch it away from Mortimer's eager hands in the nick of time. Still she had assumed it to be a mere curiousity on Mortimer's behalf; one he could be protected from. She would have never involved the children had she realised the extent of…

…stop it. This isn't about you, this concerns the Wyrde Woods and all who live in it. Focus.

What did Mortimer hope to gain by using the Tuckersham key and a blood sacrifice to unbind Ufmanna? The creature would spread terror at will, unable to distinguish between soldier and civilian, good and evil, innocent and corrupt. Unless…there was the other key, if he used that he would be lost to Priscilla forever but she doubted he would be concerned by that at all. She thought her heart would shatter into a thousand pieces by losing her second son in such a manner. Then, with a grim look on her face, she decided that she had to accept he was capable of giving in to the yearning desire for power; power to impose his will on the Wyrde Woods and plunge it into darkness. She would have to confront him and if necessary attempt to destroy her own son.

Priscilla rose to her feet slowly, feeling old beyond measure, and then walked towards the forest edge. The three archers met her there; Jasper, Jeremy and Jenny all looked at her with questions in their eyes. Priscilla swallowed.

"There's going to be a change of plans," she told the other Guardians. "We're not going to Tuckersham Church."

"Do Sarah and the Maskalls *ken*?" Jasper asked.

"No," Priscilla shook her head. "And we have no time to lose for they are in grave danger, probably as we speak."

"Ufmanna," Jeremy growled.

"Worse," Priscilla said. "Mortimer doesn't intend to just unbind him. I suspect he intends to bind Ufmanna to his own will and direct the sprite's fury at whomsoever he pleases."

"Oak's Acorn," Jasper's eyes grew wide.

"He'll be taking Sarah's lass to Gallows Hill then," Jenny concluded.

"Yes," Priscilla nodded, "to be fed to the Blood Stone."

§ § § § § § §

Maisy decided she would have to venture outside. Grip and the others were heading in the wrong direction. Joy would be alone out there. Maisy gritted her teeth, earlier disappointment replaced with a sudden anxiety. She had never been out in the Wyrde Woods at night on her own and she was plain scared.

She froze when there was a sudden knock on the front door. It was followed by more, sounding from an odd place by the bottom of the door.

Farisee? Should she stay in Joy's room if they visited? No. She had to go find Joy.

"Who's there?" Maisy called loudly.

There was an impatient grunt outside followed by renewed knocking. Maisy did not know what to do.

"Who's there?" She called out again.

"Opening the middling door would satisfy your curiosity, *surelye*," a voice complained as its owner walked in from the kitchen. "Instead of letting Master Dobbs do all the work."

Maisy's mouth dropped open as a wee bald man, half her own height and impossibly slender with long spindly limbs and a great big red nose grumbled his way to the front door.

"Wait! Master Dobbs!" Maisy called out as the *Farisee* reached for the door handle - just within his reach - and swung it wide open.

"Mistress *baint* home, what do you seek at the Owlery *disyer* night?" Master Dobbs announced rather formally whilst Maisy still stared at him in wonder. Then she forgot all about Master Dobbs as the visitor stuck his head over the threshold of the Owlery. It was Spark.

§ § § § § § §

Sarah reached Tuckersham Church just in time to see the dark figure slip into the ruins and she hastened after him until she reached the entrance after which she walked inside cautiously.

The white bundle the dark figure had been carrying lay forlorn and unmoving right in the centre of the ruins. Sarah gasped, was she too late already? She rushed forwards to the bundle and fell on her knees to unwrap the white sheet, her heart pounding. Then she frowned for the bundle contained nothing but compressed straw.

There was a metallic click and Sarah looked up to stare straight into the barrel of a hand gun.

§ § § § § § §

Fred and Betty sped down the path leading to Tuckersham Church, Hugin and Munin at Fred's heel. Fred clutched his quarterstaff with grim determination as he emerged on the dirt road which ran along the ruins of the church. He saw Sarah Whitfield disappear into a gap in the church wall where a doorway had taken centuries to erode into a wider fissure.

Fred and Betty looked left and right, trying to determine if anybody else was here but the forest around them seemed unnaturally empty. All for the owls that was, there were a remarkable number of them up in the trees hooting and screeching as if giving a dire warning. Hugin and Munin growled softly.

Then they heard a man's laughter from the ruins followed by an anguished cry and they strode towards Tuckersham Church. Ere they reached the gaping entrance though, the dogs started barking furiously at the half dozen or so men who rose from concealment behind tombs and gravestones; sneering and grinning. There were metallic clicks and Fred and Betty found themselves staring into the barrels of the rifles aimed at them.

Silas Hare stepped forward, chuckling. "Call your dogs to heel, Maskall, or I'll have them shot."

Joy was still trembling on the straw mattress. Reprieve had come at the very last moment. Someone had called down the stairs; the woman.

"Leave her be. His Lordship sent word that he's found another one. There's other plans for the *draggle-tail's chance-born*."

The man had grumbled and then backed away and slammed the cellar door shut with a mighty bang before he locked it. Shortly after she heard them stumbling about before a door was opened, shut and locked after which the house was left ominously silent apart from Joy's rapid intake of breaths.

She had not considered that another *chavee* might be chosen for tonight's offering. Who had they captured? Joy felt a shiver run along her spine. Lord Mortimer had seen one of the others on a number of occasions: Maisy. Joy pictured Maisy's beamish face, expressive in curiosity, anger, laughter and love.

Please, don't let it be Maisy. Joy fought to keep panic at bay, fought to banish images of Maisy's body prone on the grass at the foot of the Blood Stone. Whichever one of the Wyrde Warriors they had captured, Joy had no doubt as to Sir Mortimer's intentions. Blood had to flow this night. He did not just want to release Ufmanna, he wanted to bind the creature to him. His behaviour in the cellar earlier had revealed a deep level of sinister desire for power. The sort that would devour him in the end but she sensed he was already drawn in beyond that insight. *Heyoka* but not the good kind.

Joy could only hope that the Guardians would realise, as Joy had done, that Sir Mortimer's ambitions were of such a scale that he would have to revert to the Blood Stone on Gallow's Hill to raise the dark. If they went to Tuckersham they would be confronted by an awakened Ufmanna under Sir Mortimer's full control. The Owl Man would be a lethal weapon and Joy was not sure if the Guardians would be able to withstand its fury unprepared. Had Foster foreseen such a disaster?

There was a familiar scratching from the corner of the cellar and Joy bit on her lip. The rats were coming back; she could hear them scurry into the room. She grew nervous when she realised they had come in larger numbers this time, it sounded like a good dozen. Worse, they headed straight for her mattress.

§ § § § § § §

"Leon," Lizzie called to the kitchen table where the tribe had gathered in morose gloom.

Leon looked up at his cousin curiously. She had walked over to the window because she said she had heard a noise.

"Come look," Lizzie said with a calm urgency the others would not respond to. The tribe tended to do everything at once. When it was time to brush their teeth they all crowded around the sink at the same time. If one of them went to the outhouse the rest would be queueing outside in no time. However, Lizzie did not want to share this with them yet, this was something to work out with Leon.

Leon jumped up and walked to the window just as Lizzie opened it.

An owl hopped in and balanced on the sill. She was a scritch owl and looked from Leon to Lizzie and then tilted her head 90 degrees to peer at the other *chavees* inside.

"It's Joy's owl," Lizzie said in a voice full of wonder.

Leon nodded speechlessly.

"Kleak-kleak," Thallie said and then turned to face the night, rotating her head backwards to throw the two cousins an impatient look. "Kleak-kleak."

§ § § § § § §

Maisy put on her belt and checked her pouches before brushing off imagined dust from her Royal Sussex badge. Impulsively she took one of her precious cap rolls and loaded her cap gun. She sure felt she could use some of the silver bullets Lady Priscilla had referred to in her note. Maisy stuck her cap gun in her belt and put her hat on her head and strode towards the door. Spark was out in front, she could hear him fret with impatience.

Master Dobbs was still by the door. "Good luck Captain Robbins. Please bring Joy home safe."

Maisy stalled and looked at him. There had been genuine concern in his voice. He looked back at her imploringly. The little fellow really cared about Joy. Maisy dropped to her knees to get to eye level as Missus Whitfield had done earlier.

"I'll do everything I can to help Joy, Master Dobbs," Maisy said solemnly. "Cross me heart and hope to die."

The *Pook* shuddered. "Tis dangerous out there."

Maisy grimaced. "I was afraid of that."

"You should hold your left thumb in the palm of your hand and fold your fingers over it, like this," Master Dobbs showed her. Maisy did likewise and looked at him questioningly.

"Keep it like that," Master Dobbs whispered. "The *Farisee* may harass you but can't harm you that way."

"Thank you," Maisy said, looking at her clenched left hand.

"You should also wear a piece of clothing inside out," the *Pook* continued to whisper his secrets.

Maisy laughed.

Master Dobbs looked puzzled.

"I put on me own socks this morning," Maisy clarified. "They've been inside out all day. I like them that way. Thank you Master Dobbs."

Maisy rose to her feet and was about to stride outside when something occurred to her.

"Master Dobbs?" She asked.

"Yes Captain Robbins?" the *Pook* replied.

"Can you do something for me? Outside in the garden?"

"Aye, I can go there," Master Dobbs looked curious. "What do you have in mind."

"The Guardians think that Joy has been taken to Tuckersham Church. But they won't find Joy there, she'll be taken to Gallows Hill, innit? To the Blood Stone."

Master Dobbs shuddered at the name. "Tis a cursed place."

"Can you tell the bees?" Maisy asked.

"The bees?" The *Pook* looked at her with wonder in his eyes. Then he understood and he began to chuckle. "I understand, Captain Robbins. The bees will be told."

"Cracking," Maisy smiled. "Thank you."

Maisy strode outside. Master Dobbs closed the door of the Owlery behind her. Spark uttered his moody opinion on all the delay.

"Hold your horses," Maisy grinned. "That was dead useful, mate."

Maisy sat down and began to take off her right shoe. Spark rolled his eyes and grumped a grunt. Maisy ignored him and rolled down her sock. Taking a pen-knife from her pocket she proceeded to cut the closed end of the sock open.

"Gran will have a fit," Maisy confided in Spark. "But you can help me sew it back together afterwards."

Spark shook his head in exasperation.

Maisy scrambled to her feet and enticed Spark to lift a foreleg. Making sure the remnant of the sock was still inside out she slipped it over the hoof and hoisted it up until the sock was stretched tight enough not to come loose.

"See Spark, if you wear an item of clothing inside out, the *Farisee* cannot harm you," Maisy stepped back and looked at her work with satisfaction. Then she stuck her bare foot back into her shoe and tied the laces. When she was done she mounted the New Forest. A good screenplay, she figured, would call for an epic off-to-battle speech to inspire everyone. She did not have much time though and would have to settle for something shorter.

"Hi-ho Spark! Away!"

Captain Robbins of the Special Detachment of the Royal Sussex Regiment and Spark, possibly the ugliest pony in Sussex but also the most loyal mount one could wish for, rode off into the dark reception of the Wyrde Woods to find Joy.

30. Hunters in the Night

As Cynthia looked around her on top of Gallows Hill she was much reminded of the antics of Aleister Crowley and she regarded the scene with mixed emotions. Mortimer had insisted they all wear dark hooded robes. He himself was wearing one as were the five hooded men and women he had introduced as 'followers'. Cynthia herself too, was wearing one and she thought it was quite a nuisance. The robe was itchy and smelled of a previous occupant to begin with but it was hard to see anything as well. The hood had been designed to conceal a face but it kept on falling down to block sight of all but her feet. Those were not happy with the robe either, it was an effort to walk without becoming entangled with the generous folds of cloth.

She was impressed by the effect it created in the silver stage light cast by the moon; the hooded figures encircled about a menacing standing stone stained with dark moss touched an ancient archetypal recognition in her which she could not deny.

So far however, it was just theatre and Cynthia had been led to believe, by Mortimer's hints and suggestions, that he had access to some sort of power. She had half expected to be led to a hidden corner of Malheur Hall to find a weapons cache of sorts. A hidden arsenal with which to arm a highly mobile paramilitary unit that would harass any Army efforts to resist the *Wehrmacht* when the *Führer* unleashed his will onto the Sussex coast. She had allowed herself the fantasy of leading Mortimer and such a unit into an burning England lost in fear and chaos to ensure Oswald's safety. That, more than anything, would ensure Mortimer's standing in a New England; it was not inconceivable that she and Mortimer could rule a vast domain as an old-fashioned Duke and Duchess.

Instead, he had led her to Gallows Hill, south of Malheur Hall, to a theatrical scene which seemed to pose symbolic resistance only. If this were the extent of his 'power' then she would, for the first time, have to re-evaluate Mortimer's hold on reality. This was only a little better than his mother's squad of maids with broomsticks.

The one possible redemption was formed by the last person on the summit of Gallows Hill; the only one not donned in a black robe. The girl had been dressed in a simple white shift and lay on her side some six feet in front of the Blood Stone. Her hands and feet had been unbound but she lay there quite calmly, Cynthia suspected the girl had been drugged. She looked every bit the sacrificial offering in this carefully staged play of dark power. Perhaps there was something to this, for although she believed that the creatures said to be slumbering in the Wyrde Woods existed, her task was only to locate them, she had no idea how to rouse them from their sleep and perhaps Mortimer did know.

Cynthia looked at Mortimer. *Could he? Would he?*

"This is not the child I expected to see," Cynthia said.

"Ufmanna is but a test of what you wish to see unleashed upon these woods to spread terror and chaos amongst its defenders," Mortimer answered. "That child is mine now and her blood is powerful, we will need it when the time comes and it will flow."

Cynthia nodded, though she wondered if Mortimer did not have some attachment to the child and was deliberately delaying her demise. That was a weakness, however…she looked at the other girl by the foot of the Blood Stone again. If he were to transcend theatre and end a life here tonight then she had truly found a ruthless ally for her cause.

§ § § § § § §

The first leg of Maisy's journey, the path to Roreford, posed no problems. It was not even entirely dark for the moon had begun to rise and cast a remarkable amount of light already. Even so there were large patches of woodland where the light did not penetrate and the menacing darkness there gave Maisy goose bumps. Spark was undeterred though, trotting towards Roreford with calm determination. His confidence was reassuring. Maisy looked at her left hand; if she just kept her thumb and fingers in place then no *Farisee* could harm her, she kept telling herself.

They reached the point where the ridge started sloping down towards the Forgotten Road and Roreford. A fine mist seemed to be seeping up from the lower ground. It hung low but by the time that Maisy and Spark had come down the hill it was much denser so that it appeared they were approaching a lake shore. Spark slowed down and then came to a stop. He whinnied nervously.

Maisy dismounted and walked forward a bit, patting Spark on his neck and then rubbing his nose. She took a step forwards and was fascinated by the disappearance of her foot and ankle in the soupy mist.

Spark snorted.

Maisy lifted her foot back up. It was still stuck to her leg. With relief she turned to Spark. "See, nothing to it, Spark."

Spark shook his head and took a few backward steps.

"I know!" Maisy exclaimed. "But there aint much choice, mate."

Walking forwards again, both feet disappearing into the mist this time, Maisy was pleased to note that Spark followed her. The mist began to rise though and by the time they were nearing the Farisee Bridge it reached to her knees. The bridge rose ahead of them, its rounded arches an island in a white lake now. Maisy began to hum *Over the Rainbow* because it seemed quite appropriate as she was not quite sure if she was in Sussex anymore.

It really was like walking in water a little. Maisy studied the small swirls that marked her passage. There was less resistance than water, of course, although Maisy was convinced the fog offered far more resistance than it ought to. This was unlike any London fog and she had experienced plenty of those. Maisy half expected to see a fish or two weaving in and out of the long green tendrils of river grass which swayed languidly around her feet.

Maisy froze.

She looked again.

This really did look like the vegetation she had seen dancing in the current of river and stream, not proper regular grass which was far shorter in length.

Spark whinnied, his eyes wide.

"Shhh," Maisy stroked his neck. "It's fine Spark. We're safe."

She saw that the long green tendrils moved playfully around Spark's hooves as well and narrowed her eyes. She looked up and around them. Her heart started pounding in her chest when she discerned four shapes in a rough circle around them. They were for the most part submerged beneath the fog, with just their heads and backs showing as they swayed in the mist on all fours. Though they seemed to have a human physique their skin looked scaly and they had no nose or nostrils to speak of, just a little bump below eerily cold blue-grey eyes and above their somewhat elongated mouths which opened to reveal wide rows of glittering teeth. Their hair was incredibly long and drifted around them on the surface of the mist bank.

Kelpeye. Green jennies. They've crawled out of the river in their water shapes.

Maisy shivered.

They can't hurt us, they can't hurt us.

One of the jennies cooed at Maisy and two of the others burst into shrill laughter.

"Fresssh fisssh," the fourth hissed.

§ § § § § § §

"The Witch of the Owlery herself," the man chuckled. "Just as his Lordship said."

His voice sounded familiar to Sarah though his face was concealed by the hood of a dark cloak. There was no mistaking the revolver he held though.

"Where is Joy? Where is my daughter?"

"You expected her to be here," the man chortled.

"Yes, her blood to unbind Ufmanna," Sarah said, deciding that talking would buy her time and perhaps reveal the foe's intent.

"There's a lot which you didn't expect," the hooded man said with triumphant satisfaction in his voice. "All Seven of you. All that needs to be done here is to unlock a door with a key the Master happened to run across. Plus a little extra."

Sarah's blood chilled. Maisy had said that Joy had been in possession of the keys.

The man continued, "the main business will be conducted elsewhere."

Sarah's heart sank as she realised that could only be the Blood Stone on Gallows Hill. The Master her captor served was far more ambitious than they had realised.

The hooded man laughed.

"The little girl will be strangled and become part of the Wyrde Woods forever more."

Sarah groaned and made towards the man in anger but he was fast and this time the barrel of his revolver pressed cold against her forehead.

"Back," he ordered and she obeyed reluctantly.

"Strangled slowly," he drew out his syllables. "Ever so slowly to intensify the power of her passing. Your daughter will be able to enjoy every moment of it."

He started laughing, cackling like a maniac and Sarah uttered a cry of pain as she cringed.

Joy. My sweet girl.

The laughter stopped as abruptly as it had started and Sarah was sure the man sneered as he continued.

"You'll have no time to grieve, Goody Whitfield, for a blood offer will be needed here as well."

The words had no impact on Sarah, whose entire being focused on her daughter, held against her will somewhere and at the mercy of these madmen. She looked up slowly though, when she perceived the barking of dogs.

Hugin and Munin!

The barking stopped again.

"Your friends," the hooded man said. "But they can no longer help you."

His words were followed by loud gunshots which crashed their fury into the dire night.

§ § § § § § §

A most remarkable thing happened in the cellar. Joy could smell Maisy and for the first time since she had come to in her prison Joy relaxed as she gave a happy sigh. There was great comfort to be had from such a presence of her dearest friend. The pitter-pattering of tiny feet on the floor no longer filled her with dread. The rats had smelled horrible. These were not rats. Joy took a deep breath as the invaders swept around her, tasting with relish the light musky smell that was in the air. Maisy smelled like that too, as did Mus Maskall. Suddenly she could feel little claws on her scalp as one of the ferrets seized her head as anchor whilst it used its teeth to worry the knot of Joy's blindfold.

Joy giggled as similar pressure was applied to her lower back and bottom as a whole bunch of ferrets started tugging and pulling the knots of the rope which bound her hands together. The claws did not puncture her skin and tickled more than anything else as the ferrets worked out the intricate structure of the knots and proceeded to untie them. Joy suddenly understood far better why both Mus

Maskall and Maisy were so taken by the animals. They were exceptionally clever little beasts and both the old poacher and his granddaughter were drawn to intelligence like moths to a flame.

Before she knew it the blindfold fell from Joy's face and she was able to sit up. She was free to move her arms but lifting them forwards was painful and she briefly lost her strength in them halfway through the movement. A pale shape, just a little lighter than the dark – which did indeed pervade the cellar – scurried around to her front and dooked.

"Valkerie?" Joy said with wonder in her voice, slowly rubbing her wrists.

The ferret dooked some more and then, in a motion that was both familiar and strange, scrambled up Joy's arm to nest herself on Joy's shoulder.

Joy wanted to laugh and cry. She really wanted to pick Valkerie up off her shoulder and cuddle the animal but something told her Valkerie would just as happily nip Joy as come to her rescue.

"Now what, Valkerie?" Joy asked sadly. "I doubt I'll fit into the rat tunnels to crawl out of here."

Just then there was an almighty crash above them. Joy uttered a small squeal of fear, along with some of the startled ferrets. Her heart sank as she heard heavy footsteps overhead. They would just tie her up again.

"You'd better go Valkerie, take your friends," Joy whispered to the ferret on her shoulder but Valkerie just dooked again; totally unconcerned. Then a great loud voice bellowed upstairs.

"HEECHANTE!"

Joy's mouth dropped open.

§ § § § § § §

"You can't hurt us," Maisy called out waveringly.

All four of the creatures hissed and suddenly the green tentacles which swirled around Maisy's feet were withdrawn.

"Come on Spark, I've had enough of this bloody nonsense," Maisy resumed walking, heading straight for the Farisee bridge. The creatures all submerged beneath the mist but their movement caused a disturbance and Maisy could see four swirls heading for the bridge faster than she and Spark were approaching it.

Maisy mounted Spark again, feeling far safer in closer proximity to her friend. When they came to the bridge all four jennies had emerged, blocking access.

They all made crooning and cooing noises now, grinning at the joke of it.

"Here fissshie."

"Fancy a ssswim?"

"Kisss me fissshie."

"Sssweet *chavee*. Sssweet, sssweet *chavee*."

The first green tendrils swayed forwards, slithering just below the mist they made unerringly for Maisy and Spark. Maisy felt her heart pound in her chest and throat but she hid her fear. Instead, she laughed and the creatures hissed in surprise.

"Fiddle-dee-dee. You're just bullies, that's all!" Maisy exclaimed. She knew how to deal with bullies. "I aint got time for this, innit? Let me pass."

The jennies cackled.

"Now!" Maisy ordered and pulled her cap pistol from her belt. She raised it into the air and fired thrice. Instead of making the little popping noises the gun produced three sharp bangs. The jennies seemed to shrink in on themselves, withdrawing their green tentacles and showing fear on their scaly faces.

Maisy soothed Spark who shifted about nervously. Then she looked at the cap gun with admiration, Lady Priscilla had provided right fancy ammo indeed. Maisy lowered the cap gun, aiming it straight at one of the jennies. Did Lady Priscilla's cap rolls do more than just produce much better noise? The jenny screeched and Maisy raised the cap gun to aim over the creature's head. She sensed it would not do to harm a *Farisee* unless it was actively trying to tear Maisy's head off. She pulled the trigger and thought she could see something rip through the air over the jenny's head. The creature screamed and dived underneath the mist. In rapid succession Maisy aimed three shots just above the others who gyred down into the mist amidst panicked screeches.

"HEE HAW!" Maisy hollered and used her knees to direct Spark forwards. The pony understood and gave her all he had; accelerating at surprising speed. When he reached the whirling line of gyring and garbling jennies he launched himself and Maisy into the air and arced over the Farisees before pounding onto the bridge.

"Cracking!" Maisy shouted and slowed Spark down. She turned round to see the faces of the jennies spitting helpless fury. Looking back to the Forgotten Road, which stretched eastwards in front of them, Maisy's eyes grew wide and her mouth dropped open.

"Cor blimey!"

§ § § § § § §

"Chunmaniye!" Joy intended to shout but discovered that she was unable to. All she produced was a hoarse croak.

"HEECHANTE!"

"I'm down here," Joy croaked. She stood up and swayed with dizziness for a moment. Then she made for the direction of the door.

"HEECHANTE! *CHUNTAY SKOO YA!*"

Using her last strength Joy started beating on the door with her fists.

"Chunmaniye!" She cried and found within her a source of anger which allowed her to keep up the barrage of beats. His footsteps thundered down the stairs and suddenly the door handle moved.

"Heechante, stand back from the door!" She heard him call from the other side and she stepped backwards to the mattress.

"*HUNTA YO!*"

There was a mighty crash. The door was flung wide open to allow dim light and a large Lakota warrior to spill inside.

Valkerie dooked in approval.

"*Hau mushkay*, Heechante," Chunmaniye said formally after he regained his balance.

"*Han kholá*, Chunmaniye," Joy smiled. Things were beginning to look up.

§ § § § § § §

On Mortimer's signal one of the robed figures walked to the Blood Stone, a spade in his hand. The figure stalled after he had passed the girl. Mortimer could sense his hesitation.

"Get on with it," he ordered curtly.

John Hare, for it was he who was concealed by the robe, shook his head.

"The Blood Stone, Milord," he said nervously.

"The Cottage, your brother's farm," Mortimer answered, reminding Hare of the power he held and the destitution which awaited disobedience.

Hare wavered, then turned around to face Mortimer, shaking his head. The man was trembling with fear but threw down the spade none-the-less.

Mortimer glowered at him, he had not counted on this. They had talked it over many times and John's sacrifice would have been well rewarded.

"Oh bloody hell," Cynthia spoke and strode forwards towards Hare to pick up the spade. She proceeded to walk towards the Blood Stone.

Mortimer wanted to shout. A loud 'NO'. A warning to not touch the Blood Stone for it was cursed by the hundreds of anguished voices of those who had met their end atop Gallows Hill.

Someone had to do it though. Mortimer clenched his teeth as Cynthia laid her hand on the Blood Stone's surface as she positioned herself and then drove the spade into the ground before the stone.

"That is how it is done," Mortimer rumbled at Hare. "We will talk of this later."

The small box was wrapped in a waxed canvas sheet and not buried deep at all. When Cynthia brought it to him and she and Mortimer unwrapped the canvas he could see that the sturdy wood had withstood time better than its ornate decorations which had lost all shine and were covered by flakes of rust. The small key he had taken from Joy Whitfield's neck, however, slipped into the old lock mechanism effortlessly. Upon turning, the lock mechanism clicked open without resistance and Mortimer reverently lifted the lid up. There was an envelope sized fold of leather and when that was unfolded human eyes gazed upon the Blood Ruby for the first time in centuries.

The golden shine of the ring band was hardly diminished by the moon's silver light but far more impressive was the dark sparkle of the deep red ruby set in the ring – pulsating almost as if it were alive. Mortimer took a deep breath and then took the Blood Ruby and slipped it on his finger. Its power was his now.

§ § § § § §

The mist was more uneven in front of them, rising high into the trees on either side of the Forgotten Road and much lower over the road itself where it was stirred and churned by countless feet, hooves and wheels. Maisy looked in amazement at the traffic on the road: Ranks of armoured men marching in tight formation, carts carrying farmers and their kin rumbling along at a steady pace, fancily liveried horses walking, trotting or cantering to and fro, a line of chained slaves shuffling along submissively, woad-painted and furred warriors with frumious beards and everywhere gangs of children darting in and out of the traffic. They were not shadows either, all seemed solidly real. The nails hammered into boot soles scraped against pebbles on the Forgotten Road, the fresh horse poop, though it fell beyond sight into the mist, was accompanied by the smell of manure, the waggons creaked and their wheels rumbled and the air was filled with chatting, murmurs, laughter, moaning and groaning. The only thing which betrayed the ethereal quality of the scene was the incoming traffic which dissipated into strands of fog as it reached the bridge, melting into the pale blanket which concealed the road, river bank and forest floor.

Maisy was not entirely sure as to what she should do next. Spark took the lead and started walking forwards, joining the stream of traffic which flowed eastwards over the Forgotten Road towards Malheur Hall.

"How do?" A wiry old farmer on the box of a cart heading west gave Maisy a nod.

"Scratching along," she answered and the farmer nodded again before passing them entirely.

Maisy let Spark negotiate the Forgotten Road, making space for faster travellers or overtaking the slower horse-drawn vehicles or formations of people.

"You did well by the bridge," a melodious female voice spoke. Maisy glanced sideways. A woman concealed by the hood of a billowing cloak had come to ride beside her on a Chestnut gelding with a gleaming coat.

"Are you *Farisee*?" Maisy asked.

The woman chuckled, "No, I am not a *Pook*, dear."

Maisy breathed a sigh of relief. There was something about the woman which she took an instinctive liking to and she had felt a moment of anxiety about this being another intricate *Farisee* disguise.

"A *shim* then," the London girl stated.

"Not a *shim* either," the woman said. "I am me and I am where I am, you are you and you are where you are, Maisy Maskall." It sounded like the 'something of everything and everything of something' the locals were fond of using. Truth and nonsense at the same time.

"Robbins, innit? How do you know my name?"

"The bees told me," the woman answered and Maisy wondered at that. Was this one of the Guardians of the Wyrde Woods? Or had someone listened to Master Dobbs?

"You called for me," the woman clarified, "when you asked a friend to tell the bees."

"Did the bees tell you about my friend Joy?"

"Joy Whitfield has been freed."

Maisy felt a rush of exhilarating relief and a shadow of disappointment. She was not needed at all, the Guardians must have figured it out after all.

"Because there is a task she has to carry out," the woman continued. "Just as you have a quest to fulfil, Maisy of *Lunnon*."

"A quest?" Maisy's eyes grew wide. "Joy is safe?"

"As safe as can be on this night, aye. Others are not. The foe has one of your friends but that is not your concern. Your grandparents are in danger."

"Gran? Grip! Where?"

"Down this path," the woman pointed at a dirt path to their right. Maisy recognized it, it led to Lewinna's Pool, the Guardians and then...

"Tuckersham Church!" Maisy steered Spark to the right. She looked at the woman. "Will you come with me? Please?"

"At your invitation only, so, yes," the woman answered and Maisy was sure she was smiling beneath the shadows of her hood. Maisy smiled back.

"Let's go," Maisy said and the two riders and their mounts left the traffic to move along the Forgotten Road and headed south to find Fred and Betty Maskall.

31. The Blood Sacrifice

Munin snarled and made to assault Silas Hare.

"No!" Fred shouted as Silas Hare swiftly raised his rifle and fired a warning shot into the air.

"Hugin, Munin. Go! Go! Leave!" Fred shouted and the lurchers obeyed instantly, weaving between the gravestones as Hare's cronies fired shots at them.

They all missed and Fred supressed a grin at their poor shooting after the dogs had disappeared into the woods. He did not enjoy the moment for long because Silas retaliated by bringing the stock of his rifle into hard contact with Fred's nose which broke with a sharp crack. Fred sank to the ground, blood streaming over his face and Betty caught him just before he collapsed.

"Up," Hare snarled. "Away from here, back to the Guardians." He took hold of the quarterstaff and yanked it out of Fred's hand.

Betty threw a desperate look at Tuckersham church.

"The witch is as good as dead, as is her *chance-born*," Silas laughed and prodded Betty with the barrel of his rifle. "Get up."

Betty supported Fred as he stumbled down the path, both encouraged by Silas who kept on poking them with Freds quarterstaff. The path disappeared from sight as a low bank of mist crept from the woods to conceal it; lit up by the moon in places and stirred into turmoil by the party's advance. Hare's men laughed and jested, taunting the Maskalls and devising morbid terminations of the Wyrde Woods witches.

That was a mistake for they did not hear Betty as she started to speak; ever so softly but clear enough for Fred to hear.

"Sitte ge, sīgewīf, sīgað tō eorðan."

Fred understood, though he was woozy and his nose caused him great pain he spoke the next words.

"Næfre ge wilde tō wuda fleogan."

They then spoke together: *"Wudawose. Tō wuda fleogan."*

At first, Hare and his men did not notice that the mist began to swirl in places other than the wake they themselves left behind. Fred and Betty repeated the spell again and behind the party tendrils of mist started weaving together to form the twisted forms of whispering whisps.

Chunmaniye helped Heechante climb the stairs, the ferrets streaming upstairs around them.

"We'll find you something to eat and drink," Chunmaniye told Heechante.

"*Naun* time," Heechante shook her head. "It's worse than I thought, Chunmaniye. Sir Mortimer *baint* just trying to release the *Saglasa Wakinyan,* he wants to bind Ufmanna to him, to control the Owl Man, direct his actions."

"Food and drink first, you'll need strength." Chunmaniye guided the girl into the cottage's kitchen and found water, some bread and cheese.

Heechante tore into the provisions with relish despite her earlier objection.

"Your Wyrde Woods *Wicasa Wakan*?" Chunmaniye asked.

"They've been tricked," Heechante said through a mouthful of bread. "They think I've been taken to Tuckersham Church. *Howsumdever*, for what Sir Mortimer wants to achieve he needs to unlock the power at the Blood Stone on Gallows Hill. They said they had one of the other Wyrde Warriors, one of my friends. That *chavee* will die tonight if we don't stop them."

"Iya," Chunmaniye said. "A son of creation whose only goal is havoc and who feeds on the despair of others."

"Almost," Heechante replied. "This one seeks power too, power over the Wyrde Woods."

Chunmaniye nodded and followed Heechante out of the kitchen again. They left through the front door and Heechante turned to look at the house.

"The Cottage," Heechante said. "John Hare, the other must have been his wife. I know where I am now."

There was great relief in her voice and Chunmaniye wondered what she had been through during her incarceration. Whatever it had been, he decided, they had not broken her spirit.

"How did you know I was here?" Heechante asked.

"Thallie showed me the way."

"Thallie!"

"She flew off again, after she brought me here."

Although the space around the house was free of the mist which had started to conceal the Wyrde Woods this night the surrounding forest was eerily invisible. There was an ominous silence from the woods which seemed to exude hostility.

"How far is it to Gallows Hill?" Chunmaniye asked, wondering if they would make it in time.

"Too far," Heechante said, though her voice betrayed a lack of concern about the distance. Chunmaniye looked at her with surprise and saw that she was gazing intently towards the east. He followed her gaze. A boy came striding out of the mist. He was Heechante's age but Chunmaniye had never seen him before. The child had a narrow face and long dark curly hair. He wore some sort of tunic which was enclosed by a pouched belt.

"Chunmaniye," Heechante said. "This is Foster, he'll help us get to the Blood Stone."

Chunmaniye nodded at the boy who nodded back and then turned to walk towards the forest edge.

There was a forlorn chirp from the mist by their feet.

"The ferrets!" Heechante remembered. She reached down and Valkerie came scrambling up her arm to ride her shoulder. The others all scurried up Chunmaniye's trousers and then seemed to whirl round him till they had all found a place to settle on the warrior's broad shoulders or simply something to cling on to.

They followed the boy called Foster into the woodlands, not by one of the broader dirt paths but by means of a deer trail.

"There are nine *wurrelds*, Chunmaniye," Heechante told him. "Very few travel from one to the other, I don't *ken* how tis done. But the boundaries, well, they are not fixed boundaries, they shift and sometimes overlap."

"They overlap tonight?" Chunmaniye guessed and wondered who exactly Foster was. He had not heard the boy speak yet.

"Aye," Heechante nodded. "They often do on some fixed days, our celebration days. *Howsumdever*, also when someone tries to raise power; good or bad."

"And where are we now?"

Heechante smiled at Chunmaniye. "If you went back now you'd *naun* find the Cottage. Some," she indicated Foster's back, "can guide you along...other paths."

Chunmaniye nodded. They were in a *Saglasa* Spirit World then. "Best to follow the guide."

Heechante smiled. "The advantage is that elsewhere distances are measured differently."

Chunmaniye raised an eyebrow. "Meaning...?"

Foster was suddenly gone and so was the mist in the dark periphery of the forest edge Chunmaniye, Heechante and the ferrets found themselves in. The ferrets scrambled down to the ground again. Heechante laid a finger on her lips and pointed outwards. Chunmaniye's eyes followed and he saw that they were below the summit of a hill, its grass crown topped by a solitary ominous standing stone. Dark cloaked figures stood around the stone and one of them began to shout.

"*Hoka Hey*," Chunmaniye whispered.

§ § § § § § §

The mists thinned a little on the path to Tuckersham Church but reached higher yet and swirled faster in complex patterns. The forest around them was rich with the sounds of rustling twigs and cracking branches and Maisy smiled grimly as she realised they were being followed by creatures in the woods. Soon she began to spot furtive movements too for the creatures were coming closer and closer to the path. She saw something with small furious eyes which was exceptionally furry with white and black stripes. Lizard-like creatures in the shape of wingless birds or exceptionally long-legged goats. One creature was the size of Spark, with a shaggy unkempt mane of hair around its pointed snout. However, when it took a few slow steps towards them it rose and Maisy could see that it seemed to be half squatting on short hind legs while the elated fore legs lifted the upper body high into the air. The creature raised its snout at the sky and released a bloodcurdling howl.

Maisy shivered all over. She had heard those howls before.

"A boggert," she grunted.

"And gimlets, toves, borogoves, and raths," the woman nodded. Gunshhots sounded in the distance.

"Bloody hell," Maisy cursed and urged Spark into a trot. Her companion did likewise and the two hurried onwards.

§ § § § § § §

"I demand to know," the robed man at the centre of his circle shouted defiantly, "and thrice shall ask: WHO WILL STOP ME? WHO?"

The Blood Stone was a hundredfold more powerful if all living energies around it manifested willingness. The girl was drugged beyond comprehension – a well-stocked Poison Garden was a Malheur family tradition – and would not object until she started screaming her life away. By then it would be too late for it to make a difference.

The Guardians were miles away probing the defences around Tuckersham Church.

The five robed figures spread around the Blood Stone were his allies. The sixth was a new novice; a delightful creature though tainted now by the curse of the Blood Stone. His most powerful follower, the only one capable of raising the dark without Mortimer's assistance, was orchestrating the Tuckersham distraction.

"WHO WILL STOP ME? WHO?"

Mortimer could feel the power in the air now. The *Wyrd* was being drawn from an ever increasing circle of life around the Blood Stone on Gallows Hill. Tendrils of the *Wyrd,* strangely fluorescent in the darkness, drew together to form streams which were drawn into a twirling vortex around Blood Stone which starting sucking the energy in. Already it was bleeding; rivulets of dark blood streaming down its surface and dripping down onto the earth.

There was no one to stop him, Mortimer knew with triumphant satisfaction and his whole body felt attuned to Gallows Hill. He felt a thousand times more alive than usual and it sent all his senses into a dizzy spin. He flicked his hands over the swirls of *Wyrd* and saw them break course erratically there where his own energy had interfered. The Blood Ruby glittered on his finger and the girl exuded her enticing vulnerability. A knife would have been the quickest way; a swift cut across the throat, but Mortimer wanted a more visibile manifestation of his powers.

He planned to seize control of a dozen loops of the *Wyrd* spinning inwards towards the Blood Stone and use them to bind the girl to the stone. Then he would strangle her into the Blood Stone itself; something not tried for a thousand years.

"WHO WILL STOP ME? WHO?"

"THE *WUDAWYRDE WEARD!* YOU SILLY BOY." a clear voice called out and Mortimer stalled midway another flexing of the Wyrd which dissipated instantly, ebbing away beyond Mortimer's control at the sound of the challenge.

Mortimer spun round to see who had come to challenge him thus.

It was his mother, clad in an old fashioned peasant tunic with the Malheur Swan bright upon her chest. She was alone but her unexpected arrival caused some of Mortimer's followers to gasp.

"You've taken this far enough, Morty," Priscilla Malheur extended a hand. "Give me the ring and let the girl go. It's time to come home. Playtime is over."

Mortimer's mouth dropped open in a most undignified manner and Cynthia Chesterton could not help but laugh.

§ § § § § § §

Inside Tuckersham Church Sarah fought her own battles. The man had brought her into the small vestry on the other side of the tower and forced her to kneel down there at gunpoint.

Sarah struggled to stave off the deep chasm of grief she felt for Joy who had become a pawn in a deadly struggle. The whole was what mattered now, not single elements of it though Sarah wanted nothing more but to sink into the oblivion of emotion and weep for her daughter.

She fought to steel herself against the callous remarks of the man who enjoyed goading her in his speech, driving home Joy's impending sacrifice and the failure of the Guardians to protect the Wyrde Woods. He wanted to break her and she must not give into despair and surrender.

Instead, Sarah tried to reason.

"Do you truly believe your Master will share his gains with you as a reward? If you do, you are much mistaken."

The man laughed this off. "There will be a new order in the Wyrde Woods, a new order in Sussex and England. Hard to accept that your kind has no place in that new order, isn't it?"

"A new order built upon blood, think, man!" Sarah tried to keep her emotion under control.

In the distance they could hear a volley of gunshots and then awful screaming. The screams continued for a while.

"No quick end for the Maskalls then," the man said with grim satisfaction in his voice. "Sounds like gut shots, Hare is not in a forgiving mood. Such a painful lingering death."

Sarah shut her eyes tightly for a moment, willing herself to not think of Fred and Betty and continue her attempted erosion of the man's confidence. "No good can possibly come of it. There is a price to be paid for these things, it does not come free."

"I would expect such arguments from someone whose blood will be spilled tonight," the man sneered.

Sarah reflected on that, recalling now that he had previously referred to her own part in tonight's Blood Sacrifice.

"He means to bind Ufmanna to his will," she said softly "One sacrifice at the Blood Stone and one here."

"At last you understand," the man said and then fell silent. Sarah sensed an anxiety in him as he seemed to cock his head every now and then as if to pick up a signal. Then she felt a sense of relief. Timing was everything in this dark scheme of Sir Mortimer's. There was an order that needed to be followed and in this Sarah had a free choice. If she could…

"It is time," the man interrupted her thoughts and Sarah tensed. She thought her realisation had come too late but all he did was produce an old ornate key which he slid into the lock of the narrow door which led to the crypt. The lock clicked open and Sarah held her breath but the man did not attempt to open the door yet. Instead he resumed his wait and for a brief moment Sarah wondered whether he intended to kill her in the vestry or throw her into the crypt. Either way, she decided, it did not matter.

Outside she could hear the chittering and chortling of the *Lesser Farisee* as these were drawn to the old church by the promise of a Blood Sacrifice. Sarah's blood ran cold when the noise was joined by the feroscious howls of boggerts. There really was only was one escape from her predicament and ever so slowly she let her hands slide around the rubble strewn pave stones to sweep grit together.

The noise outside increased to a new crescendo as the boggerts barked and the *Lesser Farisee* screamed. Something was happening out there.

The man raised his revolver slightly, he was getting nervous and wanted it over and done with but he had clearly not yet received his signal. The time had come to rob Sir Mortimer of his timing; Sarah would force her own premature demise.

§ § § § § § §

"You're a Guardian," Mortimer hissed at his mother.

"Of course I am," Priscilla Malheur answered him. "It is the sacred task of a Lady or Lord of the Wyrde Woods to safeguard these woods. Our family took long enough in coming to understand that and I fear that you have failed to grasp it altogether."

"More of your father's nonsense," Mortimer snarled.

"Some call it wisdom," his mother said calmly.

"Enough of this," Mortimer looked away from the sparkling swan and focused on the Blood Ruby on his finger. He had set himself a task this night and this was but a minor unfortunate distraction. He gave a signal to his five followers and they lined up between Mortimer and his mother and then retrieved revolvers from their belts.

"You would have your own mother shot, Morty?" Priscilla Malheur asked with amusement in her voice. "In front of the Blood Stone? Touching it isn't the only way to be subject to its curse, Son."

"Wait?" Cynthia asked. "What curse?"

Mortimer ignored her.

"Take aim," he ordered. His instruction was obeyed and five guns were aimed at Priscilla Malheur.

"WAIT!" A clear voice rang out through the night and Mortimer rolled his eyes with exasperation as he turned to the nearest forest edge to see what new intereference the Guardians had devised.

It was the Whitfield girl who calmly strolled out of the Wyrde Woods and walked someway forwards.

"You!" Mortimer hissed and threw a murderous glance at the back of John Hare who had assured him the girl had been left securely locked.

§ § § § § § §

One of Silas Hare's men, sensing something behind him, threw a casual look over his shoulder. The whispering whisps towered above him like a multi-tentacled monster, each limb forming grotesque faces with wide gaping mouths. The man screamed shrilly and turned to fire his rifle into one of the whispering whisps.

The others turned too, including Hare, and terrified to the last man they emptied their guns at the whispering whisps which were entirely unaffected by the bullets though the creatures began to writhe angrily and bring their beaks and snouts and slavering mouths towards the men.

Fred counted the shots.

"Now!" he whispered urgently and he and Betty began to run as fast as they could. Fred half expected to hear bullets whistle by him as he ran but it seemed none of Hare's men had even noticed their captives had escaped. The unfortunates had time to reload once for another wild and ineffective volley and then they began to scream loudly as the whispering whisps sent tendrils into their mouths, nostrils, ears and even eyes and used that leverage to lift the men, one by one, into the air as the whisps engulfed their minds.

§ § § § § § §

Chunmaniye watched Heechante walk forwards and face the robed figures around the solitary standing stone on the hilltop. He recognized the central hooded figure as none other than a manifestation of Iya, the evil one. Chunmaniye stepped out of the shadows and strode to Heechante's side, followed by the ferrets.

§ § § § § § §

Soon the screams started to fade and Fred and Betty stopped their retreat. Almost immediately they were joined by Hugin and Munin who came dashing from the woods. They wagged their tails and Fred stroked their heads as they nuzzled him with moist noses.

"Back to the church," Betty said. "We need to get Sarah and Joy."

Fred nodded and then flinched as the movement sent new pain through his shattered nose. The pain was unrelenting because they began to jog back southwards and each time one of his feet landed on the path Fred would be hit by new pangs of agony. He gritted his teeth; Sarah and Joy were in danger and that was all that mattered. There was not a sign of Hare or his men when they passed the place where the whispering whisps – absent now too – had intervened. The only item there was Fred's quarterstaff and he bent down to pick it up.

An eerie silence reigned around Tuckersham Church when they got back there at last and they slowed down to catch their breath.

"I'm getting to old for this malarkey," Betty panted and Fred grimaced his agreement.

Something began to chuckle behind them and that was joined by cackling, gribing, chortling and snorting. Hugin and Munin started growling fiercely and Fred and Betty spun around.

All manner of *Lesser Farisee* were filing onto the path behind them. Crawling, hopping, gimbling and slithing towards the Maskalls menacingly. Fred gripped his quarterstaff.

"Hugin, Munin, heel," he said trying to remain calm. Frightful howls erupted from the forest and overpowered the cacophony of the creatures.

Fred paled, he knew of only one creature which bellowed and yowled like that and sure enough six boggerts came crashing out of the forest edge. The other creatures shrieked and screamed and moved away from the bulking monsters.

These broke out into renewed howling when they spotted their quarry.

"Ye Gods," Betty uttered in half a sob. "We're done for now, surelye."

Fred ground his teeth in helpless anger. Betty was right, only a miracle could save them now. Where were the other four Guardians?

§ § § § § § §

Mortimer frowned, hesitant and uncertain, as he took in the Native American warrior who emerged from the Wyrde Woods to stand at the girl's side. The girl was unforeseen but she was a local with the powers of a changeling which marked her out as a potential Guardian. He did not know which spells she had mastered but doubted her strength to impose any of their standard stock on him. He might be *willed* by the combined strength of the Guardians but not by a mere pupil of the *Wyrd*. The apparition of her ally, however, worried him. The man was formidable in size and Mortimer did not know if he was there as a warrior of the mind or the muscle.

Mortimer shrugged; he had brought his own muscle. He motioned his novice towards him. Cynthia, fortunately, understood and came to stand by his side where she would be safe. Mortimer then gestured at his other followers and three of them switched their aim towards the girl and her companion.

Mortimer looked at the girl with interest. His intentions had been made clear and he could see enough of her face in the bright moonshine to read her emotions. He wanted to see fear in her eyes. He had regretted not taking her blindfold off in the cellar of the Groundskeeper Cottage to feed on the fright in her eyes. Mortimer hoped for compensation but all he read was a small smile of pity on her lips and he started to tremble with anger.

Then the Blood Ruby on his finger started to glow and he raised his arms in supplication to be swallowed whole by an ancient power far stronger than he was. The takeover was swift. Mortimer's followers and Cynthia betrayed their nervousness as he began to intone strange foreign words.

§ § § § § § §

Chunmaniye spread his arms in reply to Iya's movements , palms faced upwards. Heechante did the same. Chunmaniye began to speak Hehaka Sapa's words. He became Hehaka Sapa of the vision, a manifestation of the spirit of the earth and he felt flowing through him now the magic of the ground and the magic of the soil; slow at first but soon lending him the strength of a deeply rooted tree. A walking tree. Next to him he sensed the predatory hunting spirit of the girl who now manifested herself as a true Owl Heart.

"*HAHO!*" Chunmaniye shouted.

Chunmaniye felt a cloud of dark angry fury directed at him. The robed foe was powerful but Chunmaniye kept his nerve.

"WANKAN TANKA!" He invoked.

The dark cloud seethed in rage and a hissing voice surrounded Chunmaniye, seeming to come from everywhere at once.

Fool! Fool! Succumbed to Heyoka!

Chunmaniye began to walk forwards as he continued to speak. The stars above seemed to flicker rapidly and the grass stirred beneath his feet. He was walking his words.

"You have been always, and before you nothing has been."

Iya snarled. *Why spill Lakota strength for these Wasichu? Why spend your spirit on behalf of those who destroyed your people?*

The voice contained a crazed malevolence which would have sent the heart of a weaker man trembling in flurries but Chunmaniye also sensed fear, it wanted him to stop.

TRAITOR.

That word caused Chunmaniye to hesitate and Iya began to laugh. The spirit's amusement turned to renewed fury though when Heechante stepped to Chunmaniye's side.

"Wakan Tanka. There is nothing to pray to but you." Heechante intoned Hehaka Sapa's words which Chunmaniye had taught her. "The star nations all over the Universe are yours."

"And yours are the grasses of the earth!" Chunmaniye refound his resolve.

"Day in Day out. You are the light of things," Heechante called out as the two resumed their slow march towards the Blood Stone.

§ § § § § § §

"Soon," Jeremy growled at Jasper and Jenny. They were concealed behind a hedge at the edge of the field, some thirty yards from Sir Mortimer and his henchmen and they had already nocked their arrows. "Leave Sir Mortimer be, focus on those with guns."

"There are five of them, and three of us," Jenny said with a grim expression.

"I know," Jeremy nodded. "Aim for the ones targeting Joy Whitfield, she must be saved."

"But Lady Priscilla…" Jasper sounded horrified.

"Tis her will," Jeremy said with resignation. "The girl is the future, Priscilla already lingers in the past."

"Oak's Acorn, what a choice," Jenny shook her head.

"Which need not be made," a boy's voice said confidently as Leon joined their rank, nocking an arrow on his bow.

"There are five Hornsby archers in the Wyrde Woods tonight," Lizzie added as she stepped forwards, arrow at the ready as well.

The three adults were speechless for a minute. Then Jeremy shook his head at Leon and growled menacingly: "We will have words about this later."

"Yes Dad," Leon looked back at his father with calm determination.

Jeremy looked at the defiance in his son's eyes for a second, secretly relishing the moment and hiding his pride, and then divided the targets.

§ § § § § § §

Iya screeched in frustration and summoned Taku Skanskan, master of the four winds who sent for his four Night Spirits. Fox, Raven, Wolf and Vulture took shape around the hooded figure with his outstretched arms but neither Chunmaniye or Heechante broke their stride.

"WAKAN TANKA!" Heechante's voice rang out.

"You are older than all need. Older than all pain!" Chunmaniye called out.

The Night Spirits detached from the hooded figure and hurled down the summit's slope towards the two.

"Older than all things on Earth," Heechante remained steadfast, ignoring the approach of the creatures. "Grandfather, all over the world, the faces of living things are all alike."

Raven and Vulture reached the two first and circled them, feigning attacks with claws and beaks but Chunmaniye and Heechante ignored them.

"In tenderness they have come above the ground," Chunmaniye continued.

"Look upon your children!" Heechante implored.

"With children in their arms, that they may face the winds and walk the good road to the day of quiet," Chunmaniye answered.

Fox and Wolf came to them and bared their teeth in savage snarls, lunging at Chunmaniye and Heechante but the two continued their steadfast progress.

Iya screamed his anger.

"Wakan Tanka! Grandfather!" Heechante called.

"Teach me to walk the soft earth, a relative to all that is!" Chunmaniye fought to refrain from flinching as Vulture's beak came within an inch of puncturing his eye and Wolf's fangs snapped at his shin.

"Sweeten my heart. And fill me with life," Heechante ignored Raven's claws which nearly gouged her cheek and Fox's teeth which nearly chawed her leg.

Iya screeched again, this time joined by the Night Spirits which howled, barked, crowed and shrieked with their master.

"Wakan Tanka!" Chunmaniye called out triumphantly. "Give me the strength to understand, and the eyes to see,"

"Wakan Tanka! Help me for without you I am nothing," Heechante finished.

"IT IS FINISHED!" Chunmaniye shouted and the air seemed to lend volume to his words. Taku Skanskan's Night Spirits dissipated into nothingness and Iya roared his helpless anger.

"*HECHETO ALOH!*" Heechante echoed with the strength of power in her voice.

The two came level with the Lady of the Wyrde Woods and repeated their last words in unison.

"Wakan Tanka! Help me for without you I am nothing. *Hecheto aloh! Hecheto aloh!*"

§ § § § § § §

Maisy urged Spark to speed up when she heard a boggert howl from the direction of Tuckersham church. Spark obeyed but whinnied nervously as the howl was repeated; this time by more than one boggert. Maisy empathised with Spark for the bloodcurdling noise sent shivers of fear running through her. Green jennies were one thing, boggerts were another and it was only the thought of Gran and Grip which kept her from turning Spark around and cantering all the way to London.

"Get ready," Maisy's companion said as they approached the continued din ahead of them.

They emerged on the dirt road which ran by Tuckersham Church and halted their mounts to take stock of the situation. To her relief Maisy saw Gran and Grip on their feet; slowly edging towards the church through the field of tilted gravestones but surrounded by boggerts. Hugin and Munin circled Maisy's grandparents barking and snarling at the smaller creatures whilst Grip swung his quarterstaff to keep the boggerts at bay.

One of the boggerts was far closer to Maisy, blocking the gap in the low wall by the church. It took a few slow steps towards Maisy and released another frightful howl.

Farisee tea time.

"Fiddle-dee-dee, they wouldn't last a minute in the East End," Maisy said, trying to sound brave.

"I wouldn't last a minute in *Lunnon* either," Maisy's companion laughed brightly. Maisy looked at her in wonder as she calmly lifted her hood to reveal long gold hair and an expression of calm determination on a serene face which seemed enhanced rather than marred by the long scar which ran along one cheek. The woman undid the clasp of her hood and the cloak fell away to reveal a long mail coat which shone fiercely in the bright moonlight.

The nearby boggert ambled forwards and Maisy turned to stare at it in horrified fascination as it opened its jaws to reveal vicious rows of vorpal teeth stained with filth; the gaps between the sharp points of its teeth emitting strains of drool. The creature stopped and looked comically surprised when it heard the noise of a long sword scraping out of a scabbard as Maisy's companion drew her weapon.

"*A-DỲDAN!*" The woman shouted and spurred her mount forwards. She swung her sword in a wide arc and snicker-snacked the creature's head right off its neck. Without pausing the warrior sped into the graveyard to tackle the next boggert, repeating her battlecry. "*A-DỲDAN!*"

§ § § § § § §

Cynthia was nauseous with confusion as she tried to make sense of the nightmare the scene atop Gallows Hill had become.

At first she had taken cue from Mortimer's continued confidence in spite of the unexpected interuptions by Lady Priscilla and then that damned girl and her incongruous companion. The guns aimed at the intruders were reassuring but then Mortimer had changed beyond all recognition as he seemed to enter a battle of strange words with the girl and the Indian. Cynthia had taken an involuntary step backwards when shapes had formed around Mortimer, seemingly from nothing and twisted and hurled around him. She did not know what they were for she could not make out their form, they were just a blur, though she had nearly pitied the most recent arrivals when the shapes had swept down the slope to envelop them in a flurry of aggression.

To Cynthia's surprise the girl and Indian continued their slow advance unscathed, calling out words in that strange tongue and when they reached Lady Priscilla the shapes disappeared into nothingness and Mortimer slumped; released from the hold of whatever had possessed him he radiated defeat. That Cynthia could not allow.

"Shoot them!" She shouted, "Shoot them!"

The five followers hesitantly raised their guns, looking backwards at their Master for confirmation.

Mortimer, fortunately, regained some semblance of self-control.

"You heard her," he snarled in a high-pitched whine. "Shoot them, finish them off."

§ § § § § § §

"FIDDLE-DEE-DEE!" Maisy shouted her own battlecry and urged Spark into the graveyard, heading for the boggerts surrounding her grandparents.

"Maisy?!" She heard Gran call out but her focus was entirely on the closest boggert which began to turn towards Maisy and Spark. It raised one of its elongated forelegs and took a clumsy swipe that seemed slow and ponderous, giving Maisy time to duck, feeling the airflow of the boggert's claw pass over her head. She then rose again and pointed her cap gun at the boggert. This time a *Farisee* was definitely trying to take her head off and she fired five quick shots in succession. The bangs were still satisfyingly loud and the boggert shuddered on each impact, yelping with indignation. Then it growled menacingly and lumbered forwards, opening its mouth to emit a waft of stale rot from its mouth that made Maisy recoil.

She aimed her cap gun at the creatures slitted yellow eyes this time and fired again. These shots sent the boggert reeling, yowling pain it rolled onto the ground and became silent after Spark delivered a fierce kick to its temple.

Taking quick stock of the situation Maisy noted that her companion had tackled another one of the creatures which only left two of them whiffling and burbling around her grandparents. Grip was whirling around each time one came too close, bringing down his quarterstaff on their outstretched claws or snout with all his might to send them staggering back in pained confusion whilst Hugin and Munin harried the other.

The lurchers dashed in as quick as lighting and sank their teeth into flanks before darting out of the range of slow and clumsy counterswipes. The boggerts did not seem fast or greatly intelligent though Maisy perceived that it would only take one successful blow of one of the powerful forelegs to throw an opponent to the ground or rip through clothes and skin.

Grip repulsed another assault just as the boggert behind him changed tactics and ignored the sniping of the lurchers, glowering at Grip with keen interest as it opened its jaws to reveal its sharp rows of teeth.

"GRIP! BEHIND YOU!" Maisy shouted just as Gran screamed: "FRED!"

Gramps turned swiftly but not fast enough and a mighty blow knocked him to the ground where he fell on his back and gasped for breath.

"NOOO!!" Maisy hollered and spurred Spark forwards as the boggert sank its claws into Grip's thigh and began to drag her grandfather inexorably towards its snapping teeth. Hugin and Munin re-launched themselves at the boggert and the creature flicked its head in irritation but did not relinquish its hold on its meal.

§ § § § § § §

"LOOSE!" Jeremy ordered and five bow strings twanged and five steel-tipped arrows flew with goose-fletched accuracy to pierce five hands.

"Nock," Jeremy said.

Three of the robed figures dropped their revolvers to scream their pain and clutch their hands, the two remaining ones, despite the arrows dangling from their hands, turned their revolvers towards the hedge.

"Draw," Jeremy ordered. "Aim at the ones still armed. Take them down."

Two gunshots sounded but the aim was wild and the bullets whistled by overhead.

"Loose," came the command and this time five arrows penetrated thick robe, clothing, skin and flesh. The two stricken figures howled in pain and tumbled to the ground.

"Nock, follow me," Jeremy said and the five Hornsby archers emerged from their concealment to approach the Blood Stone; ready to shoot their third volley.

§ § § § § § §

"It won't be long now," the man promised Sarah, though it sounded like he was trying to reassure himself.

A human voice sounded outside. "A-dẏdan!"

The man turned his head to the doorway of the vestry and Sarah could see the hand holding the revolver tremble slightly.

Good. Now. She gathered as much of the grit in her hands as she could.

When the man started turning his hooded head back towards her she rose with all the speed she could muster and flung the grit into the hood.

The man yowled and brought his hands to his face thus temporarily removing the threat of his revolver. Sarah howled like an animal and went for his throat, closing one hand around it to squeeze as hard as she could whilst clawing at the revolver with her other hand. The man used his greater strength to force the revolver down and a desperate struggle ensued between the two for control of the weapon.

The struggle ended with a gunshot and a scream.

§ § § § § § §

Maisy reached the boggert and Spark reared up, forcing her to grab his mane so as not to fall off. The boggert looked up with surprise in its eyes and Spark landed a kick on its jaw with one hoof and then the other. The boggert whimpered and took an uncertain step backwards. Spark came down and Maisy slid off his back as Spark, aided by Hugin and Munin, started driving the boggert further away whilst her companion drove her sword, the blade black with blood now, through the last boggert.

A gunshot sounded in the church.

Maisy and Gran helped Gramps sit up, his chest was heaving and he was coughing but he looked at her with wondrous surprise.

"By Callooh and Callay, Magpie," Grip chortled weakly. "You've got a mighty fine pair of balls, *sodger*."

Maisy beamed as brightly as a lighthouse, feeling immensely proud. She knew from her dad that this was how soldiers talked to each other – but only to fellow soldiers.

"It don't take those to be brave," Gran shook her head in exasperation.

"*Naun*, you're right Betty," Gramps grunted and struggled to his feet.

As they all rose they saw the last of the smaller creatures flee back into the forest, leaving the inert bodies of the boggerts behind.

§ § § § § § §

"Noooo!" Mortimer bellowed as his followers fell and Cynthia rushed to his side to support him. Whatever power he had commanded was gone, she perceived, and his normal strength seemed to be fading as he shuddered uncontrollably.

They stumbled backwards towards the Blood Stone just as the drugged girl, slowly regaining control of her senses, started to crawl towards the archers.

"Katie!" One of the younger archers shouted.

"Get her," Mortimer gasped but the two children amongst the archers dropped their bows and rushed forwards to seize the girl and half-carry and half-drag the child towards the archers.

Lady Priscilla, the woodland girl and the Indian now slowly came forwards towards Mortimer and Cynthia. Two of Mortimer's followers lay on the ground, pierced by arrows and groaning as they twisted and turned in pain. The other three were scurrying down the summit, fleeing as fast as they could.

"It is over," Lady Priscilla said softly.

"No," Mortimer shook his head. "No, no."

Cynthia looked at Lady Priscilla's party and then at the archers. The two children were huddled around the girl they had saved but the adults still had their bows at the ready.

"Mortimer," Cynthia said softly. "It's over."

"NOOOOO!" Mortimer seemed to grow taller and with a swiftness Cynthia had not anticipated he folded an arm around her and pulled her towards him whilst at the same time producing a sleek dagger which he set against her throat. The steel felt icily cold there.

"UFMANNA!" Mortimer shouted.

"MORTY, DON'T" Priscilla returned his shout. She took a step forwards.

"STAY WHERE YOU ARE," Mortimer ordered. "BACK OFF!"

Cynthia was paralyzed by disbelief.

"UFMANNA, I BID YOU UNDBOUND AND RELEASED!" Mortimer hollered and Cynthia felt the pressure of the sharp blade increase.

"Please," she whispered.

Just then, quick as lightning unseen small figures streaked towards Mortimer and clawed their way up and into his robes; screeching, biting, scratching and clawing. At the same time an owl dropped from the sky and gouged blood from Mortimer's forehead with one of its sharp claws.

"Get off me," Mortimer shrieked and let go of Cynthia to brush off the ferrets which clung to him with dogged tenacity. Cynthia pulled away, ducking to avoid the owl's claws and Mortimer made a half-hearted lunge with his dagger which pierced the skin of Cynthia's arm and cut along the length of it to release a short spray of blood which struck the surface of the cursed standing stone.

§ § § § § § §

Sarah looked down at the man who was on the ground groaning while he clutched his wounded leg. A puddle of blood was spreading on the pavestones below him and seeping into the cracks between them.

A Blood Sacrifice had been made and Sarah sensed something stirring in the crypt . She stumbled out through the door into the main part of the ruined church; self-preservation dictating that she vacated the building as fast as she could.

"Sarah!" Betty called out as Sarah stumbled from the church and her friend rushed towards Sarah to offer her support.

§ § § § § § §

The Wyrde Woods seemed to shudder around them and in the vestry the hidden door trembled violently and then disintegrated into a hundred thousand splinters; allowing fresh air to stream into the dark crypt below for the first time in centuries. Scores of owls around Tuckersham Church started hooting and screeching as the thing in the crypt opened its red glowing eyes.

Then it ululated a terrifying cry which sent more shudders to vibrate through the Wyrde Woods. Ufmanna had been awakened.

§ § § § § § §

Stars of fatigued dizziness began to dance in front of Mortimer's eyes and he stumbled. Cynthia caught him by the elbow and steadied him.

"Away," Mortimer whispered. "Away, we must go."

They made their way off the hillside and none moved to stop them. Instead one of the young archers, a boy, stood and shook his bow in the air, shouting *"Hoka Hey!"*

Others took up the shout: *"HOKA HEY!"* and the words echoed in Mortimer's ears as Cynthia led him - the both of them trembling and distraught - back to Malheur Hall.

§ § § § § § §

There was a mighty crash from inside the church and all four turned to see a black shadow rear to its full height of some six feet in the jagged gap of the former doorway.

"EEEE-EEEE-EEEECH!" It screamed. "CCHHREEEEEE!"

Ufmanna took an unsteady step forwards, its red eyes aglow and slowly it unfolded great black wings.

Maisy, Grip, Gran and Missus Whitfield cowered, their spirit instantly sapped by the pure menace exuded by the dark being. Hugin and Munin cringed and cowered and Spark whinnied and shied away from the Owl Man.

Maisy's companion was not affected and driving her horse forwards she held her sword high and shouted: "UT! UT! UT!"

Ufmanna responded with a furious screech but then, with powerful strokes of its wings, took to the sky and flew northwards away from Tuckersham Church, its angry screeches slowly fading into the distance.

The silence which descended upon the graveyard seemed surreal and none appeared to dare to believe it was over.

"We are safe now," Maisy's companion spoke with conviction.

Gramps, Gran and Joy's mum stared at her with incomprehension.

"Grip, Gran, Missus Whitfield," Maisy said. "This is Lewinna."

Maisy turned to her companion and gave her a questioning look. "Innit?"

Lewinna nodded her agreement.

"Milady!" Gramps dropped to one knee.

"There's no need for that," Lewinna decreed. She looked at Sarah. "Joy of the Owlery is safe."

"*Bethanks*, Milady," Sarah nodded formally though a relieved smile formed on her face.

"There is no one left to fight?" Maisy asked, a combination of relief and disappointment in her voice.

Lewinna laughed. "Not this night. It was an honour to fight by your side Maisy of *Lunnon*. I must go now. Rest, all of you. Ufmanna is unbound but unwilled and the Wyrde Woods are safer than they might have been."

With that Lewinna turned and rode away into the Wyrde Woods to return to her own hall.

32. Afterwards

The Hornsby Farm kitchen was crowded and seemed loud even though the mood was subdued as all and sundry talked of their personal experiences that night. Joy felt as if she could not breathe and she fled outside, wandering to a fence where she could see the edge of the Wyrde Woods. Priscilla Malheur followed her outside and joined Joy by the fence.

"What happens now?" Joy asked.

"Changes," Priscilla answered.

"Well, aye," Joy said. "Everything seems changed." She thought about adding a 'Milady' but her senses told her this was not an encounter where decorum was required.

"It is always that way," Priscilla nodded. "The part we play seems earth-shattering to us. But; the trees continue to draw water from the earth and spread their branches towards the sky to be fed by the sun's fire."

Joy nodded her understanding.

"An ancient cycle and we are but part of it, Joy," Priscilla said. "It is an ancient war too and tonight was but a brief battle, a skirmish compared to some which have been fought here."

"The war continues," Joy guessed.

"It does indeed and we will have to adapt. I must go home, to Malheur Hall, and share that with someone I no longer recognize as my own kin."

"He can't be punished," Joy mused. "Not by English law."

"Only for abduction, perhaps," Priscilla answered. "And if you wish it so I will give you all the support I can. But…"

"I understand," Joy said. "His word against mine, the Hares will vouch for him."

Priscilla nodded, "You would be presented as a simple country girl trying to make gain from false claims."

Joy grimaced bitterly. Then she set that bitterness away. She understood the need to keep at least one foot grounded in England. "Do you not hold any sort of power over him?"

Priscilla sighed and for a moment Joy felt a childish fear that she had imposed upon an adult in a most improper way. She brushed that away; they had been talking as equals so far. In that other world, not quite in England, they were equals now. Joy felt old beyond her years – something she had yearned for but now left her with a pang of sadness. There was always a price to be paid for magic and Joy wondered if it was this sudden heavy burden she felt on her shoulders.

"He holds power over me, I hold power over him," Priscilla said. "Mortimer has a plan ready. One I am not supposed to know about. A reputable panel of psychiatrists willing to determine that I am no longer sound of mind. The word of an elderly eccentric woman with a reputation of madness against theirs."

"Madness?" Joy asked softly.

"I called it Love," Priscilla smiled sadly. "He was far beneath my station according to society, and I was declared insane."

Joy did not know what to say.

"And in that," Priscilla continued, "lies the root of my power for he left me with child."

"You have another child?"

"My first-born son," Priscilla nodded. "Who passed away some nine years ago but he left a son of his own. Mortimer has desisted from executing his plan because he would dearly like me to transfer the title of Lord of the Wyrde Woods to him according to old family custom. Laws which are not England's."

Joy nodded, the title was not a legal one but it counted for a great deal in the wider Wyrde Woods.

"My grandson William has a greater right to the title, by laws within the Wyrde Woods and without."

Joy's eyes widened, "Does Sir Mortimer know?"

"He knows part of it, and no doubt plots against such a succession. The reason I am telling you this, Joy, is that the first new battles which will be fought will turn Malheur Hall into a battlefield and I must acknowledge that my position is vulnerable. As leader of the Seven, it is better now to pass that responsibility on to someone else."

"But…" Joy stammered. The Lady of the Wyrde Woods seemed a steady rock to lean on in this new world which rushed through Joy's mind like an ocean's tides.

"Sarah Whitfield is ready," Priscilla continued. "The Guardians do not always have a choice but when they do we too have our cycles. Everything must come to an end and her training has been completed."

"Mum?"

"Indeed," Priscilla looked into Joy's eyes. "With power comes a great responsibility. To know when it is time to let go. Many years from now, when you are in my position today..."

Joy made to protest but Priscilla shook her head. "...your ultimate test, Joy of the Owlery, is what you will do with the recognition that a successor is needed like a fresh green spring to replace the grey gloom of winter."

Joy shook her head as she tried to take this information in. That new older voice in her confirmed what the Lady of the Wyrde Woods was saying. Her younger self still found it impossible to conceive of ever being so old, let alone as powerful as the Lady of the Wyrde Woods.

"You will recognize the Changeling Child when she comes," Priscilla decreed. "For you too are part *Farisee*, Joy. It is not only human men who attend the Beltaine fires."

Joy felt dizzy.

"I will also, in due time, lay down – or have to lay down – my role as Guardian, Joy Whitfield," The Lady of the Wyrde Woods rose and suddenly she became Lady Priscilla again, with a commanding authority that was regal.

"Yes, Milady."

"I have chosen my successor," Lady Priscilla said. "We will meet once a week, at the Shy Maidens, for your training. I expect to see you there next Saturday at noon."

Joy looked at her speechlessly.

"Well?"

"I'll be there, Milady," Joy nodded quickly.

"Good," Lady Priscilla said and walked away, leaving Joy by the fence, gazing at the Wyrde Woods of which she was to become a Guardian.

§ § § § § §

At breakfast Sir Mortimer was pale but composed. There was a nasty cut on his forehead and his hands were covered in scratches too but his hair was combed and his mustache groomed. He averted his eyes when Cynthia gazed at him.

"I must apologize, not all went to plan last night," he said, examining the food laid out before him. "A shambles, of sorts."

Cynthia had thought long and hard. To condemn him was to return to London and report the failure of his mission. Worse, it would mean she had to leave.

"I recall but little of it," she confessed for that part was true. She saw relief in his eyes.

"You conducted yourself well," Sir Mortimer said reassuringly. "I failed to anticipate certain…outside interference."

Cynthia looked at the dark red ruby which sparkled from his ring finger. She only recalled vague snatches but she would never forget being stunned into disbelief when he had pressed the cold steel of his dagger against her throat. This was a man who would stop at nothing to achieve his ambitions. Her feelings for him were ambiguous now, she would always have to be on her guard, could never wholly trust him…but she felt bonded to him now in a manner which she could not describe. She had fallen in love with the man who had tried to kill her. The notion made her reel but she maintained her mask.

"It was…," she said, "…as you said, Sir Mortimer, a dress rehearsal. We'll be better prepared next time."

Mortimer smiled his agreement and Cynthia felt a pang of fear.

§ § § § § § §

Fred woke at dawn, curled underneath the tree in the clearing at Roreford with Maisy. Betty and Sarah had made their way to Hornsby Farm the night before so Sarah could be reunited with her daughter but Maisy had been exhausted and Fred had stayed behind with her.

For an hour or so he just looked at Maisy's face twitching in her sleep, loving the child with all his heart and barely minding his nose which still throbbed with pain. He was not the least surprised when Valkerie and the Hooligan Horde showed up; pitpattering over the Farisee Bridge they were the ones who woke Maisy when they swarmed over her.

Fred's granddaughter giggled. "Valkerie, that tickles."

Valkerie dooked. Maisy sat up and yawned.

"Grip," she smiled and then looked around her to take in the ruins of Roreford. Maisy looked puzzled for a moment, then she recalled: "We were looking for Joy."

"Who has been found and is safe and sound," Fred said with a satisfied smile.

"Oh good," Maisy said. "Spark!"

Spark snorted and gave them a foul look.

"Grip! What happened to your nose?" Maisy stared at Fred's face.

"I forgot to be cautious, Magpie, and took a fall."

"Well, you can't help that, innit?" Maisy decided.

"*Naun?*" Fred raised an eyebrow and then winced because the movement hurt his nose.

"You take after me, dontcha?" Maisy asked proudly.

Fred chuckled, "I do indeed, Maisy-mine, I do indeed."

"I had the weirdest dream, Gramps, about the Wyrde Woods. There were green jennies, boggerts even Lewinna. Can we go home now?"

"We can and we will," Fred scrambled to his feet. "You're safe now, Captain Robbins. Get on Spark and you can tell me all about your dream on the way home."

"Cracking!" Maisy jumped up, losing several ferrets as she did so but they quickly reattached themselves to the girl and kept Maisy warm in the morning's chill until the sun gained enough strength to warm up the Forgotten Road.

33. The Price of Magic

Chunmaniye was summoned to the Company Captain's office. He reported at the desk of an Officer Cadet in the front room of the farmhouse which was being used as the company headquarters. He was ushered through to the former dining room where Captain Morgan held court. The rooms felt small and cramped to Chunmaniye, who had to bend low to go through a doorway and whose head nearly touched the ceiling. The sense of confinement was increased by the number of people in Captain Morgan's office. The Captain himself was seated at the head of a table in the centre of the room, flanked to his left by Lieutenant Levesque.

Two men and a woman sat to the Captain's right and looked at Chunmaniye with a mixture of curiosity and distaste. One of them was the man who had been on the hilltop.

Chunmaniye ignored them and gave the Captain a crisp salute.

"At ease Corporal," Lieutenant Levesque said after Morgan had returned his salute. Chunmaniye noted that he was not invited to take a seat.

"Corporal, erm…" The Captain looked at Levesque for help.

"Chunmaniye," Chunmaniye said. "Walking Tree if you prefer."

The Captain looked at his Lieutenant. Those from the First Nations were generally expected to use their Christian western names but Levesque had always been tolerant with regard to Chunmaniye's preference for his Lakota name. The Lieutenant knew that the Lakota Corporal was just as fiercely loyal to Canada as he was to the Hunkpapa.

Levesque knew Morgan disapproved. He shrugged: "*C'est ça, we all call him Chunmaniye or Walking Tree, mon Capitaine.*"

Chunmaniye lowered his head to hide a grin. Morgan had strange notions about what it meant to be Canadian, he was a rabid Anglophile. All of the *Quebecois* in the Company exaggerated their French accents in his presence, throwing in a liberal dosage of French words because they knew it displeased the Captain. As a warrior, the Captain was a failure in Chunmaniye's eyes. In combat men would find it hard to rely on him. Morgan liked to preach about the rigours of combat but everyone knew he had been a Desk Wallah in the last war, riding out the horrors of the trenches in a comfortable office.

"Very well, Walking Tree it is," Morgan sighed. "THIS IS SIR MORTIMER MALHEUR."

Just about everyone jumped at Morgan's sudden increase of volume.

"HE BIG CHIEF, HE GREAT WHITE FATHER OF THE WYRDE WOODS. YOU UNDERSTAND?"

"Yes, Sir." Chunmaniye forced himself to remain impassive whilst he studied Sir Mortimer's face. Nothing on it betrayed that they had recently met on a local hilltop. Malheur was dressed impeccably in a dark suit and every dark hair on his head and in his moustache seemed to have a fixed place.

"Walking Tree speaks good English, Captain," Levesque intervened. "It is *fantastique*, better than mine, *n'est-ce pas*?"

"The Captain knows how to talk to natives, that's how we talked to the Wogs in India." The fat man who sat between the woman and Sir Mortimer chuckled. He was the eldest visitor, somewhere in his late fifties and Chunmaniye guessed Malheur trailed him by at least a score of years. The woman was probably younger though she had a hard stern face which lent her the severity of a decade.

"AND THIS VICAR FRAMSFIELD," Morgan bellowed. "HE HOLY MAN OF WOLFDEN. BIG MEDICINE MAN. CHRISTIAN MEDICINE. STRONG MEDICINE. HOLY MAN. HOLY. HOLY."

Morgan waved his hands upwards alongside of his head as he repeated the 'holy'. Chunmaniye struggled to not betray his dislike of the situation, unlike the Captain he would maintain his dignity.

Malheur was ignoring the officer completely as he studied Chunmaniye. He appeared unperturbed by Morgan's behaviour.

"AND THIS..." Morgan indicated the woman but he ran out of bluster and shut up, continuing to wave a soft flabby hand at her.

"My name is Mrs Allison Hare," The woman spoke curtly looking at Chunmaniye with as much distaste as she could. "I preside over the Wolfden Parish Christian Ladies Committee."

"I am honoured to make your acquaintance," Chunmaniye looked at all three as he said that.

"Well I'll be...," Morgan sputtered and swallowed his 'damned' with a guilty look at the vicar. "He speaks English, Lieutenant."

"*Oui, mon Capitaine*," Levesque sighed and cast an apologetic look at Chunmaniye.

"Good, then he will understand the accusations levelled against him," Sir Mortimer said crisply.

"Accusations?" Levesque asked sharply.

"Do you," Sir Mortimer ignored Levesque and looked at Chunmaniye with a triumphant gleam in his eyes. "Accept or deny claims that you have spent night times in the Wyrde Woods with a local child."

"A girl," Allison Hare spat. "All alone in the woods in the dark with a small girl."

Chunmaniye kept his face impassive though inwardly he groaned.

"I do not deny this," Chunmaniye said for the words were true even if the underlying insinuation was not. The *Saglasa* were masters of this game and he could not speak an untruth.

Captain Morgain sputtered and the vicar looked shocked. Levesque gave Chunmaniye a small shake of the head – the *Quebecois* could not protect him as he had predicted.

"I knew it," Allison Hare hissed like a rattlesnake.

"I have taught her things," Chunmaniye frowned. "I was her teacher."

As she was mine.

"That is one way of phrasing it," Sir Mortimer said dismissively. "I for one, do not care to hear the details, they nauseate me."

"Heathen savage practices," Allison Hare hissed.

"Quite right, quite right," Captain Morgan tutted.

Levesque rolled his eyes at Chunmaniye who answered with a wry grin as his heart wept.

§ § § § § § §

"I am to be sent home," Chunmaniye explained to Heechante, Ehawee and Akichita Tashunka. He had requested to meet them at their lookout point.

"Because they think that…," Akichita Tashunka stirred his ample gold hair with his hands and then looked from Chunmaniye to Joy and back to Chunmaniye,"…you and her, Joy and you…"

The boy ended with an exasperated sigh. Grown-ups were incomprehensible at times.

"You wanted to be a warrior, to fight the Jerries," Maisy commiserated.

Chunmaniye smiled, "I have become what I must and I have counted coup. The circle is complete."

Joy stood up and walked away to the two pinnacles on the very end of Hood's Gorge. The expanse of green woodlands below looked serene and peaceful, as if nothing were the matter.

"*Ey-hee!* Heechante."

Joy shut her eyes when she heard Chunmaniye approach her. Leon and Maisy stayed where they had all been seated; in mute shock.

"It's *NAUN* fair," Joy said between clenched teeth when she opened her eyes again.

"There is anger in your heart," Chunmaniye replied as he took place by her side.

"They're calling me a witch already," Joy growled. "I don't care what else they middling well call me."

"I know," Chunmaniye said. After a pause he added: "There is nothing to be done about it Heechante. I have to accept that the Army has a final say in this matter."

Joy nodded miserably. For a moment she had thought of offering him refuge. He could stay at the new fort they were building. However, she knew Chunmaniye would not be amenable to disobedience in wartime, it would reek of cowardice. He had his own people too, to get back to at Wood Mountain. She felt a short stab of bitterness. He had got his whole vision thing out of his sojourn in the Wyrde Woods and now he was leaving. Where did that leave her though?

"People come, people go," Chunmaniye smiled. "We must be grateful for the time we are given."

Joy blinked long and hard.

"I have taught you all I could, Heechante," Chunmaniye added.

"I am bloody well going to get bloody even, innit?" Joy sneered in fluent Cockney, anger seething within her now.

Chunmaniye gave her a concerned look. He turned towards her and laid a hand on her shoulder. Joy turned his way and more or less had to look straight up to catch his eyes. She calmed somewhat, feeling sheltered by his great height and safe and harboured in his presence. She would miss the comfort of that more than she could have imagined and bit her lip in an effort to keep her eyes dry.

"You have the power to get…bloody well even," Chunmaniye searched her soul with his eyes. "Do you remember what I told you about those who run with owls?"

Joy nodded reluctantly.

"Well?" Chunmaniye persevered.

"They're strong in spirit," Joy said sulkily. "*Howsumdever*, it *gwoan* either way with them. Light or Dark. There is *naun* middle road for them."

"That is my parting gift to you Heechante," Chunmaniye turned back to the view over the pool and cliffs. "A choice. Which path will you walk? It is Heechante who must decide. *He-ay-hee-ee!*"

"*Wyrd biđ ful aræd,*" Joy nodded. She had arrived at one of the crossroads of the *Wyrd* woven for her by the Norns. She had no doubt as to what path she must choose to walk if she were to become a Guardian of the Wyrde Woods. "Can't I just be *tessy*, Chunmaniye? Just for a bit?"

"No, you can't," Chunmaniye said. "That is the price you pay for power. You must know when to let Wakan Tanka direct your reactions because you cannot trust your own beak and claws. You know it is so."

"But you are my friend, Chunmaniye," Joy clenched her fists.

Chunmaniye laughed. "We will always be friends, Heechante. They cannot take that away from us. Ever. Perhaps that is why they are so angry."

Joy nodded. She spotted Maisy and Leon out of the corner of her eye. They were edging closer, looking desperately unhappy.

"The tree of life," Joy said.

"*Ai?* Yes?" Chunmaniye replied with quick interest.

"It does exist," Joy confessed. "*Howsumdever*, we *naun* show it to menfolk, never. Tis a secret."

Chunmaniye nodded with a relieved sigh. "At least I know I wasn't chasing tricksters' shadows. Thank you for telling me, *chuntay skoo ya.*"

"You *maun gwoan* looking for it," Joy added worriedly. "Knowledge of it is my parting gift. More I cannot give you."

"I have found what I wanted to in the Wyrde Woods," he said. "It has made my heart richer."

Joy smiled and beckoned Maisy and Leon over. Chunmaniye turned to them. "*Oo-oohey*, I must go now."

§ § § § § § §

"What did you two talk about?" Leon asked, as they watched Chunmaniye walk out of their lives.

"Revenge," Joy answered simply.

"GOOD!" Maisy rubbed her hands together. "Let's go get the bastards. The sooner the better, innit?"

"We're not *gwoan* to take revenge," Joy said, to Leon's surprise and Maisy's disbelief. "*All-along-of* that we should try to be *bettermost* people than them."

They had to mull over that for a moment but then nodded their understanding.

"Bugger," Maisy pouted none-the-less.

"It *gwoan* be unaccountable hard to be a *bettermost* person," Joy looked at Maisy and then at Leon. "By Oak and Acorn I want to *gwoan* hex them proper. But I *maun*. I will need your help."

"Of course," Leon answered, "We're your friends."

"That's what mates do innit?" Maisy added.

Joy nodded. She felt a wave of gratitude at the realisation that this was indeed what friends were for. She took Maisy's hand into her own, then Leon's hand too. The friends stood there in silence, drawing comfort from each other as they watched the sun transform the clouds lingering in the western sky into soft orange as it started setting over the Wyrde Woods.

34. A Boy

"A BOY!" Maisy repeated with as much righteous indignation as she could muster.

"I heard you the first time Maisy," Joy said calmly.

Maisy had not seen Joy for nigh on a week. School had started again and apparently it was truffle harvesting time again. She had been bursting to tell her friend of the disaster which had befallen her.

"From bloody Brighton, they're all daft down there you know," Maisy huffed. "I dunno what got into Gran and Gramps, we were fine as it was, innit?"

"There's a war on," Joy shrugged. "You keep telling me."

"True," Maisy brightened. "I've had some blooming good ideas, Joy. We can dig pits and put sharpened stakes at the bottom of 'em."

Joy looked doubtful and Maisy hopped back to the invasion of Maskall Farm instead. "I have to share my room with him. MY ROOM!"

"Tis a small farm, just the two bedrooms." Joy shrugged again. "Most Edgelanders share rooms. Asides, he's *fambly*, *baint* that so?"

"Well yes, but not a proper grandchild like I am, innit?" Maisy snorted. "He's Gramps's brother's grandchild; miles removed from proper grandchildren like me. Called Maskall though, Will Maskall."

"So he's your cousin," Joy secretly thought it might be fun to have a cousin. She was relishing the friendships she had acquired since Maisy's arrival and as far as she was concerned an additional soul was welcome.

"But a boy!" Maisy wailed. "What if he is a bleeding pervert? You know what lads are like, innit? What if he takes out his willy and waves it at me?"

Joy giggled. "Just laugh at it and he'll put it away again, *surelye*."

Maisy shrugged. "Blooming heck, Joy. He is dead dull. As pale as anything. Just sits there being quiet and moping all day. Hardly says a word, does he?"

"You don't mind that with Katie."

"Katie is different," Maisy dismissed the argument. "Katie'll talk, but only when she reckons there's something worth saying, innit? This Willy-boy is a right miserable git, you just lose the will to live around him. I might as well start digging me own grave, innit? Will you come to my funeral? I'd like that."

"Mayhap he's ill?" Joy suggested.

Maisy brightened. "That'd be good. Maybe the little sod will drop dead. And then Gramps..."

Joy waited for more and when it was not forthcoming she gently enquired: "Then Mus Maskall will what?"

Maisy shrugged. She looked genuinely pained for a second. "Maisy?"

"Nothing," Maisy looked away but Joy was not having it.

"You're afraid that Mus Maskall..." Joy started.

"Of course he prefers a boy!" Maisy's voice trembled for a moment. "Gramps went on and on about how he considered Willy-boy's dad his own son and all."

"Mus and Goody Maskall won't love you any less, Maisy. There is room in their hearts for the both of you, *surelye*?"

"How could they?" Maisy exclaimed bitterly. "I'm nobody, Joy. Just a loudmouth chavvie from the East End, innit? I aint polite or sweet or girly. There's not much to like, is there?"

Joy stopped walking and took hold of Maisy's arm. Maisy stopped too and looked at her friend. Joy read light panic in Maisy's eyes.

"I've seen the way Mus and Goody Maskall look at you, Maisy," Joy said earnestly, laying her hands on Maisy's shoulders now. "*Mayhap* it's unaccountable to you, *howsumdever*, they love you to bits, *surelye*. You're the *bettermost* lass in the *wurreld* to them."

Maisy looked doubtful.

"And I understand them," Joy added. "*All-along-of* me feeling the same."

Maisy smiled hesitantly and Joy hugged her. She felt the smaller girl tremble lightly and stroked her hair.

"There, there, sweetie," Joy said. "You'll be all right."

Maisy's head made a nodding movement and Joy smiled.

There was a noise in the sky and the girls separated to look up at the formation of twin-engined bombers which flew high overhead, heading for London.

"Maybe the Germans will invade today," Joy mused.

Maisy cheered up instantly. "That would be good, innit? Do you think we should summon the Wyrde Warriors?"

Joy mused this over and then smiled. "Let's do. We have a fort to finish building afore they come."

Maisy nodded, a fort to build and adventures to have. Something told her there would have to be a sequel to her *Friends in the Woods* screenplay. Colonel-in-Chief Whitfield and Captain Robbins would ride again.

THE END of FORGOTTEN ROAD

(Secrets of the Wyrde Woods will continue in HIDDEN SPRING)

Epilogues

29 September 1940
Maskall Farm
Wolfden, Sussex

Dear Mum,

Thank you for your letter, I was over the moon to hear from you. I am 'scratching along' and hope you are too.

The BBC says that the Luftwaffe are still bombing London every night. I am glad you wrote that I don't have to worry about it but I do!

There is a new evacuee. His father was your cousin George. Gran says you grew up with him. I don't remember you ever telling me about George. So you must visit so you can tell me about him.

~~I am worried sick about you and Dad.~~ Maybe you could take a holiday? Get some rest here. It's really nice here and Gran and Gramps are worried about you too although they don't tell me. But I can tell they are. ~~Mum please come home so we can be a family again.~~

Please think about it.

Your loving daughter,
Maisy Maskall

P.s. Don't forget to bring Dad when you come.

4 October 1940
Maskall Farm
Wolfden, Sussex

Dear Dad,

Did you know my Lakota name is Ehawee? I bet you didn't but now you do. ~~Joy is called Heechante and Leon (a boy) is~~ I have had some splendid proper adventures in the Wyrde Woods with my new friends Joy, Katie, ~~Lizzie and Leon~~ and some farm chavvies. ~~We got shot at by the Germans on the High Street. We nearly got killed in the Wyrde Woods. We had to run when the men came to our fort.~~ We built a hut in the woods ~~and go swimming in the lake.~~

You would really like it here! I have scouted the local pub for you. It looks medieval and they serve good ale. I was there with my soldier friends so it's okay, no need to worry.

There is another evacuee I habe to share my room with, ~~a boy.~~ who is Mum's cousin's ~~son.~~ child.

Mum wrote to tell me that you lost your new job, I was sorry to hear that Dad but I am sure you tried your best. Maybe you and Mum can come and work on the farm for a while? I would be really happy if you came. Convince Mum for me and we can all be together again. Please write back soon.

Love,

Your Ehawee

P.S. Make sure you have the right postal address because I haven't got any letters from you yet. Maybe they were lost?

Acknowledgements

Secrets of the Wyrde Wood: FORGOTTEN ROAD is, at its most basic, a Fairy Tale and it is thus befitting that it has a moral. The moral in this particular Fairy Tale is called Spark. I dedicate Spark, the Ugliest Pony in Sussex, to all those readers who do not possess the sterile characteristics of beauty imposed upon us ten thousand times a day by the media and our environment. Character is not made by physical appearance, it is built by the courage we muster, the fears we conquer, the bonds we forge, the sacrifices we make and the loyalty we display during our lifetime. It is that which makes Spark the best pony ever, not his looks or lack of them.

There are many people who had a hand in the realisation of Forgotten Road. Logistics first. I owe a great deal to Magén Klomp and Tommy Tickle for their generosity and incredible hospitality in respectively Amsterdam and Brighton. Gratitude is also due to Marcel Vankan, Gerrit Orgers, Jack Bryer and Richard Hornsby as these four gents happily accompanied me to a diverse number of Wyrde Woods locations in Sussex and Somerset. Elizabeth McHale provided the basis of a sound marketing plan which I have stuck to faithfully. Corin Spinks provided an excellent cover once again and we are both obliged to Jack Savage for inspiration. I was over the moon to receive an illustration from Kayleih Kempers as well; her interpretation stunned me. Amanda J. Norman of Dernwood Farm in Sussex is also owed a hearty thank you for her hospitality at her Dernwood Farm Wild Campsite which provided some great Wyrde Woods scenes.

Bren Hall and Lesley Bourke did a great job as editors and Leon van Assem, Hilary Anderson, Benjamin Tritschler, Robert Leaman and Mascha van Houteghem provided sound feedback which was very useful and that is an understatement. A special thanks to Liesel Lehrhaupt who casually suggested a far better end game to Forgotten Road. She claims it was a pleasant lunch time activity but it truly made for a far better story and the Blood Ruby was entirely her idea as were a few other items. Bren Hall provided the idea for Grace the Truffling Pig though she wishes to claim no credit for the nickname Bacon which I came up with. Credit is also due to Laura Coulson and her *Serious Business of Fairy Research* social media group where I picked up many ideas. Jax Atkins and Carol Homewood of the *Sussex-in-History* social media group were also very kind in letting me use their fb page as a place to elicit historical information; Chunmaniye was born there as were other characters and plot ideas. I also owe thanks to Christina Rosetti for writing *The Goblin Market (1862)* which I used for Maisy's first encounter with the *Farisees* in the Owlery on Midsummer's Night.

Last-but-definitely-not-least the people who were direct inspirations for characters. Wally Robson will hopefully recognise some of himself in Fred Maskall and the real Leon knows where Jasper got his fancy feathered hat. Lewinna is based on my friend Willeke Snijder. Barnaby Mackellow is based on a Headmaster I once had and the bad folk have characteristics of people I shant name here. I've put various parts of Marcel in Chunmaniye, though their respective cultures are far apart Marcel walks his talk and prizes honesty above all which helped a great deal.

Once again I owe a great deal to Joyce Keyzer who stood model for Joy Whitfield as she appeared in *Escape from Neverland* and *Dance into the Wyrd* and whose interests reappear in the much younger Joy. Thallie the scritch owl was created by Joyce for this book and is based on some of Joyce's owls.

Cathy Cadden has been a brilliant source of inspiration for Maisy. Hopefully Cathy will forgive me for making Maisy an East Ender for Cathy herself (and her poacher granddad) was born and bred in the countryside. Maisy's 'Maskall Touch' with animals is based on Cathy's ability to befriend just about any critter you care to think of. Valkerie and the Hooligan Horde are real and just a few of the ferrets which are given a new life at the Abington Ferret Refuge. Spark is based on two ponies Cathy had as a girl: Sparky who was a grey beauty and Bronze Boy who was the ugliest pony you ever saw as well as a great jumper. Many of Maisy's antics (nun's bloomers tied to chimney, chasing a bully with axes etc.) are based on stories Cathy told me about her youth though I may have embellished them just a little.

I was very lucky to be able to spend some time with Anna and Rozemarijn Orgers on several occasions and they provided much insight for the youthful characteristics for respectively Joy and Maisy. Anna features on the cover of this book along with Corin's daughter Melissa. Both Anna and Rozemarijn have distinct characters and refuse to hide these despite unfortunate old-fashioned public expectations as to the non-entity well-behaved girls ought to be. Kudos to the both of them, stay true to yourselves sweethearts, never let it go because it is what makes you two uniquely you and the both of you are *bettermost chavees* no matter what anybody else says.

Colonel-in-Chief Whitfield and Captain Robbins will ride again in *Secrets of the Wyrde Woods: Hidden Spring*. They will be joined by Major Maskall, familiar to readers of *Escape from Neverland* and *Dance into the Wyrd* as Willick and as the main protagonist in the historical *Will's War in Brighton* which ends on the edge of the Wyrde Woods.

Written in Amsterdam, Houvin-Houvigneul and Brighton 2015

Glossary

MAISY'S COCKNEY

bangers – sausages
barkers – guns and pistols
beef – to tell on someone, to betray them
blabber – informer
bludgers – a violent criminal
boated – to get kicked out/sent away
borrow and beg – eggs
bug hunt – robbing drunks
butchers (have a) – have a look
chapel (the) – Whitechapel area of London
chavvy / chavvies – child / children
chaunt – sing / to inform on someone
china (me old) – mate
cobblers – testicles
dabbing it up – to make love
downy – cunning/false
flue faker – chimney sweep
fly (on the) – something done quickly
gammy – false, undependable, hostile
glock – halfwit
glocky – halfwitted
gobstopper – penis
godforsaken – bacon
jemmy – clever
knackers – testicles
lush – drunk
lusheries – pubs or other drinking locations
luverly – lovely
mae bangers – best sausages
nickey – halfwit
nommus – get away! quick!
on the apples – on the display
plain brass – honest
raspberry tart – a fart
robin veg – green vegtables
tea leaf – thief
three stops down from Plaistow today – barking mad
to hold a candle to the devil – to be evil

WYRDE WOODS BROAD SUSSEX

abouten – about to
afeared – afraid
afore – before

all-along-of – because of / due to
alus – alehouse
anigh – nearby
asides – besides
atween – between
baint – is not
bellick – to shout insults
bethanks – thanks
bettermost – better/best
chance-born – born out of wedlock
chavee(s) – child(ren)
chuckle-head – halfwit
datyer – that there
dereaways – that way
dight-up – to get dressed for an occasion
dishabill – dishevelled
disyer – this here
Doby – a type of Pook
draca – dragon
draggle-tail – loose woman/girl
dunnamy – don't know how many
e'enamost – almost
enow – enough
fambly – family
furriner – foreigner (anyone not from Sussex)
gaffer – grandfather
gammer – grandmother
(by) Geemeny – used as an exclamation, like 'by Jove'.
gurt – great
gwoan – go / going to / gone
howsumdever – however
Jes-so – just so
kelpeye – an effort to Sussexize the Scottish kelpie
ken – to know
loped – run
Lunnon – London
maun – must not
mayhap – maybe/perhaps
misagift – mistaken
moil – trouble
mucking about – to make love
naun – used as no, none, not
oakum – nonsense
otherwhile – otherwise
pize – strong exclamation
Pook – goblin variety of Lesser Farisee
quiddy – what did you say? What's that?
scaddle – rogue / wild one

scorse – to exchange greetings and information
scritch – screech
scrowse – someone with a scowling unhappy face
sheere – shire, basically any area outside of Sussex
Sheere-folk – anybody not from Sussex
shim – ghost / spirit
shrucks – shrieks
skreels – screams
sodger – soldier
some-one-time – occasionally / sometimes
somewhen – sometime
somewhen-the-other-day – the day(s) before yesterday
stodge – one of the many many Sussex words for mud
surelye – surely, the spelling & pronounciation used to be very common in Sussex.
suddent – sudden
Suth Seaxna Lond – South Saxon Land
tarn – a small lake
tessy – angry
timmersome – timid
tossicated – drunk
wurreld – world
wyrm – the Sussex form of a dragon also known as knucker
zackly – exactly

OLD ENGLISH

compaignye – company
daunced – danced
entente – intent
fayerye – faeries
fynde – find
fulfild – full filled
grene – green
hir – her
joly – jolly
leeve – dear
lyven – live
mede – mead
mooder – mother
moot – must
nat – not
ofte – often
secree – secret(s)
speche – speech
speke – speak
swich – such
Wirdewode – Wyrde Woods
yeres – years
yvel – evil

No swerd or spere may do what I can
For I keep derk myght noon moot hath
The derknesse moot dwelle unbidden,
Kept sauf and cursed, I its secree holde
Releuen the stoon and thou shal fynde me
Cleuen the wode and I am ther.

No sword or spear may do what I can
For I keep dark might none must have
The darkness must dwell unbidden,
Kept safe and cursed. I its secrets hold,
Release the stone and thou shalt find me
Cleave the wood and I am there

LAKOTA

ai – yes
anp and han – light and dark
chuntay skoo ya – sweetheart
ey-hee – alas
haho – look at this
Hanwi – the moon
hau mushkay – hello female friend
han khola – hello male friend
he-ay-hee-ee – a call to the Great Spirit
hecheto aloh – it is finished
hecheto welo – it is well done
Hehaka Sapa – Black Elk
Heyoka – clown/a mental state
hohahe – you are welcome
hoka hey – it is a good day to die
hunta yo – get out of the way, something is coming
Iktomi – trickster spirits
oo-oohey – it is time
pilamaya – thank you
Saglasa – English
Tashunke Witke – Crazy Horse
Tatanka Iyotake – Sitting Bull
tokalu – fox
Wakan – life force, much like the Wyrd
Wakan Tanka – Grandfather/Great Spirit
Wakinyan – thunderbird
Wasichu – white man
Wicasa Wakan – medicine man

Wanayan maniye
Wanayan maniye

404

Tatanka wan maniye
Ate heye lo, ate heye lo.

Now he is walking
Now he is walking
There is a buffalo walking
Says the father

Kola tokile, kola tokile, kola ceyapelo.
Waziyata ki cizape
Ey-hee

My friend where are you? We made the enemy cry.
There was a battle up north.

ANGLO-SAXON
a-dỳdan – die!
Ufmanna – Owl Man
ut – out 'Ut! Ut! Ut! was the Anglo-Saxon battle cry at the Battle of Hastings
Wudawyrde Weard – A Guardian of the Wyrde Woods
Wyrd – a spiritual life force
Wyrd bid ful araed – fate is inexorable
wyrde – words

Sitte ge, sīgewīf, sīgað tō eorðan
Næfre ge wilde tō wuda fleogan
WUDAWOSE! TŌ WUDAWYRDE FLEOGAN

Settle down, victory-women,
never be wild and fly to the woods.
Wodewoses! Fly to the Wyrde Woods.

TRENCH
Corp – Corporal
Desk Wallah – a desk warrior
funk – mess up
plug – shot
windy – scared
Z-Hour – designated hour for an attack

FRENCH
Arbre-Qui-Marche – Tree which walks
Boche – nickname for the Germans, like Huns and Jerries
bonsoir Madame – good evening Ma'am
c'est ça – that's it
fantastique – fantastic
les Anglais – the English

merci – thank you
merci beaucoup – thank you very much
merde – shit
mes amis – my friends
mon ami – my friend
mon Dieu – my god
n'est-ce pas – isn't it so
non – no
oui – yes
parlais – to speak
Quebecois – somebody from Quebec
vite – quick

GERMAN
fallschirmjagers – parachutists/paratroopers
fräulein – miss
Führer – leader
guten tag – good day
hände hoch oder ich schiesse – hands up or I shoot
nicht schiessen – don't shoot
reich – empire
Stellvertreter des Führers – Deputy Führer
Wehrmacht – the German army